The
Quartet
Murders

OTHER TITLES BY J. R. ELLIS

The Body in the Dales

The Quartet Murders

A YORKSHIRE MURDER MYSTERY

J.R. ELLIS

THOMAS & MERCER

Text copyright © 2017, 2018 by J. R. Ellis
All rights reserved.

Previously self-published in Great Britain in 2017.

Published by Thomas & Mercer, Seattle

www.apub.com

Amazon, the Amazon logo, and Thomas & Mercer are trademarks of Amazon.com, Inc., or its affiliates.

ISBN-13: 9781503903098
ISBN-10: 1503903095

Cover design by Ghost Design

Printed in the United States of America

To David and Jane

Legend

It is said that Count Munsterhaven's messenger arrived at his famous destination in Cremona – No. 2 Piazza San Domenico – dusty and exhausted on a hot August afternoon in 1709. He was immediately admitted and given a refreshing glass of wine.

Having recovered a little, he was escorted up some rather rickety stairs to the workshop, seeing the apprentices at work and smelling the wood and the varnish. He passed violins and violas lined up in various stages of completion, like butterflies slowly forming in the chrysalis, before entering a tiny office where a man was sitting on a high stool at a desk looking at detailed drawings and diagrams. This was the genius himself: Antonio Stradivari, the most famous musical instrument maker the world has ever known.

The messenger bowed reverentially and handed a sealed envelope, borne hundreds of miles from Germany, to the master, who opened it and read the enclosed letter. Even though he knew of the count's wealth, his eccentric pride and his love of music, what the master read still surprised him. It was a grand commission, not for one or two or even three instruments, as he had been expecting since the count's recent visit, but for all the violins, violas and cellos of a chamber orchestra: nine instruments in all! Every string player would play a Stradivarius. The count was prepared to pay a fabulous price. Towards the end of the letter there was a neat, coloured drawing of the count's coat of arms followed by a curious request expressed in an oddly formal style:

> *So that these instruments will be forever associated with me, you will receive my everlasting gratitude if, on the back of each one, you will cause to have painted my coat of arms as it here appears. Thus they will become the 'Munsterhaven' Stradivarii and, I believe, a wonder of the world for evermore.*

Stradivari gazed abstractedly into the distance for a moment, before taking up the letter again and studying the coat of arms.

Well, my friend, he thought to himself. What a request you have given to me! He smiled and nodded. Yes, you shall have your 'Munsterhaven' Stradivarii – and I hope they will be, as you say, a wonder of the world.

One

About 500 violins made by Stradivarius still survive. They are now 300 years old. Experts still dispute the reasons why they produce such an extraordinary sound; they are the ultimate prize for collectors. Some have colourful histories and have been bought and sold for huge sums of money.

Detective Chief Inspector Oldroyd sat tensely at the wheel of his car and drove as fast as he dared through the dark, wet night, wipers swinging dementedly across the windscreen. The last thing he needed was to be stopped by one of his own officers and given a speeding ticket. That kind of a thing was a gift to the press.

It was a Friday evening at the end of November, and he was driving over to Halifax for a chamber concert in the Red Chapel Arts Centre. The internationally renowned Schubert String Quartet was playing their speciality: music by their eponymous composer. And not just any work by Schubert, but his greatest quartet: the one in D minor known as *Death and the Maiden*, with its famous second movement, one of Oldroyd's favourite pieces of music.

Oldroyd had been looking forward to this since August, when he'd been sent a copy of the Halifax Chamber Music Society programme, and had been planning to get away early from West Riding Police HQ in Harrogate. However, just as he was about to slip out, he'd received a call from Detective Chief Superintendent Tom Walker. Cursing, he went up to Walker's office, frantically thinking of ways in which he could make a quick getaway.

It had turned out to be a relatively trivial matter concerning a recent report he'd sent to the super, but often Walker used such things as an excuse for a conversation. Though 'conversation' was not quite the right word. Walker had chosen Oldroyd as his confidant, the person to whom he could regularly whinge about all the things he thought were wrong with the modern police force, modern management methods and the modern world in general for that matter. His greatest *bêtes noires* were the media, which he considered an insufferable bunch of yobs intent on making the work of the police harder, and people like Matthew Watkins, the trendy young chief constable of West Riding Police who spouted management jargon and talked relentlessly of business culture and target setting.

If only Walker could confine his rants to extended emails that could be quickly skimmed over and then deleted, thought Oldroyd as he'd sat in Walker's office trying not to look at his watch. But his boss was ill at ease with the 'newfangled gimmickry' of the digital age and preferred face-to-face communication. Another problem was that the old boy liked him and Oldroyd didn't want to offend him. He was a good boss to have, trusting Oldroyd to get on with his job. But he didn't feel he could say to Walker that he wanted to get away to his concert, if that was OK. He suspected that, if Walker had any musical tastes at all, they would not extend beyond brass bands or Shirley Bassey; what he would make of a string quartet he had no idea and didn't want to find out. As Oldroyd could think of no other plausible reason for getting away, he had to sit there while Walker railed on about Watkins.

'Do you know what the latest is, Jim?' As usual, Walker didn't give him the chance to answer. 'He's going to employ a firm of consultants to come in and "assess our work patterns". What the bloody hell does that mean? Can you imagine a bigger waste of public money? And that's not all: these consultants, apparently, specialise in banks and finance so, of course, they don't know a bloody thing about policing. And then they'll produce some jargon-ridden report saying we're spending too much on . . .'

And so it had gone on. Oldroyd shook his head to dismiss the memory. It had been nearly a quarter past six when he finally made his escape, and the concert started at seven thirty.

It was now five minutes past seven and he was passing Shibden Park, with the dark, rather sinister-looking mass of the Jacobean Shibden Hall in the distance. He drove through a steep cutting in the millstone grit under a steel bridge marked '1900', turned to the right and below him could at last see the lights of Halifax. He started to relax a little; he would probably make it.

In the small artists' room at the Red Chapel Arts Centre, the Schubert Quartet were preparing for their performance. They'd dispensed with the formal white tie and tails in favour of casual open-neck black shirts and jackets. Anna Robson, the violist, wore a white blouse and black skirt. The German leader, Hans Muller, was at least twenty years older than the others, who were all British players. The second violin, Michael Stringer, Anna Robson, and cellist Martin Hamilton had all studied at the Bloomsbury School of Music in London. They'd played together for nearly twenty-five years and won an international reputation for the Viennese classics of Haydn, Beethoven and Schubert, but especially Schubert. Their acclaimed recording of the *Complete Schubert Quartets* had won a rosette in the *Penguin Guide to Classical Music*.

In the room, there was a tension in the air beyond that normally expected before a concert. Anna Robson absent-mindedly practised short passages from the Haydn quartet they would be performing. Muller and Stringer were talking quietly, but rather heatedly. Hamilton had just returned from the building's entrance, where he'd stood just outside smoking a small cigar and tapping at his phone. They each played marvellous instruments from the Italian golden age, Amatis and Stradivarii, but Muller's violin was something truly remarkable. It was a Stradivarius from 1710, wonderful in itself, but what made it extra special was that on the back, beneath the famous varnish, a red-and-yellow coat of arms was neatly painted on to the maple wood. This indicated that it was one of only nine instruments – only six of them violins – made by the famous Italian at the height of his powers as a special commission for Count Munsterhaven in Germany, a wealthy patron of the arts in that era. It was truly priceless.

Muller impatiently waved his hand at Stringer as a sign that the conversation was at an end. He had just taken up the famous violin and was playing a few arpeggios when a Music Society official put his head around the door.

'Ten minutes, please,' the man said with a smile, and the four players made their final preparations.

Oldroyd ran down the wet streets, past the looming mass of the Piece Hall and across a cobbled road to the entrance to the Red Chapel, so called because it was, unusually for this area of millstone grit, constructed out of small eighteenth-century red bricks. It was no longer a place of worship but an arts centre – so in Oldroyd's book still a spiritual venue, especially on an evening like this. He was relieved to see people still queuing to get in.

A middle-aged man dressed in an overcoat and scarf sat at a table near the door dispensing small pink tickets. Oldroyd, out of breath but with a sense of calm and satisfaction, paid his entrance money and followed the rest inside, down the corridor and up a stone staircase that bent round to the right. He nodded to one or two of the Music Society committee members whom he knew from years of attending these concerts. They included the woman who sold him the programme and an elderly man, vaguely foreign-looking, who usually led the performers on to the stage when everything was ready and then sat by the stairs with other members of the committee. Their names were Ruth Greenfield and Frank Dancek; Oldroyd had seen them listed many times among the main subscribers to the concert seasons. He also saw Gerald Watson, secretary of the Music Society. He was wearing an old-fashioned tweed sports jacket and a crumpled tie and he was in conversation with two elderly ladies who were sitting at either side of him on the front row. Both had white hair, immaculately coiffured, and wore pearls. They looked as if, in the Yorkshire phrase, they were 'worth a bob or two' and were no doubt significant financial patrons of the Society.

Oldroyd looked around at the large square room with its high ceiling and sighed as he took in the atmosphere. A wooden floor and modern tiered seating had been constructed within the shell of the Red Chapel. The crumbling plasterwork of the eighteenth-century walls stood ghostly in the background. The seating rose up into the shadows, opposite a brightly illuminated area at floor level with four chairs and four music stands in the quartet formation.

Oldroyd's heart always leaped when he saw this evocative little tableau. He'd been coming to chamber concerts since he was a teenager and his father, an amateur cellist, had taken him to hear the Smetana Quartet from Prague play Beethoven in this very hall more than thirty years before. It held so many memories for him and it was impossible not to feel some nostalgia about his dead father and all the great music they'd heard together. Luckily he found a seat at the end of a row, near the centre and not too far back, and there was not much opportunity to dwell on such feelings. He had just had time to glance at his programme when the attendants took their seats and the quartet, led in not by Frank Dancek this time but by another member of the committee, appeared to the instant applause of the audience. The one difference to the usual layout was a small table next to Muller's seat. Recently the violinist had developed some problem with the muscles in his bowing arm and would place his precious instrument on this table between movements while he carried out some brief exercises before continuing. Because of this health problem, and the fact that he was now in his late sixties, there were rumours that he might be replaced or that the quartet would soon disband.

The concert began with the traditional curtain-raiser of an early quartet by Haydn, followed by a relatively short piece by the Czech composer Martinů, both expertly played and promising much for what was to come. Oldroyd felt all the tensions of the day ease away as he listened to the rich, resonant sound of those instruments playing the chamber music he loved more than any other. It was a sound that moved him deeply. Was it because so many of the great composers – Beethoven, Schubert, Mozart, Mendelssohn – had turned to the string quartet in their later years to express some of their most profound musical thoughts and feelings? What was it about the four strings: two violins, a viola and a cello? This ensemble had an almost holy significance for Oldroyd. There was a simplicity, yet also a depth and intimacy about it that defied analysis.

After the Martinů there was an interval, and Oldroyd went down briefly to the little bar. He drank a glass of red wine, and then returned eagerly to his seat in anticipation of the Schubert. On the wall above where the quartet sat, he noticed some mouldering plaster figures with biblical words inscribed beneath: 'Ye know not the hour'. Next to this was a window and he looked out into the darkness. There was a solitary house silhouetted on the hillside opposite, tall and narrow, and the lights of a road angled crazily up the hill. He could just make out drystone walls snaking up the fields. It was like something from a Lowry painting and he mused on how eccentric a place this was for such a concert compared to London, Paris or Vienna.

Suddenly there was applause as the quartet reappeared, bowed and took their places again. The hall was hushed in expectation of a special performance of Schubert's masterpiece. There followed an intense and dramatic first movement handled with masterful technique and power. And then the slow movement.

Oldroyd had always thought that the opening was like a funeral march; Death is stalking the Maiden as in the old legend and Schubert's earlier song. She pleads with him in a poignant and plaintive series of variations – '*Ich bin noch jung!*' – but he is implacable. The music increases in menace and drama. Death draws near, enveloping her in a dance and then striking her down. A turbulent passage of agony climaxes in death throes but then subsides slowly into quietness and calm. The final bars convey transcendence; the opening themes are repeated but transformed, uplifted. Schubert, contemplating his own early death from incurable syphilis, manages to attain a sublime and serene peace at the end. '*Sollst sanft in meinen Armen schlafen.*'

Oldroyd sat transfixed until the final chord faded out. There was utter silence. The quartet slowly lowered their instruments, and Muller gently placed the Munsterhaven Strad on to the little table.

As he did so there was a tiny thudding noise high up behind Oldroyd. A small circle of red appeared on the right side of Muller's forehead and his eyes widened. He appeared to try to stand up, still holding his bow, then plunged forward, knocked over his music stand and crashed to the floor, where he lay still. The sheets of his score were scattered around him.

There were a few strangely still seconds of complete incomprehension in the hall, before it was realised that Death had claimed more than the Maiden that night in Halifax.

Two

The 'Molitor' Stradivarius was made in 1697. It is thought to have once been owned by Napoleon Bonaparte and was named after one of his generals. It was bought in 1957 by William Anderson, who kept it under his bed in Aberfoyle Terrace, Derry, Northern Ireland, for thirty-one years. In 2010 it was sold to American violinist Anne Akiko Meyers for $3.6 million.

As Oldroyd stared down at the body, the sound of police sirens broke the grim reverie into which he'd briefly fallen. He was used to investigating murders but not to witnessing them. The brutal act had disrupted a serene moment and the shock left him feeling an odd dislocation from the scene.

In the bizarre moments that followed Muller's crash to the floor, Oldroyd was out of his seat quickly and leaping down the steps towards the players before there were shouts and screams from the audience. Suddenly everything speeded up.

Frank Dancek got to his feet and shouted: 'My God, up there!' He pointed high up into the ceiling of the hall. 'There's . . .' Then he ran off down the stairs.

Other people were getting to their feet. One of the old ladies sitting next to Gerald Watson seemed to faint, and slumped in her seat. Oldroyd sensed that chaos could quickly ensue if he didn't act.

'I'm a police officer,' Oldroyd shouted in his most commanding voice; he held up his identity pass, which seemed rather pathetically ineffective in the circumstances. 'Please try to remain calm and stay where you are. You are not in any danger – no more shots have been fired so it's likely the victim was the only target.'

After a cursory examination of the body revealed no sign of life, he placed himself in front of the corpse and turned to face the audience. He quickly looked up to where Dancek had pointed. Dancek had had a better view of the upper balconies from where he'd been sitting. There was a lighting gantry that had obviously served as a sniper's nest, but Oldroyd couldn't see any sign of anyone up there now.

Despite his reassurance to the audience, he didn't know for certain that no one else was at risk; but he had to prevent panic and a stampede out of the hall. He was aware that, behind him, the three remaining members of the quartet were leaving the hall by the smaller second staircase, which led down into the artists' room. He allowed them to go. They had been directly in the line of fire, and maybe more at risk than anyone else if there was some crazed gunman around with a grudge against string players. That seemed highly unlikely, but Oldroyd had no space yet to even begin to speculate about a motive.

A well-dressed man in his forties, another committee member, came up to Oldroyd. 'I've called the police and ambulance, explained what happened. They said they'll come armed.'

'Well done. We'll all wait here until they arrive. Don't touch anything.'

Ruth Greenfield, visibly shaking, pointed up to the same spot as Dancek and repeated what he'd said.

'The shot definitely came from up there, Chief Inspector. Frank must have gone to try to stop whoever it was from escaping. I hope he's all right; he could get shot himself.'

'I can't leave the hall until more police arrive; let's just all stay here and keep everything as calm as we can.'

Oldroyd wished desperately that he had some officers with him now. The crime scene needed to be sealed off and the search for the gunman begun, but he couldn't leave the hall. Vital minutes were being lost. All he could do was remain standing at the front looking as if he was in control. He stared down again at the body. Maybe it wasn't such a bad way to go: your last act playing the final chords of one of the greatest pieces of music ever written.

Then he heard sirens and the sound of cars pulling up and doors slamming. Soon footsteps sounded on the stone stairs. He felt relieved; at last he would be released from being imprisoned in the hall with the rest of the unhappy concertgoers. The latter seemed to have calmed down now it was clear that there was no madman on the loose. They were variously either standing warily at the side of the hall as if ready to make a run for it if necessary, or cowering in their seats too shocked and frightened to move.

Oldroyd hoped that someone he knew would appear; it would make things so much easier. This time God, in whom he found it hard to believe, was nevertheless on his side. Behind a couple of young DCs who came bounding up the stairs, both armed with pistols, Oldroyd saw a portly figure struggling and breathing heavily. He had a pronounced paunch and a balding head. His small eyes widened when he saw Oldroyd and his chubby face broadened into a smile revealing yellow nicotine-stained teeth.

'Bloody hell, Jim, what're ya doin' 'ere?' he said in a deliberately exaggerated broad Yorkshire accent and rushed over to shake Oldroyd's hand.

'Sam, good to see you. You might well ask. I was here for the concert, saw it all happen. Took charge – good job I was here, actually, otherwise it'd've been bloody chaos.'

Oldroyd had known DCI Sam Armitage since they'd been junior detectives together in Leeds many years earlier. Sam had risen through the ranks in the West Riding Force and was now based in the Halifax Division. He was a jovial character famously renowned for his unhealthy lifestyle. A heavy smoker, he was fond of lunching on pork pies laced with brown sauce and his consumption of beer easily outstripped Oldroyd's. He was still out of breath from the climb up the steps. He saw Muller's body sprawled by the upset music stand; a small puddle of red had gathered by the head and was starting to trickle away across the floor.

'Good God, so he was playing when it happened, middle of the concert?'

'Yep, picked off by a sniper up there.' Oldroyd pointed to the gantry. Armitage looked up, screwing his eyes against the glare of the lights.

'So he was shot. And then what happened, Jim?'

'I came down to the front, tried to calm everyone down. I don't think anyone's left the building – except one chap; he's always here, member of the committee. He ran off down the steps as soon as it happened. He must be still down there. I don't think there's anyone up in that gantry now, must have got down somehow or be hiding. Did you see anybody on the way in?'

'A bloke on the door and people in the bar; nobody who looked as if they'd just shot someone. What about the other players?'

'They went down those stairs.' He pointed across the room. 'They lead to the artists' room; they must be still there.' Oldroyd blew out with relief. 'It's been bloody awful; couldn't move from here until someone arrived.'

Armitage shook his head.

'I'll bet. Anyway, we can get on with it now.' He looked at the audience, who seemed even more startled now they had seen the police with guns, and shook his head again. 'We'll have to get more people over here to deal with this lot.'

He gave Oldroyd a playful smile. 'You'll be one of the chief witnesses, Jim, but at least not a suspect. I hope . . .' he added cheekily.

'Get away with thi,' replied Oldroyd, and Armitage laughed.

'Anyway, let's get on with it. Hodges, Wilson, Hepworth, start with this lot. No one leaves yet. We need to get personal details and statements from them all. See if anyone saw anything unusual. Jim, we'd better get down there and see what's going on; we just rushed past everything on the way in – they said someone'd been shot up here so we came straight up.'

The two senior detectives went quickly back down the stone steps, then through some swing doors and into the short corridor at the bottom. On the right was a door to the toilets. The outside door was in front of them at the end of the corridor. Next to it was another door, leading to the bar on the left. Two armed police officers stood by the outside door and the man who had sold Oldroyd the ticket was looking very anxious.

Oldroyd looked around, checking the layout of everything, while Armitage approached the agitated individual. 'I'm Inspector Armitage; what's your name, please? Were you here when the shot was fired? Has anyone left the building since?'

The man turned his white face towards the two detectives. He seemed to be struggling to remember the order of events.

'Stuart Atkinson. Yes . . . No, I didn't hear a shot.'

'There was no sound,' said Oldroyd. 'They must have used a silencer.'

'The first thing I heard was a scream and then all sorts of commotion up there, then Frank Dancek came running down the stairs. He was shouting: "Someone's been shot; has anyone come down here?"'

'Had anyone?' Armitage repeated his question.

'No, no one came down the stairs before Frank. I've been here by the door since the interval, clearing this board and putting new information up.' He pointed to a big notice board where events were being advertised. 'No one has gone through that door except Frank. When I told him no one had come down he looked puzzled and asked me if I was sure and then he went outside and . . . Oh – he's there. Ask him yourself.'

Oldroyd and Armitage turned to see Frank Dancek standing behind them. He seemed out of breath, and was grim-faced. He sat down on a chair by the entrance to the bar looking exhausted. Oldroyd noticed the faint Eastern European accent overlaid by Yorkshire. He must have lived in this area for a long time.

'Go back up there, Inspector; he must be still in there. The door was open. I ran down here thinking he must have made a run for it, but then Stuart said that no one had come down.' He shook his head. 'I couldn't believe it so I went outside round the streets; couldn't see anyone so I came back.'

'What do you mean, the door was open?' asked Oldroyd.

Dancek pointed back up the steps. 'Halfway up, there's a little door; it leads to a ladder that goes up to the lighting gantry. I suppose it would have been access to the Chapel loft in the old days. But, Inspector . . .' There was fear and alarm in his face. 'He must still be up there – he might shoot someone else.'

'Are there any other exits to the building?' Oldroyd was puzzled.

'There's only the emergency exit at the back of the building, but that's alarmed; he would still have had to come down the stairs to get to that and I didn't see anybody. The alarm hasn't gone off.'

'Right, let's get back up there, but no more shots have been fired. I couldn't see anyone up there, though I admit it was dark. I think if he was going to take a pop at someone else he would have done it by now.'

'Up here with us,' Armitage called to one of the armed officers. 'The assailant is probably still up there, so use maximum caution.'

The burly officer holding a pistol led the way back through the swing doors and up the steps. They had no difficulty locating the small door, which was, as Dancek had said, standing open. The officer switched on a torch, which he held in his left hand, and began to climb the steep wooden ladder followed by Oldroyd and Armitage.

He called out: 'I'm an armed police officer, and there are more armed officers in the building. Put down your weapon.'

When they got on to the gantry there was no one there.

'Here, sir: here's the weapon.'

Oldroyd walked across a narrow platform and saw a rifle. As expected, it had been fitted with a silencer. The officer continued to the end of the platform, shining his torch in every direction. It illuminated the wall and Oldroyd caught sight of another plaster figure and more words inscribed beneath: 'Vengeance is mine sayeth the Lord'.

'There's no one up here, sir,' the officer finally pronounced.

Oldroyd knelt by the rifle, taking care not to disturb anything. He found himself looking straight down to where the body of Hans Muller still lay, with the head now in a pool of red. A number of officers were slowly working through the audience taking details.

'Perfect position. Clear view; wouldn't be seen up here in the dark.'

'Is there any other way down from here?' asked Armitage.

'Can't see one, sir,' replied the officer. 'There's just the ladder we came up and the platform we're on. There's no way off at the other end; the only way is back where we came.'

'Then what the hell?' exclaimed a perplexed Armitage. 'What's going on? We need to search this building thoroughly. He has to be here somewhere, unless someone's lying.'

He shouted down to one of the DCs in the hall below: 'Hodges!' The DC looked up, startled. 'I'm up here; make absolutely sure no one leaves. The gunman's not here, but he must still be in the building somewhere.'

He pulled out his radio and spoke to the officer at the door.

'No one is to leave the building. We've found a rifle here, most probably the murder weapon; no sign of the assailant. Keep Mr Atkinson there – we need to talk to him again.'

Oldroyd followed Armitage back down the ladder, looking carefully for any clues, but saw nothing. He frowned as he ducked under the low door; this was starting to get very mysterious. When he got back to the main staircase he remembered something.

'Sam, the other players . . . they must be still in the artists' room. I'll go and speak to them.' Oldroyd returned to the hall. At the opposite side to the public entrance, the separate staircase led down into a room on the ground floor. This room and staircase had been used by preachers in the days when the building was fulfilling its original function. They prepared in this room and were then able to ascend to the main hall of the Chapel separately from the congregation. The pulpit had stood where the artists now performed. Strange, thought Oldroyd, how music and theatre have become the new spirituality for many people as the churches decline. But who wouldn't rather hear a string quartet than a bigoted old ranter going on about hell, damnation and the evils of drink?

When he reached the room he found the three of them huddled together in silence.

'I'm Chief Inspector Oldroyd.' He showed his identification. They looked at him with indifference; they seemed lifeless with shock. This has enormous significance for them, thought Oldroyd. It's not just the murder of their colleague and no doubt friend, but the shockingly abrupt end of their performing life together; the end of something brilliantly creative that they've shared for all these years. It must feel like having a limb chopped off.

'I understand what this means to you. Not just personally, but for your professional life.' He chose his words carefully, but immediately wondered if he'd said the right thing as Anna Robson put her head in her hands and started to cry. Michael Stringer went over to her and put his arm around her shoulders.

'Thank you, Inspector,' he said in a rather shaky voice. 'It's . . . devastating.'

'Have you got any idea who did it?' said Martin Hamilton, who was slumped in a chair still absentmindedly holding his cello.

'I'm afraid not; we can't find anybody, there's no one up there in the gantry and no one's been seen leaving.'

'But someone fired from somewhere and . . . killed Hans.' Hamilton sounded as if he still couldn't really believe what had happened.

'We'll get to the bottom of it. The first thing I have to ask you is: do any of you know of any reason why Herr Muller should have been killed? Did he have any enemies?'

Anna Robson had recovered a little and blew her nose gently on a tissue. She was trying to pay attention. The three musicians exchanged glances. Stringer shook his head.

'I certainly don't know of anyone who'd want to kill him. Hans was admired by everyone. He was a great musician.'

Anna nodded; she still seemed incapable of saying anything.

'There's rivalry in the music world, Inspector, like any other world where there's performance. Some people were jealous of Hans, of us being successful; you got people writing bad reviews recently, saying Hans was losing it, you know, because of his muscle problem.'

'He wasn't,' declared Anna Robson, speaking for the first time. 'You heard him tonight: magnificent.'

'Yes, it's a great loss,' said Oldroyd, sadly. 'But you'd hardly say any of those things were motives for murder, would you?'

'No.'

'I think it might have been to do with that bloody violin,' said Anna.

Oldroyd looked at her sharply. 'Why do you say that?'

'People were always pestering him about it, wanting to buy it, making offers, wanting to take photographs of it. He once told me he wished he'd never set eyes on it; but of course when he played it, it was a different matter, absolutely magical. Where is it, by the way?'

Everyone looked around the room, but the famous violin was not there.

'Didn't one of you bring it down with you?' said Oldroyd. 'It's not up in the hall.'

The players looked at each other.

'No,' said Hamilton. 'It was the last thing on our minds.'

Inwardly, Oldroyd cursed. He'd been too distracted by what was happening after the murder, and the need to control the audience, to keep an eye on the violin.

'I'd better go and have a look. Please feel free to go up to the bar for a drink – it might help – but don't leave the building.'

He went back up the stairs to the hall. The small table was empty and a quick search revealed nothing. The violin, like the murderer, had disappeared.

Oldroyd joined Armitage, who had set up a makeshift headquarters in the small bar of the Red Chapel, and they sat disconsolately at one of the tables, pints of beer in front of them. The volunteers running the bar had agreed to keep it open. It was now very late. The audience had finally been allowed to leave but only after they'd all made statements and been searched for the missing violin and any other evidence. This had taken a considerable amount of time. The three surviving members of the quartet were still in the artists' room and refreshments had been taken to them. An ambulance had arrived to remove Muller's body. Armitage took a swig of his pint and wiped his moustache. He looked comfortably ensconced in his seat and it looked to Oldroyd as if he would take a bit of shifting.

'At least this beer's good; they've got a microbrewery here. Well, I never expected a carry-on like this. No murderer and then a priceless instrument goes missing. At least we've got some idea of motive now – it must have been planned: bump off Muller and take the violin; they must be connected, don't you think?'

'It certainly seems so, too much of a coincidence but . . .' replied Oldroyd, fiddling with his pint glass and still reeling from everything that had happened. And he'd only come here to listen to Schubert! Just my luck, he thought; a wry smile came to his face and he shook his head.

'But what, Jim?'

'I don't know, I can't think straight yet, but something doesn't feel right.'

'Well, it's a very clever operation and I've no idea who might be behind it. We don't get much of this sort of thing in Halifax. You say that violin will be worth a lot?'

'No doubt about that; it's what's called a Munsterhaven Stradivarius, very rare; you'll have to find out more about it, and who was interested in it. It'll also be interesting to know how Muller came to own it.'

Armitage looked at Oldroyd, took another swig of his beer and finished it, then leaned across the table.

'I've been thinking, Jim: you seem to know about this violin thing; it's nothing in my line and you were here, you're a witness. What do you think of us investigating this together? It'll be like old times again.' His chubby face grinned.

Oldroyd had been hoping for this but hadn't liked to say. He felt he'd been made a fool of; the terrible audacity of the crime committed under his nose. His pride made him want to be involved in finding the answer.

'Well, Sam, I thought you'd never ask! Of course, I'd be delighted, but you'll have to get your super to clear it with Tom Walker. Also I'd like to bring over a DS who works with me – good lad, Andy Carter. We're going to need all the talent we've got for this one; we're totally outwitted at the moment.'

'You're right there.'

'I'll give him a call, first thing tomorrow when we've cleared it with the supers. Have your people found anything interesting?'

'No, only stuff that leaves us where we are: bloody great big mystery. The emergency-exit door is untouched; no one left through there. The whole building's been searched: no one found, no secret hiding places, no way down from that gantry except the ladder.'

'We'll have to look again tomorrow, in the light; there must be some way of getting down from there and out of the building, unless . . .'

'What?'

Oldroyd yawned. 'Nothing. I'm worn out, Sam; let's leave it tonight – we can't do any more. Are you keeping the quartet? I suppose it's a trio now . . .' he observed grimly.

'Yes. I've told them to book into a hotel. We'll need to talk to them properly tomorrow.'

'What about the violin?'

'I've got a couple of DCs searching and . . . Oh, they're here. Well, find anything?'

'No, sir, looked everywhere, even got the cellist to open his case, but there was only the cello there.'

'Great. Don't know what I'm going to tell the super: murderer and priceless instrument both disappear from under our noses. He's not going to like it.' He looked at his empty glass and turned to Oldroyd. 'Fancy another?'

'No, I'm going to check in at the Old Commercial, nearest place to here.'

'No need, Jim, you can stay with me.'

'Thanks, Sam, but I think it's better if I stay in the town, near to the scene; easy to get on with things.' Much as he liked Sam, Oldroyd didn't relish the prospect of several nights in his bungalow in Northowram, having to be sociable with his wife and family. Not that he disliked them – he just seemed to be getting antisocial these days now that he'd split up with his own wife and his kids were grown up. Often he couldn't be bothered to make the effort with people. Was it old age? Depression? Or was he just jealous of Sam's domestic harmony?

'OK, whatever you think's best.'

Oldroyd finished his beer and left. There was yellow-and-black incident tape all around the building and police officers on guard. It jarred with Oldroyd; it seemed to desecrate a place that was special to him. He wondered if he'd ever feel the same way about it again.

The Old Commercial Hotel was really a glorified pub with a few rooms attached, cheap but comfortable and right in the town centre. Oldroyd had stayed there a few times after concerts when he'd decided to have a few pints and not drive home. His flat overlooking the Stray in Harrogate didn't feel like home anyway. Sometimes he couldn't bear the loneliness of going back to the place late at night, dark and empty, and preferred to crash wherever he was.

The place was shut up but he roused the landlady, a large friendly woman who ran a popular pub. She remembered him and was eager to hear any information about what had been going on 'over at t'Chapel'. He told her what he could and then she showed him to a room upstairs above the bar.

Oldroyd sat on the bed for a while, thinking and feeling sorry for himself. It was at times like this, at the end of a hard day, that you wanted to come home to someone and snuggle up to them in a nice warm bed. He thought about his wife, Julia, and the years they'd had together as a couple and a family. He took off his clothes and got into the bed alone. He was so tired that he soon fell asleep.

Three

The 'Lipinski' Stradivarius of 1715 was named after a famous nineteenth-century violinist. In 2008 its owner loaned it to the leader of the Milwaukee Symphony Orchestra, Frank Almond. In January 2014 an armed gang attacked Almond with a stun gun and stole the violin. It was recovered shortly afterwards by Milwaukee police. It was recently valued at $5 million.

Detective Sergeant Andy Carter got the surprise call from his boss as soon as he arrived at West Riding Police, Harrogate Division headquarters the next day. Oldroyd outlined what had happened and told Carter to get over to Halifax as soon as he could.

'Halifax? Where's that then, sir?' Carter was a Londoner who had come north to join the West Riding force as a detective sergeant. He found it hard to navigate around the complexities of Yorkshire's dales and valleys.

'In the Calder Valley, Andy. It's about twenty-eight miles from Harrogate. Surely you've got a map? Go on the Bradford Ring Road and then on the Halifax Road near Wibsey; you can't go wrong.'

Carter suspected that he almost certainly would go wrong without assistance.

'It's OK, sir, I've got my GPS; I'll just follow the directions.'

Oldroyd grunted his contempt. 'Can't stand those bloody things – ruining map-reading skills; relying on technology all the time . . . Make sure it doesn't direct you over a cliff or something.'

Carter smiled at his boss's grumpy Luddism. 'Don't worry, sir. I'll be there in an hour.'

DS Stephanie Johnson was in the office. They'd met when Carter first came to Yorkshire and had been seeing each other ever since. Steph was a local girl who'd worked with Oldroyd for many years.

'What's going on over there, then?'

'Bloke shot at some kind of a concert; apparently the boss was there, saw it happen.'

'Wow!'

'Yeah I know. Anyway, apparently a mate of his is chief inspector over there in the Halifax Division.'

'DCI Sam Armitage.'

'Yeah. He wants the boss to help him with the investigation as he was sort of involved; boss wants me to come over to help as well.'

'Ooh! Lucky you!'

'Well, I . . .'

'It's OK – I'm not jealous; he knows I've got a lot on with this case at the hospital, so you're the right person to go.'

'Well, I'm going to miss you.' He gave her a quick surprise kiss on the lips.

Steph glanced around to see if anybody was watching. 'Hey, not allowed during working hours, bad boy. You'd better go.'

'What's this Halifax like, then?' he asked as he put on his coat.

'It's rather poor and run down compared to Harrogate. They've got character, though, those old mill towns up the valleys over there. See what you think.'

Oldroyd had woken up in the hotel at seven o'clock still feeling rather tired and a little confused. Then he remembered where he was, got up and pulled back the curtain slightly to see what the weather was like. He was pleasantly surprised by the sight of a bright morning. The weak early-winter sun shone on the rooftops still wet from the previous night and illuminated the green fields that surrounded the town. The sky was clear and pale blue. No chimneys churning out smoke these days, he reflected; clearer air, but with the mills shut, including Crossley's giant carpet mill at Dean Clough, had the town lost its pride and purpose?

He made himself a cup of tea using the small electric kettle supplied by the hotel. The tea didn't taste right with the long-life milk, which he managed to extract in drops from the little silver-foil-covered plastic cartons. He didn't approve of putting the tea bag straight into the cup. He took the George Orwell line on tea: it had to be made properly.

He had a quick shower and went down to have some breakfast. This was served in a little room adjacent to the bar from which aromas of beer still drifted. A cleaner was vacuuming around the tables. Oldroyd filled a bowl with muesli and milk and took a seat at a table in the nearly deserted room. There was just one other person there, a middle-aged man in a suit who looked as if he was a travelling salesman of the old type. He nodded to Oldroyd, who said a brief 'Morning'.

A girl with an Eastern European accent, probably Polish, asked him if he would like tea or coffee and a cooked breakfast. She gave him a small menu. He ordered tea and bacon, egg, mushrooms and tomatoes with toast. He immediately felt guilty, as he was constantly in something of a battle with his weight, but justified it because of the traumas of the night before. On the other mornings, however many there turned out to be, he would just have muesli and tea.

Oldroyd sat glancing at the newspaper, enjoying this little bit of unexpected luxury as he smelled his bacon frying and drank much better tea, from a pot, to which he added fresh milk. How good it felt to sit here and have a relaxed breakfast! It was like being on holiday. After he had savoured his bacon and egg, and crunched his way through a couple of slices of toast and marmalade, he reluctantly switched on his phone and called Carter.

Oldroyd and Carter met up with Armitage in the Halifax local HQ, which was a functional sixties building unlike the lovely Queen Anne-style West Riding Police HQ in Harrogate. Armitage's office reminded Oldroyd of Tom Walker's: the office of a man who disliked bureaucracy and preferred being out in the field. Armitage sat in a battered old desk chair at a desk covered in a jumble of papers. The computer was switched off. Although it must have been several years since smoking indoors had been allowed, the room still smelled faintly of stale tobacco smoke. Oldroyd wondered if Armitage still snatched a quick illicit drag now and again.

Oldroyd introduced Carter, and the three detectives started to review the case, bringing Carter up to speed.

'Everything's OK with the supers,' said Armitage. 'I think they know each other from some golfing circuit or other. Tomlinson's going to be in Walker's debt now he's released the two of you.'

'Yes and we'd better not take too long about it or he'll get restless and want us back.' Oldroyd was perched on a rather uncomfortable chair and had refused Armitage's offer of coffee as he knew it would be some dire economy instant stuff.

'Probably, but the signs aren't good for a quick solution, Jim. I mean, we've hardly begun and we've no real leads, except one thing that was found last night. One of the CSOs found it in Muller's coat pocket, but I didn't get it until this morning.'

He spread out a piece of paper on the desk. On it was a message completed with letters cut from magazines. It said: You have been warned.

'It was in this envelope. It's addressed to Muller, but here the whole name has been cut out of something so at first glance it doesn't look particularly odd. Someone must have got this to him last night; maybe left it somewhere. We need to find out if anyone took it to Muller.'

Oldroyd frowned. 'Well, that's interesting, but it doesn't tell us much.'

'No. Warned about what? It could be all sorts of things, but most likely something to do with the violin; maybe he was under pressure to sell it.'

'Could you just run through the basics for me, sir?' asked Carter, settling in by drinking Armitage's coffee and munching a digestive biscuit, but feeling a little lost.

'Of course.' Armitage looked at his notes. 'It's a good time to review what we know after all that hurly burly last night. Hans Muller was shot at five past nine by an unknown person, assuming there was just one up there.'

'I should hope so, Sam – we can't do with two of the buggers disappearing,' observed Oldroyd wryly.

'The gun's been sent for analysis, but it looked very much to me like a Russian Dragunov sniper rifle, fitted with a silencer.'

'I'll take it from you, Sam; you were always a bit of a firearms man.'

'Well, we'll see, but if I'm right it's not going to help. They've been making Dragunovs since 1963 so there are plenty around and they're not difficult to get hold of. The only thing we can conclude is that the sniper knew what he was doing: set up the rifle in the ideal position, confident enough at that short distance to hit the target without needing an optical sight. Using the silencer gave him a little more time before people reacted so that he could get away, however he did it. We searched the building thoroughly. No sign of anyone; no hiding places, trapdoors, secret tunnels, windows out of the toilets or anything like that and no other external doors he could have used. However, the person on the entrance door says no one left after the shooting except Frank Dancek, who was definitely in the concert hall when the shot was fired. The people behind the bar didn't see anybody else come down, either, and they also saw Dancek leave the building. To add to that, the violin Strad thing, whatever you call it, has disappeared; someone took advantage of the confusion to remove it. Which strongly suggests that the motive for the killing was the theft of that instrument – which you say, Jim, would be worth a lot of money.'

'Priceless. Millions anyway, to a collector.'

'The Dragunov's an old rifle, isn't it, sir?' asked Carter. 'It's not the kind of weapon you'd expect a professional hitman to use, is it?'

'Well, the model that was used at the Chapel is an old one, that's true,' said Armitage.

'So it's probably not a contract killing?'

'Well, I don't know. Obviously it's not at the top of the range, no, but there must be plenty of criminals around, particularly from the old Eastern Europe, you know – Poland, Romania, Serbia – who must be handy with the Dragunov; it was standard issue in all the armies of the Warsaw Pact countries up to the late eighties. People like that will charge less so it might be what you could call an "economy" job. What do you think, Jim?'

'I'm not sure. I'm inclined to think, like you, that the murder is related to the violin, because it's significant that the killer waited until Muller put it down on the table before shooting; that must have been to make sure it wasn't damaged. But, well, I was already half-thinking last night, it's a crazy scheme, isn't it? So many things don't add up. The assassination was efficiently done, but the idea of taking the violin in the aftermath is very chancy; there was no way they could guarantee that no one would notice; the bloody thing was there in full view.'

'That didn't stop them taking it from under your nose, Jim,' said Armitage, teasingly.

Carter smiled. 'True, but what a risk it was; the killing and the theft don't go together somehow to me. Where does that threatening note fit in? Can you imagine a professional operator leaving a note like that? Also if you were going to kill someone and steal a violin, why would you do it at a public event like a concert, which makes the whole thing more difficult?'

'We don't know why yet,' said Armitage, 'but there must have been a reason; maybe they could only perform their illusion somewhere like this and not in the street in broad daylight.'

Oldroyd looked sharply at Armitage. 'You mean disappearing from the building was a conjuring trick?'

'I'm beginning to think so. How else could someone get out without being seen? Maybe it was all done with mirrors, as they say.' Armitage didn't sound as if he believed it himself, thought Oldroyd; he was normally such a down-to-earth, practical character, the last person to suggest something as fanciful as magic. It sounded desperate, but nevertheless it made Oldroyd think.

'There is another possibility, isn't there, sir?' said Carter. 'I mean about the killer disappearing. What if there was actually never anybody up there? Could the gun have been fired remotely somehow?'

'Good point; I'd thought about that,' said Armitage, thinking privately that this lad was sharp. 'But it's not possible; all there was up there was the old Dragunov, no sign of any electronics or anything. The set-up would have to be very sophisticated; you'd need to be able to aim remotely as well as trigger the rifle. I don't see how you could do that with a Dragunov.'

Carter didn't give up; he was always eager to please Oldroyd, who he knew placed a high value on intelligence and imagination, thinking outside the box.

'Is there any possibility that the gun in the gantry was, like, a dummy, and he was actually shot from somewhere else?'

'Well, we won't know for sure until we get the report from forensics; but I'd say, from the wound sustained, the line of fire would track back up to that point – he couldn't have been shot from any other angle.'

'Maybe from the same angle but lower down, someone at the back of the audience?'

'No one reported seeing anything, and presumably they would, even if it was another gun with a silencer.'

'But that might explain how they got out, if they were actually in the audience. They just mingled with the rest of the crowd and eventually left, while you were distracted looking up in that gantry.'

Oldroyd nodded. It was imaginative thinking, but in the end how could it have been done without anyone sitting around the shooter noticing? But maybe . . . Everything had to be considered. Oldroyd decided he'd had enough for the moment and stood up.

'So that's about it, all we know. The players are coming in for questioning later on; let's go down to the Chapel, Carter, and I'll show you the crime scene. Might make a little detour on the way, show you something interesting. See you in an hour or so, Sam.'

Anna Robson sighed as she woke exhausted from a few hours' restless sleep and turned over in bed. She looked at her watch: 6.30 a.m. She sat up and sighed again, putting her head in her hands. She'd never get back to sleep again now, as all the memories of the previous night had come crashing back into her mind.

The remaining members of the quartet had stayed in the nearest hotel, part of the Quality Inn chain: comfortable, standardised and featureless. Hamilton and Stringer were in rooms further down a long corridor with its frequent fire doors. It felt more like a school than a hotel.

Anna pushed back the duvet, sat on the edge of the bed and yawned. After they'd finally been allowed to leave the Red Chapel they'd walked through the eerily quiet streets and checked in here. She'd tried to contact her partner without success and had lain awake for hours turning over the events of the evening in her mind.

She made herself a cup of tea and switched on the television and found BBC News 24. It felt reassuring to hear voices from the outside world. A female presenter talked about a row in a political party, problems in hospitals; a bomb had exploded in some far-off country and people were pictured screaming and running from the scene. Anna felt curiously detached from it all; there was nothing about Hans's murder. Was it too early yet, or had she missed it? She wanted to know what the police were thinking.

She switched the television off and went into the shower. She'd just finished dressing when there was a knock on the door. It was Michael Stringer. He was unshaven and looked exhausted.

'How are you?'

'Not good. Where's Martin?'

'Still in his room, I think.'

'OK. Come in; we need to talk.'

Martin Hamilton was indeed in his room, an identical one to Anna Robson's. He was awake, and lay in bed considering the situation, feeling a certain trepidation about the day ahead. The agitation made him turn over on to his side, and his ample belly spread out on to the mattress beneath him. They had to go to the police station later in the morning for further questioning and he didn't fancy the prospect. Like Anna, he wondered what the police were thinking. He frowned and shook his head. Why worry? He had nothing to fear. Just be straight with them. Surely after that they would be allowed to go home? He looked forward to returning to London and getting on with things, even though he knew he faced a different life now that Hans was dead and the Schubert Quartet with him. He would miss playing in the quartet but never mind: he had other avenues to pursue. He looked over to where his cello case was propped against the wall and smiled.

It was a short journey on foot from the police station to the Red Chapel. Carter walked along with Oldroyd through the streets of Halifax, some of which were still cobbled with big nineteenth-century granite setts. It seemed a funny little place to Carter; the older buildings were mostly constructed of sandstone and were yellowy in colour, except those that had not been cleaned and were still black from years of coal smoke. These were mixed with some fading 1960s and 70s geometrical tat, the usual shopping centres and multi-storey car parks. He caught sight of one huge modern building, which seemed out of context in this small town. Oldroyd said this had originally been the HQ of the famous Halifax Building Society, before mutuality had largely been abandoned in the greedy years since Thatcher. Carter smiled at his boss's political reference but it meant little to him; he couldn't remember the time before Thatcher. He looked into the distance. The town had been built among steep hills: in nearly every direction you could see across to high fields, some with sheep and cows in them, as if you weren't really in a town at all, but then suddenly the view would be disrupted by one of the few remaining mill chimneys from the textile era.

'Just down here, Carter,' said Oldroyd, taking a sharp left turn. 'There's something I want to show you.'

They walked down a cobbled lane. Carter saw a high wall ahead, then they walked through some large gates. Immediately everything opened out into an enormous square bordered on each side by a stone-built colonnade with three storeys. It was spacious and light, a total transformation from the narrow lanes surrounding it.

'Wow. Didn't expect this, sir!'

'Wonderful, isn't it? Like an Italian piazza; have you seen Venice or Siena?'

'No, sir; don't know Italy.' This was not entirely true. Carter had once had a beach holiday in Sorrento, but he didn't think that counted. He knew he was in for another Yorkshire history lesson, but he didn't mind. Against all his expectations, as a Londoner without much knowledge of the north of England, he always found what Oldroyd had to say interesting.

'It's called the Piece Hall. The "pieces" were lengths of cloth. Before the factory system started, people wove cloth in their homes and then it was sold here in a big market; must have been a great bustling place.'

'Yeah, someone must have made a lot of money out of it, too, building a place like this.'

'True,' replied Oldroyd as they walked across the huge square to an exit on the other side. 'It must have seemed amazing to the local people at the time, like a medieval cathedral to the peasants. Of course it was the merchants who got rich on it. The weavers didn't see much: they carried on struggling in their cottages – then when the factory system started they moved into the terraced houses and worked for a pittance for the mill owners. And now? Who knows what they do, but you can bet it'll be low-paid casual stuff. Nothing changes.'

'Yeah, too right, sir, but what was that thing you said when you were talking about how dirty it used to be round here in Yorkshire? "Where there's money . . ."' He tried to speak in a Yorkshire accent, which always amused Oldroyd.

'"Where there's muck there's money", lad. Aye, well done, thi accent's comin' on.'

Carter grinned. They were about to exit through another huge door when he saw something.

'Look up there, sir.' He pointed to the second storey, near the exit, where there was a sign. '"Violins, Stringed Instruments". Maybe they had something to do with it.'

It wasn't a serious suggestion, but Oldroyd looked up and seemed intrigued.

'Hmm, well, you never know; it might be worth a visit. At least they should know who's interested in acquiring violins in these parts.'

When they turned left outside the Piece Hall, the Red Chapel was visible across an area covered with old flagstones. In daylight, it looked different to Oldroyd. The events of the previous night seemed remote, as if he might have dreamed it all. But the presence of the yellow-and-black tape reminded him that it had been all too real.

They went inside, and he showed Carter everything: the entrance, the bar, the stairs up to the main hall, the lighting gantry and the separate steps down to the artists' room. He was hoping that walking through it all again might give him a fresh perspective and some ideas, but it didn't.

Carter stood in the performance area. Things had been tidied up, but there was still the dry stain of blood on the floor.

'And the bloke was shot here while he was playing?' he asked, trying again to make sense of it.

'Not exactly. It was at the end of the second movement; he'd just put the violin down.' Oldroyd thought about this again. Was that just the killer waiting to protect the violin or was there another reason? More questions than answers. He glanced around the crime scene for a last time.

'We'd better get back; we're not going to find out any more in this building. Someone who was here that night knows the answer. It's time we got to work on some questioning.'

~

Anna Robson looked decidedly nervous, thought Oldroyd, as he sat with Armitage and Carter facing her in the interview room. She was wearing casual clothes: expensive-looking jeans and top, and her dark hair was tied back. She sat awkwardly and avoided eye contact. Armitage asked her to go through the events of the previous day.

'I came up from London on the train with Michael; set off about one p.m.; changed at Leeds; got here about four thirty. We arranged to meet at the venue – the Red Chapel, is it?' Armitage nodded. 'At five p.m. we rehearsed a bit, got something to eat. We know – knew – the pieces well.' She stumbled on her words as the reality of their quartet being a thing of the past hit her again.

'Where did the others come from?' asked Armitage.

'Hans also came up from London, but he got a later train I think. I don't know where Martin had been. We don't stay together all the time, Chief Inspector. It's a professional arrangement: we only meet to rehearse and perform; we lead separate lives.'

'How did everyone seem to you? Did anything unusual happen?' Oldroyd watched her carefully. She was definitely uneasy about something.

'No, not really; things were just normal.'

'What do you mean, "not really"?'

She was momentarily reluctant to continue but then said, 'Michael and Hans had a bit of an argument – they don't get on very well – but it was nothing serious.'

'What about?'

'We all admired Hans, but we knew he was coming to the end of his career. Michael was worried about what would happen if Hans retired; he kept pressing him to say when he would go, thought we should be looking for a replacement, maybe rehearsing with someone part of the time. Hans got very angry; I don't think he wanted to think

35

about retiring. It's such a big step after a lifetime playing. He certainly didn't want anyone telling him when to go. They also disagreed about our repertoire. Michael thought we were getting a bit stale with the Viennese classics, you know; especially Schubert, though he is our speciality. Michael wanted to do more modern works: Bartok, Ravel. Hans would have none of it. I think he thought he was too old to start doing new things, so Michael's two complaints came together, really.'

'And last night?'

'Same old things: Michael saying we'd done Haydn and Schubert to death; Hans saying you could never perform the greats too much – they were the timeless masters – and so on. They were at it up to a few minutes before we started.'

'What did you and Martin Hamilton think about it?'

'We're more easy-going; we didn't mind keeping things the same until Hans gave up. Then would be the time to change.'

'Did these arguments ever threaten to become violent?'

'Not really; except once. It was Hans who got threatening, and he said something odd.' She paused again.

'Go on.'

'They were having one of their barneys. Michael had implied that Hans might be past his best. Hans stood up, furious. I thought he was going to hit Michael, but he said that when he was younger he would have had him sorted out. But nothing ever came of these rows. They would calm down and apologise to each other and that would be that.'

Oldroyd looked puzzled.

'So he said he would have had him sorted out, not he would have sorted him out himself?'

'Yes, but you have to remember that English was Hans's second language. Sometimes his expressions were unusual.'

'What do you know about Hans's background?'

'Not a lot; he never said much. He came from East Germany after the Wall came down in 1989; never talked about his life there. I remember when he arrived at the Bloomsbury School while we were still students and it was so exciting. He had this aura about him, like many string players from Central Europe.' Oldroyd saw her eyes light up at the memory. 'And he had this fabulous instrument: a Munsterhaven Strad. None of us had ever seen anything like it. It was legendary, though it became a curse.'

'Did he say where he got it from?' asked Oldroyd.

'No, never; no one liked to ask. Hans was a very private person and he could be very fierce if he felt people were prying into his life. We never asked him questions like that, especially in the early days; we looked up to him so much, felt so privileged that he selected us to form his quartet.'

'Apart from Stringer, did Muller have any enemies? Anyone who might want to kill him?' asked Armitage.

Anna reacted immediately. 'Michael wasn't his enemy; they just disagreed about things. Michael would never have harmed Hans.' Oldroyd thought she sounded very defensive. 'I said last night, I can't think of anyone who would. He lived for his music; I don't even know who his friends were, if he had any.'

'We found this in Muller's pocket after he was killed – it suggests someone didn't like him for some reason.' Armitage showed her the message. Robson looked shocked.

'That's awful. What does it mean? Warned about what?'

'We don't know. Do you know anything about it?'

'No, nothing. Do you think this was written by the murderer?'

'It could have been. Muller wasn't married?'

'No.'

'Any family?'

'None that I knew about, unless they were still in Germany. He never spoke to me about anyone.'

'Did you see anyone take the violin after Muller was shot?'

Oldroyd watched as she rubbed her hands nervously together, the strong but elegant and sensitive hands and fingers of a viola player.

'No, I asked the inspector where it was. I didn't see anything. We came to the end of the slow movement, Hans was shot and after a few seconds we left down the other staircase; we didn't feel safe up there. I didn't notice the Strad.'

'You think this is all to do with the violin, though, don't you?' asked Oldroyd slightly more firmly. 'You said just now it became a curse.'

'Perhaps. It's a wonderful thing, isn't it? But something like that can cause evil; people are jealous, they want it for themselves.'

'Are you thinking of anyone in particular?' asked Oldroyd.

'No.'

Oldroyd's long experience of interrogation and listening carefully to the nuances of people's replies told him that might not be true.

'To your knowledge,' pursued Armitage, 'had anyone made any offers to him or threats about the violin recently? Was he concerned, worried about anything?'

'No, as I said to the inspector last night, he just told me that people were always bothering him about it, making him offers, being persistent – you know; it was a nuisance.'

'You mean collectors, wealthy people?'

'I suppose so. I don't know much about it, but I think it's a murky world. Do you think that message was about the Strad?'

'It could have been. What about the rest of you? You play valuable instruments as well, don't you?'

'Yes, but not in the class of Hans's violin – and we don't own them; they belong to the school. Most professionals who play high-quality instruments have them on loan; they can't afford to buy them.'

'So Muller would have been a particular target, for people who wanted to acquire something special?'

'Maybe.'

Armitage glanced at Oldroyd, who nodded to him. It was time to end the interview, but he still had one question left. Armitage liked to keep something important back until they were, as he said, 'softened up'.

'And how would you describe your own relationship with Hans Muller?'

Oldroyd saw that the question affected her deeply. He thought she was going to burst into tears.

'It was always . . . good,' she struggled to say. 'I admired him a lot; he was one of the greatest musicians I've ever known.'

'What did you think of her, then, sir?' asked Carter when the interview was over.

Oldroyd was drinking a mug of awful, milky, weak instant coffee that Armitage had made for him. He grimaced as he replied.

'She's not telling us everything, that's for sure. My instinct is she wasn't involved in the murder but suspects or even knows something about it. There could be someone she's trying to protect. Anyway, let's see how we get on with the next one.'

Michael Stringer was brought into the interview room. He was thin, almost gaunt-looking, with short greying hair and intense eyes. Where Anna Robson had looked nervous and defensive, he had an air of anger and defiance.

'Can I just ask what all this is about?' he said before he was asked any questions. 'Surely none of us can be suspects? We were all sitting there in full view when the shot was fired; we don't need alibis or anything.'

'It's routine to question everyone,' replied Armitage. 'And you don't need me to tell you that not everyone who plans a murder carries it out themselves.'

Stringer laughed sardonically. 'Oh, so you think one of us took out a contract on Hans, thereby ruining our professional life together, and for what? The violin? Great scheme: murder someone in a public concert and steal a violin while everybody's watching.'

Oldroyd smiled; he'd thought exactly the same himself.

'Did you see what happened to the violin?' Armitage ignored Stringer's bitter sarcasm.

'No, we left the room as soon as Hans was shot. I didn't see anything, and anyway the chief inspector was there.' He nodded towards Oldroyd.

'We understand you travelled up with Anna Robson yesterday and met Hans Muller here. How was he? Did you notice anything unusual?'

'No, nothing.'

'Was there anything strange about his behaviour in the last few weeks?'

'No.'

'Did he have any enemies, people who might wish him harm?'

'Not that I know of. As Anna said last night, people bothered him about the Strad – crackpots, some of them – but Hans wasn't the kind of person to let things like that get to him.'

'What do you make of this?' Armitage again produced the note and Stringer read it.

'What on earth's all this about?'

'It was found on Muller, in his pocket.'

'I've no idea; some nutter, I suppose. Hans never said anything about it. It suggests someone was pursuing him over something, doesn't it? But I don't know anything about it.'

'You and he didn't get along too well, did you?' asked Carter, who had decided it was time to take a more active role. He knew his boss liked him to get fully engaged in any case they were investigating. Stringer looked up and frowned.

'What has Anna been saying? What have you forced out of her? You're not suggesting I gave that note to Hans?'

'We didn't force anything out of her; she simply said that you and Muller disagreed about some matters, like the things you should be playing.'

'Hans was opposed to any kind of change; he wouldn't consider any alteration to our repertoire and I disagreed. Yes, we used to argue about it sometimes – we were arguing just before the concert, actually – but that's hardly a reason to murder someone.'

'And you were worried about the future, weren't you? What would happen when Muller retired . . . And he wasn't well, was he?'

Stringer darted malicious looks at the three detectives. 'You have been pumping her for information. Yes I am – *was* – concerned about what was going to happen. Hans was getting on and had problems in his bowing arm. The others seemed quite happy to drift along, but I thought that was a mistake. You can't suddenly start playing with a stranger, especially as leader; you have to practise for a long time, develop that rapport with each other. I thought it would be better if Hans was phased out, as it were, better for everyone, but he seemed to think it an insult, said I was trying to get rid of him.'

'And were you?' asked Oldroyd directly. There was a flash of anger in Stringer's eyes.

'Of course not.'

'But he was getting to you, wasn't he? It would all run more smoothly if he was out of the way. You could get the repertoire changed and then maybe you could become the first violin and the leader.'

Stringer leaped to his feet. 'That's an outrageous suggestion! How dare you? I . . .'

'Sit down, please, Mr Stringer,' said Armitage in a deadpan voice. 'No point getting agitated.' He cut a rather lugubrious figure, slumped in his chair, hands on his belly, his large moustache drooping at either side of his face. He only needs a big pocket watch, thought Oldroyd, and he would be a perfect Victorian alderman.

The violinist sat down as his anger subsided and for the first time looked unsettled and defensive.

'Go on.'

'Well, I have no ambitions to be leader; I'm happy as second violin. I think it suits my style of playing; I'm not an extrovert player. The idea that I would kill Hans in order to take his place . . . Well.'

'What about the violin? You must have envied him playing an instrument like that?'

'So now I bumped him off for the violin?' Stringer raised his arms in a gesture of contempt. 'To be quite honest, I wouldn't want it. The worry and responsibility . . . It would get on my nerves.'

He paused for a moment and looked thoughtful.

'There is one thing. I've been thinking, you know, since what happened. We still have a connection with the Bloomsbury School; we teach there, give master classes and stuff like that. Hans always got on well with the authorities there. He was grateful to them for taking him in when he came to the West, and giving him the opportunities.'

'So?'

'Well, Patrick Jefferson – Sir Patrick: never liked him myself, pretentious so and so. Not much of a conductor either, if you ask me – he's the principal; lots of connections in the music world, always touting for money. The thing is, a few days ago, I was there working with a group of young fiddle players and took a break. I happened to walk past Jefferson's office and I could hear Hans in there raising his voice. He was clearly very upset about something and I heard him say something like: "You can forget it after this."

'Then he came storming out of the room and down the corridor in the opposite direction to me. Jefferson poked his head out of the door, looking sheepish, and glanced up and down the corridor as if he was checking if anyone could have heard what was going on. He nodded to me, rather cursorily, and then went back inside. I didn't think much about it at the time, and Hans never said anything, but when you asked if he had any enemies . . . Well, I don't know; it's not much, but it was quite a shock to hear it and he sounded really angry.'

Oldroyd had been listening intently. 'Do you have any idea what the argument might have been about?'

'No.'

'And you don't remember any tension between the two men before?'

'No. That's the point, really. I rarely saw Hans angry about anything, except sometimes with me.' He smiled wryly.

Armitage stirred himself.

'You're quite right to mention it. When exactly did this row take place?'

'It was Wednesday, a couple of days before the concert.'

'Thank you, Mr Stringer.'

'Do you think he wanted Muller out of the way badly enough to get him shot?' asked Carter sceptically, once Stringer had left the room.

'Not really – and, as he says, what a way to do it,' replied Oldroyd. 'We'll have to follow up this business at the Bloomsbury School, though; get down to London at some point. But, on the face of it, it doesn't look promising: principal of a college takes out a contract on a distinguished associate. What on earth might prompt that?'

'If Stringer was worried that the quartet might flounder if Muller stayed, that might be a motive; after all, it's his future at stake.'

Oldroyd slouched in his chair with his hands behind his head. Nothing was making much sense yet.

'Oh, I don't know,' he sighed. 'Bring on the next.'

~

Martin Hamilton seemed the calmest of the three interviewees. He sat relaxed in his chair with a faint smile on his face as the detectives asked him the same questions and showed him the note.

'No, I don't know of anyone who would have wished Hans any harm. I'm sure Anna and Michael will have told you: he was a private person, led a quiet life; didn't have many friends, I don't think, but no enemies either, that I knew of. I can't imagine who would send him a horrible note like that; it's weird.'

'We understand he and Michael Stringer didn't get along too well. What was your perception of that?'

Hamilton shrugged his shoulders. 'It was nothing, really; they disagreed about what we should be playing. Michael was worried about the future, tended to nag Hans about the repertoire and so on, but the fact is if four people are going to play together like we do, they have to get on pretty well – it wouldn't work otherwise.'

'So how would you describe your relationship with him?'

'Good; we always got on well. He was a magnificent artist and we'll miss him badly.'

'I understand you came here separately yesterday.'

'Yes.'

'Where were you during the day?'

'I was in London until the afternoon, then I drove up here. I have some business interests that I was dealing with. I buy and sell musical instruments.'

This got the detectives very interested.

'What does that involve, exactly?' asked Oldroyd.

'Through my contacts in the musical world, I get to know when instruments are going to be available and I act as a kind of agent for some of the auction houses and for some of the wealthy dealers and collectors.'

'So you would be interested in a Munsterhaven Strad?'

Hamilton smiled. 'I knew this was coming, Chief Inspector, and the answer is: yes, of course. But only if it was acquired legitimately. I'm not in the habit of bumping people off to get my hands on priceless violins.'

'Are you one of the people who harassed Hans Muller about the Strad?'

'No point, Chief Inspector; I talked to him about it, naturally, but he made it clear it was not for sale and never would be. I accepted that – and I'm not in the habit of sending threatening notes either.'

'Who were you seeing yesterday in London?'

'A client of mine. I'd rather not mention names; it's a matter of privacy and confidentiality.'

'I'm afraid that won't do, sir.' Armitage became more formal as he laid down the rules. 'We will need to speak to that person as part of the investigation.'

Hamilton looked a little uncomfortable. He frowned and his eyes darted from side to side, as if he was calculating something. Finally he said, 'Her name is Elizabeth Knott. She lives in Mayfair – 16 Belvedere Crescent; huge Georgian house – very wealthy, collects stringed instruments. She was heiress to the Elliot fortune: you remember Sir Bernard Elliot, her father? Invented those household gadgets – that vacuum cleaner and stuff. He started the collection and she's continued it. I've seen what's there and it's stunning.'

'So she might be interested in acquiring a Munsterhaven Strad?'

'I'm sure she would if one ever came on the market – which is highly unlikely, I'd say. But that wasn't what I went to see her about. She's interested in a sixteenth-century lute that's for sale; wants me to negotiate for her. We're talking about hundreds of thousands.'

'OK. Moving on, then. You say you didn't see what happened to the Strad last night?'

'No, none of us did, and your officers searched the room, didn't they? Even looked in my cello case.'

'Yes.'

Hamilton's face formed into a very serious expression, but Oldroyd, scrutinising him very closely, was not sure that it was genuine.

'So it's a bad business all round. I don't envy you: man killed and priceless instrument goes missing. Sorry I can't help you any more.'

'One more thing,' said Armitage. 'Stringer told us he overheard Muller having a row with the principal of your college, Patrick Jefferson. Do you know anything about that?'

'Absolutely nothing, I'm afraid. They always got on well, as far as I was aware.'

While the detectives were processing their first interviews and getting the investigation under way, an emergency informal meeting of some of the members of the Halifax Chamber Music Society committee was taking place in a nearby pub in order to undertake their own enquiry. They assembled in a little snug bar at the back of the building, somewhere that would have been a smoke-filled place for male beer-swilling darts players, until the British pub began to change. It was now a quiet, clean and comfortable little space, tastefully decorated, with a wood-burning stove in one corner.

Gerald Watson and Frank Dancek sat with pints of real ale in front of them. Nigel Howarth, who had called the emergency services the previous night, had a pint of lager, and Ruth Greenfield a glass of pinot grigio. None of the other committee members were available, including Stuart Atkinson, who'd been on the door for the concert and was too traumatised to leave his house.

The mood was sombre and no one spoke for a while.

'Well, what the hell do you make of it all?' began Watson at last.

'God knows, incredible,' said Howarth. 'It's the last thing you expect: someone murdered at a sedate chamber music concert. It's not exactly a drug-fuelled rock gig where arguments could get out of hand.

The police will be going over everything with a fine-toothed comb so we'd better make sure our testimonies harmonise – not that we've anything to hide.' Howarth was a wiry-framed, rather nervous character, a local solicitor who negotiated contracts with the visiting performers and tended to focus on the legal implications of everything.

'There's not much to say, is there?' continued Watson. 'There we all were, listening to a concert, and then suddenly, bang, it was all over and there was a corpse on the floor.'

Ruth Greenfield winced. 'Don't remind me.'

'How much could you see up there?' Watson asked Dancek.

'Not much – too dark – just a shape.'

'And nothing when you got down the stairs?'

'No. I still can't understand it. How could anyone get out of the building without being seen?'

'It was a bit risky pursuing the assailant, wasn't it?' asked Howarth in legalese.

'I know, but I didn't think about it; it happened so quickly and I was angry. It was just an instinct.'

'What about that fiddle? What the bloody hell happened to that? I didn't see anything,' said Watson, 'and I was fairly close.'

'Nobody did; we were all distracted. It must have all been planned, and very clever too.' Greenfield fiddled nervously with her glass and still seemed very shaken by the events of the previous night.

'What will we do about the concert that's coming soon?' asked Dancek. 'There's a piano trio in two weeks' time. Can we continue?'

'Well, you know what they say,' said Watson with a sardonic smile. 'There's no such thing as bad publicity; we might get an audience boost.'

Ruth Greenfield winced again.

'Even so,' said Howarth. 'It could be seen as bad taste; we might at least have to look at changing the venue. I don't even think the police will have finished investigating the Chapel by then, so we won't be able to use it.'

'There'll be a stain,' said Greenfield, morbidly distracted. 'A red stain on the floor where he fell; they'll never get rid of it completely. It'll always remind us.' She shook her head. 'Maybe we should move somewhere else permanently.'

'I know what you mean but we can't decide that now.'

'Whatever we do, things will never be the same again.'

'No, I don't suppose they will.'

'Well, I'm going to have a word with the police,' said Watson. 'I think we should go straight back in there and show we're not intimidated. As they say: the show must go on.'

When the interviews with the remaining members of the quartet were over, the detectives made their way back to the office.

'Let's have a spot of lunch, shall we?' suggested Armitage eagerly and his eyes lit up for the first time that day. 'I'll send someone out; they do some good Cornish pasties at Mawson's round the corner.'

As they waited for their pasties, they compared notes. Carter was drinking from a can of Coke; Oldroyd had asked for tea this time and Armitage had joined him. Outside it had started to rain again. A DC arrived with three large Cornish pasties in paper bags. They ate them straight from the bags as they carried on discussing the case.

'As far as the note goes, I don't think any of them wrote it,' said Oldroyd. 'It just doesn't seem the kind of thing that any of them would do.'

'I think you're probably right,' agreed Armitage.

'I didn't trust that last one,' said Carter. 'He was too calm for me. I prefer it when they get angry or upset.'

'Yes,' replied Armitage through a mouthful of pasty. Flakes of pastry were sticking to his moustache. He brushed them off. 'The bugger seemed to be gloating at us; saying how difficult it was and he was very sorry. Too cocky for my liking.'

'Why did he have to remind us that the artists' room had been searched?' said Oldroyd. He sipped his tea and was as disappointed as he had been with the coffee: too weak, lukewarm and very milky; exactly how he didn't like it. 'He knows that we know that. It was as if he was reinforcing the fact that we hadn't found anything there.'

'You read a lot into things sometimes, Jim.'

'Maybe, but I'm with you: he was trying to seem upset and serious but beneath it he seemed almost upbeat, as if it was something good that had happened. You'd almost think he was the one who didn't get on with Muller for some reason, and was glad to see the back of him.'

'He must have had a keen interest in that violin, more than he was letting on,' said Carter. 'Imagine dealing in things like that and every day you're sitting next to someone playing a fabulous example, something you'd just love to get your hands on. It'd be like being a car nerd and driving a Ford Focus and the bloke next to you at work comes in an Alfa Romeo every day.'

Oldroyd winced at the comparison, but acknowledged the accuracy of Carter's observation.

'I agree,' said Armitage. 'He told us he dealt in instruments but he was very cagey about the details; I think it's all a bit dodgy.' He yawned, downed the rest of his tea and looked as if he wouldn't mind a post-lunch nap.

'Anyway, we'll just have to soldier on until we get something definite. It's time we started talking to the people who were running things on the night. Why don't you go over and have a word with that Frank Dancek? I wonder if he knows more than he's letting on at the moment.'

Four

The 'Kiesewetter' Stradivarius was made in 1723. It is named after a German composer and is valued at $4 million. In 2008 it was on loan to the Russian violinist Philippe Quint when he accidentally left it in a taxi cab in New York City. The cab driver returned it and was given an award for his honesty by the city of Newark, New Jersey.

Frank Dancek lived in the top-floor flat of a large Victorian terraced house off King Cross Road.

It was well into the afternoon when Oldroyd and Carter arrived. Dancek was just on his way out, dressed in a black coat, scarf and fur-lined Russian hat; there was an unmistakeable Eastern European air about him. He smiled, seeming pleased to see the detectives. He turned round and led them back into the flat.

They sat in a rather chilly, high-ceilinged sitting room; Dancek kept his coat on. Oldroyd noticed an old stereo system, with large speakers, which had clearly evolved over the years as it contained both a turntable and a CD player. There were cabinets full of vinyl discs, cassettes and CDs. Oldroyd sympathised with the expense of having to keep upgrading to the latest technology.

'Do you live here alone?'

'Yes, Chief Inspector, I never married, you know. No one would have me, as they say.' He chuckled. Oldroyd was once again intrigued by his idiosyncratic accent, which combined foreign tones and flat Yorkshire vowels. He looked at Dancek, who had a large head with a shock of white hair, a rather hooked nose and slanting eyes.

'Where do you come from, originally I mean?'

'From what's now the Czech Republic, Chief Inspector. Where I grew up used to be called Sudetenland; we spoke German. I managed to get out to the West after the trouble in 1968, you know.'

Oldroyd did remember, though he was a boy at the time: Alexander Dubček and the Prague Spring, crushed by Soviet tanks later in the year.

'So you ended up here in Yorkshire?'

'Yes, it's been my home for many years. I love it. People have always been friendly to me.'

'You're fond of music I see?'

'Of course – and you, too, Chief Inspector. I've seen you many times at the concerts. We both love chamber music, yes?'

Oldroyd agreed. 'Can you tell me again what happened last night at the Red Chapel?'

'Certainly, Chief Inspector. I was sitting at the end of the row with people from the committee. I saw Muller fall and I was stunned at first, like everyone else. Then I looked up and saw something move up there in the gantry so I thought that must be the killer. I ran down the stairs without thinking, really. I know it was a dangerous thing to do – I might have been shot – but it was just an instinct. I was telling the others in the pub – Ruth and Gerald, you know – I think I was angry as well as shocked that somebody had done this awful thing in one of our concerts, and killed a great violin player.

'The door up to the gantry ladder was open so I thought he must have already got down to the bottom and run out of the building, but when I got there no one had seen anything; that's Mr Atkinson, who was by the door, and the people in the bar. I couldn't believe it so I rushed outside and went round the Chapel and the nearby streets to check if there was anyone there. I thought maybe there was another way out that I didn't know about, but I couldn't see anything. I came back just as the police were arriving and walked in with them. That's when you saw me. I thought the killer must be still in the building, but you couldn't find anything either.' He shook his head. 'It's very strange.'

'So how long did it take you to react and run down those stairs?' asked Carter. 'Was it long enough for someone to get down that ladder and away?'

'Yes, I think so – just, if they moved quickly as soon as they'd fired the shot. You see there was a bit of a delay before we all realised what was happening, so it gave whoever it was time to make their escape; though what happened to them, well . . .' He shrugged his shoulders.

'Did you see anyone behaving strangely? It could be important, however trivial you think it is.'

Dancek thought for a moment. 'Not during the evening, no, but I did see something odd – I mean something I didn't expect – earlier on. I'm sure it has no significance.'

'What was it?'

'Well, it was late afternoon; I was walking through the Piece Hall on my way to the Chapel. I like to get there early on concert evenings to make sure everything's OK. I got near the gate when I saw Mr Hamilton, from the quartet, you know. I recognised him from a photograph I'd seen of the Schubert Quartet.'

'What was he doing?'

'He was just coming out of that musical instrument shop on the second floor, but the odd thing was that all the shops were closed; it was nearly six o'clock. He must know the owner, which I suppose is not surprising, considering that Mr Hamilton deals in stringed instruments himself, doesn't he?'

Oldroyd glanced at Carter, who grinned; maybe the detective sergeant was about to be proved right.

'Do you know anything about that shop?' asked Oldroyd.

'No. I've been in once or twice, but there's never much in there; it's very small and they don't sell CDs, only instruments.'

'You don't collect instruments yourself, then?'

Dancek laughed. 'Me, Inspector? No, I don't have the money for that; you have to be very wealthy to do that, like Mr Shaw.'

'Who?'

'Mr Edward Shaw is the president of our chamber music society. He wasn't there that night; he doesn't come to all the concerts.'

'And he collects instruments?'

Dancek looked a little uncomfortable. 'Well, I don't like saying things about people like this, Inspector; it sounds as if I'm trying to get them into trouble and . . .'

'It's a murder enquiry, sir. You have to tell us everything you know.'

Dancek still looked unhappy. 'Well, yes, he does collect instruments, but he never talks about it and no one mentions it. I don't think anyone's ever seen his collection. We don't want to offend him; he gives a lot of money to the club. We couldn't get performers like the Schubert Quartet without him.'

'I understand. We'll be as careful as we can, but we need to talk to him. Can you tell me where he lives?'

'Well, he's a wealthy man, you know; he lives in a big old house out in the country, Bradclough Hall. It's beautiful.'

'Thank you. Is there anything else you remember?'

Dancek looked thoughtful for a moment.

'Not anything I saw,' he said at last, 'but it was strange, wasn't it, that they were playing *Death and the Maiden*?' He had a distant look in his eyes. 'I wonder if it was just coincidence or is it telling us something? And he was killed at the end of the slow movement, Schubert's meditation on death. It is – what is the English word? – "macabre", I think?'

~

In the early afternoon, Armitage informed the three musicians that they could leave the town but must remain contactable and not leave the country. Hamilton bid the other two a hasty farewell, packed his cello case into the boot of his Audi and got in, ready for the 200-mile drive down the M1. Stringer and Robson decided to travel together back down to London, just as they had travelled up. They boarded a local train at Halifax station and sat on opposite sides of a table in silence. The train plunged into a tunnel almost as soon as it left the station heading east. Robson had a pang of irrational fear as they entered the mouth and she glimpsed the small ferns and water dripping down the walls in the ghostly half-light before everything went dark. Her nerves were so strained, anything strange seemed to alarm her. She couldn't stop herself from thinking gloomy things; it seemed their lives had been suddenly flung into darkness like the train. When they emerged from the tunnel there was a tear running down her face.

'Hey, are you OK?' asked Stringer.

She wiped her face with a white lacy handkerchief retrieved from her small leather handbag.

'Not really. How can I be? He's dead.'

Stringer put his hand over hers on the table.

'I know; it's a terrible shock.'

'Have you thought that any of us could have been shot? We were so close to Hans.'

'I don't think so. There was a marksman up there; he wasn't going to miss.'

'Even so, to be so close to a bullet that hit someone.' She shuddered with the thought. 'How am I ever going to forget seeing Hans lurch to his feet like that, and the blood, and . . .' She dabbed the handkerchief at her face again and looked out of the window. They were passing some fields with cows but there were also towering mills in the valley bottom. It was a strange landscape to her.

'It's hard. I saw it all too; not something I'd like to experience again in a hurry.' Stringer also glanced out of the window. The train entered another tunnel and then started the gradual descent into Bradford.

'What were the police like with you?' asked Robson.

'OK. I made it clear I thought the whole idea of them interviewing us like that, as if we were suspects, was ridiculous. I don't envy them, though, to be honest. It won't be the easiest crime they've ever had to solve.'

'You didn't, you know, say anything, like we agreed?'

'No, nothing, so don't worry.'

They fell silent again. The train reversed out of Bradford Exchange and began the final leg of its journey to Leeds.

'What's it going to be like now?' Robson shook her head. 'It's been our lives for so long. Why did it have to end like this? What are we going to do?'

'I don't know,' replied Stringer, 'but we would've had to face it sooner or later; it's just sooner than we thought, and, well . . .' He shrugged his shoulders as if there was no more he could say. The train arrived at Leeds station and they got off, changing platforms to board the London train. Robson was glad to be back in a city and found the noise and bustle of Leeds station comforting. She felt she was putting some distance between herself and that terrible, gloomy Red Chapel building in that odd little town. Nevertheless, she was suddenly overcome with a wave of tiredness and the prospect of another nearly three hours' travelling before she arrived home was a daunting prospect.

Edward Shaw lived, as Dancek had said, in an extraordinary house in the countryside near Halifax. It was a seventeenth-century West Riding manor house in its own grounds near a small village.

The Shaw family money came from the textile trade, now almost vanished in the West Riding. Edward's great-grandfather had established the Shaw carpet mills in Halifax in the 1860s and the firm had prospered, at one time employing hundreds of people. It was he who had bought Bradclough Hall.

Edward's father had seen the writing on the wall regarding the Yorkshire woollen industry earlier than most, selling up in the 1970s and retiring early a very wealthy man. He'd also been a founder member of the Halifax Chamber Music Society after the war and had begun to collect instruments.

Edward was sent away to an expensive boarding school and there were hopes that he would get into one of the old universities and become a barrister or something. But Edward proved to be a disappointment; he was lazy at academic work and was eventually expelled from the school's sixth form. There were rumours that this was for more sinister reasons than a mere failure to complete essays. He returned home under a cloud and seemed chiefly interested in country sports and his father's instrument collection. His fascination with the latter was partly related to music, as he had once attempted to learn the violin and liked to attend the occasional concert, but more to the value of the collection, which continued to grow as his father slowly added to it, and the prices paid for rare instruments continued to soar. He also dabbled in the general antiques trade. His father set him up in Harrogate with a small business and it was there that he met his wife, Angela, the daughter of a well-to-do North Riding farmer. Although he'd now inherited the family wealth and Bradclough Hall, he kept on the antique business, staffed mainly by himself.

It was Monday morning as Oldroyd drove along the steep, narrow lanes around Norland and Greetland. He was enjoying getting out of the town and glimpsing the fields and moors. He twisted and turned between the dark stone walls until he reached the village of Bradclough, clinging to the valley side. Here he stopped to point out the old weavers' cottages to Carter: low, stone-built houses with large upstairs windows that let in plenty of light to the rooms where the looms had stood in the days of handloom weaving. They drove up a hill out of the village and finally arrived at the entrance to Bradclough Hall. Oldroyd eased the car up the short drive to the house.

'Wow, sir, this is a big pile!' exclaimed Carter, looking up at the heavy stonework and the mullioned and transomed windows. 'A bit gloomy, though.'

Oldroyd, however, gazed in admiration at the dark, atmospheric building. Rooks cawed in the black branches of the leafless trees which surrounded the house. Drystone walls enclosed a garden dominated by overgrown rhododendrons. It could have been a model for Thrushcross Grange in *Wuthering Heights*.

'Magnificent,' was all he said as they walked up to the heavy oak door, which sat beneath an unusual rose window looking out over the moors. Suddenly two shots rang out. The rooks in the trees rose up in a fluttering mass of beating wings and flew around chaotically, cawing madly. The shots appeared to have come from a copse behind the house.

Oldroyd pressed a solid and ancient-looking white doorbell and heard a faint tinkle inside. As they waited, two more shots disrupted the attempts of the rooks to settle again in the trees. The sounds made Carter uneasy. Gunshots were always bad news to a man like him, who'd spent all his life in London before joining West Riding Police and Oldroyd's team. They meant trouble; he wasn't used to hearing shotguns used for relatively innocent purposes in the countryside.

The door was opened by a blonde-haired woman dressed in expensive country casuals. Behind her, the detectives could see an oak-panelled hallway and two black Labradors lying on a Persian rug.

'Yes?' she enquired. 'Can I help you?' She smiled to reveal a perfect set of teeth in her pretty, subtly and expensively made-up face.

The detectives produced their IDs, and Oldroyd introduced them.

'We're investigating the murder of Hans Muller at the Red Chapel in Halifax. We'd like to speak to Mr Edward Shaw; I presume he's your husband?'

The smile on her face died.

'Oh, er, yes he is. I'm Mrs Shaw, but I'm sure Edward knows nothing about it. He's out in the woods shooting a few crows, I think. I'll just call him.'

She pulled a phone out of the pocket of her expensive jeans and tapped at the screen.

'Edward? Yes, you'd better come back; the police are here . . . Yes, the police . . . I don't know exactly why, but it's to do with that murder at the Red Chapel . . . Yes, OK.' She ended the call and said, 'He says he'll be here in a few minutes. Please come in.'

They followed her down the dark, rather baronial entrance hall. Carter half-expected to see burning torches and suits of armour lining the walls. As they passed them, the Labradors roused themselves and commenced a chorus of barking.

'Jasper, Tim, be quiet, what a lot of fuss! I'm sorry. Please come in here.' Mrs Shaw showed them into a spacious sitting room full of chintzy furniture. Large oil paintings in ornate gilt frames adorned the walls. They appeared to be copies of portraits and Scottish landscapes by Landseer. Or were they originals? Above a huge stone fireplace was a large, resplendently antlered stag's head. The windows, by contrast with the rest of the room, seemed small, being composed of heavy mullions and transoms. Carter felt oppressed by the sombreness of all the dark wood and subdued light.

'Please, sit down. My husband won't be long.'

A silence followed. She stroked one of the dogs rather nervously while Oldroyd gazed around the room and contemplated the artworks. Carter hoped for an offer of refreshment but none came.

'It's very quiet here at the moment,' she said after a while. 'Not for long, though: our three children will be back from Sedbergh soon; end of peace and quiet.' She didn't seem to be looking forward to it.

At last there was the sound of footsteps in the hall and a man came into the room. He was dressed in the classic country-gentleman style with green wellington boots, flat cap, expensive check trousers and body warmer. He still carried a double-barrelled shotgun, but had broken it open. He had another dog with him, a springer spaniel with large floppy ears.

'Oh, Edward, darling, this is Chief Inspector Oldroyd and, er, Detective . . . ?'

'Carter, Detective Sergeant Carter.'

'Yes.'

Shaw put the shotgun down on a sideboard and, smiling, shook hands with the two detectives.

'Very pleased to meet you. Just been out picking off a few crows, you know; damn nuisance. What can I do for you?'

Oldroyd noticed there was not a trace of a northern accent; he spoke in the plummy manner of the southern public schoolboy. It was not an endearing quality to the detective so famous for his love of his county that he had been dubbed 'Yorkshire Oldroyd' by colleagues at West Riding Police.

Mrs Shaw got up. 'I'll just take these two out for a walk, then. Come on, Jasper, Tim.'

The Labradors followed her out of the room and pattered off down the hall. Shaw sat down in an armchair opposite Oldroyd and Carter. The spaniel jumped into his lap and he began stroking it.

'I understand from my wife it's about this murder at the Red Chapel? Nasty business, but I don't know how I can help.'

'I understand you're chair of the Halifax Chamber Music Society?'

'That's correct.'

'And you contribute quite a bit of money to the concert fund?'

'Well, I help out, yes, keep the thing afloat, help them to get good performers; they don't come cheap these days.'

'Very generous.'

Shaw relaxed into the armchair. The spaniel wagged its tail.

'Well, it's sentimental reasons really; my father was a great lover of music, founder member of the club, you know. So I don't want to see it die. A lot of the old patrons, his friends, are dead; arts funding's been cut, so . . . There we are.'

'You weren't there on the night in question were you?'

'No.'

'Frank Dancek said you don't come to all the concerts.'

Shaw smiled.

'Have you been talking to him? Nice old chap; eccentric. Came over from the old Czechoslovakia I think; very keen on music – a lot of these Eastern European types are. Doesn't really do much for me, though, to be honest; I'm not like my father. I show my face now and then, of course, but it's a bit, you know, heavy going, all that chamber music.'

Oldroyd gave a rather sour smile. He could hardly say he was drawn to this man.

'But you are like your father as far as your interest in musical instruments goes?'

Shaw's face lit up. 'Ah! Now you're talking. Yes. He left me a wonderful collection and I do my best to add to it when I can.'

Carter was watching Shaw closely while Oldroyd asked the questions. He could see him driving a Range Rover along country lanes but he didn't look like a musical instrument collector.

'Where do you keep your collection then, Mr Shaw?'

'Well, I keep that a secret, Chief Inspector. It's worth a lot of money.'

'The reason I'm asking is that, as I'm sure you know, as it's been all over the papers, a valuable instrument went missing that night in addition to the murder.'

'Yes. Muller's Munsterhaven Strad, I understand.'

Shaw suddenly seemed to realise where the questioning was going. He leaned forward; the spaniel jumped off his lap on to the floor and lay down on a rug.

'But, hang on, Chief Inspector, I haven't got it; don't know anything about it.'

'OK, but I presume you'd be interested in acquiring an instrument like that?'

'A Munsterhaven Strad? Who wouldn't? Absolutely amazing – priceless, as they say – but many people would pay whatever the price was; it's every collector's ambition to get one, isn't it?'

'So I take it you don't have one in your collection?'

'No, I don't have that privilege, unfortunately, and I can't see any prospects of ever getting one. The last one auctioned went for millions, I think. I'm not in that league.'

'But you knew that Muller played one . . .'

'Yes. We all tend to know where the really famous instruments are. You know, who plays them, or if they're in someone's collection.'

'We?'

'I mean the collectors; it's an exclusive little club.'

Of very wealthy people, thought Carter.

'So do you all know each other?'

'I wouldn't say we *know* each other – people are all over the world – but we know *of* each other, put it like that. It's a kind of friendly rivalry: often you're bidding against each other; it's all a bit secretive. We don't like anything to get into the media.'

'I imagine that could get a bit nasty at times; people being disappointed, out-manoeuvred?'

'It has been known to, but I don't get involved in anything like that.'

'So was the fact that Muller had the Strad a factor in getting the Schubert Quartet to come here?'

'Well, not really. I don't decide on the programme – that's Gerald Watson's job; he's secretary. He comes to me to talk about the money involved and we discuss what I'm prepared to put in and so on.'

'But you didn't come to the concert. You missed a chance to see the violin.'

'As I said, the music isn't really my cup of tea. And I couldn't make it on Friday anyway, I'm afraid. I run an antiques business and had to see a client.'

'Could this person verify that?'

Shaw looked slightly alarmed.

'Wait, Chief Inspector, where's this going? Are you implying that I'm somehow involved in the murder of Hans Muller?'

'We have to question everyone who could have had a motive and opportunity.'

'Well, yes, I'm sure he can, in that case. I was nowhere near the Red Chapel when the murder took place.'

Shaw gave a name and number to Carter, who wrote it down.

'There is another reason why the Schubert Quartet might be of interest to you, isn't there?'

'What would that be?'

'Martin Hamilton, the cellist – he's also a dealer in instruments, isn't he? Did you speak to him while he was here?' continued Oldroyd.

Shaw laughed. 'Well, Chief Inspector, it's true that Martin Hamilton's an agent but in this day and age I hardly need to wait for him to come to Halifax in order to speak to him, do I?'

'So have you had any dealings with him?'

Again Oldroyd's sophisticated antennae noticed an almost imperceptible hesitation before the reply, as if Shaw was struggling to retain his style and calm.

'Yes, he's helped me in the past with one or two of my acquisitions, but that had nothing to do with booking the quartet for a concert. As I say, I don't need him to come to Halifax to do business.'

'So you didn't meet him when he came up for the concert?'

'No.'

'And have you had any contact with him since?'

'No, I haven't had any dealings with him for a while.'

'Do you know of any reason why Muller would be shot; anyone with a motive?'

Shaw seemed to relax as if a difficult moment had passed.

'Of course not, Chief Inspector. I mean, I didn't know the man; I only knew, as you might say, the instrument he played.'

Carter had a hunch. 'Do you have anything to do with that instrument shop in the . . . What is it, sir?'

'Piece Hall.'

Shaw laughed. 'Oh, that place! No. It's not serious; it's just a novelty shop and a place to buy cheap instruments. Went in once to have a quick look; full of parents buying second-hand guitars for their little darlings.'

A grandfather clock in the hall started to whirr and then chimed the hour. Shaw took this as a moment to try to end the interview. 'Goodness me, is that the time?' He smiled amiably and got up. 'Anyway, is that all? I've got to drive over to Harrogate, you know; keep the business ticking over.'

Oldroyd and Carter acquiesced and got up to leave. Shaw showed them out in a jocular manner.

'I hope you find out who did it. Ghastly business, but it might actually do the club some good; you know, people coming to see where the murder took place. Not sure I'd want to be the leader of the next string quartet that plays there, though, if you know what I mean.'

The two detectives walked back across the cobblestoned courtyard to Oldroyd's Saab.

'What did you make of him, sir?' asked Carter as they drove back to Halifax through the lanes. The fields dipped steeply down to the valley bottom where the River Calder and the Rochdale Canal were concealed by trees. The winter green of the fields seemed even more wan now that the sun had gone behind the hillside and the light was fading.

'Not a lot; I'm suspicious of this secret collection of his; we may have to get a search warrant. He's not interested in the music side, admitted it himself. It's all about money. But he seemed very vague about it; I don't think he knows much about the instruments either. Mind you, he doesn't need to if he's just interested in them as investments. I wonder if it ties in with this antiques business? He must be getting his money from somewhere: luxury house, three kids at boarding school. I can't think he's just living off what his father left him.'

'Maybe his wife does something.'

'I don't think so; seemed like a lady of leisure to me. I think our next visit should be to that shop in the Piece Hall, which you've rightly drawn attention to twice now. Let's see what we can find there.'

The cold evening sky was dark but clear, and the stars were shining when Oldroyd and Carter arrived at the Piece Hall. There was an eerie atmosphere in the big courtyard. Wavy lines of coloured light bulbs had been hung around the walls but did little to dispel the gloom. In the centre of the big space was a large Christmas tree with small white lights winking in the gathering darkness. Oldroyd didn't like the early onset of Christmas decorations that characterised the modern commercialised Christmas, but it was now almost December and the proper Advent period was about to begin. Workmen were busy erecting stalls for the Christmas market that was about to start.

One corner of the courtyard was more animated. A children's fairground ride was still operating despite the near-darkness. A mechanical fairground organ ground out a tune as the ride spun round and a few small children bobbed up and down on the horses, watched by their parents. One of these horses, baring its teeth in quite a disturbing manner, swung near Oldroyd as he walked past. There was a child on its back crying plaintively to get off. Oldroyd didn't blame them. As a child he'd always hated any fairground ride that rotated; the movement made him feel sick.

Carter was watching the child and smiling. 'That takes me back, sir; I haven't ridden one of them for years. I used to go on them with my sister at Margate – on holiday, you know. Amazing how small they look when you're grown up, isn't it? Sir?'

Oldroyd didn't reply. Just watching the roundabout go round and up and down was making him feel queasy. He turned away and lurched slightly as he grasped the iron railing and began to walk up the stone stairs. Carter followed. Up on the second-floor balcony, a warm glow of light shone from the instrument shop. Oldroyd opened the door. This activated an alarm that played a phrase from Vivaldi's *Four Seasons* in a tasteless electronic manner. A figure immediately appeared from a back room. It was a man in his thirties with a beer belly, a short beard and a long ponytail. He was dressed in jeans and a white T-shirt with a skull and crossbones on the front. He carried a guitar.

'Hi. How're you doing?'

Oldroyd looked around briefly before replying. There were some battered-looking guitars on a shelf, and a mandolin; two cellos and a double bass were leaned against the wall. A locked display case contained a viola and a violin. There were a number of piles of sheet music. Another wall displayed faded and curling black-and-white photographs of great string players: Heifetz, Casals, Perlman, Fournier. It was all pretty shabby. Carter looked around with incomprehension. Oldroyd produced his ID.

'Chief Inspector Oldroyd; Detective Sergeant Carter. We're investigating the murder over in the Red Chapel. And you are?'

The man looked unsurprised at their presence. He sat down on a stool and started fiddling with the tuning pegs on the guitar. 'Paul Taylor. Yes – sorry, I've got to get on with this: customer coming to collect it soon. I thought you might pay a visit over here. A rare violin went missing, didn't it? And a bloke got bumped off? Juicy stuff for you guys.' Oldroyd frowned at this flippant response.

'And how do you know about it?'

'Oh, these things get around quickly, Chief Inspector. Halifax is quite small, and the music fraternity even smaller, but I can promise you I haven't got it; bring your blokes in and search the place if you want.'

'OK.' Oldroyd looked at him quizzically. There was something about the set-up here that he found odd. It didn't quite ring true. Carter was thumbing through the sheet music. Oldroyd looked at the photographs and pointed to a couple.

'I've got Fournier playing the Bach Cello Suites but I think I prefer the old Casals version.'

'Right.'

'It's an odd place to have a stringed-instrument shop, isn't it?' continued Oldroyd. 'What's trade like?'

'You'd be surprised. We get lots of parents buying guitars and violins for their kids to learn on. I don't keep much here in the shop; I order stuff for people. We get students from the music school at Huddersfield; that's where I studied – my old tutors send people over.'

'What about the trade in collectors' items? I don't suppose the average parent or student can afford to get into that.'

Oldroyd thought he detected a slight uneasiness. Taylor started to strum the guitar before replying.

'Not much through the shop here; it's mostly done online these days. I don't keep much here. I have stuff at home.'

'Do you know Edward Shaw?'

'The Edward Shaw who collects instruments? Yes, of course; he comes in occasionally.'

'He must be one of your main customers, surely; there can't be many collectors like that round here?'

'Well, not really. I mean, I have got things for him occasionally, but he's a big player; he deals all over the world.'

'Can I ask you where you were on the night of the murder?'

Taylor laughed. 'Does this mean I'm a suspect?'

'Not necessarily.'

'Closed at five o'clock and went home as usual; Friday night, went out to the Fleece for the jazz.'

'You went straight home at five?'

'Yeah. Why?'

'We have a witness said he saw someone leave this shop after six o'clock that evening,' said Carter, who came over to join Oldroyd and exert more pressure.

Taylor had been strumming and tuning the guitar, much to Oldroyd's annoyance, but at this he stopped abruptly.

'Leaving here? Who? And who said it?'

'I can't name the witness, but they claim that they saw Martin Hamilton from the Schubert Quartet leaving here. Do you know Mr Hamilton?'

Maybe Taylor was a little rattled but he was trying hard to conceal it.

'Met him once or twice; he's a different level from me, though; international stuff, isn't he? Very big money. But he certainly wasn't here that night.'

'Are you sure about that? It would seem strange that he would be here in Halifax and not pay a visit to a fellow dealer in the area, even just to exchange information and so on.'

'Well, he might well have been going to come in on the Saturday, for all I know; I presume you guys were questioning him instead, then he probably went off back to London.'

'Why would we be questioning him then, sir?' asked Carter.

'He was there, wasn't he? When the bloke was shot?'

'Yes, and when the violin disappeared,' cut in Oldroyd abruptly as he leaned towards Taylor. 'Did you get him to steal it for you? Was that what you were arranging at that meeting?'

'What meeting? I've told you, he never came in here. Ask him.'

'We will, sir,' said Carter. 'So it's in your interest to tell the truth now.'

'He didn't come here.'

'Has anyone else approached you about a violin since the murder? Offering anything for sale maybe?'

'No, they're not likely to come to me with something like that, either; as I've already told you, I'm not in that league and I don't have any dealings with stolen goods.'

Oldroyd glanced at Carter.

'So if anyone does, you'll get in touch, won't you?'

'Yes, of course. You can trust me,' he said, in a tone that implied the opposite, and then took up the guitar again to resume his strumming. The two detectives left.

'What do you make of all that, sir?' asked Carter as they descended the steps into the near-deserted courtyard where the roundabout was now shut, still and in darkness.

'Not a lot. The place is phoney. "Violins, Stringed Instruments"? It's a farce. There's nothing in there and he knows nothing about classical music. It's a cover for something; all the real deals take place behind the scenes, you can bet.'

'I agree sir; I was looking at the music. Load of rubbish; stuff for piano and trumpet, all dusty like a stage prop, makes it look like a bona fide shop. So what do you think he really does? Drugs?'

'Maybe. He could be in the instrument business as well as other things, especially if Hamilton did come here, but you can bet it's shady stuff, stolen.'

'Why does he bother to have a shop at all, sir – and why here? I mean, it's not exactly the centre of the musical world, is it, Halifax?'

'Steady on,' said Oldroyd. 'There are long musical traditions in this part of the world. Haven't you heard of the Huddersfield Choral Society? The Brighouse and Rastrick Band? The Colne Valley Male Voice Choir? The School of Music in Huddersfield and the Contemporary Music Festival?'

Carter grinned; he hadn't heard of any of them.

'I know what you mean, though,' conceded Oldroyd. 'But it's deliberate. No one expects to find an operation like that here – they expect it in London; so it's not as suspicious. And nowadays with so much done online, it doesn't really matter where you have your base, although it's handy to have one if you want to see people face to face. People are getting nervous about emails and phones and stuff being hacked. He invited us to come and search the place, but that would be pointless and he knows it; there'll be nothing valuable or incriminating in that shop.'

'It would be a great coincidence if he wasn't involved in some way wouldn't it?' mused Carter as they made their way back to police HQ. 'I mean, a violin goes missing and there's probably a dodgy set-up dealing with instruments virtually next door.'

'True, very suspicious, but almost too easy; coincidences do happen. It's important not to jump to conclusions; too many police forces have done just that over the years and ended up getting innocent people convicted.'

Despite this Oldroyd had become convinced that the answer to the mystery lay with the missing Strad. Just how was still very far from clear.

On the way home, Oldroyd decided to stop at one of his favourite fish-and-chip shops. At Stump Cross on the way out of Halifax, the shop was nestled eccentrically into the wall at a junction of two main roads, one of which climbed steeply from the junction while the other went slightly downwards.

The shop was brightly lit and warm on the dark winter's evening, but the most enticing thing was the distinctive smell, one of the most evocative Oldroyd knew. It smelled of crisp batter, juicy fish, tasty chips with vinegar and delicious mushy peas. It suggested childhood, when he'd gone to the fish shop for a bag of chips and 'bits' of crunchy batter. No meal was more satisfying to a true Yorkshireman!

He stood in the queue and listened to the local banter. Two men still in work overalls were chatting with the server, who was wearing a white smock. Behind him there was a sudden bubbling and roaring sound as a bucket of chips was tipped into the fat fryer. A cloud of steam billowed up.

'What the hell's goin' on at that Chapel place, then?'

'You mean that bloke getting shot?'

'Aye, at one o' them posh concerts; they said he were playing a violin.'

'Aye, and som'di told me he were a German, one of them that came over when that wall went down.'

'Aye, well it's not a surprise, is it? Who knows what some of them were up to before they came across?'

'Well, they needn't be bringin' their trouble here; we don't want it.'

The server turned to Oldroyd. 'Yes, sir?'

Oldroyd, a little distracted for a moment by what he'd heard, replied with his order. He applied salt and vinegar and took the warm packet out to his car; chip shops no longer wrapped food in newspaper, thanks to Health and Safety, but it smelled the same as ever. He ate his fish and chips out of the paper and was able to submerge himself, if only for a relatively brief time, in bliss.

~

Armitage and his officers were still slogging through the routine interviews of everyone who'd been at the Red Chapel on the fatal evening but their efforts had yielded very little. No one's evidence contradicted the basic outline of what had happened. Nothing suspicious before the moment when Muller was shot. Dancek ran down to the entrance and out. He then came back when the police arrived. No one had seen anyone else leave the building. No one had seen what happened to the violin. They had searched for CCTV footage of the area but nothing showed the Chapel itself and the key streets around it. Armitage was getting frustrated.

'Have you got anything, Jim? We're banging our heads against a brick wall with this one.'

They were assembled in Armitage's office again the next morning and Oldroyd was enduring the abysmal coffee.

'There's something going on with these instrument dealers and collectors. I'm sure Edward Shaw and Paul Taylor know each other far better than they're saying. If Hamilton did visit that shop it might mean that all three are involved in something. They all play it down, but it could be serious money. We know people will pay a fortune for these things and they prefer to do it secretly.'

'What do you think's really going on, though, Jim?'

'I don't know exactly. Smuggling in a stolen instrument from abroad; avoiding import taxes; who knows? There's also that woman, Elizabeth Knott. It could be four or more people in some kind of ring; international, big money and dangerous too.'

'Bloody hell. And part of it here in Halifax?'

'Yes, Sam, but I was saying to Carter, that's the beauty of it. No one suspects anything here.'

'So you think there might have been some kind of plan, a conspiracy to bump off the violin player to get the instrument?'

'I think that's looking likely; this has the hallmarks of a sophisticated operation even though we don't yet know how it was done. What looks clumsy may turn out to be for a reason. In fact, although the whole thing looks odd, you'd have to say it's worked, at least for the moment: Muller's dead, the violin's gone and we've no idea where it is or who committed the murder. I don't need to tell you that where there's a lot of money involved you get some very clever and ruthless operators.'

'But, sir, if there were several of them involved, which of them was going to get the prize?' asked Carter. 'Only one of them can keep the violin.'

'True, but who knows what deals were going on? There may be other instruments involved that could be traded. Once you've got something like a Munsterhaven Strad in your possession, you've got a powerful bargaining tool.'

Armitage sighed.

'Perhaps you're right, perhaps not. Who knows? Nothing makes sense and we've no real bloody evidence for anything. It's enough to drive you nuts.' He rubbed his eyes and shook his head. 'We'll just have to start again, interview everybody and keep at it till we find something. Jim, how do you fancy going down to London? Take this lad with you. He'll be on his home territory. I've had to let the three musicians go, no evidence against them, and they all live down there. You'll have to see that Elizabeth Knott, and the principal of that Bloomsbury School. I'd prefer to stay up here and see if I can get to the bottom of what was going on that night; I think we need to know a bit more about the victim too, so have a look round Muller's flat. And to be honest . . .' He pulled a face. 'I'm never that fond of going down there; it's not my scene. Anyway, I've cleared it with Dave Newton of the Met. He'll give you a hand if you need it.'

Carter grinned. 'Do you feel out of your depth in the capital then, sir?'

Armitage smiled back. 'No, you cheeky bugger, I don't, but it's too bloody big and busy; I can't make sense of it. Here I know everything and everybody; you could never say that in London could you?'

'No,' said Oldroyd. 'But go on, we'll risk a trip down there; send a search party in a while if we don't report back.'

'Aye, I will,' replied Armitage, looking somewhat relieved. Maybe, thought Oldroyd, it's because he thinks he can't get good pork pies down there.

Armitage's phone went. He picked it up. 'Detective Chief Inspector Armitage.'

'Oh yes, Chief Inspector.' An elderly, genteel-sounding female voice was on the line. The kind of voice Armitage called 'posh Yorkshire', from an era when many of the sons and daughters of the well-to-do middle classes were encouraged not to develop local accents and instead to adopt southern vowels. The 'broad' Yorkshire vowels, however, had a habit of finding their way back into their speech, much to the chagrin of their aspirational parents.

'My name's Gertrude Dobson; I'm sure you've heard of me. My father owned the carpet mill.'

Indeed, Armitage had. Dobson's massive mill had been one of the main employers in Halifax's textile era. The business had lasted into the 1980s. Gertrude, who'd never married, was the heiress to the Dobson fortune.

'Yes,' he replied. 'How can I help?'

'Well, you see, I was at that dreadful concert the other night. Dreadful, I mean, because that poor man was killed, not because it was a bad concert, you understand; the playing was absolutely heavenly until . . . Well, you know what happened.'

'Yes, I see,' said Armitage, wondering what he was in for after this rambling opening.

'I was there with my dear friend Liza – Eliza Bottomley, that is – and we were sitting with Mr Watson, you know, the secretary. He was very kind to us when the nasty thing happened. I mean, Liza nearly passed out, poor thing; hardly surprising after what happened. It was such a shock. Fancy going to a music concert and that happening. I don't know what my father would have said. Still it's what we have to expect in the world today.'

'Yes,' said Armitage patiently. He glanced over to where Oldroyd was looking at him questioningly and shook his head. 'So, what can I do for you?'

'Well, if you'd like to come round to see me I think I have information that might be useful. I know what you're going to say: I've already made a statement. Yes, I did, to that very nice young officer; he was very polite to us and Liza said he looked just like her nephew.'

Armitage sighed inaudibly; he didn't have time for this.

'You see, I've remembered something I saw; it might not be important and I don't want to waste your time, but, anyway.'

Drat! thought Armitage. She's probably right – it might be nothing – but I can't take the risk; I'll have to go over to see her.

'That's all right, Miss Dobson; I'll be over as soon as I can.'

After further assurances that she was not wasting his time, he was eventually able to put the phone down.

'I have an idea who that might have been,' said Oldroyd grinning.

'Some old dear who was at the concert; thinks she has information.'

'I thought so. I bet it's one of the women who always sit at the front at the concerts dressed up in their pearls. They were sitting with Gerald Watson the other night. They give a lot of money to the Music Society.'

'Gertrude Dobson and Eliza Bottomley; their fathers both owned textile mills.'

'They're the ones.'

'That was Gertrude – Miss Dobson, I should say. I'll have to go over to see her. As far as I remember she lives in a big Victorian mill-owner's house up near Savile Park.'

'Well, let's all go. We've no other burning leads to follow here at the moment. It should be quite an experience to savour before we head down to the big bad capital.'

'Right you are,' said Armitage as he reached for his battered over-coat. As they left HQ, Carter mused on what an extravagant use of resources this was: three detectives including two Chief Inspectors going off to interview an old lady. He'd learned to expect these differences from his old life in the hectic and pressurised world of London policing, and he'd also learned that somehow, with DCI Oldroyd, things seemed to happen in very unexpected ways.

Armitage drove through the town in the direction of Sowerby Bridge. He had an old Mercedes that retained some of its style despite the unwashed exterior and the rather scruffy interior, which smelled strongly of cigarette smoke. Oldroyd opened his window halfway down to get some fresh air despite the freezing temperatures. Luckily Armitage didn't smoke on the way and add more to the fug.

They turned on to a wide, tree-lined road.

'This is the street; great big mansions, bit gloomy for my taste. They certainly got some brass out of those mills,' said Armitage.

Carter looked out. Between the tall, mature trees he could see large, grand Victorian houses set back from the road in spacious grounds.

'Aye, by paying their workers a pittance,' replied Oldroyd.

'All right, Karl Marx,' laughed Armitage. 'Don't say that to Miss Dobson or you'll be insulting her father.'

'It wasn't his generation who were the worst; it was the ones who started the mills in the 1840s. Had children working more than ten hours a day until people like Richard Oastler campaigned against it.'

Armitage, who had little interest in either politics or history, did not reply.

'Who lives in these houses now, sir? There aren't many mills left now, are there?' asked Carter.

'Not many; most of these mansions are split up into flats now. Miss Dobson's pile must be one of the few left that's still owned by the original family.'

'Here we are,' said Armitage as he turned into a gravel drive, and swept up past leggy rhododendrons and overgrown lawns to the door of a rather faded Victorian mansion built of the local millstone grit.

They got out and pressed a large white button by the door, which looked as if it was made of ivory, with the word 'Press' engraved in the centre, in black. Some things were similar to Bradclough Hall but in a much worse state of repair. Carter noticed that the paint on the old window frames was peeling. This was what was presumably known as 'genteel poverty'. There was the very distant sound of a bell ringing and then a voice saying, 'Just a minute.'

Bolts slid back, and the door swung open. Gertrude Dobson was there: an elderly, thin figure dressed splendidly in a black-and-white houndstooth dress with a set of large white pearls hanging around her neck. She looked as if she was about to depart for a grand dance in the 1930s; all she needed was a white fur stole.

'Please come in, gentlemen.'

Oldroyd could detect the unmistakeable traces of the Yorkshire vowels in the voice. They followed her across a large cold hall and their footsteps echoed on the marble floor.

'Through here; it's draughty; can't afford to heat it all these days. We'll snuggle round the fire in this room.'

She led them into a high-ceilinged sitting room with deep skirting boards, ornate coving and picture rails. There was a baby grand piano in one corner. A high-backed sofa and some armchairs were grouped around a big fireplace framed by an elaborate, baronial-style mantelpiece. A fire was burning in the grate.

'Please, sit down.' She sat on a chintzy armchair next to the fire; Oldroyd sat opposite her, leaving Carter and Armitage to occupy the sofa. 'Can I get you a drink of anything?' The detectives politely declined. She seemed pleased to have visitors but also a little anxious. She looked around the room and frowned.

'I'm sorry, this room has seen better days.' She gestured towards some huge and ancient-looking radiators. 'I can't really afford to have the heating on. I only live in three of the rooms and it costs a fortune to heat up this old place. It's so inefficient, no insulation like they have in modern houses.' She turned to the detectives with a wistful expression. 'I remember, when I was a girl, my father used to have wonderful parties here, with roaring fires in every room if it was winter. The local joiners used to come and take all the doors off so people could move more easily between these downstairs rooms. He used to hire a dance band and waiters came round with drinks on silver trays.' Here she leaned forward with a mischievous smile on her face and lowered her voice.

'My sister and I were supposed to be in bed, but we used to creep out on to the landing and peep through the balustrade at the people below.' She giggled. 'We loved watching the women in their glamorous ball gowns.'

'Your father loved classical music as well, didn't he?' asked Oldroyd.

'Oh indeed.' Her face brightened at the memories. 'That was his first love in music. He helped to form the Halifax Chamber Music Society and of course I like to support it now, partly in his memory.' She looked around the room again. 'Famous musicians, string quartets and the like, used to practise in here. My father had them to stay here when they came to Halifax to give a concert. Oh the house was full of that glorious sound when they played!' She pointed to where they'd come into the room. 'I used to peep round that door to have a look at them; I saw some of the greatest quartets in the world, though I didn't realise it at the time – too small. Some left London during the war; wasn't safe there with the bombing, you know. Also some were in exile from Europe, from the Nazis. I remember the Hungarian Quartet and the Busch. Adolf Busch was a very kind man. He let me hold his violin and even draw the bow across and it was worth a fortune; a Stradivarius of some kind.'

Armitage and Carter were beginning to tire of these reminiscences, but Oldroyd was fascinated. 'Was your father interested in the instruments?'

'Not particularly. He played the cello quite well; formed an amateur quartet with some of his friends. I remember them playing in here too; they had a lot of fun.'

'How about you?'

'No. Piano's my instrument, Chief Inspector.'

Oldroyd glanced at the baby grand.

'I went to the Royal Manchester College, you know. Became a teacher; taught scores of pupils at that piano . . . Can't play like I used to, I'm afraid.' She looked down at her hands, which were lined with veins but still looked very elegant.

'Did your father own an expensive cello?'

'It was an Amati, I think, but he sold it when he got too old to play and times were harder; the business was doing badly and he had to sell up.'

'So he never collected instruments?'

'Not to my knowledge.'

'So, er, Miss Dobson . . .' Armitage had had enough and wanted to move things on. 'What is it that you have to tell us?'

She turned to Armitage.

'Ah yes, well, it was just something I saw. Well, I didn't actually see anything, but there was something odd, if you see what I mean.'

Armitage didn't and felt as sceptical as ever about the value of this particular enquiry.

'Can you take us through it?' suggested Oldroyd helpfully.

'Yes of course.' She closed her eyes and seemed to be making a big effort to recall the events of the fateful evening.

'You see, it was after that poor man was shot; there was a terrible commotion, Chief Inspector, and you came down to the front and took control. You were very commanding, I must say. It was so fortunate that you were there, but I know how regularly you've supported us over the years.'

Armitage glanced at Oldroyd and raised his eyebrows. Oldroyd nodded smugly to Gertrude Dobson.

'Liza fainted I think; she was slumped over to one side and Mr Watson was attending to her. I was leaning over to speak to her, asking her if she was all right, but I also kept an eye on what was happening down where the quartet had been sitting. He was lying on the floor and you were standing in front, partially obscuring the body. Behind you I could see the violin on that little table where he'd just put it before he was shot. Then someone moved in front of that table with his back to me. I looked quickly at Liza, who seemed to be coming round, and then back. The table was visible again, but the violin had gone.'

Armitage had sat up. So maybe the old dear had seen something important after all.

'So you think that person could have taken it?' he said.

'Well, I wouldn't like to say for sure, but it seems like it, don't you think? I mean, I'm absolutely positive it was there and then seconds later it wasn't.'

'And who was it?'

'It was definitely the cellist, Martin Hamilton.' As soon as she'd delivered this revelation she seemed to shrink from the implications of what she'd said.

'I don't know if it means anything. I didn't actually see him *take* it, as it were, because he had his back to me; it could have just been a coincidence. I don't know if anyone else noticed, it was so chaotic.'

'But you saw the violin and then it disappeared after he'd stood in front of the table?'

'Yes, but – oh dear – I don't want to get the poor man into trouble if I've made a mistake.'

'I'm sure there's no mistake,' said Oldroyd reassuringly, 'and you just leave it to us to find out what was going on. Did you see anything else?'

'No. Mr Watson and I revived Liza, and we just sat there until that nice young policeman came to talk to us. I know I should have told him at the time but I didn't think of it. Eventually Mr Watson rang for a taxi to take us home. It was only later when I saw the reports saying the violin was missing that I realised that maybe I'd seen something important.'

Armitage got to his feet.

'Well, thank you very much, Miss Dobson; that's been very helpful. You stay here by the fire now and we'll see ourselves out.'

Miss Dobson, however, insisted on seeing them to the door and looked quite sad that they were leaving.

'I think she's a lonely old bird,' commented Armitage as he drove back to police HQ.

'Yes, it's a shame,' replied Oldroyd, who had some personal sympathy. 'Wonder why she never married? Probably the war: killed thousands of young men in this area; not enough to go round after that.'

'Not sure about the poverty tale and not putting on the heating; Dobson's Worsteds must have been worth millions.'

'Well, maybe she's just frugal, doesn't want to waste money. She still gives plenty to the Chamber Society, which is why Gerald Watson makes a fuss of her. What did you make of her, Andy?'

'Seemed a nice old dear, sir; can't see she would make anything up, so isn't that our first real lead on what happened to that violin?'

'I think you're right; we'll have to pay Mr Hamilton a visit as soon as we get to London.'

Five

The 'Duke of Alcantara' Stradivarius of 1732 was named after a Spanish nobleman. It belonged to the University of California and in 1967 David Margetts, second violinist in a UCLA quartet, borrowed it for a rehearsal. Either he left it on the roof of his car or it was stolen from the car, but it was missing for twenty-seven years before being recovered from an amateur violinist who claimed it had been found at the side of a motorway.

Anna Robson owned a small but very expensive terraced house in the Barnsbury Estate in Islington: delicate early-nineteenth-century brickwork and a small garden. She'd bought it with her husband, Christopher, who was a journalist and currently in America.

It was a fine but cold-looking morning, and she stood in the house gazing out of the window. She hated being alone in the emptiness and quiet. All she could hear was the gentle thrum of the central heating and the occasional creak and groan of the house shifting around as it warmed and cooled. It was enough to drive you mad. It was also quiet outside; occasionally someone passed by, and then the postman walked up to the door. The letterbox rattled but she stayed where she was. She couldn't be bothered to go and pick the mail up. The postman retreated, and she turned back to the room where her music stand stood and her viola was laid on the table in its case. She should have been practising, but she didn't have the energy. She sighed and put her hands up to her face. There were so many things she regretted, but she knew the feeling was pointless; you could never change the past. She felt something brushing against her knee. It was her poodle, Mollie. She smiled; it was good to have a friendly dog as a pet when you were by yourself.

'Come on then, madam, let's go for a walk,' she said, ruffling the dog's ears. She went into the hall and started to put on her shoes. Mollie barked in anticipation. Anna picked up the mail and put it on a table by the door to be sorted later. Then she put on her coat, attached the lead, grabbed a key and some doggy waste bags and opened the door. She was pulled forward by Mollie, who strained with enthusiasm.

'Hey, careful, girl; who's taking who for a walk?' They got on to the pavement outside the house. 'Right, let's go down to the canal.'

She walked through the pretty streets of restored terraced houses down to where the Regent's Canal came out of its tunnel before crossing the railway lines out of King's Cross. As it was quiet, she let Mollie run up and down the towpath, which gave her time to think.

Hans was dead. She'd both loved and hated him. When he'd first arrived in London she'd been mesmerised by him and infatuated; this glamorous and mysterious figure from Eastern Europe who played so brilliantly on a wonderful violin. They'd soon become lovers, even though he was more than twenty years older. The relationship had lasted for several years, until she met Christopher, though she'd come to sense that Hans had grown distant from her. She later discovered that he'd conducted numerous affairs, mostly with young musicians at the academy. He'd obviously used the same charms on them as he had on her.

She could have forgiven him that, if he'd been able to let her go, but he seemed to resent her leaving him to marry Christopher and was constantly trying to lure her back to him – telling her she was the real love of his life, how much he missed her and so on.

She'd had no intention of being unfaithful to Christopher, but her marriage had not gone particularly smoothly and she'd made the mistake of not telling her husband about her long affair with Hans. Christopher was an insecure man, jealous and suspicious. Hans seemed to sense this and dropped hints about what had happened in the past and even suggested that things might still be going on. It was malicious and Anna was furious. Unfortunately, it had the effect that Hans intended: it drove a wedge between her and Christopher. They had rows; he said he couldn't trust her. Now she feared even worse repercussions.

Anna was walking under one of the numerous bridges over the canal. A runner went past wearing headphones. Anna called out to Mollie and sighed at the unpleasant memories. She blamed the man who'd once been her lover for the problems in her marriage. She could never forgive him for that and it had become more and more difficult to play with him in the quartet. She had really wanted to see the back of him, although she'd been careful not to let the police know just how hostile she had become towards the dead man.

She sat on a bench for a while, making Mollie sit still and wait. She was trying to train the dog, which was still little more than a puppy. She got out her mobile phone and scrolled through her texts. Messages were still coming from friends and acquaintances around the world expressing their sympathies and condolences. None of them really knew what a complex and painful situation it was. She was sitting near the railway bridge that took the trains away from St Pancras. A long passenger train powered its way across the bridge, taking people to destinations in the Midlands. She felt it would be nice to escape for a while, maybe visit a friend in Los Angeles or Paris, but she knew that was not possible while the investigation continued. She was permanently on edge waiting for the next contact from the police and very anxious about the future. She looked at the still grey water of the canal and felt misery welling up inside her. She looked at the phone again. She would have to call Michael Stringer: he would reassure her; she'd always been able to rely on him. They went back a long way. She tapped in the number and the phone rang; she was disappointed to hear Michael's voice in a recorded message. She left a brief message for him and, with a sigh, got up and walked back down the towpath towards home. The dog trotted after her, happily unaware of its owner's state of mind.

As Anna Robson walked by the canal, Martin Hamilton, dressed in a silk dressing gown, bustled about his apartment in Notting Hill with a spring in his step. It was three days after his arrival back in London following the remarkable events in Halifax. He'd not seen the other members of the quartet since they'd got back; he'd been too busy. He sang softly to himself as he spooned fragrant ground coffee into his coffee machine and switched it on. He slipped two slices of bread into his toaster.

Sitting at his pine kitchen table he glanced at the morning paper while the gadgets did their work. The murder of Hans Muller was still causing quite a stir in the press. There was a long article that included an interview with Chief Inspector Armitage, in which he employed the usual evasive police phrases: 'pursuing several lines of enquiry', 'no arrest imminent' and so on. He also asked for anyone with information about the missing violin, which had a distinctive design on its back, to come forward.

Hamilton was smiling as he read this when the door buzzer sounded. He was expecting someone, but this was a little early. He pressed the button and said, 'Hello?' while still half-reading the newspaper.

The visitor spoke a code word, so Hamilton pressed another button to release the lock on the outside door. His toast popped up and the gurglings of the coffee maker reached a crescendo as he ambled down the short hallway and opened the door to the apartment. A figure dressed in black immediately barged in, knocked the portly cello player against the wall, raised a gun with a silencer and shot him between the eyes. Hamilton's expression was frozen in surprise as his legs gave way. He slid down the wall and came to rest sitting by the door, his back propped against the wall. The Schubert Quartet was now reduced to two.

Andy Carter stood at the entrance to Martin Hamilton's ground-floor apartment, and looked through the open door at the elegant and characterful street outside. The apartment was now swarming with SOCOs, and the entrance up the Georgian stone steps was cordoned off with black-and-yellow tape. Little groups of people were gathering across the street, fascinated by the presence of all the police cars.

It felt strange to be back on his home territory. He hadn't expected the case to take a turn like this, but it was now clear that there was some kind of organised crime involved. The big boys in London were fully in on the case. The body had been removed, but blood was congealed on the varnished wooden floor by the door. It seemed like another contract killing, brutal and efficient. He walked back into the living room to join Oldroyd, who was comparing notes with DCI David Newton from the Met, one of Carter's old bosses. The apartment was an utter mess; every room had been thoroughly ransacked. It suggested that the intruder had had difficulty finding what they'd been looking for, if indeed they had found it.

'It has to be connected to the violin in some way,' said Oldroyd as Carter came in.

'If you say he told you he was a dealer, I would agree,' replied Newton, a tall, powerful figure dressed in a smart suit, 'but do you think he had it here in the flat?'

Oldroyd gazed around the room and sighed. This case was becoming more dangerous and complicated by the day. He and Carter had made a very early start from Halifax, and had got to the London area on their way to see Hamilton and Elizabeth Knott when the call came through that Hamilton had been murdered. Two members of the quartet killed in a similar manner: both clinically taken out by gunmen who knew what they were doing, and it looked now even more as if the violin was the motive. Oldroyd and Armitage had agreed that they would work with the Met. The press were now going mad, and the world of classical musicians was in hysteria at what seemed like an unprecedented attack on their profession. The pressure was intense and Oldroyd was desperate for some kind of lead. All he could see in the stylish but devastated flat were books, smashed ornaments, overturned furniture and Hamilton's cello next to its case. Why hadn't they taken that? Too conspicuous? Not valuable enough? It looked as if they'd taken it out of the case. That case was there on the night of Muller's murder. What if . . . ?

'Andy, let's have another look at that cello case.'

Carter and Newton looked puzzled.

'There's nothing in there, is there, sir? Wasn't it searched the other night?'

'Yes, but just come over here.'

Dutifully, Carter went over to help his boss as Newton watched sceptically.

Oldroyd turned the case over, looking at the outside and then the inside. He seemed to be measuring using his hands. He shook his head.

'There's something not right here. Hold it open.'

As Carter did, Oldroyd fiddled around with the inside of the casing as he muttered, 'It'll be very well concealed.' He felt around the rim and seemed to find something. 'Yes!' he cried. He pressed a catch and a panel in the back of the case sprung open. A neat, thinly padded space was revealed, just big enough to hold a violin.

'Bloody hell, sir,' said Carter, and Newton whistled. Oldroyd pointed to the case.

'If you look at this, there's obviously a cavity there; it's too narrow on the inside compared to the width of the outside. You can bet that's where the violin was concealed. So our Mr Hamilton did take it the other night. He saw his chance when everyone was distracted. Miss Dobson was right, Andy: he must've picked it up, hidden it under his jacket or something and then put it straight into this hiding place where it's probably been ever since. It fooled us, but the killer obviously knew where to look. All this mess is a diversion to get us to think the motive was an ordinary burglary; they've got what they wanted.'

'Do you think Hamilton planned the whole thing, then, sir? It still doesn't really make sense, does it? The chances of someone seeing him pick it up were high – in fact they did, didn't they?'

'No, Andy, I don't think he planned it at all; it was just opportunistic. Maybe he got to the violin before someone else and this is their revenge. Or he's offered it to someone dodgy and he's been double-crossed. He was clearly involved in shady stuff, as we suspected; he'd had this compartment specially constructed for the purpose of moving things about in secret.' He looked at the case again and then at Carter. 'It's time we paid a visit to Elizabeth Knott.'

Visiting Elizabeth Knott turned out to be quite an experience. The house in Mayfair was a spectacular Georgian mansion of three storeys in a very select square with a private garden in the centre. This must be worth millions, thought Oldroyd, as he and Carter ascended the stone steps, passing elaborate wrought-iron work at either side. The windows were huge and Oldroyd noticed that one on the first floor was fitted with steel security bars. The door was flanked by two black ceramic tubs containing ornamental box trees that had been shaped like cellos.

'We're clearly at the right place,' observed Oldroyd as he pressed the doorbell. Inside they could hear the buzzer sound and almost immediately a voice was heard from a metal box on the wall.

'Turn round; I can't see you,' a peremptory upper-class voice was heard to say. Oldroyd and Carter were momentarily confused and gazed in all directions.

'To your left, above the speaker.'

They looked up and saw the lens of a small CCTV camera.

'Ah, that's better. Who are you?'

Oldroyd explained.

'Police? What on earth do you want with me?'

'We're conducting a murder enquiry and . . .'

'Murder! Oh how thrilling, but I don't know anything about a murder. Who's been murdered anyway?'

'Two people, one I think you knew quite well: Martin Hamilton.'

That seemed to silence the voice for a few moments.

'You'd better come in, then. Hold your identification up to the camera, please.'

Oldroyd and Carter did as requested. The buzzer sounded again and the door opened. They found themselves in an opulently furnished hall with a polished wooden floor. A luxurious carpet covered a wide staircase; crystal chandeliers hung from the high ceiling and antique furniture lined the walls. Drifting in from a room to their left was music that Oldroyd recognised as a Beethoven string quartet: Op. 59, No. 1, *Rasumovsky;* end of the first movement, to be precise. Oldroyd quietly congratulated himself on recognising the piece.

'In here!' called a voice and they entered a large rectangular sitting room with similarly expensive furnishings, including long William Morris curtains at the tall windows. At one end of the room were a pair of Quad electrostatic speakers, and at the other end a large armchair, in which was ensconced the figure of a woman. She was small and thin, dwarfed by the size of the chair; with her legs curled up on the seat, she didn't need the adjacent footstool. She was wearing a short black lacy dress and fishnet tights. Her feet were bare. She had straight hair dyed purple, and her face was heavily made-up, including bright-red lipstick. Beneath the black mascara, a pair of sharp eyes glared at the detectives above a curved, beak-like nose and a wide mouth with the lips turned down in a frown. On her lap was a large white long-haired Persian cat, which she stroked languorously from time to time.

As the detectives entered, she touched a remote control and the volume of the music decreased, although it remained in the background throughout the subsequent conversation.

'Sit down.' She nodded towards a sofa. As he descended, Oldroyd thought he was going to disappear into its luxurious softness.

'What on earth's happened to Martin?' Her voice was surprisingly deep and commanding, considering her size. Oldroyd felt that he was the one being interviewed.

'He was found dead this morning in his apartment. Shot. We believe Mr Hamilton had the violin that belonged to Hans Muller and the killer took it from the flat.'

Oldroyd saw the eyes narrow imperceptibly.

'Poor man, how perfectly dreadful. You mean he had the Munsterhaven Strad? But how?'

'We believe he stole it on the night of Muller's murder. He had a secret compartment in his cello case.'

'Good heavens! But how dramatic: a man is murdered, his friend steals his violin and then gets murdered himself; it's the stuff of fiction. But what brings you to me?'

'We're already investigating the murder of Hans Muller. Mr Hamilton told us about you in connection with his musical instrument business.'

'Humph, that Muller: frightful man. Yes, I knew Martin for many years, got hold of some wonderful instruments for me; excellent cellist too.'

'Was it just a business relationship?' asked Carter. The keen eyes were turned on him.

'I'm sixty-five years old and haven't had anything to do with men in that way for years. Not since my last husband croaked while he was on top of me; disgusting business, tends to put you off. Anyway, men are overrated. Decided I was better off without them and never looked back.'

Carter could think of no reply to this. Oldroyd continued.

'Apparently he was acquiring a sixteenth-century lute for you.'

'I was hoping so; doesn't look as if I'm going to get it now.'

She seems more concerned about that than about Hamilton's death, thought Oldroyd.

'Has Hamilton been in contact with you recently?'

'The last time we spoke was last Friday, I think.'

'He obviously intended to dispose of the violin to one of his clients. So are you sure he didn't contact you about it?'

'No, and the reason is that he knew that I would never get involved in anything illegal.'

Oldroyd wondered if 'knowingly get involved' might be nearer the mark. Every dealer and collector they'd encountered in this case immediately denied being involved in anything illegal, which probably meant that in fact they all were.

'Did he ever offer anything to you that seemed shady?'

'No.'

'Where did he get his instruments from?'

'I don't know; it was none of my business.'

'So was it a case of "ask no questions hear no lies"? You must have some idea where he got the stuff from?' The frown intensified and the eyes glared.

'I hope you're not making allegations against me? I can assure you that everything in my collection was acquired legitimately. Martin also dealt with other collectors who wanted to buy and sell, but it's all done very discreetly. A lot of people involved in this are very wealthy, but they're also very private, don't like drawing attention to themselves. Martin did the negotiations very quietly: no auction houses, no press people.'

'And a lot of money changed hands.'

'Of course. Sometimes millions.'

'And he would get a percentage?'

'Usually about ten per cent, as far as I know.'

'That's a big cut.'

'It's worth it to people who want to stay out of the limelight and can afford it. Sales through Martin always seemed to go smoothly; everybody satisfied, no publicity.'

'He must have made a lot of money out of it.'

'I couldn't tell you. Part of his discretion was that he didn't talk about his other clients or deals he'd made. He just made you aware of what was available, or he'd conduct a search for you if you were after something specific. It seems he became involved with dangerous people and got out of his depth.'

'Do you mean online?' asked Carter. She laughed again.

'Nothing is done online – too risky; it's all done in person. Look,' she said, suddenly interrupting the questioning. 'It seems as if this is going to go on for a while. Can I get you a drink? Coffee?'

Oldroyd wondered if she was trying to take the heat off herself. Normally he refused such offers from people he was interviewing; it wasted time and was a distraction. But he thought this might be an unusual experience.

'Yes that would be good: coffee, please.'

He turned to Carter, who nodded.

'And what kind of coffee? Espresso? Latte? Americano? We've got a big espresso machine down in the kitchen, came from Italy, far better than the muck they serve you in most of the cafés.' Both chose Americano.

A long finger adorned with purple nail varnish snaked out to press a button on a box on a table at the side of her chair. It was an intercom.

'Yes, madam.' A woman's voice with an Eastern European accent was heard.

'Lydia, two Americanos for the visitors and a small espresso for me.'

'Yes, madam,' was repeated mechanically in the same tone.

'While we're waiting for the coffee, I'd rather like to show you my collection. There are instruments there that Martin got for me. You might find it interesting.'

Again Oldroyd hesitated. He felt he was being diverted from his main purpose, but the prospect of seeing what was in her collection was tantalising, so why not? She obviously enjoyed showing it to people.

'I'm sure we will, thank you.'

'Down you go, Godetia.' She lifted the cat from her knees and placed it on the floor. She climbed down from the chair and headed out of the room.

'Come with me.'

Oldroyd and Carter followed obediently. As Carter walked past the cat he leaned down to stroke it. When his hand got near, the creature uttered a loud growling, hissing noise and swiped at Carter's hand, scratching across his palm and drawing blood.

'Shit, you little . . .' exclaimed Carter as he quickly drew his damaged hand away.

'She doesn't like being stroked by strangers, I'm afraid,' said Elizabeth Knott as she climbed the wide staircase.

Oldroyd gave Carter a wry smile as the latter sucked at his scratched hand.

When they reached the first floor, Elizabeth Knott approached a solid-looking door that Oldroyd saw was steel, skilfully engineered to look like wood and harmonise with the rest of the old furnishings. She tapped at a keypad on the wall, waited a moment and then opened the door. As they entered, lights came on automatically, producing a subdued, subtle light. Looking at the steel bars across the window, the detectives realised they were in the fortified room they'd seen from the street. Inside, the room was set out like a museum, with closed glass cases and cabinets. There was wooden panelling on the walls. Elizabeth picked up a remote control and pressed buttons, and instantly doors slid back to reveal the contents; small lights came on within the display cases, angled on to the instruments and highlighting their contours and colours.

Oldroyd and Carter were impressed by the technological slickness and by the unexpected richness of the display before them. The cabinets and cases were all packed with stringed instruments of various sizes and colours, all looking of antique quality and extremely valuable. There were violins, violas and cellos by Stradivarius and Amati, an ancient double bass and guitars, lutes and viols, some of which, thought Oldroyd, must have been more than 400 years old. Even Carter, who was unfamiliar with it all, shook his head in disbelief.

'It's magnificent,' said Oldroyd after some quiet minutes spent looking around.

'It's been growing for over fifty years. Daddy started it and I've made it my life's work to continue and make it into one of the greatest collections in the world, if not *the* greatest.'

She began a tour of the collection, giving a quick description of the highlights, explaining how each was acquired and how much was paid. She took one or two out of their cases and allowed the detectives to hold them briefly. After his initial sense of awe, a kind of sadness came over Oldroyd. Although it was wonderful to see the fine instruments so close up, so well kept and cared for, there was something impersonal about it. They were all clinically arranged museum specimens. It was like looking at old butterfly collections where each insect was pinned on to a board; the beauty of their wings was preserved, but those wings would never fly again, never again would that sinuous, fluttering flash of colour pass by a wondering person. Similarly with the instruments, you could admire the craftsmanship and the beauty of their shape, but they were silenced, unable to express the glorious sound for which they were made. He turned to their 'curator'.

'You were listening to Beethoven when we arrived.'

'I was.'

'So you don't just collect these instruments, you appreciate the music they make?'

'Of course; I'm a regular at the Wigmore Hall. When I was little, Daddy used to have private concerts here; we've got a big music room – in those days, quartets from Eastern Europe were eager to come here and perform for a smallish fee.'

Oldroyd gave her a thoughtful look. 'Don't you think there's something a bit sad about this?' He pointed to the display cases. 'All these great instruments, all silent.'

She laughed. 'You're not the first person to say that, but jealousy plays a part, I think, for some people. Who wouldn't want to own these?' She looked towards her treasured possessions and her eyes gleamed. 'Anyway, there are plenty more being played; no one misses mine.'

'Don't you ever lend them to players?'

'Good gracious, no, there's no telling what might happen to them; they stay here, safe and protected.'

'But when you hear a great violin being played by a master, say like Hans Muller, don't you feel that its greatness lies in its voice, as it were, that we ought to hear it?'

She thought for a moment. 'To be perfectly frank, when I hear a great instrument I want to possess it; I want it to join the others here and sit proudly in my collection. I feel it's the destiny of these marvellous things to be together here, under my guardianship. This collection is a wonder of the world.'

'I take it then you'd be keen to possess a Munsterhaven Strad? I don't see one here.'

She gave Oldroyd a wry smile. 'It's the aim of every collector to own a Munsterhaven Strad; they're unique – but unfortunately all accounted for at the moment, and unlikely to come up for sale. It was Daddy's biggest regret that he never managed to acquire one.'

'You know where they all are, then?'

'Every one of them. I know who has them and how long they've had them and who had them before that; there's a whole history to each of those instruments going right back to when they were first made. It was a tragedy of course that after the count's death the collection was split up and sold off, but they had to do it; his extravagance had built up enormous debts despite his wealth. Just think of it, though: a whole string ensemble playing custom-made Strads; it must have sounded extraordinary. He could have made a fortune charging people to attend concerts, but apparently he never did; thought that was all too vulgar. They only ever played for him and his guests.'

A far superior attitude and value system to yours, mused Oldroyd.

'It must have been quite tantalising for you, then, to know that Muller possessed one of them, and that your agent Hamilton played in the Schubert Quartet with him, so was in close proximity to a Munsterhaven Strad all the time.'

Elizabeth Knott pressed the control again. The lights went out, the panels slid back over and, sadly to Oldroyd, the great instruments were imprisoned again like birds in cages.

'It could have been if I'd dwelled on it, but I've known for a long time that Muller would never part with that violin. Oh, I got Martin to ask him all right, several times, but nothing doing. And now they're both dead.' She shook her head. 'Quite extraordinary. By the way, it's interesting how Muller came to possess it. He came from East Germany, I'm sure you know; there was a Munsterhaven Strad owned by a Jewish family in Berlin before the war, and it disappeared during the Jewish persecution. I'll wager that's the same one – "Nazi gold", as they say, not pleasant. Of all the Munsterhaven Strads, that's the one I'd least like to own; it's got a dirty past, if you see what I mean.'

'Well, if we're right, people are being murdered for it now so it does seem to have a kind of curse on it, if you believe in things like that.'

'Not me. I'd still give it a home here if I had the chance, despite its history. Anyway, we'd better go back down; the coffee will have arrived.'

On their return, the detectives saw that a large silver tray had been placed on the walnut coffee table, complete with the coffees ordered and a selection of mini pastries. Oldroyd seemed to have completed his questioning and started to converse with Elizabeth Knott about chamber music while they sipped their coffees. Carter felt rather excluded so he worked his way through the pastries, which were delicious but only a mouthful each. After the coffee they left.

'If any of your contacts give you any information about the missing violin, I'm sure you'll let us know,' said Oldroyd as Elizabeth Knott showed them out.

'Of course,' she replied. 'We wouldn't want the poor thing to disappear now, would we?' She gave Oldroyd a smile that was very hard to interpret.

'She must be absolutely loaded, sir,' said Carter as they made their way through the quiet and opulent streets of Mayfair. 'All those violins and stuff must be worth a fortune, never mind the house itself.'

'Yes, and that collection is very important to her. In fact, it seems like the most important thing in her life. She's more interested in that Munsterhaven Strad than she's letting on; she'd like to get her hands on it all right.'

'Do you think she's involved, then? In the murders?'

Oldroyd stopped and looked up at the majestic façades around him; this was a world where money was everything, regardless of its aspirations to pre-eminence in the world of high culture.

'I don't know; not directly. She would be absolutely ruthless in getting what she wanted but she would keep any dirty work at a judicious distance. I didn't buy all that about her acquisitions being legitimate; I'm sure she'd take anything, never mind how it got to her.'

'So we should get Inspector Newton and his team to monitor her movements?'

'Yes, but low profile. I think, if we're careful, she might lead us to it. Anyway, before we go to see Jefferson we'd better take a quick look at Muller's apartment.'

As soon as she closed the door on Oldroyd and Carter, the ambiguous smile left Elizabeth Knott's lips. She went straight back to the sitting room, shooed off the cat which had sat in her chair, sat down and dialled a number on her phone.

'Yes?' growled a male voice.

'It's me. Have you got it?'

'Got what?'

'Don't play games with me,' snarled Elizabeth Knott. 'You know what I'm talking about. Hamilton was shot and it's been taken.'

She tapped her foot on the floor while she listened to the reply.

'I don't know whether I believe you, but if you haven't got it you'd better get hunting for it if you ever want to get a penny out of me.'

There appeared to be an outraged response from whoever was listening.

'Don't give me that. You'd better use all your contacts, all those lovely people you know in the underworld, because I'm paying you nothing until I see that violin nicely placed in my collection upstairs. So get moving.'

She pressed the button to end the conversation, and sat grim-faced in her luxurious armchair. The rejected cat peered at her, wondered about jumping back up on to her knee, but decided against it, curling up underneath the chair instead.

Muller had lived in an apartment owned by the Bloomsbury School of Music, not far from the School itself, in another elegant street of Georgian houses. When Oldroyd and Carter entered, the last of the December sunlight was shining through the window of the sitting room, which looked out on to the street, but the apartment was chilly as the heating was switched off. In the corner there was a baby grand piano and several music stands. The walls were lined with bookshelves upon which were dozens of volumes on music and art, many in German. A number of shelves contained a large collection of sheet music. There was also a writing bureau and Oldroyd opened the drawers to reveal stacks of papers.

'Well, there's plenty of stuff to look through here,' he said rather wearily. It had been a very long day. 'We'll have to get Newton's lot to go through it carefully, but we'll have a little preliminary search. Off you go and look around the other rooms; I'm going to have a look at this stuff.'

'OK, sir.' Carter went off to the kitchen while Oldroyd sat at the desk and sorted through the papers. It was mostly receipts, bills, bank statements and other mundane stuff, but as he delved a little deeper into the recesses he found some things that were of more interest; two things in particular. One was a piece of paper containing a stark message composed of letters cut from magazines:

Nazi scum you've got stolen property, give the violin
back or you'll pay

Oldroyd felt a tingle of excitement. At last some links were starting to form, however vague; there had to be a link with the other message found in Muller's pocket after his death.

The other thing was a black-and-white photograph, which had been carefully placed in an envelope for protection. It was a portrait of a young woman smiling into the camera; her hairstyle was from the 1960s. There was nothing written on the back.

He called Carter in. 'Look at this.'

Carter read the message. 'Interesting,' he said. 'Sort of confirms what she was saying: his violin was taken from Jewish people; someone else obviously knows about it.'

'Yes, and if it relates to that other message, it looks as if they pursued him all the way to Halifax. We need to tell Newton to investigate this and find out if there are organisations in London devoted to recovering this Nazi gold. Oh, and there's this.' He showed Carter the photograph.

'Must be an old girlfriend. Looks a long time ago; good taste, though – he must have been up to more than just practising his fiddle in those days.' He grinned as he handed the photograph back to his boss, who slipped it into his pocket.

'I wonder what else he might have been up to, if anything?'

Oldroyd wandered around the quiet flat trying to get a sense of the man who'd lived there. He was a person of some mystery. The people in the chip shop had made him begin to wonder. What had happened in the first forty years or so of his life in the old East Germany? The message said 'Nazi scum'. Muller would have been a baby during the war but maybe he had other things to hide? How had he acquired the violin? Did he know about its history? Oldroyd silently interrogated the rooms, but discovered no answers.

It was late in the afternoon and already dark by the time Oldroyd and Carter got to the Bloomsbury School of Music. The school was housed in an early 1960s building constructed following the demolition of a crumbling but elegant 1840s façade, which, according to the governors of the school at that time, who were eagerly embracing the modernist zeitgeist, concealed an interior dominated by gloomy staircases and corridors and was thus unfit as a place to study music. Consequently, another piece of heritage had been obliterated and the new construction sat very uncomfortably alongside the elegant buildings of earlier times.

These were some of Oldroyd's thoughts and surmises as he surveyed the building. Carter was just enjoying the sensation of being in the lively London streets again and the architecture didn't really register. They entered through glass and metal doors and found themselves in a light and airy concourse that, Oldroyd had to concede, was quite welcoming, although he did detect a kind of faded tiredness in the fittings and flooring, cracks in the ceilings and general deterioration in the window frames, as if the building may already have been coming to the end of its short life. It was a flimsy, almost temporary structure compared to the solidity and grandeur found in the buildings of previous ages, which seemed to mature and improve with age like good wine. However, he decided he wasn't in the mood to share any of this with Carter, who he sensed would be a rather unresponsive audience.

They had already contacted Patrick Jefferson to arrange an interview, so at reception they presented their badges and the young receptionist, who looked rather intimidated, called through to the principal and directed them up to the office on the first floor. As they mounted the stairs, they were passed by a number of young students carrying instrument cases of various sizes.

'Did you ever learn to play anything, Andy?'

'I can do a bit on the guitar, sir. Mostly chords and stuff. I had a battered old Fender Stratocaster once. Me and a few mates formed a band; we were going to storm the world and be the next great boy band – you know, girls shrieking at us, millionaires before we were twenty. You know what it's like when you're a teenager. How about you, sir?'

'Nothing so exciting, I'm afraid. My father tried to get me going on the cello but I wouldn't practise. It's a shame; I regret it now.' There were several other things in his life he regretted too, but he shrugged off those thoughts. This was no time for self-pity.

Patrick Jefferson turned out to be a tall, thin, dapper, rather old-school character wearing round, steel-rimmed glasses. He welcomed Carter and Oldroyd into his office with a scrupulous but rather formal politeness and then sat behind an expensive-looking wooden desk with neatly organised bookshelves behind him. On the wall opposite were a number of black-and-white photographs of famous luminaries of the Bloomsbury School. Carter and Oldroyd sat on the other side of the desk. It felt a little as if they'd been called to the principal's office for a dressing down, but when Oldroyd searched Jefferson's face with his keen eyes he detected a tension there that Jefferson was trying hard to control.

'I presume you're here because of Hans's murder.' The voice was very precise and rather clipped. 'Absolutely dreadful business, but I don't know how I can help. Where was it, Halifax? Or somewhere or other up there?'

'Things have become more serious today,' said Oldroyd, bridling at the implication that Halifax was in the back of beyond, and emphasising his Yorkshire vowels to counter Jefferson's public-school plumminess. 'I'm afraid there's been another murder. Martin Hamilton was found shot in his flat this morning.'

'What?' Jefferson leaned forward in the chair and put his hands on the table. He seemed genuinely shocked. 'Another member of the quartet dead? That's terrible; this is going to be so bad for the school. Two of our most illustrious alumni murdered. What on earth will people think?' He shook his head, raised his arms in a theatrical gesture and then seemed distracted, as if he'd temporarily forgotten the detectives were there.

'I'm sure you're aware that Muller's violin was stolen from the murder scene.'

Oldroyd's question jolted Jefferson out of his reverie.

'Yes, I knew the violin was missing.'

'We're pretty certain now that it was taken by Martin Hamilton. He smuggled it away in a secret compartment in his cello case and then it was taken from him by his murderer.'

This came as another severe blow to Jefferson.

'My God! Martin, a thief? But this is terrible. The publicity will . . . And the Strad's gone missing again, you say?'

'Yes. Were you aware that Hamilton was a dealer in rare instruments?'

'Well yes, but I didn't think he would do anything illegal. I mean it's absolutely against our ethos here, to . . .'

'That may be so, but the existence of that compartment in his case means that he must have regularly moved violins and smaller stringed instruments around in secret. Why would he do that unless he had something to conceal?'

Jefferson shrugged.

'It's very puzzling, but I can assure you that we had nothing to do with that here at the school.'

'Going back to Hans Muller. Did he have any enemies that you were aware of?'

'Hans? No, certainly not here, Chief Inspector. He was always welcome. One of my predecessors, Andrew Lipton, invited Hans to the school when he came over from Germany. He was an outstanding player, very experienced, and he brought that amazing instrument with him. He worked with our young musicians and three of them formed the quartet with him.'

'Did he ever tell you where he got the Strad?'

'No; he never talked about his life in Germany. I don't know why. Maybe he just wanted to start a new life here and forget the past. He did come from the East, which may not have been that pleasant.'

'Would you say that you personally got on well with him?'

'Yes I would.'

Oldroyd and Carter exchanged glances.

'You see, we have a report that there was a row between yourself and Muller, here, just a few days before he was killed. Is that true?'

There was a pause. For the first time, Jefferson seemed to be on the defensive.

'Yes, it's true that we exchanged words and Hans got rather upset.'

'What was it all about?' asked Carter.

'Well, I . . .' he stuttered and seemed perplexed. 'These matters are confidential, and . . .'

'This is a murder enquiry, sir. You must tell us.'

Jefferson sighed and sat back in his chair. 'Well, the truth is – and this is not my doing, as I hastened to tell Hans – that the school wants *wanted*, I should say – to terminate Hans's contract here. It's part of the cuts we have to make. Hans was on quite a significant salary for not doing a great deal, really, as he spent most of his time with the quartet, just a bit of teaching. We always thought it was worth it to retain such a prestigious figure. He'd had this contract since he first came to the school. However, the governors decided that it couldn't be justified any longer. Hans was getting on a bit. His health was not good and that would inevitably have affected his performance at some point. He was offered a generous retirement package and he would still have done some teaching, but on a casual contract. There was a proposal to set up an award named after him in recognition of his contribution over the years.'

'But he didn't like it?'

'No, he didn't, and I can't say I blame him. It felt like we were casting off someone who'd done so much for the school just because they were getting a bit older. Hans was a proud man; he was very upset by what was proposed. He got very angry, said he would cut all links with us, we were so ungrateful, etcetera. He stormed out of the office. I'd been thinking ever since about how I could bring him round, make him see that maybe it was time to step back a little, but I never saw him again.'

'So you had no contact with him after that?'

'I'm afraid not.' Jefferson sank into the chair looking completely deflated.

'This has obviously come as a great shock,' said Oldroyd, watching the man carefully.

'Yes, apart from the, er, personal loss; to lose two members of the Schubert Quartet so quickly and in such . . . circumstances, I . . . I just don't know what will happen. I don't know what the board will say; the quartet's destroyed and the school is being mixed up in criminal activity. It's just . . .' He raised his hands in a gesture of hopelessness. 'We may never recover from this.'

Oldroyd and Carter were intensely weary after this final interview of the day. They made their way slowly back to the Met to report back to Newton before they departed for the north.

'I don't like any of these people,' muttered Oldroyd gloomily. 'They're all more concerned about themselves than the fact that people have been murdered. Elizabeth Knott wants to get her hands on the violin and Jefferson's worried about the impact on the reputation of the school. I'm not sure what Stringer and Robson really think either, or how they're involved if they are, and Taylor and Shaw are up to something.'

'You're right, sir. Who would have thought the world of classical music and beautiful instruments would have been so murky? It's supposed to be rock musicians who are the bad boys, isn't it?'

'Maybe, but something dramatic like this has certainly lifted the lid on an awful lot of goings-on in that genteel world. I don't think we know the half of it yet.'

At about the time Oldroyd and Carter were leaving the school, Michael Stringer eventually checked his phone and heard a message from Anna Robson. He'd been busy at the school with his pupils all morning and was on his way back home. He listened to her message before plunging down to get the underground at Russell Square. He was sorry he'd missed the call; he was very fond of Anna and she still sounded very distressed. No wonder, after what had happened. He'd often hoped that he and Anna could get closer but there never seemed to be any chance of it; there was always someone else – first Hans and now Christopher Downton. His face twisted into an expression of contempt; Downton was an arrogant, volatile ass. He couldn't understand what Anna saw in him.

Having lost concentration, he fumbled with his Oyster card at the ticket barrier and then returned to his thoughts while going down in the lift. Downton seemed to spend a lot of his time abroad pursuing stories for his newspaper. Maybe, now that Hans was gone, Anna might start to see things differently, especially if he played the role of supporting her while Downton was conspicuous by his absence. A sardonic smile came on to his face; every cloud had a silver lining. There was also the promise of a new beginning for the quartet: Hans had been such a dead weight on the possibility of change.

He got on to the train and sat down, resting his violin case on his lap. The train seemed to be mainly occupied by young people, probably students, listening to music through headphones. It was a normal scene and one that Stringer witnessed regularly on his travels to and from the school. The events in Halifax seemed very distant, almost dreamlike now, but he had a feeling there was more to come. Where was Hans's Munsterhaven Strad? He glanced at the case on his lap, which contained his own violin, a modern one. He was a bit of a sceptic about the so-called unique sound of the Stradivarius; he believed that modern violins could sound just as good. Hadn't that been virtually proved by blind tests? Of course the sound wasn't the motivation of collectors; it was their mystique and special status that ensured the Strads had enormous value.

Stringer's phone had no reception while he was travelling underground, but as soon as he arrived at Hampstead station and got to the surface he discovered that his plans for the future of the Schubert Quartet were destined never to be realised. His phone rang; it was Anna again.

'Michael! Thank God! Where have you been?' she sounded utterly distraught.

'Yes, what's the matter, I'm sorry I didn't get your message earlier, I—'

'It's Martin, Martin!' He could hear her sobbing.

'What? What's happened?'

'He's dead, he's been shot!'

'What?'

'The police called; they'll be trying to contact you.'

'But . . .'

'Michael, I can't stand it. First Hans, and now Martin. What's going on and what are we going to do?'

Six

The 'Lady Blunt' Stradivarius of 1721 was named after one of its owners, who was Lord Byron's granddaughter. It is in near-original condition, having spent nearly 300 years in collections and being played very little. In 2011 it was sold in an online auction for the record price of £9.8 million, with the proceeds going to the Japanese Earthquake and Tsunami Relief Fund.

On the way back from London, Carter drove. Oldroyd sank into one of his depressive moods and went quiet; he hated the monotonous four-hour drive up the M1. Carter brought up Jefferson and Knott again as they reached the motorway.

'I think you're right: she might lead us to something, sir; and I got the feeling he wasn't telling us everything.'

'Maybe, maybe not; he seemed genuinely shocked.'

It was an uncharacteristically dull and laconic response. He was tired and he'd had enough for one day so he started to think about other things instead: depressing things, like how intensive work on cases like this and spending time away from home had ruined his marriage; how the resulting loneliness had caused him to live even more for his police work; how he could not see much future for himself, an ageing detective living in his rented apartment overlooking the Stray in Harrogate. He shook his head and tried to banish the self-pity.

A couple of hours later they pulled into a service station in the Midlands for a break. Oldroyd was thinking about his wife, Julia. They'd been happy together for many years but she was a mystery to him now. Since they'd separated she hadn't formed any other relationships as far as he knew, which gave him hope that she might one day have him back. But she remained aloof. They met in Harrogate every couple of months to talk about their children, Louise, who'd followed her parents to Oxford to study history, and Robert, who worked for an engineering firm and lived with his girlfriend in Birmingham. Other than that, she gently resisted all his attempts to meet her socially and maybe make a new beginning. As he sat at a table in the café on the bridge, with the headlights of cars and lorries shooting past on the motorway beneath, he got out his phone and started to inexpertly tap out a text to her suggesting that they meet. Carter came over with two cups of tea.

'Are you OK, sir?' Carter asked as he sat down opposite his boss.

'I'll be better when we get back. Can't tell you how much I detest this motorway – and look at this place; it's like a nightmare of all I hate about modernity.' He pointed to the lines of people queuing up for fast food. 'Plastic food, plastic tables, great big soulless room, cars and lorries hurtling beneath; it's all built around car worship and everything's hard, ugly, fast; nothing soft, attractive, welcoming.'

'Steady on, sir; it's only a motorway services. What do you expect? People just stop for a cuppa; they're not looking for great cuisine or wonderful architecture.'

'Yes, but people are so passive; they accept what's given to them. We still have a wartime mentality: don't complain about anything, it's unseemly. And what's this thumping music?' He waved his hand in the air dismissively.

'Bob Marley, sir; it's great. Surely you like a bit of reggae?'

Oldroyd shook his head.

'I've heard of Jacob Marley, and I feel like a bloody ghost sometimes.'

He returned to his clumsy texting. Carter smiled, drank his tea and then excused himself to go and make a call to Steph. He stood in the corridor on the bridge outside the café area listening to the hum of the traffic passing underneath.

'How's it going? Visit to London given you any clues?' It was nice to hear her voice.

'Not sure really; bloke was definitely done in for the violin; that makes two. Boss found a secret compartment in his cello case where the bloke'd hidden the violin after he'd pinched it. He is amazing, isn't he?'

'I know.'

'Anyway, still no sign of the bloody thing. We reckon there's some serious people involved; it was a clinical execution, straight between the eyes. Then we went to see this old bird who collects instruments. Bloody hell, what a place! Talk about marble halls, everything dripping in money; she showed us her collection, lots of old violins and stuff, worth a fortune according to the boss.'

'How is he?'

Carter knew that Steph took a kind of daughterly interest in Oldroyd. She'd worked with him since she joined the force as a detective constable and had always admired and respected him. She also knew his weaknesses and they'd confided in each other over the years about their family problems: Oldroyd's separation and Steph's now-absent father, who'd terrorised the family when she was a girl. Oldroyd was the nearest thing she had to a father and she cared about him.

'Not too good at the moment; it's been hard going. Set off at six this morning; went to Muller's flat after Hamilton's place and then ended up going to see the principal of the music college. Not much doing with any of it really. Then we had to report back to Newton and get on to the M1; traffic was awful as usual. He must be tired and not just because of today; he's been at it non-stop since the first murder and that must have been a special stress, you know, being there when it happened.'

'Yeah, I'm sure it was. Anyway, you look after him; be cheerful; try to keep his spirits up. He likes you.'

Carter laughed. 'Problem is, it's all getting a bit messy and out of his control and he doesn't like that; we've got two forces involved now and it's spread to London and he's not really in charge.'

'No, he won't be happy with that. He likes to do things his way; but the thing is, he's usually right.'

'Yep, but I think we've a long way to go on this one yet. Anyway, see you soon, shouldn't be too late back.'

'Bye, love you.'

Carter dropped the phone back into his pocket and felt the warm glow of being in a good relationship. Against all his expectations when he'd first come north, he much preferred his present settled life in Harrogate to the relative wildness of his time in London when he was growing up, and later working for the Met. He got plenty of teasing from his London friends – such as Jason Harris, a financier who thought Carter was fast becoming middle-aged and boring – but he didn't mind. He was more concerned about Oldroyd; he felt his boss didn't deserve the loneliness and depression that clearly dogged his life at the moment. When he got back to the table he found Oldroyd still tapping at his phone.

'Any luck, sir?'

Oldroyd looked at Carter and sighed. He had told him a certain amount about his personal life, though it was rarely mentioned; he knew the young man was sympathetic.

'Nope,' was all he said and they returned to the car.

After Carter had driven a few miles in silence Oldroyd said, 'Sorry Andy; this case is getting to me and Christmas will be here soon; it's a hard time of year for me.'

'Don't worry about it, sir.'

On the last leg of the journey, Oldroyd fell asleep.

It was after ten o'clock when they arrived back in Harrogate. Although his flat opposite the Stray often seemed lonely, Oldroyd had had enough of the Old Commercial in Halifax and decided he would commute for the duration of the case.

Carter dropped him off. It was very quiet in the winter evening. He could just hear the sound of a television in a neighbouring flat as he entered his. The door pushed against a pile of mail and a draught of cold air greeted him. He switched on the light, grimaced at the sudden brightness, and looked around. It all had the forlorn feel that came with everything being exactly as he'd left it. No one else had been in to tidy things up and put the heating on. This was no one else's space; he didn't share it with anybody.

He put the kettle on, and half-heartedly sorted through the mail. The days-old milk was off. He tipped the stinking, gloopy liquid down the sink and drank his tea without it. He sat down in the small living room and thought about switching on the television. There would probably be something on the news about the case, but not involving him. One advantage of working for these other forces and divisions was that Armitage and Newton had to handle the media and he could stay in the background, even if they had enjoyed the idea of a detective chief inspector being present at a murder and being outwitted. He'd seen some headlines – 'Musician Murdered Under Noses of Police' and the like – but he wasn't going to take the bait. He had too much to do and think about to get involved in energy-sapping press conferences when he didn't have to.

Having rejected the television, he didn't know what to do with himself. He'd slept on the journey up, so he wasn't particularly tired and he wasn't relaxed. He put some music on low volume, a Beethoven String Trio, and decided to make a call. She would still be up; she never went to bed before midnight. He took his phone and tapped in a number.

'Jim!' said a voice he found immediately calming. 'How are you? This is a bit late for you.'

It was his sister Alison. She was a vicar in a picturesque village near Harrogate called Kirkby Underside. She was a few years older than him and a great source of wisdom and strength.

'Just thought I'd give you a call. It's been hectic recently with all this stuff in Halifax. We've been down to London today. Another member of that quartet has been murdered; it's all getting very serious.'

'Yes, I've seen it on the news, as I usually do. And you were there at the concert when the first victim was killed?'

'Yes, he was shot at the end of the slow movement of *Death and the Maiden*.'

'That's dreadful, and also strange. Did that have anything to do with it?'

'What do you mean?'

'Well, why then, at that particular point in the performance? Couldn't he have been shot at any time in the concert?'

'Yes, but we're pretty sure the gunman waited until the violin Muller was holding was put down safely. He didn't want to shoot him while he was playing for that reason. It was all about the violin, you see, it's a priceless instrument.'

'I see, but that still doesn't explain why then. Why not after the first movement, or the third?'

Oldroyd thought and then smiled. He often got help with cases from his sister. She had such a sharp mind, and she came at things from a completely different angle. She was uncluttered by police procedures and standard ways of looking at things and so she helped him see things from a different perspective. She never deliberately offered advice; it was just her observations that he often found enlightening. She was always interested in the people involved and what motivated them.

'I've no idea, but you've got me thinking about it now. I'd assumed it was arbitrary but maybe not.'

'Well, I'm assuming it was all well planned so it's unlikely to be chance.'

'True.'

'Anyway, how are you, Jim? I hope you're looking after yourself. You must be exhausted. That must have been an awful shock even for someone like you, seeing someone shot in a place like that; last thing you were expecting.'

'Oh, I'm OK, seen plenty of blood in my time. The problem with this is it's a brain teaser: murderer disappeared from the building, no trace, and the violin's still missing; we're not really getting anywhere with it.'

'Well, it'll come to you; it always does. Are you doing OK in that flat?'

'Can't complain, it's not exactly family life, but . . .' his voice tailed off. He didn't need to explain it to her.

'I know. Heard from Julia?'

'Not much; I'm trying to keep in contact, show her that I still care, but I don't get much response.'

'What do you expect? She wants to be sure you're really serious about wanting her back. I take it she hasn't found anyone else?'

'Not as far as I know.'

'Well, you'll just have to be patient. How are Robert and Louise?'

'Fine, don't hear much from them either.'

'Are you feeling a bit sorry for yourself tonight?'

Oldroyd smiled. 'Yes, I can't keep it from you, can I? But enough of that. How's the old parish?'

'Oh fine, as good as it'll ever get. It's not really me, as you know. Too sedate.'

Alison had accepted a move from inner-city Leeds, where she'd been heavily involved in social action, to the countryside 'for a sabbatical', as she described it, after her husband had died of cancer. Her own struggle with loneliness had deepened the bond between her and her brother still further.

They chatted on for a while and Oldroyd arranged to pay her a visit before he rang off.

As if she'd sensed they'd been talking about her, Oldroyd immediately received a text from his daughter Louise:

Hi Dad
Running a bit short this month, any chance of a bit of a loan? £50?
Pay you back over Christmas, going to get a holiday job.
    L. xxxxx

This brought a wry smile to Oldroyd's face. Louise had always had cash-flow problems, and she usually turned to Dad, who transferred money to her account on quite a regular basis. He didn't really expect that she would ever repay the money, though he believed she did intend to. It was just that she never generated a surplus, no matter how many holiday jobs she got. Julia was not aware of these 'loans', and would not have approved. Her view was that Oldroyd was indulgent and his behaviour was not teaching his daughter the value of money; nor was it fair to Robert, who was much more prudent with money. But Oldroyd took no notice. He switched on the computer and immediately transferred the money. He texted back:

Hi
£50 from Bank of Dad on its way; don't spend it all at once!
Dad xx

Was it guilt because he thought he'd neglected his children when they were young by working too much? Who knew? He was too weary to think about it and at last he felt drowsy. It had been an absurdly long day, but the drama was not quite over.

That night he was troubled by a strange dream. He was deep in a forest in winter and he had the impression it was somewhere in Eastern Europe, maybe even the Vienna woods that Schubert would have known. He could hear *Death and the Maiden* playing. A large moon, covered by a thin veil of mist, shone through the black, twisted branches. There was snow on the ground and everything was in black and white. Suddenly a young woman, long hair streaming behind, came running through the forest casting anxious glances behind her. She was out of breath and started to stumble. In the distance he saw a ghostly white carriage, pulled by spectral horses, flitting at great speed between the trees.

With an expression of despair, the woman stood exhausted against a tree as the glimmering carriage stopped and a macabre figure emerged from the interior. It was a skeleton dressed in the tattered remnants of clothes. It held out its arms in welcome as it strode purposefully towards her. With a shock, Oldroyd realised he was watching the ancient motif of *Death and the Maiden* played out in this winter forest. There was no sound other than that of the string quartet, which reached the dramatic fifth variation; it was like watching a silent film. The Maiden was pleading with Death, but he took her hand and they began a terrifying dance of death in the snow. With surprising and grotesque agility, Death whirled her around as the music reached its frantic climax, at which he grasped her in his arms. She seemed to look towards Oldroyd; was she asking him for help? Then she went limp. The words came again to Oldroyd as they had on the night of the concert: '*Sollst sanft in meinen Armen schlafen.*' Gently, Death cradled her in his arms and laid her body on the snow. As he sat beside her she was transformed into a skeleton like him. The music subsided into its tranquil ending.

Oldroyd woke abruptly and sat up in bed. The room was completely dark and silent. He lay down again and tried to go back to sleep, but he found it difficult to forget that young woman, the Maiden, who had succumbed to Death. He had a strange feeling that she was trying to tell him something.

After a poor night's sleep, Oldroyd was tired when he arrived at the police station in Halifax, even though Carter had driven them over from Harrogate. Armitage remained his dogged self despite the fact that he'd had to deal with the press again. They were in top gear over a double murder and a missing violin; it was a wonderful, dramatic puzzle and they were milking every exotic twist. It was all right for them, Armitage reflected ruefully: they didn't have to solve the wretched thing. In fact, the longer the thing remained a mystery the better it was for their sales.

'Got some useful information, Jim,' he said as he settled himself in his usual chair.

Oldroyd had declined the offer of coffee and was drinking water. His head ached and he felt that a single mouthful of Armitage's brew would make him vomit.

'We've been finding out a bit more about Hans Muller, to see if that'll give us any clues. I've been on to the police in Germany and they've sent some stuff over. It's in English so don't worry.'

He pulled his screen around so that Oldroyd and Carter could see, and opened up a file. A photograph of Muller came up, along with paragraphs of information. He looked much younger and the picture had probably been taken when he came to England in 1990.

'He was from the East, of course, and so the early part of his life is a bit unclear. In fact, the authorities are reliant on his own account of that part of his life. I suppose there must be records somewhere that were kept in the old regime, but they're not mentioned; could've been destroyed after the Wall came down.

'Anyway, according to Muller, he was born in East Berlin; family seem to have been fairly well off. His father was quite a high-ranking official in their equivalent of the civil service. He went to the Hanns Eisler Academy of Music and then played in orchestras around East Germany; details of that are a bit sparse. What I'm interested in is how and where he got that violin. Remember Anna Robson said he would never talk about it? I can't see how his family could have been so wealthy as to acquire one for him – and anyway, was it even legal to trade in things like that in the Communist regime?'

'Elizabeth Knott thinks it was Nazi gold taken from a Jewish family in Berlin, who are on record as having owned a Munsterhaven Strad before the war, and it's never been traced since.' An image came into Oldroyd's mind of a wealthy, musical family, treasuring the violin, playing it at family events; they probably all ended up in a death camp, the instrument confiscated by some Nazi official. 'What's more, we found a few things in Muller's flat.' Oldroyd told Armitage about the threatening letter.

Armitage raised his eyebrows.

'Interesting. If that's the case then it would explain his attitude: too ashamed.'

'Or too wary. I've asked Newton to investigate if there are any groups around who track down things like that. We know they do it for Nazi war criminals; maybe they do it for this so-called Nazi gold as well.'

'So you think it's a real possibility that some kind of organisation had Muller bumped off as revenge for taking the violin?' asked Carter.

'And to get it back. Martin Hamilton could have been in league with them, or could have taken the violin himself, which would explain why things got nasty.'

'It would make some sense; as much as anything else does in this case. But why wait so long? He's been in Britain for twenty-five years, and his possession of the violin's not been a secret; surely they would have made the connection long ago? Do we know how long he'd had that letter?' asked Armitage sceptically.

'No, but again we'll get the Met on to it. Could just be some crank, but they seem to know quite a bit.'

'Yes, and the other interesting thing about the violin is this: I've been on to Muller's solicitors to see if there's anything notable about his will. Do you know who he's left the violin to, if we ever find it?'

'Go on.'

'The Bloomsbury School of Music.'

This brought Oldroyd to a state of alertness for the first time that day.

'Now that *is* interesting; that would make his argument with the school and Jefferson potentially much more significant.' Oldroyd briefly explained to Armitage what Jefferson had told them about the incident. 'We need to find out if they knew Muller was leaving the violin to them, because if they did . . .'

'They could've been worried that he might change his will and so had him bumped off before he could do it.'

'Exactly,' said Oldroyd. 'Maybe Sir Patrick was not telling us everything he knew. The acquisition of a Munsterhaven Strad would be a wonderful boost to them, and its loss a major blow.'

'Surely Muller would have discussed it with someone there; told them he was leaving it to them?' said Armitage.

'Maybe he didn't, or they wouldn't have been as keen to pension him off. Anyway, we need to try to find out who knew what.'

'Yes, and remember the state of his health. If he thought he was going to get to the point of not being able to play, he might have thought about selling the violin.'

'To finance his retirement?'

J. R. Ellis

'Possibly, and that might be another reason why the Bloomsbury School would miss out, unless he could be stopped.'

'I'll contact Newton and get him to question Jefferson again. We're also reliant on him now to track down the violin,' said Armitage.

Carter thought about this for a moment and then said, 'Sir, if you don't mind me making a suggestion? Maybe I should go back to London and work with the Met on this until we get somewhere. I can report back to you on a regular basis, and I know the people and the area and stuff.'

Armitage looked at Oldroyd.

'What do you think, Jim? The lad's got a point. It would be useful to have our own man down there.'

Oldroyd frowned. He'd got used to Carter as his sergeant. He liked his cheery presence and his eager willingness to learn. The prospect of losing him made him feel even lonelier, but he could hardly present that as an objection and he could see the sense in the suggestion. It would also mean he wouldn't have to go down to London himself again. He'd once found London exciting; nowadays he found it relentlessly urban and exhausting.

'OK, good idea, but let them do the legwork looking for the violin. That's not our main concern. We've got a murder to solve.'

'But if we find the violin will that not lead us to the murderer?'

'Maybe Hamilton's killer, but that may not be connected to Muller's death, and by now the violin may have changed hands again, maybe more than once, and whoever's got it may not have been involved at all. It's still all a mess.'

On his way home, Carter thought Oldroyd had seemed uncharacteristically downbeat. He was usually keen and up for the challenge. There seemed to be something about this case that perplexed him, as if he somehow couldn't get any purchase on it. He would love to achieve a breakthrough for his boss and maybe during his time in London he could do it. But first he had to go Christmas shopping with Steph; she would never forgive him if he went off to London so soon before Christmas, leaving her to do it all by herself.

It was pre-Christmas late-night shopping in Leeds, and the city centre was very lively on a clear, cold evening. Carter and Steph were sitting in the beer hall of the crowded German market eating roast duck with sauerkraut. Steph had a glass of Glühwein and Carter a large foaming German beer. Steph was making a present list while they talked.

'So the boss wants you to go to London to help follow up the leads there?' she said.

'Well, I volunteered actually. I thought it would speed things up if I liaised between the two groups.'

'Yes, well done. I'm sure he was impressed at your keenness.' Steph often teased Carter about his desire to create a good impression with Oldroyd. Then her tone changed. 'Take care down there, though, won't you? There're obviously some dangerous people involved.'

'There always are when there's a lot of money at stake and you get competing gangs involved.'

'I'm sure your mum'll be really pleased to see you just before Christmas, especially as we're staying up here this year.'

'Yeah, and I want to get all this finished off before then. Anyway, how are you doing at the hospital?'

'Oh, it's tricky; an allegation that a nurse has been deliberately harming patients; very difficult to prove and you've got to be extremely careful. Inspector Moore is heading it up. He's OK, but it's not like working with the chief inspector.'

'No. Nothing's ever straightforward or dull with him, though sometimes it's such a rollercoaster you wish for an easy case or two.' They both laughed.

'Anyway,' said Steph. 'This isn't getting us anywhere on the present-buying front. I've started a list, look.' She pushed the piece of paper over to him. 'I suppose you'd like to get some stuff to take down to London with you?'

'Yes, ideally, but you know what I'm like; I never have a clue what to get.'

'Well, think then, and jot some things down while you're finishing your beer. Then we need to get off.'

Carter looked at the list and his mind went blank. If it were up to him, they'd stay there drinking beer and wine. He smiled wanly at Steph.

'Oh, give it back to me,' she said. 'I can think of a few things. Men: you're bloody useless!'

The next day found Oldroyd walking across the Stray in Harrogate to Montpellier Hill. It was a fine, crisp December morning with a weak sun shining through the bare winter trees. Christmas decorations adorned the streets and Oldroyd could hear the sound of a brass band playing carols. The build-up to Christmas was well under way, but he did not feel any excitement about it. In fact, the whole 'festive season' could easily become another source of self-pity if he allowed himself to dwell on happy times in the past and so on. For the last few years he'd spent Christmas with Alison in the vicarage at Kirkby Underside, which could have been worse, as they enjoyed each other's company, but as they were also both leading lives of enforced solitariness, their moods often dipped and they ended up reminiscing about Christmases in their childhood.

Oldroyd was allowing himself what he called a 'research break' from the investigation. But it wasn't really a break at all. It just meant that he was exploring background information on the case instead of interviewing suspects. He'd told Armitage he wasn't going over to Halifax today, but he didn't want to go to North Yorkshire HQ either as he knew once he set foot in the door he would be called in to give a report to Tom Walker and that would lead to another of the latter's diatribes against management.

Montpellier Hill went down steeply from the main road. It contained an elegant parade of shops, in one of which was located the northern branch of Coopers, the famous auctioneers of fine art, furniture and musical instruments. Oldroyd had been on their website and found that they now branded themselves as an 'international art business' – presumably to try to distance themselves a little from the stark, monetary unseemliness of rich people trying to outbid each other before the hammer fell.

Oldroyd had used Coopers before in his research while investigating art thefts, and his contact, Neville Adamson, was a specialist in musical instruments. It would be interesting to talk about the Munsterhaven Strad to someone who wasn't a suspect, and who had genuine knowledge, not like those collectors who seemed mainly interested in money and acquisition.

An old-fashioned bell tinkled as Oldroyd entered the building, and he immediately saw Neville Adamson behind a wooden-panelled counter at the entrance to a large room, the walls of which were adorned with paintings, like Edward Shaw's drawing room, but these were much more varied and tasteful. Adamson was a portly, middle-aged and rather dandified figure wearing corduroy trousers, a colourful jacket and a bow tie. He had a carefully groomed moustache and hair plastered back over his balding head.

'Ah, Chief Inspector! I've been expecting you! Quite a situation you're involved in over in Halifax, isn't it? I thought you might want to come in and talk violins at some point.'

Also like Edward Shaw, Adamson spoke RP without any suggestion of Yorkshire vowels, although, to be fair, Oldroyd didn't know if he originated from Yorkshire or not. Anyway, he liked the man, who was always cheery and helpful. Oldroyd just found it irritating to hear those vowels in Harrogate; it reminded him that, for so long, the local accent had been regarded as inferior to the RP of southern origination. So much so that boys he knew at school had been sent for elocution lessons to rid them of the accent and dialect that was their heritage.

'Yes, well, I thought it might be useful to get a bit of extra information.'

'You're very welcome. Come and have a seat, while I find a few books. I've been doing a bit of research in preparation for this.'

Adamson directed Oldroyd to a comfortable armchair by a marble-topped coffee table in the corner of the room. This, thought Oldroyd, must be where Adamson chatted up his potential clients and maybe sometimes persuaded them to part with their prized possessions.

Adamson fussed around some bookshelves behind his desk for a minute, talking to himself.

'Yes, that'll be useful, and that.'

Eventually he sat down opposite Oldroyd and placed a pile of books on the coffee table.

'The Munsterhaven Strads; yes, one of the most amazing stories in the history of music and art. They were the only instruments that Stradivarius personalised like that. The only ones to have anything painted on them in that manner.'

He opened one of the books and showed Oldroyd a picture. It was the back of a Munsterhaven Strad showing the count's coat of arms painted on the wood beneath the varnish.

'Wasn't that an unusual thing to do?' asked Oldroyd. 'I mean in the sense of mightn't it affect the sound the violin produced?'

'Good question, but it doesn't seem to have done. In fact, there are people who argue the Munsterhaven Strads produce the finest sound of all. The paint is thin, protected by the famous varnish, and of course they were using natural pigments in paint then, no damaging chemicals.'

'Is it still thought that it's the varnish that makes them special?'

Adamson laughed. 'The varnish, the wood, the preservatives – take your pick; there're lots of theories, and some people think it's all nonsense anyway, that a modern instrument can sound just as good. They did some blind tests once and prominent musicians seemed to be unable to distinguish the Strad from the modern violin.'

'What do you think?'

'Well, Chief Inspector, I'm not a musician or an artist either; I just deal in fine works of art of all kinds, but to me it wouldn't change anything if somehow you could prove that a Strad wasn't any better as an instrument, because that wouldn't remove the mystique, would it? It's because these amazing pieces of craftsmanship are still being played after three hundred years, and they still produce such a fine sound. There'll always be a fascination with them.'

'Which is why they're so valuable?'

'Of course. Here's a picture of the man who started it all: the count.'

Adamson pointed to a reproduction of a painting and Oldroyd saw a fat man with a trim beard, dressed in an ornate costume and posing majestically on a large throne-like chair.

'He was fabulously wealthy, and a great patron of the arts. He loved music most of all. Bach and Handel stayed with him. He had one of those fairy-tale castles on the Rhine. The story goes he heard a Stradivarius being played and was so impressed he travelled to Italy to see for himself how they were made. After that he had to have some at his court and that's when he gave Stradivarius that extraordinary commission. Imagine a whole string ensemble playing customised Strads! They would have been worth a lot then, but now, if it was possible to gather them all together, their value would be beyond anything in the world of art and music, even the *Mona Lisa*. No one could calculate what that collection would be worth.'

'That's never going to happen, though, is it?'

'Not possible, Chief Inspector. There were eleven of them altogether: six violins, three violas and two cellos. Only seven of them have survived into the twenty-first century. One of the violins and one of the cellos were lost at sea in the nineteenth century when a ship went down crossing from Europe to America. They belonged to a wealthy American businessman who apparently never recovered from his loss; went into a depression and later hanged himself.'

'They seem to have brought misfortune to people,' remarked Oldroyd. 'Is there talk of a curse?'

'Not really. Because of their great value, they attract people with money, some of whom are in the media spotlight, and if anything goes wrong it's always in the press. You see, not only are they Strads but they're special Strads; unique within unique, if you see what I mean.'

'I do. So what do we know about the remaining seven?'

'Well, the ownership and whereabouts of most Strads is public knowledge; just google it and you'll find lists telling you who owns the "Lady Blunt" and the "Madrileno" and so on; they all have names they've picked up over the years, except the Munsterhavens themselves – they're just known as Munsterhavens, plain and simple.'

Adamson consulted another book, a sort of catalogue.

'I still deal in hard copy for certain items. Some information doesn't get online; too sensitive. So one violin and one cello are in Japan, owned by a music foundation. Of the three violas, one is owned by a Texan oil billionaire, one is owned by the Paris École de Musique and one is in a museum in Rome. Finally, two violins left, so there's Muller's and then another that's been missing for many years. It was stolen in 1963 from its owner, Stefan Schwarz, who played in an orchestra in Vienna. He'd had the violin bought for him by his uncle, a wealthy industrialist. That poor man died later from cancer while he was still young, but there's no suggestion of a link with the Strad, unless you think the illness was caused by guilt. I suppose he must have thought he'd let his uncle down by not taking greater care of his special present, even though the uncle was dead by then.'

He passed the book to Oldroyd, who looked at the list and the photographs of various instruments. It was amazing to think of the strange histories many of them had, and how they'd survived to the present day despite being jealously desired, fought over, hidden away and rediscovered.

'How many of them are actually being played?'

'Quite a few: all those owned by schools of music and foundations are played by students and professionals; the Texan generously loans his to a concert violinist; up to now Muller was playing his. The only one not being played is the one in the museum.'

Oldroyd was thoughtful. 'Does anyone have any idea where the missing one might be?'

'No one who's prepared to say anything. It's most probably been squirrelled away in someone's private collection and they're not going to let on because they know it was stolen. And it's a long time ago; if it was going to reappear it would more than likely have done so before now, although of course it's not impossible.'

'And if someone were to acquire two of these Munsterhaven Strads?'

Adamson whistled. 'Well, that would be unprecedented.'

'It would instantly raise that person's collection, whoever that person was, to pre-eminence; it would become the world's greatest collection.'

'It would indeed.'

'But it's not likely to happen because, from a collector's point of view, the situation is not good in terms of any of them coming up for sale. They're either owned by organisations who put them to use, or by people who are not likely to sell.'

'I think you're right,' agreed Adamson.

'However, Muller was getting older and it was not clear, at least to the public, what was going to happen to his Strad after his death. As he was not hugely wealthy like the Texan, maybe he could have been persuaded to sell it,' suggested Oldroyd.

'If what you say is true then Muller would have been closely watched by a number of people around the world. You'd be surprised at the lengths some of the more fanatical collectors will go to acquire something like a Munsterhaven Strad.'

Oldroyd thought about the bodies of Muller and Hamilton and was not surprised.

'What do you know about those people? The ones who have the desire and the money to buy things like that?'

Adamson shook his head. 'Companies like mine only deal with public auctions; no private deals. We occasionally auction something valuable enough for it to attract the attention of the press. There was a Strad auctioned recently that sold for over nine million pounds. It's often done online these days and when something like that happens everyone thinks what powerful brokers we are. But I tell you, Chief Inspector, what we do is paltry compared to what goes on in private: deadly rivalries between ruthless, obsessive people who will stop at nothing to get what they want.'

'Yes, we've seen evidence of that. Do you know any of these collectors?'

'Not personally, no, but I know of them. I've been involved in auctions where people have been bidding by phone. They're very shady characters; they try to stay out of the limelight.'

'What about Edward Shaw, the local chap? He has an antiques business here, doesn't he?'

Adamson smiled.

'Well, I've heard he collects instruments but I don't know how serious he is. If it's anything like his antiques shop it'll be a bit of an amateur carry-on.'

'Do you know anything about an instrument shop in Halifax at the Piece Hall? Seems to be run by someone called Paul Taylor.'

'No, never heard of it.'

'How about Elizabeth Knott, in London?'

Adamson raised his eyebrows. 'That's a different matter. She's a serious player all right. I've met her once or twice at auctions, but I'd hazard a guess that auctions are not her main source of acquisitions; very determined character. Have you seen her collection?'

Oldroyd nodded.

'Extraordinary, isn't it? She enjoys showing it off; took a group of us round a couple of years ago after an auction in London. I found it all a bit creepy, though; all those fabulous instruments in glass cases like specimens – they really ought to be played.'

Oldroyd smiled and nodded again: it was good to have his own response echoed by someone who, even though artworks and instruments meant money to him, still valued their aesthetic and artistic qualities.

'One more thing: you know that the Nazis were notorious for stealing artworks and other stuff? Is there any evidence that they ever got their hands on a Munsterhaven Strad?'

'Why do you ask?'

'Elizabeth Knott thinks that Muller's Strad could have been "Nazi gold", as I think it's called. She says that there's a record of a Munsterhaven Strad being owned by a Jewish family in Berlin before the war.'

'Well, I don't know about that, Chief Inspector, but I can make some further enquiries for you. It wouldn't surprise me. Wonderful though those instruments are, they've been associated with more than their fair share of drama and tragedy.'

When Oldroyd left the office of Coopers, he decided to have a look at Edward Shaw's antique shop. He made a quick call to Armitage first.

'Sam, how's it going?'

His old friend's voice seemed even broader on the phone, but also a bit muffled. 'Not much further on, Jim.'

'What're you eating?'

'Oh just a Poor Ben; they're still my favourite gums.'

Oldroyd smiled; he was partial to the black liquorice and aniseed sweet himself, although they were more difficult to get now outside traditional sweetshops.

'Anyway,' continued Armitage. 'The press are making a bloody nuisance of themselves as usual: "Mystery Killer Still Eludes Police" and rubbish like that; the tabloids are going for this bonkers supernatural stuff about the "Curse of the Munsterhaven Strads" – sounds like a horror B-movie from the 1950s. They're dredging up all sorts of stories about people who died after owning one of these things. I think they want people to think there was no murderer in the Red Chapel; Muller was killed by a ghost or some tosh like that. Maybe they think the same ghost knocked on Hamilton's door and shot him when he opened it. I always thought ghosts could walk through walls, no need for the door.' Armitage laughed.

'That's the way to treat 'em,' replied Oldroyd. 'Send 'em up, don't let 'em get to you. Anyway, I've been talking to a contact of mine about the violin and he's making more enquiries for me so we might have some real information soon – and nothing to do with ghosts.'

'Thank goodness for that.'

'Anyway, I'm about to speak to Edward Shaw if he's in his shop. Did we establish his alibi for the night of the murder?'

'Hold on a minute.' Oldroyd could hear Armitage muttering to himself.

'Yes; the man whose name he gave, a Colin Benton, backed up the story, said he was with Shaw at the shop in Harrogate at that time, negotiating a price for an antique table; unless of course he's in on it all too. You can never tell in this bloody case.'

This time Oldroyd laughed.

'Not to worry. Keep at it Sam; I'll be over tomorrow.'

'Right. Has that lad of yours gone back down to London?'

'Yes.'

'Good. Well, let's hope he can unearth something down there; we could do with it.'

The antiques shop was smaller than Oldroyd expected and rather shabby. There were some small, ornate tables and chairs on display and various vases, ornaments and lamps. Shaw was semi-reclined on a chaise longue, reading a book and looking extremely relaxed. He glanced up and removed his reading glasses.

'Ah, Chief Inspector. I didn't expect to see you here. How's the investigation going? Things have got more complicated, haven't they, since we last spoke?'

Oldroyd inwardly bridled again. There was something faintly smug and patronising in the man's tone.

'Yes, well, I thought I'd come to see you at work as I was just passing,' he said, gazing around the shop.

'Very nice. What can I do for you?'

'We're pretty sure that this valuable violin is central to the case. I'm sure you're aware that there's also another missing Munsterhaven Strad?'

'Missing?'

'It was stolen in Vienna over fifty years ago.'

Shaw smiled.

'Well, yes, Inspector, that's a well-known story; but I'm sure you don't think I had anything to do with that. I wasn't even the proverbial twinkle in my father's eye in the early sixties.'

'Of course, but have you ever heard anything about where it might be now?'

'No, unfortunately, and I'm not the only one who wishes he knew either. Why do you ask?'

'Just researching a little, finding out about these instruments; see if we can unearth any clues, you know.'

'I see.'

Oldroyd glanced around again. 'Do you make a good living out of your business here?'

'Yes, keeps the wolf from the door, you know; can't complain.'

'It's quite small, isn't it?'

'Ah well, this is not the only stock, Chief Inspector. I have other things in storage.'

'And where do you get it all from?'

'Oh, it's all a question of buying in a judicious way. I travel all over the country and abroad, viewing things for sale.'

'Far away?'

'Not really, mostly northern Europe, where there are more wealthy people to acquire expensive items that I might be interested in.'

'How often do you get out of the country?'

'About once a month if I'm lucky; I always look forward to it – makes a nice change, you know.'

'Yes. Apparently Hans Muller left his Strad to the Bloomsbury School, so that one won't be on the market either. If we ever find it, of course.'

'I see. Well, let's hope it turns up, Chief Inspector.'

'Indeed. By the way, it seems that your alibi was proven for the night of the murder.'

'Good, well I'm very relieved.' Shaw chuckled.

'We shall, though, need to see your collection at some point.' Shaw didn't seem quite so sanguine about that.

'Well, of course, if you insist, but I don't know what you'll gain from it.'

'We always have to be very thorough; we won't disclose any details about the location or the contents.'

Shaw didn't reply.

'So we'll be in touch.'

'Very well.'

When Oldroyd had left, Shaw watched him walk away across the Stray until he was out of view, then he opened a door in the corner.

'You can come out now,' he said, and Paul Taylor, owner of the Piece Hall shop, emerged. 'How much of that did you hear?'

'Most of it.'

'It's a good job we saw him coming; it wouldn't do for him to see you here. Did you hear what he said about seeing my collection?'

'Yes,' replied Taylor, who was laughing. He sat on the chaise longue and put up his feet with their dirty trainers.

'I fail to see what's so amusing. What am I going to do about it? And please put your feet down – that's valuable.'

Taylor slid them on to the floor.

'I haven't a clue; you'll just have to keep stalling them.'

'Until when?'

Taylor shrugged his shoulders.

'Until all this has blown over and the police aren't crawling all over the place.'

'And when the hell is that going to be?'

'Who knows? But what choice have we got? I'm expecting them back sniffing around my place again before too long. All we can do is ride it out; answer their questions but don't give anything away.'

'And you're sure we can get through it?'

'Why not? We just have to keep our nerve.' He grinned at Shaw. His hair was lank and greasy and his T-shirt, straining over his belly, was stained with food. Shaw looked away in disgust.

Later that evening, Oldroyd was listening to Dvořak's 'American' string quartet and drinking a glass of wine when Adamson called.

'Well, I think I've found something interesting for you, Chief Inspector. I spoke to Frederick Hawkins, he's an instrument historian at the V&A. It seems Elizabeth Knott was right: she knows her stuff, that woman. There was a Jewish family who owned a Munsterhaven Strad. Their name was Lerner. Jacob Lerner owned an engineering factory in Berlin and became pretty wealthy. He bought the violin for his son Itzhak in 1932. The boy was a brilliant player, apparently; everyone thought he would have a great career. Then the Nazis came to power, and everything collapsed. First the business was taken from them, their wealth was confiscated, and finally they were all sent to Ravensbrück, a camp north of Berlin. Tragic. It's not known for certain what happened to the violin, but it was most likely taken by the Nazis; they were great looters of works of art, as you said.'

'Very interesting.'

'Yes, and the thing is, by a process of deduction, it seems to me almost certain that that is the same Strad that Muller had. The fact that he came from East Berlin, which is most likely where the violin ended up. Also we know much of the history of the others, though we don't know for certain where those violins that got to America and Japan were before they got there. The odds must be on this being the same one. Do you know anything about his life before he came to England?'

'Not a lot, but I think he was well connected in the old East Germany, so that would tie in.'

'Hawkins said that in that regime items as valuable as this often ended up with high-ranking officials if they weren't given to a conservatoire.'

'Yes.'

'There was another curious thing you might find interesting. Hawkins said that someone else had been asking about this quite recently.'

'Who?'

'Man phoned him. Didn't give a name; wanted to know about this Berlin Munsterhaven Strad. So Hawkins gave him the same information he told me; said the caller was very grateful. Do you think it's connected?'

'If not it's a big coincidence, but they do happen. Anyway, thank you for your help.'

'A pleasure, Chief Inspector. Any time.'

Oldroyd went back to his chamber music and mused a little on who that caller might have been. It was getting quite late when there was a knock at the door, which was unusual. He didn't get many callers and certainly not at night. He opened the door and was surprised to see his daughter, Louise. She was carrying a big shoulder bag.

'Louise! Come in, love.'

He gave her a big hug; she put her arms round him. Then he looked at her face. A tear was running down her cheek.

'What's wrong? Sit down; can I get you a drink of anything?'

'No thanks; I'm OK. It's just that I've had a big row with Mum and I walked out; got the last bus. Is it all right if I stay here for a bit?'

'What about?' She wiped her face with a tissue. Oldroyd hadn't seen her since the end of September, just before she went back to Oxford for the Michaelmas term. She was wearing jeans and a stripy jumper; her hair had grown longer. She looked beautiful: a little older and more like her mother than ever, though there had always been a strong resemblance. He realised with a shock that she was almost the same age now as Julia had been when they'd met at Oxford in their second year.

'Oh, usual stuff: money, not being tidy, not helping. You'd think she'd be glad to see me after eight weeks but all she does is nag, nag, nag.'

'So who says I won't be nagging you if you're not tidy?'

She laughed. 'You don't, though, because look at this place – it's not exactly neat, is it?' She pointed to the piles of newspapers and unwashed mugs on the coffee table.

'Hey, cheeky! And what about your poor mum by herself, and it'll be Christmas soon?'

'Well, that's her fault. If she wants me to come back, she can apologise and treat me better. Robert and Andrea will be coming up for Christmas so she won't be by herself – and anyway, you're by your-self all the time. What are you doing at Christmas, going to Auntie Alison's?'

Oldroyd took a few seconds to unpack the information she was giving him about Julia, albeit partly unwittingly. There was obviously no sign of another man in his wife's life, which always came as a relief and a reassurance that his long-term aim of getting back with her was not without hope. What was her mood? She sounded negative, stressed; maybe that was the effect of the long autumn term teaching at her sixth-form college, or maybe she was unhappy? Was this the time to make a more explicit move than his discreet invitations to plays and films? He couldn't properly consider these questions now.

'Yes, I suppose so. There's nowhere else really and we enjoy one another's company, you know.'

'Auntie Alison's great; why can't Mum be more relaxed, like her?'

'It might not be the same if Auntie Alison was your mother.'

'Maybe.'

'How's the political activism? Have you been doing anything reck-less? You know Mum gets worried about you.'

Oldroyd was proud of the fact that his daughter had been actively involved in campaigns on various issues since her mid-teens. This had sometimes involved direct action; she'd had a few run-ins with the police when she'd been part of groups that had picketed shops and occupied squares.

'Too busy; you know what the Oxford term's like. We have a stand outside the clothes shops in Cornmarket on Saturdays, protesting about sweatshop labour, but it's all peaceful. Don't worry, I haven't been arrested.'

'Thank goodness for that.' Oldroyd was relieved. It would be yet another gift to the media if a chief inspector's daughter got into serious trouble with the police, but he'd never used that to discourage her from acting on her beliefs, most of which he agreed with anyway. 'But if you've been so busy where's the money gone?'

She laughed. 'Well, you know me, can't keep out of the pubs and clubs. Drinks are so bloody expensive. The loan they give you's rubbish anyway.'

'So how about that Christmas job? It's going to be more difficult if you're here in Harrogate.'

'Yeah, I know, but I'll go round the cafés and bars tomorrow, see if they need anyone; they often do over Christmas.'

'Does Mum know I sent you money?'

'I didn't tell her.'

'I bet she suspects; no doubt I'll be in trouble.'

'Forget it. It's none of her business anyway, what I do with my money.'

'She's only thinking of your best interests; she just wants you to be sensible with it.'

Louise threw back her head. 'God! Sensible! That's what the system wants, isn't it? We all slave away earning money, save it up and spend it on what society tells us are sensible things – houses, cars, clothes, stuff, stuff, stuff – and then we sensibly go back to work and earn some more.'

Oldroyd clapped. 'Very fine speech; but the speaker's a hypocrite as she's financed by the Bank of Dad, which gets its money from the same wage-slave system.'

'Dad, get lost!' She laughed again, picked up a cushion and threw it at him.

He looked at her archly. 'There's something else, though, isn't there? You were upset when you arrived; it's not like you to cry over having a row with Mum.'

Her expression turned serious.

'Yeah, something else happened this term; made me think.'

'What?'

'Girl at college, I didn't know her all that well . . . Killed herself. She had bad depression, apparently, but kept it to herself.'

A chill went through Oldroyd and an image of the young woman in his dream and her meeting with Death flashed across his mind.

'That's bad.'

'Yeah, well, it just made me think about the people I care about, you know. I know it's a big cliché, but I thought about you and Robert and Mum and then when I got back I seemed to get straight into a row with her and I just hate it.'

'The problem is you're too much alike.'

'What, me and Mum? You're joking! She just has a steady, boring, middle-class life, never does anything radical.'

'You're forgetting her background; she came from a very well-to-do Home Counties family, big house, stables, everything. She turned away from all that and came up north with me to work as a teacher; her family didn't approve, I can tell you, and it took some guts to do it. She might not be much of an activist, but she's got a social conscience; she cares about things.'

'Maybe. She never seems like that to me.'

'That's because she's in the parent role with you. It's a lot easier for me, remember? She's been bringing you up since we split up. I'm more of an indulgent grandparent than a parent.'

His daughter looked at him.

'You always stick up for her, don't you? I think you still have a soft spot for her.'

'Of course; I always will have.' He didn't want to say just how strong his feelings still were.

She shook her head.

'Oh, Dad!'

'Anyway, early start for me tomorrow – got to get over to Halifax – so I'm off to bed. You'll have to make up that bed in the spare room.'

'Fine. I've just got to text a few people, tell them what's going on, so goodnight.'

'Night.'

Oldroyd got into bed feeling more relaxed and less lonely than he had for some time. Although he felt guilty thinking this way, he was glad his wife and daughter had had the row. It felt good to have someone else in the flat, even if it was only for a limited time.

Seven

The 'Kinor David' Stradivarius of 1734 was in the possession of the violinist Eugène Ysaÿe when it was stolen from a dressing room in St Petersburg in 1908. It turned up mysteriously in a shop in Paris in 1925. It is now played by the leader of the Israel Philharmonic Orchestra.

The church in Notting Hill was packed for the funeral of Martin Hamilton. It was a dull, cold day but the church was brightly lit. Some of his pupils played cello pieces and one of them delivered a moving tribute, describing what an inspirational teacher Hamilton had been. The recent revelations about the deceased's criminal activities were judiciously ignored by all present.

Anna Robson and Michael Stringer sat together towards the back. It was the second funeral they'd been to recently, but at least this was much better attended than the one for Hans. As had been expected, no one had come from Germany so it had just been his fellow musicians and his pupils and representatives from the Bloomsbury School. The same people, including Patrick Jefferson, were here again today. Stringer caught Jefferson's eye, but the latter looked away.

Afterwards they paid their respects to Hamilton's family, which consisted of a brother and sister. Sad, thought Stringer, how he himself was the only member of the quartet to have a family of his own; he had two sons at high school, though he was divorced from his wife. It was often the case with successful musicians, as it was with actors. The incessant travelling and the punishing performance schedules put enormous strains on relationships and family life.

Afterwards Stringer and Anna went to a nearby café. Anna looked very pale and said she wanted to talk. A goatee-bearded waiter wearing a striped apron took their order: a cappuccino and pain au chocolat for Stringer and an espresso for Anna. Stringer looked round as they waited. The café was called NY55, and the walls were exposed brick, hung with black-and-white photographs of New York scenes of the 1950s; the chairs and tables were metal and glass. Jazz was playing softly in the background. There was silence until the waiter brought the drinks and the pastry.

Stringer took a knife, cut his pain au chocolat in two and took a bite from one half. The warm, flaky pastry and the melting chocolate formed a satisfying combination. Anna still seemed distracted. He reflected ruefully on the funeral they'd just attended. It had been a most unwise move of Martin's to steal the violin like that and he'd paid the price. He'd never been that fond of Martin, to be honest, never trusted him. He glanced at Anna and saw that her hands were shaking.

'Are you OK?'

'Not really. What the hell's going on, Michael?'

'I know; it's terrible.'

'But . . . now Martin, too; I can't believe it. I'm just . . . I'm in a state.'

'I don't blame you.'

She looked at him with a face lined with strain.

'You look calm; I mean how do you know it's not going to be one of us next? I don't feel safe in the house; I'm thinking of going away.'

'I think you're overreacting. Martin stole Hans's violin and then it was taken from his apartment. He was obviously killed because of that. Neither of us is involved in the criminal world, are we? I don't think some maniac's out to massacre the whole of the Franz Schubert Quartet.'

'What about Hans, though?'

Stringer looked at her quizzically. 'Do you really think Christopher could have been involved?'

She put both hands rather pathetically around the tiny cup of espresso as if hugging it for warmth. 'I don't know what to think; I'm confused. Christopher's still in America; I've had a short conversation with him. I told you in Halifax. I've been worried about him ever since he found out about me and Hans. He's volatile and you know his past.'

'Yes, but he wouldn't do a thing like that.' Stringer suppressed his dislike of Downton in order to reassure Anna. 'It's a wild idea that he would arrange a hitman to bump Hans off at a concert, in Halifax of all places; does Christopher even know where that is? I mean, it's ludicrous.'

'I suppose so. You're sure you didn't say anything to the police?'

'No, of course not, but I did tell them about Hans having an argument with Jefferson at the school; they'll have a good time investigating that, though I can't see anyone at the school having Hans murdered either. Can you imagine Lord Bromley, our distinguished chair, ringing up the mob and hiring a hitman? He'd never soil his aristocratic hands with something so sordid.'

Stringer picked up the last piece of his rapidly cooling pastry and popped it into his mouth. His attempt to lighten the mood had not really worked, Anna still looked haunted.

'But, Martin . . .' She shook her head. 'He was dealing with stolen stuff all the time and we never knew.'

'It appears so, though I like to think most of his dealings were above board.'

'I've read the reports; the police found a secret compartment in his cello case. He must have had that made to transport instruments around in secret, stolen stuff. I can't bear to think about it. All these years we've known him and worked with him and he was really a criminal. I . . .' She burst into tears. Stringer put his hand over hers.

'He wasn't just that; he was a great cellist and our friend. I'm sure . . .'

'Friend! He stole that violin while Hans was lying there dead. How could he? It makes me sick to think about it. I knew he would have liked to have got that violin from Hans, but I didn't tell the police about it. Now I'm not sure. Maybe I should have, maybe he *was* involved in Hans's death.'

She dabbed her eyes with a tissue and then suddenly looked at Stringer. 'You didn't know he'd taken it, did you?'

'Hey, of course not! Are you getting me involved now, too? I was too shocked by what had just happened to notice anything; so was everybody else. He must have just slipped it inside his jacket, couldn't resist the temptation. I admit it's not a nice idea but, come on, calm down or soon you'll have created a massive conspiracy where even the bloke who sold the concert tickets wanted Hans dead.'

For the first time a faint smile crossed her face.

'I'm sorry; I just don't know what to think or who to trust anymore. It's as if my world is disintegrating. Just a few weeks ago we were all playing together and now we've been to two funerals and . . . and it's all a horrible mystery.'

'I know; it's very difficult for us and I wouldn't fancy being the police either. They must be tearing their hair out over this one.'

'Is it true they don't have any leads?'

'I don't think so; apparently they don't even know exactly how Hans was killed, or at least how the killer escaped.'

She stared down at her coffee, and then took a sip.

'Have you thought about what you're going to do now?' she asked.

'You mean as far as playing goes?'

'Yes; obviously the quartet's finished. We can't replace two people.'

'No, that's true. But you and I could found a new ensemble, recruit two new players from the school. We'd have lots of interest.'

'I don't know; it's too early. I wonder whether it would ever be the same.'

'No, it wouldn't be the same. We could play a different repertoire, more modern; it would appeal to young players.'

She peered up at him. 'That's what you always wanted, isn't it? A different repertoire. Maybe; I can't think about it, haven't got the energy.'

'I understand; we'll talk again later.'

'I'm going to stay with my sister and her husband in Brighton for a while. I can't stay in the house by myself and Christopher's not back for a few days.'

'Is he not coming back early after all this?'

'Says he can't; the paper want him there until he finishes his assignment.'

'What's he doing that's so vital?'

'He's in Washington, covering the midterm elections to the senate.'

Stringer drank the last of his coffee.

'OK, well, I have to be getting off; got some pupils to see.' He put his hand lightly on to hers again. 'Call me from Brighton and take it easy. I'm sure the police will make a breakthrough at some point.'

She smiled wanly and nodded.

'OK.'

He left some money and she watched him leave the café. Her mood darkened again. Michael was always a help, but she was finding it hard not to be suspicious of everything and everybody. He'd always been a rather cool person, not given to showing his feelings, but even for him he seemed strangely unaffected by what had happened. She knew he'd never liked Hans, and she'd seen them have those awful rows, but that couldn't have been enough to . . . And what about Martin? Surely? She shook her head, paid the bill and left.

Sir Patrick Jefferson knew it was only a matter of time before the police came back again. The governing body of the Bloomsbury School of Music had held an extraordinary meeting in the boardroom to discuss recent events. It had been a grim affair, dominated by a sense of crisis. Not surprisingly, the governors, led by their chair, Lord Bromley, were very keen to minimise adverse publicity and Jefferson had had to reassure them that he was doing everything he could to distance the school from the criminal investigations, reports of which were plastered over the front pages of every tabloid newspaper. The biggest difficulty, as they all realised, was the fact that on Muller's death the school inherited the Munsterhaven Strad. Wonderful as this was – or would have been, had the violin not disappeared – it obviously looked as if the school would have benefited from Muller's murder. This was perfect material for unscrupulous journalists looking for the next sensational story.

'If it emerges that we were intending to pension him off, however generously, and that he didn't like it, we're in trouble,' said one of the governors, a corpulent businessman who chaired the committee concerned with sponsorship and private-sector involvement. 'It's going to look as if we could have got rid of him to make sure he didn't change his will.'

'But that's monstrous,' replied another governor, a retired soprano who had been famous in her time. 'Who on earth would think such a thing of such a reputable institution as this?'

'Journalists don't think twice about it; any half-baked story and they're off. In fact, the better your reputation, the better they like it;

the more sensational it is. The bigger they come the harder they fall, so to speak.'

'Well, did anyone know about the situation with Muller other than us?' intoned Lord Bromley in his near-caricature of an aristocratic accent.

'Only the police. I had to tell them,' said Sir Patrick. All eyes were turned on him. 'They were asking questions; Michael Stringer told them that Hans and I had had a row. I couldn't just deny it; they find these things out eventually and then you're in serious trouble.'

'So what did you say?'

'I told them we were going to retire Hans and that he didn't like it; that's all; just as I reported to you at the last meeting. I didn't tell them about the will, though I wish I had because they'll dig deeper and discover it. Then they'll be back. You've also got to remember that the violin is missing again, so it's big news after Hamilton's murder. There's no way we could quietly take possession of it, even if it hadn't disappeared.'

There was much sighing and shaking of heads.

'It's an absolute mess,' said the businessman. 'What do you suggest we do?' The eyes turned to Jefferson again.

'The best strategy is to stay calm; we'll have to confirm that there was a disagreement between the school and Muller, but make clear that's all it was. If we continue to firmly deny all knowledge of anything else, then I think they'll tire of trying to link us to the crimes. As you pointed out . . .' He nodded to the female governor. 'It's a far-fetched idea that the Bloomsbury School of Music could be going around hiring hitmen, and I think the media will realise that and drop it after a while. Hopefully the police will produce some other suspects, which will help to take the attention away from us.'

'That sounds very reasonable to me.' Lord Bromley seemed to draw a line under the matter. 'Shall we move on? There are one or two matters I wanted to raise while we're all together.'

Sir Patrick felt some relief at this point and everyone else seemed pleased to go on to a new topic. When the meeting came to an end he had a discreet word with Lord Bromley in private.

'It's fine,' said Bromley quietly, and with rather more steel in his voice than was suggested by his public persona. 'None of them suspect anything. I think we're in the clear.'

'Good.'

'Have you heard anything?'

'No, but give them time.'

'Be careful, Jefferson: these are dangerous people.'

'We all know that after what happened to Muller and Hamilton, but what's the alternative? Rely on the police?'

Lord Bromley shook his head.

'Very well; I just hope you know what you're doing.'

When Carter appeared for his second meeting with Sir Patrick, the latter felt better prepared. Carter on the other hand had little enthusiasm for the encounter. He didn't favour the idea that the School of Music had anything to do with it all. To him, professional murders like these meant hardened criminals, ruthless characters, not these genteel types who played musical instruments. Yes, money was a great corrupter, but he couldn't see them being capable of taking out one or even two of their own people, people who'd done so much for them in the past: that was brutal gangsterism. Nevertheless, they had to follow up everything and the boss wanted Jefferson interviewed again.

'So, sir, the reason I'm back is that I don't think you told us everything the last time we were here, did you?'

They were in the principal's office, and Jefferson was quite glad that the older man, the Yorkshire chief inspector, was not there; there was something sharp and penetrating about him that made it difficult to conceal anything. Carter was accompanied by Detective Constable Jenkins from the Met.

'I take it you're referring to Muller's will?'

'Yes.'

'Well, I was shocked by what had happened, and by you telling me that Martin Hamilton had been murdered; it slipped my mind.'

'So you knew that Muller had left the violin to you in his will?'

'Yes.'

'And you were obviously pleased about that?'

'Of course, having a Munsterhaven Strad would put the school on a level with the other music academies around the world who own such special instruments.'

'You wouldn't want to do anything that jeopardised it coming to you?'

'No.'

'So wasn't it risky to offend Muller by giving him the push? He was a sensitive kind of bloke, wasn't he, and a bit volatile?'

'Well, as I told you before, we were offering him a good retirement package and he could have continued teaching here.'

Carter decided to go for the kill.

'But he didn't like it, did he, sir? In fact, he threatened to change his will and not leave the violin to you and that, I put to you, was what you were really arguing about that day when Stringer overheard you.'

Jefferson retained his cool. 'Yes, all right, Hans was very upset and he said some wild things, but . . .'

'So what did you decide to do about it, sir? Did you panic and decide that it would be better if Muller left the scene before he could change his will?'

Jefferson smiled; it was a rather crude attack. 'That's rather wild too, Sergeant, if you'll forgive me. We were confident that Hans would calm down and see reason. I assume you know he had health problems and probably couldn't go on playing much longer. I'm sure deep down he wanted the school to have the violin so that someone would play it; he wouldn't have wanted it to go to a museum and into a glass case. With the money he was going to get from us he would have been financially secure and wouldn't have had to consider selling it.'

'Who's "we", sir?'

'I discussed it with Lord Bromley, the chair of governors.'

'And did he agree?'

'Yes.'

'So you were prepared to just play it cool despite his threats? That was risky, wasn't it?'

'No, I don't think so; I don't think there was any real danger to our inheritance.'

Carter paused. He somehow felt that he still wasn't getting the full truth.

'You told us before that no one here knew that Hamilton was dealing illegally with instruments.'

'Of course not.'

'That would have been a scandal, wouldn't it, if it had ever become known?'

'Yes.'

'So did you find out what he was doing and then take steps to stop it?'

Still Jefferson remained unruffled. He smiled patronisingly at Carter.

'What do you mean, Sergeant? Are you accusing us of having Martin Hamilton murdered now? This is the Bloomsbury School of Music, not the Sicilian mafia.'

'But maybe you knew what was going on and then when Hamilton stole the violin that was the last straw. After all, that was what you've just described as your inheritance.'

'So we had him killed to get the violin back? Well, I have to hand it to you, Sergeant, you're certainly persistent.'

'Maybe, sir, but you can't deny you certainly had a motive.'

'I suppose that's true but I wish you the best of luck in proving the ludicrous idea that we had anything to do with the murders of two of our most illustrious musicians – and in the meantime I also wish you luck in recovering our inheritance, as you put it, for us.'

Carter had decided that was as far as he could take things and was getting up to leave.

'Before you go, Sergeant; there is one thing that I think I ought to mention. I ought to have told you before, but it's a . . . well, a delicate matter.'

Carter sat down again.

'Go on.'

'You asked me before if I knew if Hans had any enemies.'

'Yes.'

'Well, there was a problem with Anna Robson. Not so much her personally but her husband, Christopher Downton.'

'In what way?'

'Hans and Anna had a relationship over quite a long period, but then she met Christopher and broke it off with Hans. Apparently Hans wouldn't accept this. I don't know the details, but it was fairly well known among people here that there was friction. Downton once turned up here in a rage, confronted Hans, threatened him. This was in front of a number of people.'

'How did Muller react?'

'Defiantly, according to the witnesses: laughed at Downton, called him a "puny man" or something. Hans could be quite haughty and arrogant at times; no one intimidated him. He seemed to think he was above reproach.'

'So that conflict wasn't resolved?'

Jefferson hesitated.

'No. And the other thing is, Christopher Downton has a record of violence. He was prosecuted for assault and served six months a few years ago, and that was to do with his girlfriend of the time. I think someone was harassing her in a bar, and Downton smashed a bottle over his head; seems like he's a jealous character, and acts quickly on his feelings.'

'OK, sir. We'll leave it there for the time being.'

Carter and DC Jenkins left the school, passing the groups of arty-looking students in the lobby carrying their instruments as they chattered to each other. Despite the information Jefferson had given him about Christopher Downton, Carter was feeling disgruntled and outmanoeuvred. Maybe the Bloomsbury School did have something to hide. On the way back to the Met, he called Oldroyd and told him what Jefferson had said.

'Apart from that, I didn't get any more out of him, sir; don't know whether he was telling me all that about Robson's husband to deflect attention from himself. Bit of a cool customer; denies any involvement of himself or anyone at the school in the murders of course. I must admit, I think it's a bit far-fetched myself.'

'Sometimes the most unlikely explanations prove to be the ones that turn out to be true.'

'Yeah, and I do get the feeling that he's still keeping something back.' Carter had been working on his instincts, his antennae. He'd learned through observing Oldroyd that, when things got difficult, you sometimes had to go with your gut and then look for the evidence, often in unlikely places. But you also had to remain open, be prepared to accept that your theory was wrong and that you had to start again from scratch.

'What do you think that might be?'

'Don't know, sir, but he's a smug git, if you'll pardon the expression; he seems to enjoy the fact that we've nothing really on him. I wonder how genuine all that shock was when we first interviewed him; it just seems to me that there was so much at stake, you know, if they'd lost that violin.'

'Do you think other people at the school are involved?'

'Don't know, sir, it's all speculation.'

'Do you think they know where the violin is?'

'Who knows? All I can say is he seems very calm for a man whose prize inheritance is missing, maybe for good.'

'OK. And how's it going with the search for Hamilton's killers and the violin? Has Newton got any leads?'

'He's got a team working on it. They're pretty good: know all the gangs who deal in stuff like that; they're using all their contacts to get information. The airports and ferries are on the alert for anyone trying to take it out of the country.'

'Good. Well, getting back to Robson, you'd better go and talk to her again about this husband of hers and her affair with Muller; she kept that from us so there must be something she's trying to hide.'

'It sounds like another long shot to me, sir. I mean, it's one thing to lose your temper and whack somebody over the head in a pub, but this was a clever premeditated job and more than a bit dangerous; what if the gunman had missed and hit Anna Robson? Would you put your own wife at risk?'

'I know, but let's see what she has to say, and also talk to Stringer again and find out what he knew. Call me again when you've got things to report.'

'OK, sir.'

Carter ended the call. DC Jenkins was driving the car. Carter looked around as they went down Gower Street, past the British Museum and on to New Oxford Street. It was good to see the streets of London again and get the vibe, but he'd forgotten the kind of pressure such a relentless urban environment produces. He felt a bit claustrophobic; he'd got used to being able to drive out into the countryside within minutes. He was staying with his sister, who lived in Croydon, not far from the house they'd grown up in. He could have contacted Jason Harris, and stayed in his flat while he was in London, but had decided that was not sensible due to the wild lifestyle of his old friend, who was still making and spending piles of money in the City. He didn't have time for that now, nor really the inclination anymore. He hadn't even told Jason that he was in the capital. The car headed down Whitehall back towards New Scotland Yard. He needed to report to Newton and find out where Robson and Stringer lived. After that he could ring Steph and see how things were back in Harrogate – or, as he was increasingly thinking of it, back at home.

The next day Oldroyd returned to Halifax, driving again over the same route he'd taken on that fateful night. It was a fine day with a pale-blue sky; the sun was so low that one half of the Calder Valley was in shade and would remain so all day. He decided to go a different route and took the road out of Bradford, which climbed up to Queensbury. Here there were panoramic views of the moors and hills in all directions. He stopped, got out of the car briefly and inhaled the bracing air. It was good to get out of the towns and up to what seemed like the roof of the world; somehow it gave him a perspective on things.

In Halifax, the Christmas atmosphere was intensifying; decorations festooned the streets and vans were selling hot chestnuts. Oldroyd's absorption in this case was making him feel rather detached from it all. He arrived at police HQ and reported his findings about the violin to Armitage. The latter was chewing his way through a packet of jelly babies and he offered one to Oldroyd.

'I'm not sure it gets us much further in narrowing down the field, Sam,' said Oldroyd. He put the green baby he'd chosen in his mouth and chewed the soft, sweet gum. 'We still haven't got any definite links between anybody and the criminal things that happened that night apart from Hamilton – and he's dead. But the most interesting thing is that someone else has been asking about Muller's Strad.'

'Do you think they could have been the killer?'

'Possibly. But like just about everything else in this case we can't be sure. I'm interested in this background story, you know, where the violin came from.'

'You mean all that Nazi stuff?'

'Yes, now Adamson's confirmed it all, and how it came to Muller.'

Armitage stuffed another jelly baby into his mouth and looked unconvinced. 'Do you think it lends weight to the idea of some organisation taking revenge?'

'I don't know, but I think we should check the backgrounds of people. What about Frank Dancek? He came from somewhere near that part of the world. He could be concealing things about himself.'

'You mean he's really Jewish? Sounds unlikely.'

'Who knows? Let's face it: we've got to follow up every possible lead, however slender. We need to know about the pasts of everyone involved with the Red Chapel. It must have been someone who knew the place and had access.'

'OK. I'll get people on to it.'

'I presume you've already spoken to Gerald Watson and the rest of the committee?'

'Of course; we've seen them all and they've made statements like everyone else there that night. Nothing's come of it. No one saw anything we don't already know about.' He offered Oldroyd another jelly baby. This time he took a red one.

'I think I'll go and talk to Gerald Watson again; after all, he was the one who booked the quartet to come here.'

Armitage shrugged. 'Fine, if you think it'll do any good; all we can do is keep rummaging around and follow our instincts.'

Oldroyd got up rather wearily, chewing lethargically on his jelly baby. They seemed to be almost as directionless as ever, mired in information that didn't lead anywhere. Maybe even more sugar would inspire him.

'Sam, how about a few of those for the road?'

'You're welcome,' Armitage replied and poured some from the packet into Oldroyd's outstretched hand. At least his sweets are better than his tea and coffee, thought the latter as he made his way out of West Yorkshire Police HQ, wondering how Armitage managed to retain any of his teeth.

Gerald Watson was a true Yorkshire eccentric. He lived in an old manor house in the village of Longstalls, high up in the hills to the west of Halifax above the Calder Valley. From here he ran his own one-man engineering company, supplying finely crafted individual metal parts to bigger companies that were geared to mass production. He had few hobbies other than music. He was a fine amateur violin player and a longstanding supporter of the Halifax Chamber Music Society. He was unmarried, lived rather frugally, and his personal wealth was difficult to determine. However, he was always generous in respect of the society and keen to engage the finest ensembles.

Oldroyd enjoyed the drive up from Halifax. The weak sun illuminated the fields with a slanting light. He liked this part of the West Riding. It was not as gloriously beautiful as the limestone dales further to the north, but it had a rugged, windswept, bleak attractiveness and a unique atmosphere. In the small valley towns were the remnants of the textile industry, with many of the chimneys gone and mills demolished or converted into apartments. Narrow winding roads with millstone grit walls led up to villages and hamlets where many old solid-stone weavers' cottages stood.

Oldroyd relished the unusual names: Thick Hollins, Choppards, Wash Pits, Thurrish Rough, Dog Kennel Bank, Totties, Flush House, Dockery; hamlets called Paris and Egypt. He loved the sheer stubborn determination and bloody-mindedness that had built farms on these high moors, eking out a living from the peaty ground with sheep and cattle. But people were mistaken if they thought this was a place lacking culture and sophistication. As well as the musical traditions, this was the land of the Brontë sisters and the poets Ted Hughes and Simon Armitage. As he drove along he glanced over at the hills to his right and knew that up there somewhere was the ruined farmhouse of Top Withens, almost certainly the model for the eponymous home of Cathy and Heathcliff in *Wuthering Heights.*

He wound his way up and around the hillside. The hardy sheep stood in the damp and scratched at the frosty fields to get at the cold winter grass. Panoramic views across miles of countryside and up to wild moorland summits kept appearing before him. He saw the obelisk of Stoodley Pike on the horizon and also thought he could pick out Heptonstall church, where Sylvia Plath was buried on a hillside above the town of Hebden Bridge. Eventually he saw the sign 'Longstalls' and was suddenly forced to the right up a severe gradient. He saw that the road was called 'Back O'th'Hill' and then he was in a quiet, narrow street with weavers' cottages at either side, still climbing up towards the dark tower of a church.

He was looking for Longstalls Manor House and eventually found a low building slightly set back from the road. He parked in the street, walked through a little formal rose garden and knocked on the solid-looking door, above which the date 1704 was carved into the stonework. After several tries there was no response so he decided to go down a lane at the side and see if he would have better luck at the back of the house. He passed through an iron gate and into a bare yard flagged with huge squares of millstone grit. He could hear the noise of machinery coming from a low stone extension with green wooden doors. Light was shining through a dirty window. He walked across the yard and knocked on the door. Inside, the noise was louder and there was no chance that anyone would hear him. He opened the door and eased his way in.

A man dressed in blue overalls and wearing large goggles was standing over a machine and holding some kind of tool against a piece of metal, which was spinning at great speed. As Oldroyd watched, the tool was moved in closer; there was a high-pitched grinding noise and an impressive shower of sparks flew up, some of which landed on Oldroyd's head. He quickly and vigorously tried to brush them off. This movement caught the man's attention. He switched everything off and pushed up his goggles to reveal a smiling face smeared with oil. He seemed totally unsurprised by Oldroyd's appearance.

'Ah, Chief Inspector! I thought you might be paying me a visit afore long.'

Everyone seemed to be expecting him, thought Oldroyd. How was it that in this case he somehow felt a few steps behind all the time?

Watson put his equipment down on a bench and offered Oldroyd a rather greasy hand, which the latter took.

'I know we've never met formally, but I've seen you many a time at t'Chapel. Didn't you used to come with your father years ago?' The accent was broad, as befitted someone who'd lived all his life up here in a moorland village.

'Yes.'

'Me too: my dad loved chamber music; used to bring me along, reluctantly to begin with, but I learned to love it. I remember you sitting with your dad; bald-headed chap with a moustache, wasn't he?'

'You've got a good memory.'

'I have for people's faces; can't remember names, though.' He laughed. 'Old age again I suppose. I'm a few years older than you I think. Anyway.' He pulled the goggles completely off his head to reveal a thinnish face with a scrawny beard. 'Let's go inside; can I get you owt to drink?'

'A cup of tea wouldn't go amiss.'

'Right.'

Oldroyd followed his lean figure as he walked in a sprightly manner across the yard and into a large kitchen, which felt a bit like entering a time warp. The doors were painted and grained, 1950s style, in a dull brown colour. There was an old Rayburn cooker with two mongrel dogs asleep on grubby-looking mats at the side. Old wooden cupboards were built into the walls, which were covered with faded wallpaper, and on the floor were expensive but ancient and stained carpets. These had almost certainly been made in Halifax in the heyday of the woollen industry. Worn sofas were partially occupied by piles of magazines and strewn with dog hairs. It all had the rough-and-ready appearance of an old bachelor life, but seemed nevertheless very cosy and comfortable.

Watson filled a kettle, put it on the Rayburn and then cleared a space on the sofa for Oldroyd, who noticed that the magazines were from a rifle club. Watson then sat down in an armchair despite his oily overalls.

'Well, what can I do for you? I presume it's about t'murder. I told that constable everything. Didn't see any more than you; then I was looking after Mrs Hurst, who passed out – couldn't leave her. Thought you did a grand job of calming things down till the others joined you.'

'Thank you. Did she recover all right?'

'Yes, she's fine – nearly ninety, mind you; not sure she'll be coming again. Said it was a disgraceful carry-on, people getting shot at a concert and in a chapel too. What was the world coming to . . .' He laughed and shook his head. 'Some of the old people can never accept it's not a place of worship anymore. I think she used to go there in the old days when it was a Methodist chapel. Aye, it's a shame: she was a generous donor; not without a bit o' brass, you know. Her husband had an engineering company in Sowerby Bridge, though he's been dead a few year now.'

'I know you made a statement at the time, but I wanted to ask you again if you saw anything unusual that night or in the days leading up to that concert. Anything at all.'

Steam billowed from the Rayburn; the kettle was boiling.

'Just a minute.'

Watson got up and mashed several spoonfuls of tea in a big brown pot. He stirred it round and poured the dark-brown liquid into two huge mugs.

'Milk and sugar?'

'Just milk, please.'

Watson splashed the milk in plus a couple of spoonfuls of sugar into his and passed a mug to Oldroyd, who sipped the potent brew. It was the strongest tea he had ever tasted, but a relief after the awful stuff that Armitage made. He noticed that the inside of the mug was stained brown, presumably from prolonged soaking in the stuff.

Watson sat down again. He opened a battered tin and offered the contents to Oldroyd.

'Fancy a chocolate digestive?'

Oldroyd declined, but Watson munched his way through several during the conversation that followed.

'There was nowt odd that I can remember; just a normal concert. Everybody was excited, you know, Schubert Quartet being that famous, we were lucky to have 'em.'

'How did you manage to book them? They must have been expensive.'

Watson dunked a biscuit in his tea.

'It's mainly due to Edward Shaw; he always coughs up a lot of money. I mean, we all put in money on the committee, you know, but we couldn't really continue without his contributions, not and get anybody decent. I always plan the programme with him and we were looking at information from the agents. I said what a good quartet they were and he read through the stuff about them and said, "Let's have 'em", and I wasn't going to argue.'

'Did he say anything about the Munsterhaven Strad? You know he's an instrument collector?'

'Yes, but he never says much about all that. I suppose that might have been the attraction for him, but then it's odd if he was wanting to get a look at it that he didn't come to the concert. Mind you, he doesn't always come; I don't think he's that fond of the music, not like his father was.'

'He admitted as much to me. So why do you think he keeps paying so much towards the concerts, then?' asked Oldroyd.

Watson shrugged. 'Don't really know and don't ask either; as long as he keeps giving us the money that's good enough for me, no questions asked. I think it's to do with his father – thinks his father would want him to keep supporting the society.'

'Does he have any contact with the ensembles when he does turn up?'

'Yes, well, he's president, so he has the right to meet them. He usually goes into that artists' room and has a chat.'

'What about?'

'Well, when I've been in there it's always been about the instruments they're playing, as you'd expect.'

'Did he ever make any offers to any of them to buy their instruments?'

'Not that I ever heard.'

'What about you? I think you're a fiddle player, aren't you?'

Watson laughed. 'Me?' He got up and went over to a cupboard, from which he took a violin and bow. Abruptly he put the instrument up to his chin and rattled off a passage that Oldroyd recognised as from one of Bach's unaccompanied violin suites. It wasn't at all bad for an amateur.

One of the dogs woke up and barked as it walked over to Watson.

'Shut up, Trixie. Oi! Calm down, you stupid dog! She doesn't like the sound of me playing; it always upsets her. Maybe she's got a musical ear.' He laughed again as the dog's noise subsided to a growl and she slunk back to the Rayburn.

'I play with a few friends. We're all getting on a bit now; we have a go at one or two of the easier Haydn quartets.' He looked at the violin. 'It's a nice old instrument, Chief Inspector, but I don't imagine it's worth much. I don't think Edward Shaw'd be interested, put it that way, and neither am I, really. I don't go in for collecting 'em like he does.'

Oldroyd took a long drink of his tea.

'What's the routine on a concert night?'

Watson sat down again.

'Well, I meet the performers at about six o'clock, usually, and take them to t'Chapel, down into that room, make sure they're settled in, get 'em drinks and stuff and then leave them to practise.'

'Did everything go as normal on that night?'

'Pretty much.'

'How did they seem to you?'

Watson shrugged. 'OK. You don't get much time with them really. The woman, Anna Robson, she was very nice and that cellist who was shot later; the other two didn't say much, didn't look too happy.'

'So after that, what happened?'

'I left them to it. The other committee members started to arrive about half past six; we all have a job, you know, Ruth sells t'programmes, Stuart is usually on t'door checking tickets, poor bugger. That turned out to be quite a job that night; I take it he still swears no one went out o' t'building except Frank?'

'Yes.'

'So t'murderer vanished into thin air?'

'So it appears, but we'll find out what happened, however long it takes. And then the concert started?'

'Yes, I was sitting at t'front with the two old ladies. I like to make a fuss of them, you know; after all, their contributions are significant too. I'm not sure how we'll manage without when they're not around.' He leaned forward and dropped his voice to a whisper. 'I'm hoping they've both remembered us in their wills. Anyway, the first part of the concert went well.'

'And that was all before the interval?'

'Yes, then went down to the bar. Saw you there. Went back up and then they started the Schubert. You know the rest.'

Oldroyd finished his tea and put the mug down. He looked at the piles of magazines at his side.

'I see you're interested in guns.'

'Yes, I've got a few old rifles. I go with some friends to a rifle club; blast away at the targets. It's all above board, I've got the licences if you want to see them.'

'No, that's fine; wouldn't mind seeing the rifles, though. I presume you've got them locked up?'

'Of course; the gun cupboard's through here in the hall.'

He got up, and led Oldroyd into a rather dark hallway where there were two grandfather clocks ponderously ticking away and a wooden cupboard. Watson took a key and opened the cupboard.

'There you are. Three beauties there, my pride and joy. I can get them out if you like.'

'No, that's fine. I can see everything's in order. I'll be off now – thanks for the tea.'

'Aye, you're welcome. I'll come out with you. Back to work, got to get those bearings finished.' He showed Oldroyd out through the front door and the detective stood for a moment considering the December rose garden in which a few pinkish flowers still hung on in the cold.

When Oldroyd got back to the car he dialled Armitage's number.

'Any luck, Jim?'

'Probably not; he seems a harmless sort of bloke, can't see any kind of motive. There was just one thing.'

'What's that?'

'He had a Dragunov sniper rifle in his gun cupboard.'

Carter had woken up with a bit of a hangover. He'd given in to temptation in the end, got in touch with Jason and arranged a night out. They'd toured various bars in Soho and met up with some mutual friends, all of whom were delighted to see Carter. There was constant teasing of Carter as a 'northerner'.

'Aye by gum, it's Andy Carter t'Yorkshireman', delivered in clumsy parodies of a Yorkshire accent. 'Have yer been on Ilkley Moor, bar whatever-it-is, lad?' 'How's them Yorkshire lasses, swooning for the London stud, I'll bet?'

He took it all with a smile and didn't even try to explain what it was really like and how he'd come to love it. Nor did he mention Steph; he didn't want a lot of ribald banter about her. He played the evening judiciously and drank well but not to excess. Nonetheless it was well into the small hours when he got back to his sister's in Croydon and he felt well and truly knackered this morning. Maybe he just couldn't take it any more: too old. But that was a fact of life, wasn't it? Much better to accept that you're getting older and make the changes than try to live an eternal and increasingly sad youth, like Jason.

'Feeling a bit rough, Sarge?' said DC Jenkins, who was again driving the car as they headed towards Islington. He grinned at Carter, who was yawning and looking rather pale.

'Yeah, it was a good night; had to celebrate being back in London with my old mates.'

'So you're up north now?'

'That's right, Harrogate, West Riding Police.'

'That's a posh place, isn't it? A bit like Cheltenham?'

'Don't really know Cheltenham, to be honest, but Harrogate's a nice town, lots of green.'

'You don't get bored then, you know, with it being so quiet.'

'Not really, I work for a very interesting bloke, and unusual things happen. It's different.' He thought of telling the constable about his first case, where the body was found in a pothole, but the effort of explaining about what potholes were, and how the body came to be found where it was, was too much in his present state. He was quite relieved when they arrived at Anna Robson's house and he had to summon up the effort to conduct the interview.

Anna Robson was expecting them and she showed them into a living room that was like a smaller version of the one in Muller's apartment, with its baby grand piano, music stands and shelves lined with books. She remembered the handsome young detective from the interview in Halifax.

'You've caught me just in time, Sergeant. I'm leaving London tomorrow, going down to Brighton to stay with my sister for a while; it's all getting a bit much here, as I'm sure you'll appreciate.'

Carter shuffled a bit uneasily and tried to remember how Oldroyd would conduct an interview like this. He still found interviewing educated, articulate people difficult; he was more familiar with thugs and burglars from the harder parts of the city.

'Yes I can; quite a bit's happened since we last, er, spoke. Going to Brighton is fine just as long as you don't try to leave the country.'

Robson looked alarmed.

'I just mean that until we've concluded the investigation, everyone, er, involved has to stay available for questioning.'

'You make it sound as if I'm a suspect.'

'You weren't entirely frank with us when we interviewed you in Halifax.'

'How?'

'We know you had a relationship with Muller in the past and that your husband didn't like it; also they had a row.'

Anna Robson sighed.

'Who's been telling you this?'

'Patrick Jefferson, but he claims it was widely known.'

'He should mind his own business.'

'Is it all true?'

Carter looked at her and saw her expression was resigned, as if she partly welcomed the air being cleared.

'Yes, it's true that Hans and I had a relationship over several years and that Christopher didn't like the idea.'

'Was your relationship definitely over when you married your husband?'

She looked at him sharply.

'Yes, of course, and if anyone says anything different they're lying.'

'How did Muller feel about it?'

'He wasn't happy either.' She laughed sardonically. 'Two men fighting over you: a woman's dream. Hans was quite possessive, didn't want to let me go, said he'd always love me, that I reminded him of someone he'd known when he was younger who he'd lost. I'm not sure that's really a compliment; it made me feel I was a substitute for someone else.

'Hans was a lot older than me. I felt the relationship was over. It had always been a lot to do with a young woman's infatuation with this charismatic figure, a brilliant player who came from what had been East Germany while we were students; all very exotic and exciting. When I look back now I think Hans exploited his position.'

'How?'

'To impress young female students. I wasn't the only one he slept with, and I know he was seducing students while we were together.'

'OK, but coming back to your husband: couldn't he accept that your relationship with Muller was over?'

'I made the mistake of not telling him about it. I knew he had a tendency to be a bit jealous and insecure. He found out from someone else, and Hans was always reminding him about the past.'

'According to Jefferson, your husband once threatened Muller in public at the Bloomsbury School. Is that true?'

'I don't know what Jefferson's trying to achieve by telling you all this . . . But I can't deny it, there were plenty of witnesses.'

'What happened?'

'I think Hans had been making remarks about me, and it was passed on to Christopher. He flew into a rage, came to the school and confronted him; warned him not to say things like that.'

'Or what?'

'Nothing. The thing about Christopher is he's all bark and no bite; as soon as he's calmed down he's sorry for losing his temper.'

'That temper did get the better of him at least once, though, didn't it? He was done for assault.'

'That was when he was a lot younger and he was drunk. Look, I imagine what you're driving at here is that my husband had a motive to kill Hans. I can't say it hasn't crossed my mind, but Christopher's not the kind of person to cold-bloodedly plan something like the way Hans was murdered. He's been in America for several weeks, so he would have had to hire a killer and . . . Well, it's just not possible.'

'Well, it's possible, but you're saying not likely.'

'OK.'

'Have you spoken to your husband since the murders?'

'Yes. He's shocked like everyone else and his shock is genuine.'

'What about Martin Hamilton? We haven't spoken since his murder.'

She put her hands to her head as if she could not stand much more questioning about things she found so upsetting.

'That's also very shocking and frightening. It's the reason why I'm leaving London and going into a kind of hiding. Two members of our quartet killed: who knows what will happen next?'

'Did Hamilton have any enemies to your knowledge?'

'No, Martin was always very genial with everybody, but now we know he was dealing in instruments illegally, so who knows who he was involved with?'

'Did your husband know Hamilton?'

'No, he'd met him, but didn't really . . . What are you implying now? That Christopher and Martin somehow were involved in this together and now my husband, having got rid of his rival, has also bumped off his accomplice and run off with the violin?' She was starting to sound angry and a bit hysterical. Carter tried to calm her down.

'No. These are just routine questions that we always have to ask; every possibility must be followed. So I have to ask you: where were you on the morning of Hamilton's murder?'

'What?' she laughed contemptuously. 'You're not seriously suggesting I'm a suspect too?'

'Maybe you helped your husband.'

'Who's been in America for several weeks and . . .' She flung up her arms in contempt. 'All right, I was here, probably walking the dog or something. My cleaner was here, I think.'

At this moment Mollie the poodle came bounding into the room. Carter, remembering his experience at the home of Elizabeth Knott, looked around warily. The dog ran straight to her owner, but then turned and growled at Carter. Clearly I don't have a way with pets, he thought to himself.

'Calm down, girl, calm down. It's just a man come to ask me some questions. It's all right.' Anna stroked and reassured the dog.

Undaunted, Carter continued.

'Did you know that Muller had left his violin to the Bloomsbury School?'

She looked up with an expression of surprise.

'No, Hans never discussed anything like that with me.'

'Does it surprise you?'

'Not really; people did wonder what might happen to the violin after Hans had gone. I know Martin was interested in it, not surprisingly, but I didn't want to say that to you in Halifax because I had no evidence against him. Now we know he took it, but I want to say to you: I still don't believe he had anything to do with Hans's murder.'

'You think he just took his opportunity and picked it up?'

'Yes.'

'How about you? Wouldn't you have liked to own one of those Minsteroven . . .'

'Munsterhaven Strad,' she corrected him with a smile.

Damn, thought Carter, I'm making a fool of myself; the boss would never make a mistake like that.

'Not really.' She looked down at the dog, which she was still stroking. 'As I said to you before, that violin was almost a curse to Hans. Wonderful though it is, I think it would be more trouble than it's worth to own.'

'You also said in Halifax,' said Carter, consulting his notes, 'that Muller never said anything about where he got the violin.'

'No.'

'We have some evidence that it once belonged to a Jewish family in Berlin. Thereafter it was probably taken by the Nazis and then by the East German government after the war.'

She frowned.

'What happened to the family?'

'Sent to the concentration camps.'

'God. How horrible!' She stopped stroking the dog and looked at Carter thoughtfully. 'If what you say is true then no wonder the violin caused him trouble, whether he knew its history or not. I think it really is cursed.'

Eight

A Stradivarius violin manufactured in 1696 was owned by South Korean violinist Min-Jin Kym when, in 2010, it was stolen from her by a team of opportunist thieves who snatched it from the floor of a café at Euston station, London, while she was distracted. Being unaware of its value, they tried to sell it to someone for £100. The violin was eventually retrieved undamaged three years later, in 2013, and sold that year for £1.4 million. It is now known as the 'ex-Kym'.

DCI Sam Armitage sat in his office at police HQ in Halifax. There was a pint mug of tea on the desk and a packet of ginger snaps. He munched on the biscuits as he pondered on the baffling nature of this case, which was enough to tax the abilities of a more imaginative mind than his. He was used to fairly straightforward stuff: domestic argument, one partner kills the other; fight in pub – knives drawn, someone is stabbed and the blood mingles with the spilled beer; nephew bumps off his old aunt to get the inheritance, but cack-handedly leaves a trail of clues for the police to follow . . . Maybe he'd become a little too stuck in his rut of routine cases. He didn't mind a challenge, but this was something else, so strange and offbeat that he was glad of Jim's help. He knew Jim had a sharper and more inventive mind than he did, and he always seemed to attract these unusual cases where nothing seemed to make sense. And all this stuff about violins and string quartets was not really his thing. That lad from London was proving useful too, with his Met connections, especially as it seemed they were dealing with professional criminals from way outside the Halifax area.

The media pressure and speculation was intense, but he knew from experience that you just had to grind this out until you made some kind of breakthrough. That was his main quality: his dogged persistence. The media, of course, had no patience; they wanted a story. They would move on if there was no new material for them to use. He was more worried about the longer term. It was always a bad feeling when cases went unsolved: it felt like a defeat, as if you'd let people down – families of victims and so on. Cases could remain in this state for decades and detectives became obsessed with them, forever revisiting the evidence and turning it over in their minds. Sometimes they went to their own graves with things still unresolved. He hoped that wouldn't happen to him.

There were other problems on his mind. It was now well into December, and Christmas was fast approaching. This case was taking up so much time that he couldn't fit in any Christmas shopping, and lurking at the back of his mind was the annual problem of what to buy for his wife. The issue troubled him again when it was her birthday, but luckily that was in June so he had a welcome six months in between. He hated shopping at the best of times and left most of it to her. She even bought most of his clothes for him, an embarrassing fact that he tried hard to conceal from everyone at work. His forays into present buying had not been the best experiences of his life; he'd given up on clothes and jewellery as he inevitably got the wrong style or colour and his heart sank when he saw her open the package and her smile fade. But what were the alternatives? He was turning this over in his mind when Oldroyd appeared. Maybe he would be able to offer advice.

'Morning, Sam.' Oldroyd sat down and Armitage wondered if he had the same problems with presents. Didn't most men of their generation find it difficult, especially buying for women? Then he remembered that Oldroyd was separated from his wife; he felt sorry about that but at least it must relieve the present-buying pressure. Oldroyd, however, launched straight into work stuff.

'So: Watson had a Dragunov in his gun cupboard.'

'Do you think it means anything?'

'Not really, just clutching at straws, but it's an odd coincidence: he has the same type of gun as the murder weapon, and he obviously knows about guns.'

'Would he have shown you the guns if he'd had anything to hide?'

'Probably not, but who knows? Anyway, what did you find out about Dancek?'

'Not much. I got on to Immigration; they confirmed that he came to Britain in 1971. The record says he came from Czechoslovakia, as it was then. We let a number of people in from behind the Iron Curtain in those days if they managed to get out of their Eastern Bloc country, especially after the uprisings in Hungary and Czechoslovakia. There's very little detail about his past or his family. I get the impression the authorities didn't ask too many questions about their pasts; they were seen as defectors to the West and were welcomed. It's not like asylum seekers and immigrants now and all the suspicions after the Iraq War and all that. It's always possible he could have made up things about his past, but I don't think there's any way of verifying anything at this distance of time.'

'It might be worth getting on to the Czech Republic and seeing if there are any records of him. I know it's a shot in the dark, but we need all the help we can get.'

'I'll try.'

'And I'll talk to him again at some point, but I'm going to try the bloke who was on the door – Atkinson; see if he's remembered anything from that night. I presume you've got statements from the people in the bar?'

'Yes. Two volunteers clearing up after the interval; they both agree with Atkinson – only Dancek left the building.'

'And they were all positive it was him?'

'Yes.'

Oldroyd shook his head; it just couldn't be right. 'Well, we'll have to talk to Atkinson again; he was the closest to the door. While I've been driving around the moors, Carter's been grafting away in London.'

'He has, Jim, and the lad's done well; we have some new leads, though I don't know whether they're taking us very far. There's still a question mark over the Bloomsbury School, who didn't want to lose their inheritance, and then we've got Anna Robson's jealous husband, who has a history of violence. Also I'm waiting for Newton to send me their file on Nazi hunters; apparently there is a group who've spent years campaigning for works of art, instruments and stuff like that to be returned.'

'Good. Carter's going to pursue Robson and he'll talk to Stringer again. How are we getting on at this end?'

'Not much further: we've got Edward Shaw and Paul Taylor, and the suspicion of something shady with musical instrument deals going on. Then, apart from Dancek, there's Gerald Watson, who has a Dragunov, and Stuart Atkinson, who insists that only Dancek left the building; he also said there was a bloke came in to buy a ticket during the concert and hung around for a while. It's all a bit thin, isn't it?'

'Atkinson could be mistaken about Dancek.'

'But other people saw him running out of the building too.'

'I know, but maybe the person who ran out was disguised or something.'

'But if it wasn't Dancek, who was it? And in that case, what happened to Dancek himself, because you saw him leave the concert hall and run down the steps? That means they would have seen two people come down the steps and go out and then Dancek was back in the building when we arrived.'

Oldroyd shrugged. He had no answer, but he wasn't about to give up. 'We need to look wider; you said there was nothing in the statements of the audience that was suspicious?'

'No, and I can't see how any of them would have had the means or the opportunity to set up a thing like that; we must be looking at somebody who was on the committee, an official who had access to the building and could move around without looking suspicious.'

Oldroyd sighed and frowned.

There were a few minutes of silence during which Armitage's mind strayed back to considering when he might ask his friend's advice about Christmas shopping.

'OK,' said Oldroyd at last. 'There's another thing I think we should do at some point: go to the archives and see if we can find the original plans for the Red Chapel. There might be something there that might help us.'

Armitage shook his head. It all sounded pretty desperate, but Oldroyd got up and rubbed his hands as if trying to spark off some energy. 'So come on, we've plenty to do; let's start with Atkinson.' He was clearly ready to set off immediately.

'I'll come with you,' said Armitage, putting on his coat. 'I need to get out of this office for a bit.'

Stuart Atkinson lived in a terraced house not far from Frank Dancek's home in King Cross. When Oldroyd and Armitage called, his wife opened the door. She looked worried and harassed.

'Stuart's just having a lie-down; he's been off work since the murder. The doctor told him to rest. He's never been that good with his nerves; this has all been too much, with all that questioning from the police. Do you have to go over it all again?'

'I won't be hard on him; it's just that we have to keep talking to witnesses to see if they remember anything later that they forgot at the time.'

She sighed but didn't reply and led them into a living room that looked out on to the road. Atkinson was lying on the sofa, but roused himself as they came in. Mrs Atkinson spoke softly to him.

'Stuart, this is Chief Inspector Oldroyd and Chief Inspector Armitage; they want to speak to you again.'

He sat up and looked from one to the other in alarm.

'God, two of you! I've said everything already; why do you people keep asking me the same things again and again? I'm not going to change my mind about what I saw. Do you think I'm suddenly going to remember a hooded gunman running past me on the door?' He waved his arms and his face had a haunted look.

'Calm down, Stuart, I'm sure they're not going to harm you.'

'Not at all, sir,' said Oldroyd, adopting a deferential style. He nodded to Armitage, who took the hint and sat down on a chair at the side of the sofa, leaving the questioning to Oldroyd. 'I'd just like to ask you again about what happened that night, in case you remember something else, something different, however trivial it sounds.'

Atkinson sighed and shrugged his shoulders.

'Just take me through it again very carefully and tell me everything.'

Atkinson lay back against the cushion and closed his eyes.

'OK.' He sighed again as if this was a huge effort. 'It was thirty minutes after the interval; I knew the second half was well under way.'

'Why were you not in the concert hall listening to it?'

'The committee has a rota; one of us stays downstairs first of all to sell tickets to latecomers. I could have gone up to listen to the second half but to be honest I'm not fond of Schubert: too gloomy especially all that *Death and the Maiden* stuff; it's too much like a death march to me.'

Oldroyd profoundly disagreed, but this was not the time to pursue it. 'So you stayed downstairs?'

'Yes. I helped them clear up in the bar a bit and then hung around the door; we sometimes get people making enquiries and wanting to buy tickets for concerts coming up.'

'Did anything happen before the murder?'

'No.'

'Did anyone come into the building before that moment?'

'A man came to ask about the next concert, a piano recital; bought a ticket, paid cash.'

'Did you recognise him?'

'No, never seen him before.'

'What was he like?'

'Middle-aged, average height, dark hair, wore an overcoat.'

'Did he stay at the door, or come into the building?'

'He came in, said he needed the toilet.'

'So he went out of your sight for a while?'

'In the toilets, yes, but I saw him come out and leave the building, before there was any trouble.'

'How long was he out of your sight?'

'Not long – can't remember exactly; I got talking to one of the people in the bar – but I definitely saw him go out.'

'And then what happened?'

'It was all completely quiet except you could just faintly hear the music playing; I was messing around with the notice board, then the music stopped and seconds later I heard screaming. We all heard it and I was just about to go up the steps to investigate when I heard someone clattering down, and Frank Dancek appeared.'

'How did he look?'

'Shocked. He said had anybody come down the steps just now before him and I said no, and he looked puzzled; then he said someone had been shot from the lighting gantry and the killer must be trying to escape. Then he looked round desperately and said he was going to look outside, and asked was there another way out of the building. I said no, and then he ran out.'

'And it was definitely him?'

Atkinson looked exasperated. 'Yes, no doubt; I was standing speaking to him, looking right at him. I've known Frank Dancek for a long time; it was him, right down to the accent, which was a bit thicker that night . . . I expect because of the stress he was under.'

'OK, carry on.'

Oldroyd frowned. It didn't look as if his idea that the person leaving might have been disguised and somehow mistaken for Dancek was going to stand up.

'So after that, we didn't know what to do. It didn't seem wise to go upstairs if there was a gunman around, so we just waited near the door ready to bolt for it if anyone appeared with a weapon, but nobody did, and then the police arrived and went upstairs.'

'Then we came back down to speak to you and Frank Dancek was there; he'd come back in from his search.'

'Yes. He told you about the door up to the gantry and you went back up. That's it; that's all that happened. It was all over pretty quickly but it was a nerve-racking experience and I don't react well to things like that. I've been feeling bad since that night. I have a history of anxiety and depression; being involved with the Music Society was supposed to be a way of relaxing, and now this. Don't know whether I'll ever be able to go into that Chapel again.'

'I'm sure you will, given time. How well do you know the Chapel building?'

'As well as anyone; we're all like caretakers of the place. It's mostly run by volunteers; we clean it, maintain it and all that.'

'So you've no knowledge of any other ways in or out other than the front door where you were and the fire escape which was still sealed?'

'No.' He looked weary again. 'I've told all this to the police already. There are no other doors, no tunnels or secret passages; it was a chapel, for God's sake, not Dracula's castle. Anyway, even if there were, there wouldn't be any starting in mid-air from that gantry, would there? Unless the murderer disappeared through a portal into another dimension.'

'No. So, final question, sir, then I'll leave you alone: did you notice anything else unusual on that night?'

Atkinson paused and shook his head slowly as if acknowledging the mystery confronting them all.

'No. It was mostly the usual people who went in at the beginning, no one suspicious-looking; that bloke came in to buy a ticket, but I'm sure you won't get anywhere with that, and then it all happened as I said. It was a perfectly ordinary concert night until I heard the scream. After that, nothing makes sense.'

The young violinist's face had an expression of intense concentration as he skillfully danced up and down the octaves of one of Bach's unaccompanied partitas for violin. Michael Stringer sat languorously on an easy chair and listened with satisfaction. His pupil had made good progress under his tutelage.

'That's excellent, Adam, but don't try to go too fast – you're losing detail a little in some of those runs – but much better tone and you seem much more confident.'

The pupil grinned and nodded.

'OK, we'll leave it there for today. We'll have a detailed look at the second movement next week so start to practise it. I've got to go now; the police are coming to see me.'

'Is it about the murders?'

'Of course, what else? They haven't caught anybody yet.'

Adam wanted to ask more questions, and pass on juicy bits of information to his fellow students, because the murders of Muller and Hamilton were electrifying the school with rumour and gossip.

However, he knew that this was potentially a very touchy subject for his teacher, who could be quite irascible at times anyway, so he packed up his violin and left without another word.

Stringer walked back to his office at the Bloomsbury School where he'd arranged to meet Carter, the young detective sergeant. No big guns this time; he didn't merit a chief inspector. What did that mean? Maybe they had de-prioritised him; he was not a suspect. He was heartily sick of this business now. It was impossible to do anything. He was besieged by media requests for interviews. People at the school and also outside in cafés and in the street were pointing at him and whispering. He was worried about Anna, but at least she had had the sense to leave London and hide away from media attention. He was glad to take the brunt of it for her. If only she hadn't got together with that brute of a journalist, but then who knew how things might turn out when the truth of all this emerged?

Carter and DC Jenkins were waiting for Stringer in his office.

'So, Sergeant, what can I do for you this time? Still no luck finding the killers?'

Carter winced. He hated it when people made remarks like that. It was almost as if they were enjoying seeing the police struggle. He thought of Oldroyd and made a big effort to control his feelings.

'The investigation is ongoing, sir. I need to ask you about some new issues that have come up.'

'OK, Sergeant, fire away.'

Carter began with Muller's will.

'Well, I didn't know anything about that. Hans always kept his cards very close to his chest.' He smiled in a rather unpleasant way. 'Poor old Patrick; the violin's left to the school and then it goes missing after Martin pinches it. What a right old mess!'

'You're sure that you weren't interested in that violin yourself?'

'Certainly not, as I told you before. And Hans would never have left it to me, anyway.'

Carter moved on to Anna Robson's husband and his jealousy of Muller.

'Yes, I was aware of all that.'

'So why didn't you tell us when we first interviewed you and asked if Muller had any enemies?'

Stringer was thrown on to the defensive.

'Look, I saw Anna that morning in the hotel and we agreed that we wouldn't mention Christopher.'

'Why?'

'Well, it's an absurd idea that he would have organised something like that, and we didn't want to give you any ideas that might have made the situation worse for Anna.' Stringer held up his hands. 'OK, I know it was probably wrong; withholding information and so on.'

'Yes, it was, and can't you see it makes us more suspicious if you keep stuff back like that? It looks as if you've got things to hide.'

'It was difficult. Christopher can be . . . volatile. If we said anything it would seem to him as if we were accusing him just on the basis of one incident with Hans.'

'So you left us to find out about it by ourselves?'

'Yes, so Christopher can't blame us, and in particular Anna, if the police come to him asking questions.'

'It sounds as if she's frightened of him.'

Stringer shrugged. 'As I say, he can be short-tempered. Absolutely charming man most of the time and very interesting; amazing knowledge of international affairs, but . . . Anyway.'

'Were you a bit surprised when they got together?'

Stringer looked up at Carter. Maybe he'd underestimated the young detective: that was a very perceptive question.

'And disappointed?' That was even more perceptive. He laughed a little nervously.

'Yes, I admit it. Sometimes there's no accounting for taste, is there, Sergeant? But I hasten to add that there's never been anything between me and Anna.'

'Do you wish it were otherwise?'

Stringer was now finding this very uncomfortable.

'Look, I'm not sure how relevant this is. I've always got on well with Anna, and yes I find her attractive, but, I repeat, there's never been anything between us. I'm not even sure what she thinks about me, in that way, as it were.'

Carter was enjoying seeing Stringer squirm a little. The rather irritating, superior tone of condescension had gone. He decided to move on.

'Since we last spoke, Martin Hamilton has been murdered. Were you aware that he had any enemies?'

Stringer was relieved that the questioning had moved away from his personal life.

'No, none at all. Of course I knew he did instrument deals, but not that he was involved in illegal stuff. He must have known some dodgy characters, maybe he got out of his depth. But it's been another terrible shock. No wonder Anna's scared.'

'How about you? Aren't you worried that whoever it is might strike again?'

'You make it sound like some terrible serial killer is on the loose. I don't know why Hans was killed, but it's pretty certain that Martin was killed because he had that violin. Whether it's all linked together, I don't know, but I can tell you that I had nothing to do with any of it.'

'So where were you on the morning of his murder?'

'I was here teaching. I'm sure I can get one of my students to verify it if necessary.'

Carter returned to the Met feeling a little despondent; he felt he was letting Oldroyd down. He'd been entrusted with interviewing Robson and Stringer, two of the suspects, and had not made a very good job of it. They were sharp and intelligent. Not that he wasn't – it was just that he knew Oldroyd would have pressed them more searchingly and maybe discovered something significant. Anyway, he'd done his best and he knew he was still learning. Now it was time to report back again.

Oldroyd and Armitage had just arrived back at police HQ in Halifax when Carter called.

'No great revelations from Robson and Stringer, sir, but some things we might want to consider.'

'Go on.' Oldroyd had just refused Armitage's offer of a cup of tea and was sipping from a bottle of mineral water he'd taken to bringing with him.

'First there's the business of Robson's husband. They both admitted that he is potentially violent and that they weren't open with us when we interviewed them in Halifax. This bloke, Christopher Downton, is supposed to be in America, works for a newspaper, been out of the country since before the first murder, but I think we need to check that. Did he actually go, or was that a cover? Maybe he's been here all the time and involved in all this. And are Robson and or Stringer in on it? They gave me alibis that will need to be checked. He claims he was at the music school, but he could have slipped out briefly. She was walking the dog.'

'Can you get Newton to follow up on those? He can also speak to Downton's paper, make sure this American trip is real.'

'OK. The other thing is there's clearly some feeling between Robson and Stringer, at least on his side. I got him to admit he's fond of her.'

'Well done. That can't have been easy; he's a bit of a spiky character.'

'Thanks. What I'm thinking – I know this is a bit complicated – but if Stringer wanted to get rid of Downton, what better way than to get him implicated in Muller's murder?'

'While apparently doing the opposite.'

'Yes.'

'Hmm, sounds a bit far-fetched, to be honest, and he's not got very far with his plan, has he? He hasn't given us any real evidence against Downton.'

'Well, I think we're supposed to discover it ourselves as we investigate, so it doesn't look as if it came from him. Let's see what we find.'

'OK, Andy, well, you know I like a detective who thinks about things, however . . . *imaginative* . . . his theories are.'

Carter laughed. 'Thank you, sir.' He rang off.

Suddenly Armitage exclaimed, 'Bloody hell, Jim, look at this!'

Oldroyd rushed over.

'This is the file from Newton on that group who track down Nazi art thefts. Seems they've had some run-ins with the law – and look at these mug shots.'

Oldroyd looked at the screen and saw a series of standard police photographs of arrested people.

'Look there,' said Armitage. He pointed to a picture of a woman.

'Good God!' said Oldroyd.

It was a photograph of Ruth Greenfield.

The police car driven by one of Armitage's detective constables sped out of Halifax in the direction of the upper part of Calderdale. On the edge of the town it passed the Tower of Spite, a famous landmark in the region and a typical piece of Yorkshire eccentricity. It was meant to be a chimney but had been completed as an ornamental tower with a striking cupola at the top and never used for its original purpose. There was a legend that it had really been built so that the owner could look over on to his rival's land. Today the top was illuminated by sunlight and it looked like a watchtower surveying the valley. Oldroyd had once trudged up the 400-step spiral staircase inside the tower to get to the viewing platform at the top. The views had been worth it.

Sadly, there was no time for such leisurely exploration today as the car continued down through the edge of Sowerby Bridge and into Luddenden Foot. Ruth Greenfield lived in Hebden Bridge, further up the valley.

Armitage turned to Oldroyd. 'Do you get up here much these days, Jim?'

'Not as much as I'd like; it's quite a way from Harrogate. I tend to go up the Dales when I'm walking.'

'Aye, well, Hebden Bridge is a trendy place now; full of artists and vegetarians and stuff like that. They say there's more lesbians per head of population there than anywhere else in the country.'

Oldroyd had to smile at this edifying little description.

'It's not like it was when my uncle had a dye works in the bottom,' continued Armitage, 'and dumped all the muck straight into the river.'

'No.' Oldroyd reflected again on the transformation of so many of these formerly dirty, smoky, polluted little mill towns into green and desirable places for the middle classes to inhabit. But where had this gentrification left the old working class, whose labour over the centuries had built these places and the famous textile industry? Seemingly forgotten or banished to run-down estates in the bigger towns and cities.

Ruth Greenfield lived in the end terrace of a row of weavers' cottages on a narrow road above the town. The DC manoeuvred the car around tight corners and up steep gradients, passing four-storey houses built into the hillside where the top two and bottom two floors were separate dwellings. They found the address and managed to squeeze the police car into a space by a gate that opened into a field.

There was a small front garden rather overgrown with grass and what were probably wildflowers in summer and clay pots from which the remains of herbs still sprouted. Small pieces of sculpture peeped out of the grass. Armitage knocked on the door, but there was no response. Oldroyd walked down the side of the house. There was a steep and narrow back garden and views over the town and the valley. A train sounded its horn as it left Hebden Bridge station. There were some narrow boats on the Rochdale Canal and in the distance he could again see the lonely pinnacle of Stoodley Pike on the hill above Todmorden. He turned to look through the window; there was a kitchen with a pine table and a wooden bowl of fruit. On the wall was a large picture, vaguely impressionistic in style but clearly of two naked women embracing. He smiled as he contemplated Armitage's response to this if they ever got inside.

'Good afternoon, Chief Inspector.'

He turned abruptly to see Ruth Greenfield at the door of a small shed in the garden. 'No need to gawp through the window; you can come in – and I assume you're not alone. This way.'

She was dressed in an orangey-red print skirt and a brown corduroy jacket, and she held a bag that contained some onions. Presumably she stored them in the shed in winter. He looked down the garden and saw that it was mostly dug over for growing vegetables. There were still some carrots and Brussels sprouts in the damp ground.

He followed her through the back door, through the kitchen and down a narrow hallway that was lined with posters from various campaigns, mostly around gay rights and animal welfare. Oldroyd noticed one that had a caricature of a Nazi officer with a swag bag holding paintings and musical instruments. The caption said 'Return Nazi Swag Now'. Greenfield opened the front door to let in Armitage and the DC.

'In here.' She led them into a sitting room and invited them to sit on a battered but very comfortable-looking sofa with deep cushions. The DC perched on a wooden chair with a wickerwork seat. In one corner there was a cello propped against the wall. Oldroyd noticed a table with framed photographs, many showing Greenfield with another woman. In one they were holding hands and looked radiantly happy.

'That's my partner, Jo, Chief Inspector, she's an artist. She's down at her shop and gallery in the town at the moment.'

Armitage shifted uncomfortably, and seemed to sink deeper into the sofa.

'Now, what can I do for you? I've already told you everything I can remember about what happened on that night.'

Armitage and Oldroyd exchanged glances and the former nodded. He didn't relish having to question this woman.

'I'm afraid we have reason to believe that may not be entirely true,' said Oldroyd and produced the police file that Newton had sent. Greenfield glanced at it and immediately realised what the detectives had discovered. She gave a wry smile and Oldroyd saw that she was not particularly surprised or frightened.

'I see you've been busy. Once you're on the police files, you're marked for life, aren't you?'

'So I think you know what we're interested in. We know you're in this group that campaigns to have stolen art returned, and we also know that Muller's violin was almost certainly stolen from a Jewish family during the war.'

'It all fits together, doesn't it? But I'm sorry to disappoint you, Chief Inspector: I didn't kill Muller or the other one – Hamilton, wasn't it? And no one in my group would either.'

'Maybe not, but I think it would be a good idea if you told us all about this.'

She frowned at Oldroyd and seemed reluctant. She obviously had little time for the police, thought Oldroyd, but she was too sharp not to realise that refusing to cooperate with a murder enquiry would be foolish.

'OK, but I'm telling you now it's got nothing to do with these murders.'

'I think we'll be the judge of that,' said Armitage. Greenfield gave him a filthy look.

'Well, you say you've been researching things so you know that the Nazis, in addition to sending six million people to the gas chambers, also stole a lot of priceless art works and musical instruments from people, mostly Jewish. Talented people.'

'Why are you interested in all this?'

'I'm interested in any kind of injustice, but I find this particularly painful because I'm a musician myself.' She glanced towards the cello. 'I've been playing since I was five; I started on a quarter-size instrument. I've played in several orchestras, but I got fed up of the travel. Jo and I settled here in Hebden Bridge fifteen years ago. I teach cello and she has her little business and her art. We get by OK.'

'And?'

'I'm Jewish. The real version of my name is Greenfeld. I don't practice anymore. I don't want anything to do with any religion; they're all misogynistic and homophobic. Do you know Jo and I would probably be stoned to death in some countries?'

'So you got involved with this group?'

She looked at Oldroyd defiantly. 'Yes, I did. Because another thing you should know is that my grandfather was sent from Hungary to a death camp. He was a brilliant cellist, apparently, and he had an Amati cello that the Nazis stole. He managed to get my mother, who was only a small child, away to England.'

'How?

'No one knows; my mother doesn't remember anything about it. Her earliest memories are of being in England. She must have been smuggled out somehow; small children were sometimes hidden in suitcases, things like that. He and my grandmother died in the camp. She was their only child and they never saw her again.'

There was a brief silence. It was an agony beyond words.

'Is she still alive?'

'My family live in north Leeds. There's a sizeable Jewish population there, as I'm sure you know, but I don't want to be part of that and I don't know how they'd react to me and Jo.'

'So you slightly altered your name and came out here to be away from it.'

'Yes, but that doesn't mean I don't care about my family and what happened to the Jewish people in the war. There's been plenty of people hunting down the Nazis themselves – people like Simon Wiesenthal – but very few pursuing all those art thefts.'

Oldroyd consulted the documents from Newton. 'You joined the RNATN. What does that stand for?'

'Return Nazi Art Thefts Now. It was started by an Israeli artist and musician, a brilliant man: Abel Ashkenazi. He's used his Israeli contacts, including Mossad, to track down paintings, sculptures, instruments that were stolen – and then we campaign to get them returned.'

'Isn't that difficult? Haven't many people bought them legitimately, not knowing they were stolen?'

'Yes, but it's only like any other stolen goods; they have to be returned.'

'And are the original families still around?'

'In many cases, yes, and sometimes it makes a big difference. We were able to return a rare violin to a family in America who were very poor; they decided to sell it and they were able to pay for hospital treatment for the wife, who had kidney failure.'

'What happens when you can't find anyone?'

'It's our view that the instrument should be sold and the proceeds used to help victims of political oppression as suffered by the Jews in the war.'

So far Oldroyd found himself agreeing with everything, but what about the methods?

'Do you always campaign peacefully on this?'

'Yes, I believe we do.'

'What happened to get you into trouble with the police?'

'We do put pressure on people who won't cooperate. There was this wealthy banker in Mayfair. He had a painting that we could prove had been taken from a Jewish house in Berlin in 1938, but he wouldn't have anything to do with us, wouldn't even have a discussion. So we picketed his house continuously day and night, chanting slogans, pasting posters on the walls. He complained and we were ordered to stop, but we wouldn't so we were arrested for breach of the peace. That's all it amounted to; we never use violence.'

'Do you threaten people?'

'No.'

Oldroyd produced the messages found in Muller's apartment and in his coat pocket after his death. This time he saw that she was quite shocked and she didn't reply straight away.

'Do these have anything to do with RNATN and, more precisely, with you?' Oldroyd's tone hardened and his manner suddenly became much more hectoring. 'Because if so, that is threatening behaviour and it's an offence.'

Her expression was now very serious. She seemed to be thinking hard, making a calculation.

'All right. This is what happened. We'd identified Muller's Munsterhaven Strad as a stolen instrument.'

'Did anyone contact the V&A about that recently?' asked Oldroyd, remembering what Adamson had told him about another person asking questions.

'I wouldn't have thought so. We have our own sources of information. We don't work through British museums, but if you've been researching you'll know about the Lerner family. Abel said he'd suspected Muller's Strad ever since he'd arrived in Britain, but that he'd recently found more information that proved conclusively that his Strad was the one taken in Berlin.'

'What kind of information and where from?'

'It was something to do with records from East Germany that had come to light. Abel never discloses his sources but we trust him. He's never wrong and he wouldn't falsify evidence.

'We approached Muller, but he was utterly contemptuous; said he'd earned the right to the violin. Not sure what he meant by that, but he would have nothing to do with us.'

'So?'

'This was a tricky one because we didn't want to create a lot of trouble for the Bloomsbury School. I studied there myself and so did others in the group. We didn't want to make it hard for the quartet either; such a wonderful ensemble. We're not philistines. It's not just about the value of these things. What we hoped was that we could intimidate Muller into giving up the violin or at least acknowledging where it came from, and that it was wrong for him to have it.'

'Would that have been enough?'

'I don't think there's any trace of the Lerner family. They all went to the gas chambers, so we couldn't return it. We're flexible; we're open to suggestions as to the way forward. He could have sold it for a lot of money and part of that could have been given to the causes we support, in recognition that a wrong had been committed.'

'But he was having none of it so you decided to send him the threatening messages?'

'Yes; we knew he'd probably know who they came from, but we made them anonymous and nasty, hoping he would be scared and put feelers out to us.'

'The first was sent to his apartment, but it had no effect.'

'No, it didn't.'

'And the second?'

'By coincidence, the Schubert Quartet were coming to Halifax. It was too good an opportunity to miss. I wrote another message. When the quartet was in the artists' room, I went in with drinks for them, and I slipped it into his coat. The irony is he probably never saw it.'

'You understand that it was threatening behaviour?' repeated Armitage. She shook her head.

'Maybe, but I can assure you the only things we were threatening him with were exposure, embarrassment; we weren't threatening violence.'

'You may not have been,' said Oldroyd, 'but how do you know about the others? Are any of them capable of violence?'

'No, none of them; we believe in correcting injustices, Chief Inspector. Muller may have been an unpleasant, arrogant man, but, after all, he wasn't the one who stole the violin and murdered the family, so how would it be fair to do him any physical harm?'

'So did you have anything to do with Martin Hamilton stealing the violin after Muller's death?'

'That would presuppose I knew the murder was going to happen and therefore was in some way involved, so, again, no. I didn't have much time for Hamilton. He was a dealer. Those people reduce wonderful instruments to commodities. I'm surprised at a man like him, such a wonderful player. It's depressing how money can come to dominate even a fine artistic temperament like his. How could he play that beautiful cello of his the way he did, and at the same time be constantly thinking about the monetary value of such things? And mixing with those dealers and collectors; they're the people who trade in stolen things and they don't ask any questions about the history of any of it.'

Oldroyd studied her closely. She was highly intelligent with strong moral convictions. Sometimes convictions like that enabled people to justify dubious actions for what they saw as the greater long-term good.

'So if you had nothing to do with the murder of Muller or the theft of the violin from the Red Chapel, did you or any of your group have anything to do with Hamilton's murder?'

She gave him an acid smile. 'You're determined to get me one way or another, aren't you, Chief Inspector? No. We don't kill people to get works of art back. People were murdered in the past and things stolen from them. It would hardly be fitting for us to do the same.'

'And where were you a week ago on the day of Hamilton's murder?'

'Here in Hebden Bridge; my partner can vouch for that. We went shopping and to our favourite café, so a lot of people would have seen us.'

'Do you know of any other organisations or groups who might do things differently?'

'No. We have nothing to do with violence of any kind. You need to look among the greedy people I mentioned before: the dealers. When there's money at stake some will do very nasty things. I think Hamilton got too involved in that world and paid the price.'

Oldroyd had finished for now. 'We'll have to ask you to accompany us to Halifax to make a statement about those notes; a decision will be made later about whether to press any charges.'

She nodded. Oldroyd found that he liked her and admired her for her principles. She reminded him of his daughter. He decided to end on a positive note.

'You might like to know that, in his will, Muller left the Strad to the Bloomsbury School; that's where it will go if we can retrieve it.'

She'd got up and was putting on a coat.

'Good. In that case I wish you all the best in finding it. That will be a very fitting home and I'm sure the Lerner family would have approved.'

Every December Elizabeth Knott held an elegant early-evening soiree at her home in Mayfair. It was champagne and soft drinks only with a kaleidoscope of savoury and sweet canapés served by hired waitresses and waiters. Formal attire of tuxedos and evening gowns was required. An invitation was much sought after among the wealthy elite of Mayfair because the hostess was such a famous, if eccentric, local celebrity. The soiree provided an opportunity to meet unusual people and the climax of the evening was the viewing of the near-legendary instrument collection. Nobody minded that Knott's security staff submitted everyone to a thorough check. It was a prized feather in the cap of one's social accomplishments to be able to say that one had seen *the* collection, and by special permission of the owner.

By six thirty the evening was in full swing. Lights blazed from the windows on the ground floor of Knott's house. She preferred not to have curtains drawn on these occasions and the sparkling chandeliers and mingling guests were visible from the street, together with a barely audible hum of conversation. The first floor, where the collection was housed, remained in darkness, although the security bars on the windows were just visible.

The hostess, expensively dressed in a low-cut black silk cocktail dress, was flitting around the ground-floor rooms, champagne glass in hand, greeting her guests. These were an exotic collection of minor aristocrats, bankers, ambassadors, foreign oligarchs and a sprinkling of famous musicians. She spoke to Lord and Lady Westerby, an ageing titled couple who owned a massive Georgian pile in the next street. Nevertheless, their chauffeur-driven Bentley had brought them the few hundred yards round the corner. Lord Westerby was over ninety, thin, stooping and very deaf. He had the habit of turning to his wife, Lady Westerby, when he didn't catch whatever was said to him.

'How are you?' asked Knott, in what she thought was a fairly loud voice. Lord Westerby, however, immediately looked towards her ladyship, who sported a diamond-studded tiara on her immaculately coiffured hair.

'What did she say?'

'She's asking how you are,' Lady Westerby bellowed at her husband.

'Oh, very well, thank you,' replied his lordship, but to no one in particular, as if he couldn't remember who had asked him the question. Suddenly he headed off towards a pretty waitress in a tight black skirt and white blouse who was holding a tray of canapés. Knott smiled at her ladyship and moved on to a balding man with a bulging paunch and miserable expression who was chief executive of an investment bank.

'And how are you, Simon?'

The man continued to frown. 'Could be better; down on my luck recently; got outbid at the auction. There're too many damned Russians and other foreigners throwing their money about.'

Knott knew he was referring to a vintage sports-car auction where cars from the 1950s and 1960s went for millions. Not that that was a problem for him, as his annual bonus alone would run into millions.

'I was hoping to get my hands on a 1962 Aston Martin; it went for three million. I mean it's just ridiculous.'

Not as ridiculous as you bellyaching about your lot in life, she thought, but played the part of the sympathetic hostess.

'Oh dear, poor Simon. Well, better luck next time, darling; you've got to know the opposition, take it from me. Why don't you have another drink?'

The banker grunted and still refused to smile. He took another glass of champagne from a tray and knocked it back in a petulant, greedy gesture almost of contempt. Knott moved on again.

In a corner of one of the reception rooms, a group was gathered in conversation by the shiny grand piano. There was a large, muscular, brutish-looking man with a shaven head, a large nose and a scar across his face who looked more like a bouncer from a night club than a guest at a party like this. Next to him was his opposite: a small and rather frail man with a shock of white hair. He wore a permanent smile but his eyes were cold. The third person was younger with dark hair and slim build. He had an angry look on his face as he addressed the big man and was struggling to keep his voice down.

'I don't believe you, Djaic; I think you know exactly where it is. In fact, I think you took it from Martin's flat after . . .'

'Careful, my friend.' The big man laughed, apparently unconcerned. 'Careful what you are saying. I have Mr Bartlett here as a witness if you slander me.'

'I don't care if . . .'

'Steady on, Tony,' said the older man in a rather wheezy voice. 'Don't jump to conclusions; just because our friend here has a reputation of a certain kind doesn't mean he had anything to do with this business.'

'Oh, Felix, I know you are meaning a reputation for honesty, straight dealing,' said the big man facetiously and the old man laughed.

'Those aren't the qualities that immediately spring to mind. Where's that waiter? My glass is empty.' He looked around with rheumy eyes while the big man clasped his hand to his forehead in mock outrage.

'Felix! And I thought you are my friend.'

'I've had enough,' said the young man contemptuously, and turned away. He walked across the room to the door and almost collided with Elizabeth Knott, who was just coming in.

'Ah! Tony, I'm glad I've found you.' She looked at him with an expression of concern. 'And how are you?'

'Elizabeth, thank you. OK, I suppose; be feeling better if I hadn't got talking to them.' He nodded towards the outlandish-looking pair, who were still by the grand piano. Knott looked over; her eyes narrowed and became steely and her lip curled with contempt.

'Very unfortunate; I'm sorry you've encountered such inappropriate company. Not people I'm fond of, but I have my reasons for asking them.' She turned to him. 'Did they tell you anything interesting?'

'Not likely, but I told Djaic what I think.'

'Which is?'

'I'm sure he knows where the missing Strad is, whether or not he had anything to do with Martin's murder or Muller's.'

Knott looked across the room again at the big man. 'Novak Djaic, one of the godfathers of the trade in stolen art. He's had more works of art and musical instruments pass through his grubby hands than the British Museum, and all illegally; too clever to get caught, though.'

'And Felix Bartlett, your great rival in the London world of instrument collecting.'

Knott snorted with contempt. 'He thinks he is, but his collection can't hold a candle to mine, which is why I invite him every year: to gloat. The amazing thing is he always comes.'

'Who wouldn't? The champagne and the food are too good to miss.'

'Oh, it's not that. I think he secretly hopes that one day he'll be able to get me to part with something if we stay on good terms. What do you know about those two anyway?'

'Not much. I met them both through Martin, but I never talked to him much about that side of his life.'

'You didn't like it, did you?'

'No, I didn't. I wasn't the only one who found it odd that a man like him – so brilliant and successful as a player, you know – would want to mess about dealing in that kind of stuff, with people like that. It was all right with straight deals with people like you, but . . .' He shook his head. Knott looked at him with a hint of a smile on her face.

'Maybe it was the excitement, the sense of danger or . . . Oh, Tony, I'm sorry, I didn't mean . . .' She saw that there were tears in his eyes.

'I know,' he said, wiping his face with an expensive and very soft white napkin. 'But they were so . . . *uncaring*. They don't know I was his partner, but they knew we were friends, and they just laughed at me.'

'They're brutes; don't take any notice. Here, have another drink.' She clicked her fingers at a passing waiter, who refilled Tony's glass.

'What really upsets me is that he brought this on himself. I mean, what was he thinking of, stealing that violin, and after Hans Muller had been murdered?'

Knott looked at him with an expression of pity. 'I suspect the temptation was just too great; a Munsterhaven Strad there in front of him and the owner dead. I don't think he thought about the consequences.'

Tony shook his head. 'Exactly. He wasn't thinking about me.' He looked at Knott. 'Did he contact you about that violin?'

'No, he didn't, because, as I told the police, he knew I wouldn't have anything to do with anything dodgy. Have the police been to speak to you?'

'No, I don't think they know anything about me; we kept our relationship fairly secret – it was a very private thing, and we lived our own lives. I'm always off travelling with the orchestra, and he was with the quartet; always kept our own apartments too. I saw Michael and Anna at the funeral, but I don't think even they knew just what the relationship was between me and Martin.'

'Well, I'm not going to say anything.'

He gave her a wan smile. 'Thanks. I think I'm going to get off now. Thanks for inviting me.'

She gave him a peck on the cheek. 'Thank you for coming. It can't have been easy, I know.'

'No. Martin used to love coming here; he looked forward to seeing the collection.'

'Well, he helped me with quite a lot of it. I'll always be grateful to him.'

Tony looked to be on the verge of tears again. He forced another smile and then went to retrieve his coat and scarf from the security people at the door.

Knott watched him go and then turned to frown at the two men still in conversation by the piano. She walked over to them.

'Ah! Elizabeth!' exclaimed Bartlett, toying with his glass. 'When does the viewing commence?'

'Not yet; you'll just have to be patient. I know it's the only reason you're both here, but I think you could be a little more polite and convivial with my other guests.'

'Do you mean Tony Mason?' laughed Bartlett.

'Yes.'

'But, *Eleezabeth*,' protested Djaic theatrically, 'he is not nice to me; he accuses me of stealing Martin Hamilton's violin, even of killing him. This is right, Felix?'

Bartlett laughed again; they clearly both thought it was a joke.

'I'm sure you were shaking in your shoes,' said Knott. 'He's just a naïve boy, doesn't know anything about what goes on, and he was very close to Martin.'

Djaic carelessly shrugged his shoulders.

'Elizabeth,' said Bartlett, in a placatory but rather wheedling manner, 'I'm sure Novak meant no harm. These are strange times; we're all reeling from the sad and tragic events.'

'Yes, I'm sure we are,' replied Knott, rather sarcastically. 'And I'm also sure that it hasn't escaped you that there's a Munsterhaven Strad on the loose and you would give a great deal to get your greedy mitts on it.'

Bartlett maintained his affable smile but the eyes became even more piercing and icy.

'And you too, Elizabeth.'

'I think we understand one another,' she replied and walked off.

In the adjoining room another distinguished guest, Sir Patrick Jefferson, was in conversation with a group of academics. He saw Elizabeth Knott enter and, making his excuses, moved across to intercept her. 'Elizabeth, lovely evening, looking forward to the viewing, just wanted to have a word about . . . *things*, you know.'

Knott regarded him quizzically. 'What things would they be, Sir Patrick?'

The principal seemed to be uncharacteristically at a loss for words. 'Well, I know you must be taking an interest in what's been happening, and I wondered if you'd, well, discovered anything.'

'I take it you mean the violin. Do I know where it is?'

Jefferson hadn't expected such directness; he looked around and laughed rather nervously. 'Well, you've come straight to the point and no mistake. I just meant . . .'

'Is this just general curiosity, or is it something more serious?'

Jefferson continued to fumble. 'I just think it would be a tragedy if it disappeared. You know, one of the "wonders of the world", as they were called.'

'Indeed, but I'm afraid I can't help you, Sir Patrick. These are criminal matters. I don't get myself involved in things like that. I'm sure the police will find the culprits and the Strad in due course.'

'Quite, well, I'm sure you're right. No offence, I just thought that as you're always alert to these things and so on, you might have heard rumours about what happened.'

She smiled at him rather sourly, and he excused himself and walked off. Later she saw him in conversation with Djaic. What was Jefferson's real interest in the Munsterhaven Strad? Was it to do with the reputation of the Bloomsbury School or more than that? Whatever his motivation, the number of people wanting to track the Strad down was growing and that was not good. However, she had no more time to speculate as it was time for the grand viewing. The lights sprung up on the upper floor and, after going through security, the guests trooped upstairs to be admitted into the inner sanctum. The stunning collection was duly admired, Knott presiding and accepting the adulation from people who'd been invited for this very purpose and knew it. It was like an annual ritual observed by members of an ancient cult, welcoming the opportunity to view the sacred relics and pay obeisance before the high priestess.

As people were leaving, Knott cornered Djaic by himself. She came very close and lowered her voice. 'So what have you found out?'

'We're still working on it, don't worry. We'll find it. I have a good idea which gang is involved; just be patient.' His face contorted into a chilling smile.

'Look, Djaic, I told you when the police visited me that I'm going to have that violin in my collection one way or another; this is probably my last chance to get a Munsterhaven Strad, even if I have to keep it a secret for the rest of my life.'

'You're not the only one,' smirked Djaic, whose English was much better when he was being serious, rather than playing the role of the ignorant-sounding Serb. 'Jefferson seems very interested, I don't know why, and of course old Felix would love to get his hands on it before you.'

'Don't be ridiculous,' she hissed. 'You know I'll pay much more than them and I won't ask any questions.' She sighed. 'If only Hamilton had come to you or me first. What was he thinking of?'

'I told you, he may have been going to, but once the word got out that he had a Munsterhaven Strad he was in danger. He must have been hawking it round trying to play us all off against each other, but he never got to us.'

She looked at him sceptically. You couldn't trust anyone in this dark world.

'Of course I've only got your word for any of this. You could've had Hamilton killed and be sitting on the violin at this very moment . . .'

Djaic threw his arms apart. 'Elizabeth, what do you think I am? A cold-blooded gangster?'

She wanted to reply 'Yes', but thought that might be too provocative.

'You'd just better get a move on, or I might see if anyone else can help me and then you'll get nothing.'

When all her guests had gone, Knott sat stroking Godetia with one hand and drumming the fingers of her other hand on the arm of the chair in frustration. It was so tantalising to be so near at last to the ultimate prize. She thought of her father, whom she'd always idolised. What would he have thought of her acquiring a Munsterhaven Strad? He wouldn't have been too worried about the circumstances either; not all of his own business deals had been exactly ethical. She smiled: she was her father's daughter despite her avowals of probity. She wanted that violin badly, for herself and for Daddy. She would stop at nothing to get it.

Nine

The 'Lincoln' Stradivarius made in 1695 is the only Stradivarius that belongs to a city. It was given by the Honourable Mrs Dudley Pelham to the people of Lincoln, England, in 1970 on condition that it was loaned to the Hallé Orchestra for the use of the leader. It has been valued at £2 million.

Armitage and Oldroyd were deep in the vaults of the local archive, where a very helpful assistant had dug out a tattered portfolio of old plans and maps from the eighteenth century. They had put on thin rubber gloves and were now scrutinising the original architect's drawings for the Chapel from 1778. Oldroyd enjoyed the atmosphere of musty quiet and scholarly enquiry. It was just the kind of setting for a ghost story by that master of the genre M. R. James. A bit of supernatural help would be useful to them now.

He attempted to gently flatten the yellowing sheets of paper as he and Armitage searched the plan for clues.

'What are we looking for?' asked the doubtful Armitage.

'Anything unexpected.'

The drawings were marvellously neat and orderly. They were somehow redolent of the classical eighteenth-century mind with all its balance, proportion and symmetry. However, there appeared to be nothing unusual in the representations of the external part of the buildings. Turning his attention to the drawings of the inside of the Chapel, Oldroyd finally found something interesting.

'Yes! Now look at this, Sam. You see these wooden joists and rafters and so on holding up the roof? I wonder . . . And also look here . . .' He pointed to a small square drawn on the plan. 'What's that? It looks as if it could be a hole in the floor, where there was a trapdoor. Hold on: there's something written beside it.' He held a magnifying glass over the place and tried to make out what had been written with a quill pen in elaborate but tiny eighteenth-century script, all those years ago, but it was too faded.

'But my officers have searched all over the building and they swear there are no trapdoors or anything like that.'

'Nevertheless, it's worth another look,' said Oldroyd.

Further examination of the documents, even with the aid of a magnifying glass, revealed nothing more, so the two men left and made their way the short distance back to the Red Chapel. The streets, bustling with Christmas shoppers, seemed bright in the winter sun after the gloomy archive. A brass band could be heard in the distance playing carols in a characteristically rather slow and mournful manner.

The Chapel was now returning to normality. All incident tape had been removed and there was no sign of any police officers. Inside it was quiet as Oldroyd and Armitage ascended the stone stairs to the deserted concert hall. Oldroyd now looked upon this space with a mixture of fond memory and horror. Sadly, he'd accepted that coming to concerts here would never be the same again. He had with him a photocopy of the relevant page of the plans, which he consulted.

'OK, let's go over here.' Armitage followed reluctantly. He couldn't see where this was leading.

Oldroyd walked right to the back of the hall and kneeled down, examining the floor. 'Well, it should be here, but of course this new wooden floor's on top of it.'

'Do you really think there's some kind of hole or trapdoor under there?'

Oldroyd grunted with frustration. He felt around on the floor, checking if anything was loose. 'Something's marked on the plans, but how do you get to it now?' He shook his head. 'I'd get your lot back and see what's underneath here and also if this floor comes up easily somehow; someone may have prepared a getaway route. The interesting thing is: look where we are.' Armitage looked around. 'We're behind all the seating,' continued Oldroyd, 'and it would have been very dark during that concert. If the gunman could have slipped down off that gantry behind the audience and got to here, he could maybe have got out this way.'

Armitage was deeply sceptical. 'But even if there is a hole of some kind under there and he could have got to it, where does it lead to?

'That's what we need to find out.'

'We must be above the bar here. You're not telling me he dropped down into there and calmly ordered himself a pint.'

Oldroyd grinned.

'I'm not sure anything would surprise me, Sam. Anyway, my other idea . . .'

Oh dear, not more of this, thought Armitage as he followed Oldroyd back into the centre of the hall.

'Was to have a look upwards, as it were, instead of downwards.' Oldroyd craned his neck to look up into the high ceiling. 'Yes, look up there.'

'What is it, Jim?'

Oldroyd pointed. 'You see at that section at the back? There's a framework of joists. I just wonder if, instead of dropping down off the gantry, he climbed upwards on to those joists – it would have been very dark up there – and somehow got on to the roof.'

'And then what?'

'Well, he could have shimmied down the drainpipe in time-honoured style.'

'Wouldn't he have been seen in his Spider-Man outfit?' Armitage wasn't sure just how serious Oldroyd was being. These ideas seemed pretty outlandish. Was the pressure getting to him?

Oldroyd laughed. 'OK, Sam, I know none of it sounds very convincing, but we've got to think the unlikely. Whatever's not actually impossible has to be considered. There are no obvious explanations. You know what Sherlock Holmes used to say.'

'What?'

'"When you have eliminated the impossible, whatever remains, however improbable, must be the truth."'

Armitage grunted and shook his head. It seemed to him at the moment that everything *was* impossible, but he might as well go along with his friend, who he knew to possess a very imaginative and analytical mind.

'Fine, I'll get a team on to it. We'll examine the floor and up in those rafters and I'll even get someone on the roof, but if we draw a blank, as I think we will, what do we do then?'

Oldroyd just smiled and shrugged his shoulders.

Armitage had another reason for acceding to Oldroyd's request. Maybe now was a good time to call on his old friend for help.

'By the way, Jim,' he said rather sheepishly, 'I've been meaning to ask you . . .'

Oldroyd looked up questioningly, not quite sure what to expect.

'Have you any ideas about what I can buy Janet for Christmas?'

When the two detectives eventually arrived back at police HQ there were two people waiting for them: Gerald Watson and Frank Dancek. They were taken into Armitage's office.

'We're here about Ruth, Chief Inspector,' began Watson, who looked agitated. 'Ruth Greenfield.'

'What about her?' said Armitage.

'She is an important member of the committee,' said Dancek, though the detectives were not quite sure of the relevance of this.

'News travels fast around here, especially in our little music community,' continued Watson. 'We hear you've brought her in for questioning about the case.'

'She's innocent,' declared Dancek rather dramatically. 'Ruth would never do anything violent.'

'Wait a minute.' Armitage held up his hand. 'I think rumour's getting things more than a bit distorted. You seem to think we're about to arrest her for the murder of Hans Muller or Hamilton or both.'

The two men were silent.

'Well, we're not, but as you're here you can tell us all you know about her involvement with this Jewish organisation, this "getting Nazi artworks back" business.'

'Who told you about that?'

'She did.'

Watson and Dancek exchanged glances.

'We knew she was involved with them,' said Watson. 'She felt strongly about it and we agreed it was a good cause.'

'But we warned her not to do anything stupid,' added Dancek.

'Like sending threatening notes?' interjected Oldroyd abruptly.

'What do you mean?'

'Her organisation sent a very hostile note to Muller in London, and she put another one in his pocket here in Halifax before the concert.'

'Saying what?'

'Demanding that Muller return his Munsterhaven Strad. They believed it had been stolen from a Jewish family during the Nazi period in Germany.'

'Did they threaten violence?'

'Not specifically, but that doesn't mean they weren't intending to if Muller didn't cooperate.'

Dancek shook his head.

'I'm shocked and disappointed with Ruth. She told me she wouldn't do anything like that. But it doesn't make her a murderer. She was sitting at the front of the hall when the shot was fired. You saw her, Chief Inspector.'

'We can't rule out that she may have been part of an organisation that planned it, and the same goes for Hamilton's murder. The organisation she's involved in has had at least one brush with the law and she was once arrested.'

Watson and Dancek looked perplexed and puzzled; they hadn't expected this.

'But surely you don't think they arranged the murders of two famous musicians like that. I mean, Ruth is a musician herself. It's just not credible.'

'Our views don't come into it. We proceed simply on the basis of the evidence,' said Armitage, 'and now I think we need to get on with the investigation.'

After the two men had left, shaking their heads, Oldroyd and Armitage sat in silence for a while. The investigation was actually still very much in the doldrums. Armitage had constructed a diagram on the wall of his office, with photographs of the people involved and lines indicating connections. Both men gazed at it, looking for inspiration.

'Let's have a quick run through the possibilities,' said Armitage without enthusiasm.

'Fine.'

'So, in terms of motive; the people who might have wanted to get the violin were Knott, Shaw, Taylor, Jefferson and the School of Music, and Hamilton. It's possible that some of them could be working together.'

'And fell out, which resulted in Hamilton's death.'

'Yep, then other motives for Muller's murder were the jealousy of Robson's husband, Downton; this Jewish organisation Greenfield was involved with, taking him out because he was hanging on to Nazi gold; and perhaps Stringer's resentment of Muller in terms of the direction of the quartet.'

'And means and opportunity?' Oldroyd had sat back in his chair with his eyes closed.

'The interesting point there is that none of them had either. They were all either sitting in the audience that night or were elsewhere with watertight alibis – so the phantom murderer, as I call him, must have been either an accomplice or a professional hitman that we don't know about. You say Watson has a Dragunov, but it wasn't the one used in the murder, and Watson was sitting smack in the front row. As far as Hamilton's murder goes, the same thing applies: all the people I've mentioned had alibis.'

Oldroyd sighed wearily. They'd been through all this before. They were just circling around the same facts and getting nowhere. It was like being in a maze where every possible exit, however tantalising, leads disappointingly to a dead end. And this was even before they'd solved the mystery of how the murderer escaped from the Chapel. He felt completely outwitted and didn't like the feeling.

'What do you think of it all, then?' asked Armitage, reaching for a bag of mint imperials and putting three into his mouth.

'Not a lot; nothing hangs together. These leads don't seem to take us anywhere. There's no pattern; none of the possibilities convince me.'

Armitage frowned.

'So where do you think we should go next?'

'Well, the murders weren't random. They were well planned, particularly the first, so I'm sure the answer lies with the people we know already; no one else with any kind of motive has emerged. We must be missing something. The only thing we can do is keep probing until we get a breakthrough. I've asked Carter to investigate that Jewish outfit. I'm also thinking about that character Taylor. He's a shadowy figure, and there's definitely something not right about his so-called musical instrument business. I think he's the next one to go back to, and let's do a background check. He claims he was at the Huddersfield School of Music, but I didn't get the impression he actually knew much about music.'

'OK.'

'We also need to get a warrant to look at Edward Shaw's instrument collection; you never know what we might find. He was rather cagey about that – just the opposite of Elizabeth Knott, who was keen to parade hers.'

'If he's got that violin he's not going to put it on show is he?'

'No, but there's nothing wrong in applying pressure, showing we have suspicions. Criminals start to make mistakes when they know the heat is on.'

'True.'

'So where does Paul Taylor live?'

'It'll be an interesting visit for you. He lives in a narrow boat on the canal.'

Dusk was falling as Oldroyd walked along the towpath of the Rochdale Canal out of Sowerby Bridge towards Luddenden Foot. He'd parked his car in the town so that he could walk by the still and peaceful water of the canal, now used mainly for pleasure craft and not to transport the loads of coal, wool and cloth for which it had been constructed. He went near the edge of the path on to the massive blocks of millstone grit that had been there forming a strong bank since the eighteenth century. In the water were small groups of mallard huddled together and looking rather listless in the winter cold. On the far bank a grey heron stood hunched and completely still, peering into the water.

He went under a bridge where the towpath narrowed rather alarmingly and thought about the horses that used to pull the boats along, trudging on this path. There was a tall stone warehouse, now empty, with an ancient crane hanging out over the water. He came to a lock and was delighted to see that a boat was going through. With a boyish enthusiasm he watched as the sluice gates were cranked open and the water rushed in. The boat rose slowly from the rather frightening depths to the top of the lock, and was almost twenty feet higher than when it had entered at the bottom. It was such a simple but ingenious device and always satisfying to watch. The top gates swung open and the boat puttered off through the calm water.

Oldroyd continued down the towpath. A train clattered past, hidden in the trees up to his left, and on his right in the valley bottom was the River Calder. Streets of terraced houses climbed up the steep valley, some at crazy angles. There was something Gothic about this landscape, which had been one of the earliest places in the world to be industrialised. Oldroyd, like Armitage, remembered it when it was smoky and dirty, when the giant mills were full of rattling looms. The valley was now much cleaner, the air pure, the rivers ran clear; there was more greenery and tourism was developing. How strange would previous generations have found that! They had decamped for their brief holidays to Blackpool or Scarborough to get the bracing sea air and to escape the grime.

A little further on, Oldroyd came to a kind of marina. There was a chandler's shop selling all kinds of provisions for boats, including rope, varnish and bottles of gas, and some permanent moorings, as well as toilets, showers and facilities for disposing of rubbish. Oldroyd's phone rang and he took a call from Armitage before going into the shop to enquire which was Taylor's boat, and being directed to a rather shabby-looking narrow boat that looked as if it had been moored in the same position for some time. Nearby, just off the path, was a motorbike, chained to a metal post and covered with tarpaulin. Oldroyd lifted the cover; it was a Harley Davidson. The light had nearly gone as he clambered on to the deck to have a look round, and he trod carefully so as not to trip on anything and fall in. He wasn't sure what he was looking for, but you never knew. There was a door into the cabin, which was locked. He peered through the grubby windows and saw the outlines of rooms with a table, bed, chairs. On the deck were some rectangular flower troughs containing dead geraniums and overgrown with weeds. Absentmindedly, he pulled some of the weeds out.

'Thanks, Chief Inspector.'

He turned round rather startled to see Paul Taylor standing by the narrow boat. He was wearing a black leather jacket and heavy boots. His ponytail hung down his back. 'I'm not much of a gardener, as you can see. Things usually die when I get my hands on them.'

'I used to enjoy gardening when I had a garden, but I live in a flat now,' replied Oldroyd.

'Bet it's expensive. You want to get on to the water. Very cheap. Anyway, didn't expect you here. Good place for a murder, though, isn't it? They've found a few bodies in this canal over the years. Just think, I could knock you over the head and kick you into the water.' He raised one of his legs, displaying the boot quite threateningly. 'And who would know? You'd drift downstream and they'd probably find you by the lock.'

'You've got quite a morbid imagination for a musical instrument dealer.'

'Always liked a good murder on the telly, you know. The more gruesome the better. Anyway, come in.'

He stepped on to the deck, unlocked the door and flicked a light switch.

Oldroyd followed him in, down a short flight of steep wooden stairs and into a narrow corridor. At the end was a small sitting area with fitted wooden benches around a table. The benches were covered with dirty cushions.

'Have a seat. Fancy a drink?'

'Not for me thanks.' Oldroyd sat down. He could see out of the rather grimy windows on to the bank. Two serious-looking cyclists wearing helmets and cycle shorts passed by, pedalling vigorously. Taylor lit a stove and filled a kettle with water. Then he came and sat opposite Oldroyd.

'What can I do for you?'

Oldroyd looked at him. Often, the jauntier the suspect was, the more they had to hide.

'Wanted to check again if anyone has contacted you offering a violin.'

Taylor smiled.

'It's still missing, then? And that cellist I was meant to have seen in the shop got shot?' He shook his head. 'Bad stuff, but no, as I told you before, I don't deal in things like that.'

Oldroyd looked around.

'Very comfortable here, isn't it? Very compact, though, not much space for storing things, I shouldn't think.'

'It's fine.'

'But you told us last time that you didn't have instruments in your shop in the Piece Hall; you said you stored them at home. How do you manage that here?'

Taylor's jaunty confidence was suddenly a little diminished.

'I didn't mean here. I have another place. It's part of a flat I used to live in and I store the stuff there.'

'I see. We'd be quite interested to have a look at some point.'

'Why? There's nothing in there that will interest you.'

'We have to be thorough in an investigation like this.'

'Fine. If you just let me know so that I can, you know, sort it out a bit. Excuse me.'

The kettle was boiling, and Taylor seemed glad of the temporary respite from Oldroyd's questioning as he returned quickly to the kitchen area. Oldroyd waited patiently. Taylor returned with a mug of tea and Oldroyd continued.

'How long have you been interested in musical instruments?'

Taylor looked a little hesitant, as if he was not quite sure where Oldroyd might be going. 'Since I was a student.'

'At Huddersfield?'

'Yep.'

'What did you study there?'

'I was doing a music degree and learning guitar.'

'But you didn't complete the course, did you?'

209

'No.'

'Why was that?'

'Just got fed up, you know, with student life. Dropped out.'

'That's not exactly true, is it?'

Taylor looked rattled. 'What do you mean?'

'I had a call from my colleague just before you arrived. You were expelled from the University of Huddersfield because of drug dealing. So why are you lying to me?'

Taylor squirmed, and fiddled nervously with the handle of his mug. 'OK, congratulations on the research. It's not something I'm proud of. I'd rather forget about it.'

'So are you still involved with drugs, then?'

'You don't expect me to answer that.'

'Why?'

'Pointless question. You coppers know that millions of people smoke stuff, and more. It's against the law but you can't stop it. If I say yes, you can take me in, but if I say no, you won't believe me anyway.'

'You know what I mean. Are you involved in dealing?'

Taylor laughed.

'Same question, same answer.'

'OK, so what happened to your musical career after you left Huddersfield?'

'Joined a band, tried to go on tour. Classic, isn't it? Every teenager's dream. Didn't get very far with it; we weren't good-looking enough. Then my uncle had this little shop in the Piece Hall and he was retiring, so I inherited the lease from him and started the instrument business.'

'So you seem to have done quite well out of it, judging by the brand-new Harley Davidson out there?'

Taylor raised an eyebrow. 'You don't miss anything, do you, Chief Inspector? Biking's a hobby; had to save up for that beauty. I don't exactly live in luxury here, as you can see.'

'All right.' Oldroyd got up from his seat. 'That'll be all for now, but we'll be back to see your collection, so if you could get it ready for us, as it were, that would be most cooperative.' There was an unmistakeable sarcasm in his tone.

Taylor nodded, but didn't get up from his seat as Oldroyd climbed up the stairway and exited back on to the towpath. He walked back into town, noticing barges and boats on both banks. The glow of lights from behind curtains and the smoke coming from the small chimneys suggested cosiness on the winter evening.

Everything about the interview confirmed what Oldroyd already thought: there was something deeply suspicious about Taylor.

Oldroyd thought about ringing Armitage, but he was tired; he'd had enough. It was dark and cold and he wanted to go home so he got into his battered old Saab and drove back to Harrogate, following the same route as the one he'd taken on the night of the first murder, only in reverse. Since that night he'd worked almost continuously, travelling around the Halifax area and down to London. It had been exhausting but the effort had so far yielded no real breakthrough. The clues that he normally uncovered in such cases hadn't appeared, unless he was missing them. He had the uncomfortable feeling that somehow their lines of enquiry were off track, like the terribly misguided Ripper investigation of the 1970s that went off on the wild-goose chase of trying to locate a killer with a Geordie accent.

As he entered Harrogate, he saw the Christmas lights again on the Stray and felt a pang of guilt, as he'd done nothing yet about cards or presents. Julia had always taken care of all of those kinds of things – and not properly appreciated by him, as he now realised. But when was there time for any personal life when he had a case on like this? It was the same old dilemma with which the job had always tormented him.

The flat was in darkness and he found a note from Louise on the table:

Hi
Gone into Leeds, meeting up with Jenny, Chris and
the old crowd from college, back sometime!!
L. xx

He was just looking in the freezer to see what there was to eat when
the phone rang.

'Hi, it's me.'

It was a rare phone call from his wife.

'Oh, hi, er . . . How's things?'

'Not that good, obviously. Is she there?'

'No, gone into Leeds, meeting up with her old friends.'

'Is she expecting to come back here to crash out?'

'No, don't think so.'

'Well, how's she getting back to Harrogate when the clubs are shut?'

'No idea; she'll probably stay over somewhere.'

'Yes, probably with that Ben and his girlfriend. Apparently they live
in a filthy student house in Hyde Park and smoke weed all the time.
They got Louise into smoking it in the first place.'

'Why are you getting so sanctimonious about that? We used to
smoke it quite a bit in the old days.'

'Yes, Jim, but we weren't so . . .'

'What?'

'I don't know. She's just a bit too much on the wild side; you never
know what she's going to do next. She worries me, and it won't look
good for you if she keeps getting arrested on these demonstrations.'

Oldroyd knew that now wasn't the time to talk about how he
admired his daughter's activism. Why was his wife getting so narrow-
minded and conservative? He wanted to remind her how rebellious
she'd been with her parents in rejecting their Home Counties lifestyle;
the awful rows he'd witnessed from the embarrassed sidelines. Maybe it

was the stress of her job as a history teacher, or was it a sign of a deeper discontent, a loneliness?

'She's nearly twenty now. You know as well as I do that you've just got to let her go her own way; the more you try to control her the worse it will be.'

'You wouldn't think she was twenty from the way she behaves here; bags of stuff all over the place, wet towels and underwear on the bathroom floor, dirty cups and plates in the living room; she's more like a fifteen-year-old.'

'She's got lofty issues on her mind; she can't be bothered about keeping the house tidy,' laughed Oldroyd, trying to get his wife to lighten up a little and see the funny side, but it didn't work.

'It's OK for you to say that; you always let them get away with everything – when you were here, that is. It was always me who had to set some rules, boring mother. No wonder she runs off to you.'

'Look, it's not like that. I told her she wasn't being fair to you; that you'd always had the responsibility of looking after her and Robert, and it wasn't easy.'

'And a fat lot of difference I bet it made. I know she thinks I'm just a dull, nagging middle-aged woman and I . . .'

She stopped, and Oldroyd could hear gentle sobs on the other end of the line. It upset him deeply. He wanted to reach out and take her in his arms, but he couldn't and she probably wouldn't let him anyway, even if he'd been there with her. He had to try his best with words.

'Julia, please don't. I know she loves you. I know I said she's twenty but that's not really that old, she's still half a teenager. They say and do hurtful things that they don't really mean, you know that.'

'Yes, but . . .'

'But what?' He was hoping she would say, 'But it's so lonely here by myself and hard to cope with so please come back.'

'Oh, I don't know. Anyway, tell her to ring me tomorrow just so I know she's OK.'

'Right.'

'I'd better go now. Bye.'

'Bye.'

She rang off, leaving Oldroyd looking at the phone and thinking about all the things he would have liked to have said to her.

Anna Robson stood nervously near the arrivals gate at Heathrow airport. It was 8.00 a.m. and she'd come up from Brighton to pick up her husband, Christopher, returning from his trip to Washington. She was then going to return with him to Islington. Getting away from London for a while had calmed her down but she still had a residual fear that her husband could have been involved somehow in the terrible events. It was going to be very tricky to broach that subject without provoking his anger.

Tired, jet-lagged passengers started to wander out of the baggage hall and through passport control. She saw Christopher wearing dark glasses and dressed in jeans and a jacket, looking a little bedraggled but handsome with his stubbled face and trim figure.

'Chris, here!'

She ran over to him, and they kissed. He took her hand with one of his and pushed his case with the other.

'God I'm knackered, been awake all night; can't ever sleep on a plane.'

'Don't worry, we'll go straight back. You can go to bed if you want.'

'Well, I wouldn't mind that,' he said, giving her a smile and a lingering look.

'Hey! I thought you were tired!'

'Never too tired for some things. It's been a long time.'

'Yes.'

They were silent as they went up escalators and along walkways until they got to the car park. Anna drove. Downton slumped into the car and looked as if he might go to sleep but then he spoke.

'Anyway, how are you, darling?' he said, rather casually she thought in the circumstances. 'You've had an awful time; two murders! I don't blame you for getting out of the way to Brighton. How're Amy and Harry?'

'Fine. They've been really good.'

'Fantastic. They're such great people.'

She glanced at him just as she entered the busy carriageway. Did he really understand what she'd been through? He seemed very cool about it; it worried her.

'I could have done with you being around.'

'I know; they just wouldn't let me come back early. You know what Jeremy's like.'

She looked in the driving mirror and sighed. Maybe this was the time to tackle him, when he was too tired to get angry.

'You did contact him, didn't you?'

He looked up, puzzled. 'Of course. What do you mean?'

'It's been very traumatic. I don't think you realise how bad. Two of the quartet, my friends and . . . essential to my working life, both murdered. It's . . . it's made me feel frightened in . . . in different ways and strange . . . and . . .'

He sat up.

'Look, darling, I do understand, it's just that I'm tired at the moment. I . . .'

She turned towards him and said abruptly, 'You didn't have anything to do with it, did you?'

'What?'

'Did you, Christopher?' She was shouting now.

'Watch it!'

She swerved suddenly to avoid a parked car she'd been about to drive into. The car behind blazed its horn at her.

'Turn left here and pull in. You're going to get us killed.'

She turned left without warning and provoked more horn blowing from behind. She drove into the quiet side street and stopped at the side of the road. She turned off the engine and promptly burst into tears. Downton put his arm around her and let her cry for a while.

'Look, what's this all about?'

'I . . . I've been so scared about everything,' she said between sobs. 'And so confused . . . and . . .'

'Go on.'

'Well, I know you and Hans never got on, and . . . Well, all sorts of horrible things go through your mind. The police know that you threatened Hans and you were in prison that time; I just thought . . .' She started to cry again.

Downton sighed. 'OK, I understand. You're worried that I might have had him bumped off.'

'Oh God, I'm sorry; it sounds so awful and ridiculous when you say it like that.'

He laughed grimly and shook his head.

'Not really; my behaviour in the past hasn't been exactly perfect, has it? I know I've got a nasty temper. I've only myself to blame, and you've been under so much stress, but come here.'

He turned her face tenderly towards his and looked her in the eyes. 'I swear to you I had nothing to do with it. I didn't like the bloke and he made it clear he didn't like me, and I hated him for causing trouble between us. But that's all a while ago now, and it's behind us. I can't say I'm sorry he's gone, but there it is.'

'I'm sorry,' she repeated.

'Don't be. I deserve it and it actually shows you care for me or you wouldn't be worried.'

'Yes.'

'I assure you I'm not some kind of gangster.' He smiled. 'And I wouldn't know how to hire a hitman even if I wanted to. Unless you think that I teleported myself from Washington to Halifax and did him in myself.'

She had to smile at that.

'And surely you don't think I would have Martin killed?'

'No, of course not.'

'So let's forget about all that. I promise you I'm going to look after you now I'm back, starting now. Get out of the driver's seat; you're not fit to drive.'

'But . . .'

'No buts.'

They got out of the car and changed over. It was a relief not to have to drive. She sat with her head resting against the window during the journey back to Islington, feeling a measure of relief that was nevertheless not total. She believed him, but such was her state of turmoil now that it would only be once the police had actually caught the real perpetrators that she would be able to even contemplate feeling relaxed again.

Carter and DC Jenkins drove to Golders Green to seek the location of Return Nazi Art Thefts Now. It was not a part of London he was very familiar with, but he knew there had been a significant Jewish community there for a long time. They passed a number of synagogues as they went up Golders Green Road.

'Must be a bit of a shame, being Jewish at this time of year,' said Jenkins, observing what he considered to be a paucity of Christmas decorations around the streets.

'You mean they don't get to stuff their face and watch telly after falling out with the family they hate and only see because they have to?'

'That's a bit jaundiced, Sarge; I've always liked Christmas, you know, ever since I was a kid.'

'Yeah, I was only joking. It's good, I like it too. Good excuse for some boozing! I'm sure a lot of Jews and other religious types have a good time at Christmas, don't they? I mean it's not much to do with religion anymore, is it? Just a holiday and a big party.'

'My family's a bit on the religious side; we have to go to church on Christmas Day or my mum and dad aren't happy.'

'Then you don't go again for the rest of the year,' laughed Carter.

'Yes, at Easter when the family's together again.'

'Right – slow down – we're nearly on it.'

The address was on the main road, but there was no sign of the organisation. The building seemed to be a pizza takeaway. Carter went inside to enquire and was directed to the back of the building. Jenkins drove gingerly down a narrow back alley, between shabby back entrances and lock-up garages, and parked up. There was a buzzer by a door with RNATN scrawled faintly beneath it. Carter pressed it and waited for some time before he heard a voice behind the door.

'Who is it?'

'Police, this is a murder enquiry; we need to ask you some questions.'

'Murder? What murder?'

'Two murders, two musicians have been killed, one here in London, one in Yorkshire.'

'What's it got to do with us?'

'I think you need to let us in.'

There was a brief pause and then the rattling sound of bolts and locks being opened. A man's face peered around the door and looked at them suspiciously. He was bearded, and wore a kippah. He asked to see their ID and then let them in and directed them up a staircase.

'We've got to be careful. There're skinhead groups, fascists, round here; they're always ready to smash things up. That's why we don't advertise our presence here.'

'I wouldn't have thought what you're doing was that controversial.'

'Jewish people claiming *anything* is not popular with everyone, even if you're only asking for stolen things to be returned. It's not generally realised how much anti-Semitism there still is. Synagogues, Jewish businesses, they regularly get bricks through the window.'

Carter felt a point was being made: probably that they could do with more support from the police.

'Anyway, come in here.'

He opened a door to reveal a room that was clearly the nerve centre of their outfit. There were several desks with PCs and people working, filing cabinets, old black-and-white photographs on the wall of paintings and musical instruments and also some rather poignant ones that looked as if they were of Jewish families before the war, looking happy and blissfully unaware of what was to happen to them.

On one wall was a banner proclaiming 'Justice is Still Justice However Long It Takes'. Two or three very earnest-looking people were tapping away at keyboards.

'I understand that this is the office of Return Nazi Art Thefts Now,' said Carter. 'Who's in charge?'

'Me,' said the man who'd let them in. 'Adam Rabin. Please sit down.' He gestured to a couple of desk chairs in front of a workstation that was obviously his. 'I don't have an office; it's all open plan – a team effort, no hierarchies.'

'OK,' said Carter, perching on the rather small and uncomfortable chair. 'So we're investigating the murders of Hans Muller and Martin Hamilton; also the disappearance of a rare violin, a . . .' Carter looked carefully at his notes so as to get it right this time. 'Munsterhaven Strad.'

'A Strad that belonged to the Lerner family in Berlin before the war and was stolen from them by the Nazis.'

'Are you sure about that?'

'Yes, I'll show you.' He clicked on the screen while he was talking. 'We've spent years tracking down this kind of stuff.' He swivelled the screen to reveal a faded black-and-white photograph of a young man in formal pose, smiling into the camera and holding a violin.

'That's the only surviving picture of Itzhak Lerner, the young man who played that Strad, and there he is holding it. If you look carefully you can just see a bit of the Munsterhaven coat of arms on the back, which makes those instruments so famous.'

'And valuable.'

'Of course, all the more reason they should be returned to their rightful owners.'

'How did you find out about all this stuff?'

'It wasn't me; it was Abel, our founder.' He pointed to a photograph on the wall behind his desk. It showed a portly, rather elderly man with a greying beard wearing a suit and a kippah.

'Abel Ashkenazi. He's in New York – that's the headquarters – though he's over eighty now and doesn't do much anymore. We run the London office. He started the organisation in the 1970s. His family had a wonderful art collection that was taken by the Nazis. He began by trying to recover those paintings that had been dispersed over Europe. Then he realised just how widespread the problem was, and that he wasn't the only one looking for stolen stuff. So he started RNATN.'

'But you can't be absolutely sure that that's the same violin as the one owned by Muller.'

'Not one hundred per cent, but the odds must be on them being one and the same,' said Rabin, echoing Adamson's words to Oldroyd.

Carter consulted his notes again.

'One of your members, Ruth Greenfield, says that Abel Ashkenazi has some information that confirms that they are the same instrument.'

'Maybe, but you'd have to ask him. I don't know whether Ruth knows something I don't. I'm sure Ruth has also told you that Abel has developed a network of contacts over the years; many of them are secret and he doesn't share the identity of his sources with anybody, even us. But we all trust Abel, so if he says he knows that's the same instrument as the one owned by the Lerners then we believe him without asking how he knows.'

'OK. So you believe that that violin should be returned to the family?'

'It would be nice if that were possible, but they were all wiped out in the concentration camps. In those circumstances our policy is that musical instruments should be given to music schools so that young musicians get a chance to play them. If by any chance they're sold, the money should benefit certain charities that we promote. I'm sure Ruth will have told you that.'

Carter looked at Rabin, who was leaning back casually in his chair. He radiated confidence and certainty and the cause seemed a just one. But when did campaigning zeal become fanaticism? How far would this organisation go in their pursuit of what they regarded as justice?

'The violin that belonged to Muller was taken by Martin Hamilton, one of the quartet, and then by whoever murdered him.'

'So I understand from the press. Getting rather lurid, isn't it? All kinds of speculation going on.'

'Yes, but has your organisation had anything to do with it?'

Rabin smiled and looked unruffled.

'We don't go in for murder, Sergeant.'

'But you have gone in for intimidation, haven't you?'

'What do you mean?'

'Come on, don't play ignorant: sending threatening messages, protesting outside houses, harassing people; some of your members have been arrested for breach of the peace. You know that Ruth Greenfield herself was questioned about sending a threatening note to Muller on the night he was killed. That's very suspicious, isn't it?'

Rabin shook his head.

'Ruth would never physically hurt anybody. You're wasting your time. We look upon these things as simply pricking the consciences of people, getting them to realise the injustice involved in them possessing stolen property.'

'It's a bit heavy-handed, isn't it?'

'Some people need the message to be made forcefully before they will respond.'

'So does that extend to more than messages in the case of someone like Muller? Because he was a stubborn old so and so, wasn't he? He wouldn't have anything to do with you, would he? So did you arrange for him to be shot as the only way you could separate him from that instrument? And then you had to kill again to get the violin from Hamilton. Where is the violin now?'

'I repeat: we do not use violence and I've no idea where that violin is. But I know where it should be and that is not in the hands of some greedy, acquisitive collector. You're making wild allegations.'

Carter was inclined to agree; maybe he shouldn't have gone so far, but he had to press on now.

'I need to know where you and all your colleagues here were on the night of the first murder and the day of the second. Every member of the organisation will have to come down to the station to make a statement. We also need you to disclose all the information you have about the violin and its history.'

Rabin remained composed. 'Fine. You'll get full cooperation from us. We have nothing to fear. But you'll have to contact Abel in America if you want to find out what he knows.'

'We will, but if you or anyone here knows anything about the murders or the whereabouts of the violin you need to tell us.'

'I only wish I could help you, Sergeant. I want to know as badly as you do.'

'Well, the Czech authorities had nothing new on Dancek. Disappointing but not surprising, I suppose. He's been here a long time and he left the old Czechoslovakia under the Communist regime. Probably the records have disappeared. He's a dark horse, isn't he? We know nothing about him except what he shows us.'

'Yes, it's mysterious, but we're probably reading too much into it.'

Oldroyd and Armitage were holed up in the latter's office again. Oldroyd was weary of the whole thing: travelling from Harrogate; not being in his own domain and having to endure his friend's clumsy hospitality; the frustration of not getting anywhere. He was beginning to regret ever agreeing to get involved, but he could hardly have refused under the circumstances. Anyway, it was too late now, he was deeply involved and he couldn't stop until the thing was solved. It wasn't so much his pride as the impetus that had always driven him on; the sheer fascination of wanting to know what had happened; the who, how and why.

'No,' he replied to Armitage. He's one of those people, reflected Oldroyd, who is always on a level. If he won a million pounds or contracted a serious disease, he'd sit there just the same, sucking mint humbugs taken from a paper bag in his lap just as he was doing now. 'Carter didn't unearth anything with the Jewish organisation, but he's pursuing them for alibis and so on. That's one of our problems: we've got too many suspects. We can't prove any of them did anything wrong – except Hamilton, who stole the violin, and he's dead – but we can't quite eliminate any of them either. None of them could have actually shot Muller, but any of them could have arranged it, and Hamilton's murder for that matter.' He thumped the table in frustration. 'And we still don't bloody well know how the first murder was done.'

'On that score, I'm afraid none of your ideas about hidey-holes and escape routes have led to anything either. I've had people go over everything again, including on the roof. There are categorically no hiding places under the floor, no trapdoors and no secret exits to the building. There's no way of getting on to the roof from that gantry even if you somehow managed to get up into the rafters. And if you did get on to the roof, there's no way down; it's too high and too steep. We spoke to a bloke who did some roof work there and he said they had to use scaffolding to get up and down; ladders were useless.'

'Great,' murmured Oldroyd dejectedly. 'Well, I suppose it was a long shot.'

'We've got the warrants to search the premises of Taylor and Shaw,' said Armitage consolingly but without optimism. Oldroyd looked up. 'Good. Well, let's get to work on that, then. There's definitely something fishy about them both.'

At this point a DC knocked on the door, came in and handed a dossier to Armitage, who quickly glanced through it.

'Well, have a look at this, Jim. Very interesting. I had Shaw tailed when he went on his last trip to Europe to see where he ended up and who he met. I've got a useful contact in the Dutch police.' He handed a sheet of paper to Oldroyd.

'Well done, Sam; this makes it more urgent that we get on to him.'

It was early morning in the village of Longstalls. It was barely light and the weak December sun had not yet broken through the clammy winter mist. The long main street was deserted, except for two furtive-looking figures dressed in padded jackets and balaclavas. They walked slowly up towards the manor house, repeatedly looking around and checking the names and numbers of the houses. One of them was carrying something bulky. When they finally reached the manor house, the other checked something on his phone, pointed at the house and nodded. After another glance up and down the street, they approached the door and knocked. Immediately there was the sound of dogs barking inside the house and then Gerald Watson's voice.

'Na then, calm down! Come on! Jess! Trixie!'

The barking stopped and Watson fumbled with the door and opened it. As he peered out, there was a flash of light.

'What the bloody hell?!'

The cameraman took several more shots in quick succession as the other reporter began to fire questions at Watson.

'Gerald Watson? We're from the *Daily News*. Is it true that you know what happened to the Munsterhaven Strad?'

'No, I bloody don't, now bugger off!'

'But you organised the concert, didn't you? Did you plan to have Muller killed in order to get your hands on the violin?'

Watson was red in the face with anger. 'I'm warning you, get lost now or I'll set t'bloody dogs on ye.'

'Did you have anything to do with Hamilton's death, Mr Watson? Was he in the way when he took the violin? That wasn't fair, was it, when you'd had the dirty work done on Muller? How did your mistress react? Did she encourage you?'

Watson was so bemused by the question that he'd answered before he could stop himself. 'Who the hell do you mean?'

'Anna Robson, in the quartet; you were having an affair with her, weren't you, Mr Watson? Did you do it all for her?'

Watson's face progressed from red to purple. He turned abruptly back into the house. Undeterred, the reporter continued to hurl questions after him.

'Have you sold it, Mr Watson? Will you and Anna go away together when all this has died down? Will . . .'

He was halted by the spectacle of Watson returning to the door brandishing his Dragunov rifle. He shouted at them.

'This is my final warning: get off my property now or I'll bloody well give you something to think about.'

The two reporters finally retreated backwards down the path, but not before the cameraman had taken a picture of Watson with the gun, which would appear in the newspaper the following day with the headline 'Double Musician Murder Suspect Threatens Reporters with Gun'.

As they reached the gate a final question was called out.

'Is that the same type of gun used in the murders, Mr Watson? You seem to know how to use it.'

It took all of Watson's self-control to prevent himself from taking a pot shot at the man. Instead he abruptly went back into the house and slammed the door. Muttering, he picked up the phone and made a brief call. Then he pulled on an old green Barbour jacket and a pair of boots, went out into his backyard and got into his battered old Land Rover. He shot up the lane at the side of the manor house, out into the main road and drove at speed along the damp country lanes, diesel fumes belching out of the exhaust pipe. The sun was low in the pale-blue sky and in the distance the hills above Huddersfield were still blurred and misty. But Watson hardly noticed. He was on his way to Bradclough Hall to see Edward Shaw. He needed to discuss this situation with him. If things were going to continue like this, he would have to resign as secretary of the Halifax Chamber Music Society.

At Bradclough Hall, the atmosphere was rather strained even before Watson's arrival. Angela Shaw was concerned about her husband, who obviously had something on his mind. He was uncharacteristically moody and quiet. He had long phone conversations in his study and sometimes she could hear him shouting. She'd tried several times unsuccessfully to persuade him to tell her what was wrong. She had some dark thoughts that she was trying hard to persuade herself couldn't possibly be true. Her face was strained as she brewed coffee while the dogs lay on the kitchen floor.

Shaw was in the study now working at the computer. Maybe if she took coffee in she could get him to talk to her. She couldn't stand this atmosphere any longer. As she waited for the percolator to complete its process, she looked out of the window at the curving herbaceous borders, pergolas and smooth green lawns, which were such attractions at the rear of the house.

They were not the result of her labours nor of those of her husband. They employed a professional gardener for two days a week, three in summer, at considerable cost, just as they employed a cleaner for a full day each week and occasionally a chef who prepared meals when they were entertaining. It was a comfortable lifestyle to which she had grown accustomed and, as the children were mostly away at boarding school, it left her free to take long walks with the dogs and to pursue a social life with other women of similar means in the area. She'd never taken the slightest interest in how the whole thing was financed; that was Edward's domain. She was quite happy with her traditional female role as home maker, especially as most of the 'making' was done by other people, so any suggestion that anything may be amiss, any possible threat to their position, made her feel alarmed. The only work she'd ever done was modelling, and she was too old for that now.

In the study, Shaw was sitting in a padded desk chair gazing at the computer screen, which was switched off. After a while he took his phone and dialled a number.

'Hello. Yes, I've thought about it and I've decided, no, there's nothing else we can do. I'm going to tell them . . . What do you mean I can't . . . ? I'm bloody well going to and I've got an excuse worked out too. You haven't suggested anything else . . . Well, I don't know what you can do; we never expected this, did we? It's our bad luck, but it's every man for himself now. You'll have to work out your own salvation.' He ended the call as there was a tap at the door.

'Ed, darling, can I come in? I know you're busy but I've just brought you some coffee.'

'Of course.' His wife came in and put a tray with two cups down on a small table. He swivelled in the chair to face her as she sat opposite him, her face uncharacteristically pale and tense.

'How's it going?' she said, and gave him a thin smile.

'Fine, just a few of the old money-flow problems; nothing to worry about.' His tone was unconvincing.

'Are you sure? You know you've not been yourself for a while, ever since that ghastly business at the Chapel and . . .' She tried to drink from her cup but her hand was shaking. 'Look, you didn't have anything to do with that, did you, Ed? I mean . . . did you?' She was on the verge of tears. Shaw put his hand on her knee.

'Darling, no, of course not. You don't think . . . ?'

'I didn't know what to think; you've been behaving so strangely, and then the police came and I . . .'

Suddenly there was the sound of a vehicle coming up the drive, seemingly at some speed.

'Damn,' said Shaw. 'Who the hell's that?'

A car door slammed and then there was an urgent knocking on the door of the house.

'I'll go,' he said, giving his wife's knee a reassuring squeeze.

Shaw strode down the hall feeling some relief. He was glad to escape from his wife's questions. He opened the door to reveal an agitated Gerald Watson.

'Gerald? What on earth? What's wrong?'

'I've had enough, Mr Shaw, I really have.' He stumbled over the threshold. 'I'm a private person, can't be doing with it. I don't know why they've picked on me.'

'Who?'

'T'bloody newspapers, never away from t'door; they were round early this morning, taking photographs, accusing me of all sorts of stuff.'

'Come in, let me get you a drink.'

'Thanks, I'll just wipe me feet.'

Watson attempted to remove some of the mud and general filth from his boots and then followed Shaw down the hall and into the

sitting room where Oldroyd and Carter had recently sat. Shaw opened
a cabinet, took out a decanter and poured whisky into two glasses. He
could do with a drink himself. He handed one glass to Watson, who
took a big gulp and held the glass with both hands, leaning forward and
resting his elbows on his knees.

'I've just had enough,' he repeated. 'I'm being hounded, just
because I'm secretary and my name's on stuff and I organised the concerts. They're trying to say I was involved, I arranged it.'

'That's ridiculous.'

'That doesn't make any difference to them. They got me so worked
up just now, like an idiot I got my rifle out and threatened them.' He
shook his head and put his hand up to his temple. 'So now they've got
a wonderful story about me being trigger-happy. No doubt they'll find
out it's a Dragunov, like the one the police say was used by the sniper.'

Shaw sipped his whisky. 'How can I help?'

'I've just come to say that I'm going to resign as secretary if this
goes on.'

'How will that help?'

'I can take a low profile. I'm thinking of going away for a while. I've
got a cousin, has a farm in Northumberland. I can stay with him for
Christmas and into the New Year. It's miles from anywhere.'

'It might look as if you're guilty and running away. The media are
very good at tracking people down.'

'Maybe, but at the moment I'm an easy target; they know where
I am. At least I can make it a bit harder for 'em, and they might try
someone else instead. I was thinking, Mr Shaw, maybe you could take
over for a while.'

'What do you mean?'

'Well, just be there at the concerts and supervise things, meet the
artists beforehand and make sure everything's OK, stuff like that. The
programme's all arranged for the rest of the season. Hopefully after a

few months it'll all have blown over and I'll come back and get to work on next year.'

Shaw took another sip of his whisky. 'I see. Well, I suppose . . .'

He stopped as there was the sound of another car coming up the drive.

'What the hell's going on this morning? Who's this? Excuse me, Gerald.' He put down his whisky glass and went back into the hall, feeling that the pressure on him was mounting. When he opened the door there was nothing to reassure him, because on the doorstep stood Detective Chief Inspector Oldroyd and Detective Chief Inspector Armitage looking purposeful and implacable.

'Oh, good morning, gentlemen; I wasn't expecting you,' he said lamely, as he struggled to compose himself.

'There are some things we need to discuss with you, Mr Shaw,' said Armitage.

'I see. It's not really convenient, I have a visitor you see, can we . . . ?'

'We need to come in and talk to you now.'

Shaw swallowed nervously. 'Well, you'd better come in, then.'

The two detectives entered the hall as Gerald Watson came out of the living room looking puzzled.

'Mr Shaw? What's going on? I thought I recognised the voices.' He turned to Oldroyd and Armitage and pointed his finger at them. 'What you lot should be doing is protecting law-abiding members o' t'public from t'bloody press instead o' wasting your time harassing people like Mr Shaw here.'

Shaw moved between Watson and the detectives, who did not respond to Watson's outburst.

'Steady, Gerald. Look, it's better if you go now and I'll give you a call later, OK?'

'Aye, all right then.' Watson continued to dart angry glances at Oldroyd and Armitage as he left the house, mumbling to himself.

Shortly after, they heard the roaring sound of the old diesel Land Rover starting up and then disappearing off down the drive.

'Come in,' said Shaw, gesturing to the living room and feeling very flustered. At that moment Angela Shaw appeared at the door of the study.

'Ed? What's going on? I heard Gerald Watson so I left you to . . . Oh it's you. Why are you here again?'

'It's OK, darling, they just want to ask me a few more questions. Why don't you go upstairs and have a lie-down for a while?'

Angela sighed and went back into the study.

'So, how can I help you this time?' asked Shaw, when the three men were in the living room and the detectives had refused all offers of hospitality.

'We've come to inspect your musical instrument collection,' announced Oldroyd with a hint of sarcasm.

Shaw had been expecting this but he still looked rattled. He desperately tried to deflect them. 'But it's not . . . ready. You didn't tell me you were coming.'

'Come on, Mr Shaw, you knew we would want to see it sooner or later. You've known that since we first spoke to you,' said Armitage.

'The problem is,' said Oldroyd before Shaw could think of an answer, 'you don't have a musical instrument collection, do you?'

This rapier thrust seemed to puncture Shaw. He crumpled and sat down heavily in a chair.

'No, it's true. I don't.'

'So what's going on, then?' asked Armitage.

Shaw looked at the two detectives and smiled. He seemed to rally himself a little as if he had an answer ready.

'You see, I sold it all.'

'All of it?' asked Armitage.

'The lot, I'm afraid, bit by bit over the years. Everything my father collected. We just needed the money. You must have wondered how we keep up this lifestyle. I'm not exactly a high-powered earner; not in my father's class – bit of a lightweight really. I know I was always a bit of a disappointment to him, after all he spent on my education and all that.'

'So why do you preserve this fiction that you retain a collection?'

Shaw looked a little sheepish. 'I suppose it's partly out of guilt. I know Father would be furious if he was here and knew I'd sold it and also . . .' He glanced at the door and lowered his voice. 'My wife doesn't know; she thinks all the money comes from the business.'

Oldroyd and Armitage exchanged glances. 'But actually, Mr Shaw, your income comes neither from selling musical instruments nor from your antiques business,' continued Oldroyd.

'What do you mean?'

'You get money from your *real* business, which isn't anything to do with antiques or musical instruments, is it?'

'What?'

For the first time Shaw looked genuinely alarmed.

'Being an antiques dealer and an instrument collector, they're just useful covers for your trips abroad. We never really bought it, you know. You haven't got the slightest interest in music, and that antique shop in Harrogate is a joke. No, your *real* business, Mr Shaw, is drugs.'

Shaw stood up. 'That's ridiculous; what kind of an allegation are you making?'

'Sit down, sir,' said Armitage, becoming more formal.

'You go abroad to collect drugs and smuggle them in – maybe in antiques sometimes, who knows? You have an aura of respectability and nobody suspects you.'

Shaw was now desperate and wild. 'You can't prove anything,' he shouted.

'Oh, but we can,' said Armitage calmly and he produced some photographs from a folder he was carrying.

'This is you recently in Amsterdam; we followed you from England, and this man you're talking to is Karl Neeskens, a notorious drug dealer. He imports the stuff from South America and distributes it around Europe. You're one of his agents, you and your partner.'

'Who do you mean?'

'Paul Taylor; he's another one using his so-called instrument business as a cover. He doesn't have a collection either. We've also seen you and him together. The problem is, he's got form in being involved with drugs – that's what put us on to you. You're the respectable face of the operation who brings the stuff in, and he's got all his links at this end to sell it on. Links he's been building up for years, ever since he was a student.'

Shaw was silent. The door opened and Angela Shaw came in looking worried.

'Ed? I heard shouting; what's the matter?'

Shaw looked at her with an ashen face. 'Darling, I'm afraid I've got something to tell you.'

'What?'

'It's about—'

'I'm afraid there isn't time for that now; we're taking you in. We have enough evidence to charge you.'

'Edward!'

Shaw said nothing as he was led out to the police car except to ask for his solicitor.

'You need to come down to police HQ as well, Mrs Shaw. We'll need to interview you too, and then you can talk to him briefly,' said Armitage, feeling some sympathy for the woman whose comfortable world was about to be abruptly shattered.

'But what has he done? It's not to do with the murders, is it?'

'No. Please follow us down when you're ready and we'll speak to you later.'

'Edward!' She was nearly hysterical now. 'What's all this about?'

But the police car door was shut and the vehicle moved off. Oldroyd glanced out and his last image was of Angela Shaw slumped on the steps with her head in her hands.

~

At about the same time as Armitage and Oldroyd arrived at Bradclough Hall, Paul Taylor was in his shop at the Piece Hall. He'd a reasonably good morning as it was nearly Christmas and parents were buying the cheap guitars he sold as presents for their offspring, who would probably soon discard them after the excitement of receiving them on Christmas morning had dissipated. As there was a lull in the number of customers, he went out for a cigarette on to the balcony, where he could look over the expansive courtyard. The Christmas market was now busy and the coloured lights were on everywhere. It was very colourful, with stalls selling everything from German stollen to wooden toys and Santa outfits. Smells drifted up from frying potatoes and mushrooms and the spices of mulled wine. The roundabout was in full swing and the mechanical noise of the fairground organ was mixed with the laughter of children.

He was savouring the scene when suddenly he heard the noise of a siren, and a police car drove quickly through the huge gates of the Piece Hall. It was heading towards him. He stubbed out his cigarette. Damn! This didn't look good. He thought he'd put that detective off the scent, but it looked as if they were coming for him again. What had Shaw been saying? The man was a coward and an upper-class twit!

He hurried back into his shop and locked the door to the room at the back. He couldn't allow the police to search there at the moment. He pulled on his jacket and hastily announced to the two potential customers in the shop that he was closing due to an emergency. He locked the door and walked along the balcony, away from where the police car had stopped. But he was too late: police officers had run up the stairs to his level and saw him leaving the shop.

'Paul Taylor,' one of them shouted. 'Stop!'

Taylor ran for it. If he could get away and lie low he might be able to get back to the shop and remove the incriminating evidence; then the police could search to their heart's content. He would say they panicked him or something, so he ran off.

He continued round the balcony until he came to another set of stairs, which he jumped down several at a time. At the bottom he was met by more officers and zig-zagged to avoid them. He ran behind some of the stalls, knocking a stand of clothes over.

'Hey!' shouted the owner, making a lunge at Taylor but missing. Police officers were converging from various directions and there were gasps from people as it was realised that there was a chase on. He was trying to get to one of the exits, but as he dodged between stalls he caught his leg on the wooden support of a trestle table. He fell on to the adjacent stall and upset its contents, ending up sprawled on the floor covered in Santa masks.

'Ho-ho-ho, sir,' said a sarcastic police officer, as Taylor was yanked to his feet.

'Shall we go back to your shop and see what Christmas presents you have stored away in there? I'll bet they're not ones suitable for children.'

Taylor was frogmarched back up on to the balcony and forced to open up. It didn't take the police long to find the stash of drugs freshly brought over by Shaw from Amsterdam and hidden at the back of the innocent-seeming little music shop, prior to being distributed by Taylor to his numerous contacts in the area. A clientele that, as Oldroyd had rightly suspected, he had been assiduously building up since his decadent student days.

Ten

The 'Lauterbach' Stradivarius of 1719 was in the National Museum in Warsaw in 1939 when the Nazis invaded Poland. It was hidden behind a wall by the museum's curator, but the hiding place was discovered. In 1948 an American officer found it in the home of a former member of the SS. Records suggest it was sent back to Poland but the Polish authorities claim that it never arrived. Its current whereabouts are unknown. As it was constructed by Stradivari in his 'golden period', it would be worth several million pounds if it is ever found in good condition.

Oldroyd had made a rudimentary effort at decorating his Harrogate flat for Christmas. He'd put a small artificial tree on a table next to his TV screen and had hung some tinsel around pictures on the wall. Surveying the rather paltry effect made him wonder why he'd bothered, but there was something he didn't want to see die. Even though he was in the flat by himself, he could try to maintain links with the past, to happier times when he was a boy and then when his own family were young. If a bit of festive decoration could keep those memories alive, then why not? The alternative, which was sitting in an unadorned flat while Christmas happened all around him, was too bleak to contemplate.

'Well, it looks very nice in here, Jim; you've made a real effort.'

Oldroyd had invited his sister Alison round for a meal. Louise was there, too, eating with them before departing for Leeds. They sat together on the sofa, the elder woman wearing an elegant dress, which she confessed to having bought in Oxfam, his daughter in jeans and T-shirt. Oldroyd admired and loved them both.

'Thanks. Well, why not?' Oldroyd knew his sister was over-praising deliberately in order to encourage him to take an interest in things and not become depressed. She'd worried about him ever since his separation from his wife.

Oldroyd worried about her, too. She was also on her own after the death of her husband.

'I'm not going to become a grumpy old curmudgeon just because I'm by myself.'

'More grumpy than usual, you mean, Dad,' laughed Louise. 'And anyway you're not by yourself this year: I'm here,' she said and gave him a wry and affectionate smile.

'Of course and I'm very glad.'

The question of where Louise would spend the Christmas holiday period was still unresolved. Oldroyd didn't want Julia to think that he was putting any pressure on Louise to stay with him; that could make things even more difficult between them.

'Maybe you'll both come over to me on Christmas Day,' said Alison.

'That would be great,' replied Louise. Oldroyd smiled. He always enjoyed going to the old rambling vicarage at Kirkby Underside over Christmas. He went to the Christmas Day service at the church, conducted by his sister, and then they had Christmas dinner together. It would be even better if his daughter was going to be there, at least for part of the time, but he couldn't help thinking how much better still if Julia, Robert and his partner Andrea could be there too. They would be at Julia's house in Chapel Allerton. How silly and unnecessary that separation seemed; how strange families could be. And yet it was all really his fault.

He went into the kitchen and then announced: 'It's ready.'

He was enjoying a rare opportunity to act as host. They all sat at the table and Oldroyd served the food: mushroom pâté with crusty bread, vegetable lasagne – in deference to the preferences of his two female companions – with a green salad, and lemon torte, all of which he'd bought at Waitrose and Marks and Spencer's, along with a bottle of cabernet sauvignon. His culinary skills were limited and somehow these days he couldn't be bothered.

'How's the church, then, Auntie Alison?' asked Louise, picking at her portion of lasagne. She never seemed to eat very much, which worried Oldroyd.

'Oh, it chugs along, you know, and I occasionally stir them up. I had gay marriage services put on the agenda of the last PCC meeting.'

'Wow, I bet that got them going up there!' laughed Louise.

'Indeed it did. Retired Major Hawkins came to the vicarage before the meeting all steamed up. Grey toothbrush moustache, demeanour stiff as a board. He's like a stereotype of the "disgusted, Tunbridge Wells" school. I had to reassure him that I only intended to discuss the implications of the new legislation and wasn't planning to introduce gay marriage at St Bartholomew's. Not yet anyway.' Her eyes twinkled. 'I'm sure he knows I'm in favour of it, but the Anglican Church is still lumbering on well behind society and I can't really break canon law until the Church accepts it. Anyway, what kind of a term have you had? Have you been doing naughty things and got in trouble with the police again? If not, why not?' They both laughed.

'Haven't been arrested again, much to Dad's relief.' She glanced at Oldroyd, who pretended to wipe sweat from his forehead. 'But there's quite a bit of active stuff going on in Oxford.'

'I'm glad to hear it.'

'There's some really interesting people around; I went to a talk at Balliol by this sort of radical priest who's also an economist. He was actually a banker then he gave it all up. He was saying, like, the whole financial system is just built on greed and it just favours the people at the top, you know.'

'Very true and it's getting worse. A lot of this prosperity talk is just disguising greed anyway. It's this acquisitiveness that is such a cancer in the world and it's all over, isn't it? I was reading about the fights in shops when the sales began, people pushing each other out of the way to get at stuff. How can we live as a community if people behave like that? Meanwhile the poor are ever more excluded.'

Here's a sermon developing, thought Oldroyd, but he couldn't disagree with the arguments.

'People don't think,' replied Louise. 'They're seduced by capitalism, advertising. They're made to feel as if they're inferior if they haven't got the latest things.'

Oldroyd smiled. Here he was with his 'red' sister and daughter, and it was great; he was proud of their militancy and their courage in standing up for their principles.

After the meal, they returned to the sofas.

'Jim, how's this case with the violin coming along? Are you going to get it all finished before Christmas?' Alison always took an interest in Oldroyd's work, though on this occasion he wished she hadn't raised the subject. The combined effects of the meal, the wine and the company were making him feel relaxed for the first time in a while and he'd finally got his mind off work.

'It's bogged down, very complicated. We've virtually eliminated two suspects who were dealing in drugs, not musical instruments, but that's about it. My detective sergeant's down in London. The Met are trying to track the instrument down. We're pretty sure the violin will lead us to the killers. It's relevant to what you were saying earlier, really: greed, acquisitiveness, rich people wanting to get more. Apparently some of these collectors can be very ruthless in trying to get what they want. But why? They just keep them hidden away; wonderful instruments that could be played.' He was thinking of Elizabeth Knott and her beautiful but somehow lifeless collection.

'Well, they might as well collect matchboxes,' said Alison in disgust. 'This collecting business is another strange aspect of human psychology, isn't it? Accumulating stuff or squirrelling things away for no apparent reason.'

'It's very common, though,' remarked Oldroyd. 'Almost everyone collects something, don't they? Remember I used to collect train numbers in the great days of trainspotting.'

'I can't believe you did that, Dad,' laughed Louise. 'Why? What was the point? You just wrote down the numbers?'

'And underlined them in our Combine, to record that we'd seen them.'

'In your what?

'The Ian Allan Railway Combined Volume. Never mind.' He waved at her in mock contempt. 'You'll never understand; you'll only laugh. Only those who lived through it can appreciate the great days of the steam locomotive.'

'It was a bit bizarre, Jim, looking back, but you certainly weren't the only one.' Alison smiled.

'The only one! Every station and railway embankment and junction in the land was full of boys in short trousers with their notebooks.'

'I know! The point is, yes, people collect all manner of stuff, but like lots of things in human nature it can get out of hand. To spend all that money just to possess those instruments for no reason other than to possess them. There's something pathological about it.'

'And that's why we think one of these fanatical instrument collectors is behind all this. Maybe even someone calling the shots from a distant country.'

Alison sipped her coffee and considered this for a moment. 'Have you got any further with the problem of the murder at the Red Chapel?'

'Not much, I'm afraid; it's baffling.'

'I still think it was such a strange thing, to shoot someone in the middle of a concert like that. It makes you think.'

'What do you mean, Auntie?' Louise was texting as she sat listening to the conversation.

'Oh, well, I don't know really, I'm no expert on these things.'

'I don't know about that.' Oldroyd knew his sister had a penetrating understanding of people and how they behaved, and she had a fierce independence of mind.

'It's always easy to think about things in a kind of trammelled way. It happens in the Church all the time – orthodoxies that have been around for centuries, but that doesn't necessarily mean they're true. People don't want to think outside the box; we take our cue from other people and don't question things, especially if there seems to be a consensus. But sometimes, even though the evidence may point in a certain way, that solution turns out not to be true in the end. It takes the people who are prepared to question, and not accept what they are told or how a situation appears to be, to finally reach the truth.'

Shortly after this, Louise departed to get the bus to Leeds, where she was meeting friends at a club. Oldroyd and his sister were left to finish the wine before she got a taxi back to Kirkby Underside.

Later, Oldroyd lay in bed thinking about what his sister had said. Outside, a strong wind was blowing and rain beat against his bedroom window. The raindrops tapped relentlessly on the glass just as his doubts nagged at his mind. Was he making assumptions in this case? The main thrust of their investigation seemed sound. Who else would've been prepared to kill for a valuable instrument? It had to have been organised by someone powerful and rich. Once they recovered the instrument, that must lead them to the murderers. It all made sense. Nevertheless, Alison had created doubt and he lay awake until the small hours turning it over and over in his mind.

It was mid-morning of the next day at the Knott residence in Mayfair. Elizabeth Knott was sitting restlessly in her grand living room, nervously stroking Godetia and waiting for news from Djaic, or others in her vast retinue of instrument hunters and dealers, of the missing Munsterhaven Strad. The buzzer sounded and she sighed as she pressed the button to answer. She was not in the mood for visitors.

'Yes.'

'Hello. Arrow deliveries. I have a package for Elizabeth Knott.'

Knott looked at the CCTV image and saw a man dressed in overalls that had 'Arrow' printed on them.

'Put your ID up to the screen.'

She looked at the card presented and checked the photograph.

'OK, I'm coming down.' She pressed the door release and put Godetia on the floor. She liked to receive packages herself; they often had valuable things in them. She walked down the stairs, turned to face the door and froze. A figure dressed in black with a balaclava covering his head and face was standing by the door pointing a pistol with a silencer at her. On the floor in front of him the Arrow delivery man lay spread-eagled, blood flowing from a head wound. She cursed herself for falling for the trick. He must have kept just out of sight of the camera with his gun trained on the poor man, whom he'd probably just abducted from a street nearby while he was making a delivery.

'Let's go upstairs, shall we?' said the killer.

'Who are you working for? Did you kill Hamilton?'

'I don't think you're in a position to ask questions.'

'You're hardly going to shoot me before I've let you into my collection are you? I assume that's why you're here.'

He waved the pistol impatiently. 'Upstairs – now.'

She turned round and walked up with the intruder close behind, keeping his pistol close to her back. When they reached the entrance to the room where the collection was held, she tapped in a number and opened the door. He followed her in.

'Put on the lights.'

She obeyed. Suddenly the reinforced glass cases were illuminated.

'Open them up.'

'They open from this side.'

He walked around to where she was standing, still with the gun trained on her.

'I need that remote control to do it.' She pointed to a black box on a table behind them.

'OK.'

Knott picked up the box and with a quick movement pointed it at him and flicked a switch. He gasped and slumped to the floor. The box was not a remote control but a Taser with a charge strong enough to render an unwelcome visitor like him unconscious. Calmly she took a tissue from a container on the table and knelt down to pick up the pistol, which had fallen to the floor. She got out her phone, pulled back the balaclava and took a photograph of his face. Then she switched off the lights and left the room, locking it behind her. On her way down she heard a scream. Clearly poor Lydia, the maid, had discovered the body of the unfortunate Arrow delivery man.

This could prove a very useful development. Before she rang the police, she would make a few of her own enquiries and see if she could find out who was behind this intrusion. If it turned out to be Djaic there would be hell to pay, but she didn't think so. More likely to be the gang who had killed Hamilton. Anyway, at last there was going to be some action.

Carter was part of the team that was sent to the Mayfair residence. The gunman was found slumped on the floor, still groggy. Refusing to answer any questions, he was handcuffed and led away to Scotland Yard.

'Well done, madam; that must have been a very frightening experience.' Carter congratulated Knott as he sat with her once more in the opulent sitting room. Godetia was sprawled luxuriously by the large open fire, which this morning was burning sweet-smelling logs.

'Oh, don't worry about me. I can look after myself. These bully boys always underestimate me because I'm an elderly woman and small. They have no idea how tough and ruthless I can be.'

Carter looked at the diminutive but wiry frame and the hawkish expression and decided he could well believe it himself.

'I assume you'll break him down and find out who's behind this?'

'Most probably; these people often squeal to try to save their hide. They don't fancy taking the rap for their bosses. We can often get some deal to do with what they're going to plead in relation to information they can give us. Mind you, the interesting thing here is that if that gun turns out to be the one that killed Hamilton, then we're into different territory.'

'My guess is that they will be connected; someone's got overconfident after their success in acquiring the Munsterhaven Strad and miscalculated that they could help themselves to a few more. It suggests that they have a purchaser, doesn't it?'

'Yes, but aren't there always people waiting for things like that to become available?' Carter looked at Knott knowingly and the latter raised her eyebrows. This young detective was no fool and he was rather good-looking too, she thought, as she noted again his strong frame and handsome features. It was quite a pleasure working with the police when they looked like this. Pity she couldn't prolong the interview by telling him what she'd found out: that there was indeed a connection between the crimes and she was getting nearer to discovering the whereabouts of the missing Strad.

It was drizzly and cold in Halifax. Oldroyd walked through the wet streets in the half-light of an overcast December afternoon. It was at times like this that you saw how poor a place the town was for many people. He bought a *Big Issue* from a vendor and passed a number of beggars in doorways. Bedraggled and depressed-looking young women pushing prams were heading into an All for a Pound shop next to some boarded-up properties. Regeneration after the collapse of the textile era still had a long way to go. At this time of year it seemed positively Victorian to see poverty on the streets while so much stuff was being sold. He veered off the street through a large entrance gate to escape the rain and find somewhere more congenial.

Halifax Borough Market was always a cheery, brightly painted, bustling place. Oldroyd loved old markets like this; the cornucopia of different things all bundled together, noisy and colourful. He loved the traditional foods you could still buy: tripe, pork pie, brawn, Cornish pasties, sold to you by red-faced, portly butchers. How could a butcher not be portly and red-faced? They had to look as if they enjoyed feasting on their own meat pies! The only problem today was that while enjoying the Dickensian Christmassy colour and liveliness in here, he could not forget the Dickensian poverty close by outside.

He'd come into the market to do a bit of shopping to take back with him to Harrogate. The hall was additionally adorned with Christmas decorations, especially around the ornamental clock, which stood in the centre under a cupola in the roof. Oldroyd wandered around soaking up the atmosphere and buying bits and pieces: apples, onions, a few more Christmas baubles for his tree and some black pudding, which he rarely ate but found irresistible in its black sausage-like coils in the butcher's display. He was gazing at the fish laid on crushed ice at a fishmonger's, alongside an enormous lobster, which he hoped was now dead and would not suffer the fate of being boiled alive, when he heard a voice behind him.

'Hello, Chief Inspector.'

It was Ruth Greenfield. She was dressed in jeans, a long coat and a multicoloured scarf. Her hair was tied back. She was carrying a woollen shoulder bag that looked as if it was full of shopping.

'It's pretty gruesome, isn't it?' she said, nodding towards the lobster. 'Could you pop that into boiling water if it was still alive?'

'That's quite a coincidence; I was just thinking about that and no, I couldn't. But I'm a cowardly meat-eater nevertheless. I eat the stuff but couldn't kill anything.'

'That's no worse than most of the population.'

'No, I suppose not.'

'How's the investigation going?'

Oldroyd looked at her with interest. It was still possible she could be charged with threatening behaviour after sending that message to Muller, and she would get at least a caution, but she seemed very sanguine about it and clearly bore him no ill will. She was the kind of woman who . . . Well, no point thinking that way, given her sexual orientation. He remained in perpetual hope of getting back with his wife, and remaining celibate seemed to be part of that for him; the patient, faithful wait for the moment he believed would someday come. Maybe he was just badly self-deluded, as there seemed no sign of it yet.

'So-so. We're waiting up here for news about the Strad. It's only a matter of time before the London people track it down.' He checked himself before he said any more. He shouldn't really have said even that to someone who had not entirely been eliminated as a suspect. Likewise, he would like to invite her to go for a coffee somewhere but that would not be wise either in the circumstances.

'Good. Well, I hope when you find it, it's not damaged; that would be a great shame. There's always a chance of that when something so valuable, I mean in artistic terms, is in the hands of people who are only interested in money.'

'I suppose that gives them an incentive to look after it, as they know no one is going to buy it if it's damaged.'

'I just hate to think of something wonderful like that being the plaything of the rich.'

'Even though many of the families you campaign for were wealthy?'

'Yes, but they bought their instruments to be played and their art-work to be displayed and shared. They appreciated them. They never put them in collections and kept them secret.'

'None of them?'

'Not that I'm aware of; it would go against all Jewish artistic traditions.'

He looked at her with even more admiration.

'What about Muller's murder?'

'The investigation continues,' he said judiciously and for the first time became very slightly suspicious. Was she trying to find out things for a purpose?

'I'd better be off. I hope you do find who did it. If I can be of help . . . well . . .'

It was a little embarrassing given her behaviour the night of Muller's murder, but Oldroyd thanked her nevertheless and watched with curiosity as she disappeared into the crowded market.

Carter hunkered down in the passenger seat of the unmarked police car. He and DC Jenkins were parked in a side street near King's Cross station. Other police cars were placed strategically around the area. They sat silently waiting for the signal to move in. Armed plain-clothes officers were already in the massive station concourse patrolling unobtrusively.

The potential breakthrough had finally come with a call from RNATN. Carter had taken the call. It was from Adam Rabin.

'We've had information from one of our agents that there's going to be a handover of the violin: King's Cross station, Friday two p.m. Someone must be paying good money.'

Carter was sceptical.

'That sounds very precise. How do you know that?'

'We're not just a band of worthy campaigners fighting for a good cause, Sergeant; we get down and dirty with the people who trade in the stuff we're interested in. We've infiltrated some of these gangs so we can monitor what's happening. Sometimes we take action ourselves, and sometimes we let the police do it.'

'So what do you get out of this? The violin's not going to be handed over to you if it's recovered; it'll go to the Bloomsbury School – that's where it legally belongs now.'

'Well, which laws are we talking about, Sergeant? That violin was stolen from a Jewish family, so we'll be continuing to campaign for it to be returned to its rightful owner, if one can be traced, but of course it's much better if the violin is kept safe in the meantime and we know where it is.'

'OK, but I'm warning you: there are stiff penalties for wasting police time.'

'I'm sure there are, Sergeant, but it's not in our interests to get into trouble with you on a matter like that. It's reliable, I assure you.'

Carter had immediately taken this information to DCI David Newton, and the decision had been taken to mount an operation aimed at intercepting this handover.

But it was a dangerous and difficult thing to do, thought Carter as he waited in the car. Not only would the criminals most likely be armed, but they had to take possession of the fragile instrument without damaging it. He'd spoken to Steph the previous night, but had decided not to mention what he was going to be involved in today. No point worrying her. People thought the police didn't worry about such things because they were professional and trained; of course they bloody did! Who wouldn't worry if their partner might be involved in a shoot-out?

Suddenly Newton was on the phone to him.

'I think we're on to it; we've identified someone in the station concourse. Terry Nash. He's a thug with form as long as my arm; done time for armed robbery. We wondered what he was up to, so it seems he might have got in with some gang specialising in this kind of stuff. Anyway, he's sitting at a table outside a café and he's got a holdall with him that would be ideal for carrying the violin.'

'So we're watching to see who turns up for the transfer?'

'Exactly. I'll let you know when that happens. So far it looks as if that lot at RNATN are right.'

Carter put down his phone and passed the information to DC Jenkins. Who on earth would appear to collect the violin? It would probably not be long before they found out.

Oldroyd arrived back at police HQ with his shopping to find Armitage in a familiar pose, slumped in his desk chair looking at the screen of his PC. Outside, the light had just about faded away.

'Did you get your shopping, then?'

'Yep, went into the market. They've got some nice food stalls in there, all fresh local stuff.'

'My wife gets all our food at the supermarket. Can't be bothered with it, to be honest – leave it all to her.'

'It's time you started taking an interest. Eat better, get a bit fitter. We're not getting any younger, you know.'

Armitage stretched and his belly pushed up against the desk.

'I know. Never been much for healthy eating. Maybe it's the boring salads we used to have on a Sunday afternoon when I was a kid. Do you remember those?'

'I do. Lettuce, tomato, celery, with tinned salmon or luncheon meat, all plonked on your plate separately with nothing on it except salad cream.'

'We used to have vinegar on our lettuce.'

'Good God! Uncivilised!' They both laughed.

'And then it would be bananas and custard or tinned fruit with Carnation milk poured over.'

'Ugh, don't remind me!'

'Anyway, thinking of food, it'll be bloody Christmas soon,' said Armitage with an obvious lack of enthusiasm. 'Not a good time for your dieting. I'd hoped we'd have got through this business before then. You doing anything interesting over Christmas?'

Oldroyd winced at this latest reminder that these family occasions were not the same for him anymore, and that he was not really looking forward to the season of goodwill.

'Not much. It's not really like it used to be, you know.'

'Oh yes, sorry I forgot. It must be . . . er, difficult for you.'

'Yes.'

'Mind you, the old family Christmas isn't exactly all it's cracked up to be. We'll be having Janet's mother to stay, and mine, and they're both as deaf as posts. So the conversation will consist of me bawling at them, and them misunderstanding what I've said. The kids, not kids anymore, will be off out with their partners as soon as is decently possible, leaving me in the geriatric ward. I'll have to console myself with the whisky as usual.' His face brightened at the prospect of that.

Oldroyd was anxious to move the conversation on. 'Anyway, anything to report?'

'Not much. I sent some DCs round to look at Watson's firearms collection and you were right, he does have a Dragunov. But the problem is: so what? As I said before, it's a very common rifle and he bought it legitimately. He had the proper certificates for it and for a shotgun. There's no evidence that he possessed the one we found at the murder scene and, although he knew how to use one, he obviously wasn't the murderer as he was sitting just in front of you.'

Oldroyd didn't reply. It was clear that his shot in the dark, so to speak, had landed nowhere of any significance.

'And by the way, we tracked down Atkinson's mystery man who bought a ticket for another concert that night. All bona fide, just a random member of the public who came in; nothing to link him with anything.'

There was silence for a while. Armitage picked a wine gum from a paper bag and popped it into his mouth; he offered the bag to Oldroyd, who declined.

'Do you think Shaw and Taylor can be eliminated now?' asked Oldroyd, eventually.

Armitage sighed.

'Again, there's no real evidence against them. Now that we know what they were really up to, and that the musical instrument thing was just a front, we've even lost a motive for them being involved, never mind the old means and opportunity.'

'Did anything emerge about Anna Robson's husband?'

'Christopher Downton. Well, I've liaised with David Newton. They've established that he was definitely in New York when the murder took place. So with him, it's the reverse problem. He has a motive, because he hated Muller and he's a bit of a hothead, but he has no means or opportunity – unless we think he hired a hitman or something, but it seems unlikely. And why have it done at a concert in Halifax?'

'No, I don't think he had anything to do with it. It has to be someone closer to home, someone who knew the Red Chapel well. By the way, I saw Ruth Greenfield in the market.'

'Right, did you speak to her? She's still a suspect.'

'I know. Don't worry; I was circumspect. She intrigues me, though.'

'Why? Or should I not ask?'

Oldroyd ignored the tease.

'She came straight up and asked me how the investigation was going, even though we took her in not long ago. She's not fazed by anything. I got the impression that she was trying to find out what she could.'

'People in those campaigning groups are tough and determined. She's already had some brushes with the law, so I don't think she's intimidated by us.'

'True, and her organisation seems to be batting for us; they gave the tip-off for this operation in London, according to Carter.'

'Hopefully that's the breakthrough we've been waiting for.'

'Yes.'

'So what's bugging you, then?'

'Nothing really, but she's intelligent and she's deep. She seems to inspire admiration and loyalty in people. You remember how Watson and Dancek came straight away to defend her?'

'So?'

'I just think she'd be capable of organising and leading some-thing . . . something clever and dangerous.'

'Is there any evidence that she has?'

'No,' admitted Oldroyd. He put his head in his hands. 'There's something we're missing, Sam. There're all these people who were there that night: the rest of the quartet, Watson, Dancek, Greenfield, Atkinson on the door . . . There has to be some link somewhere that we've not yet discovered. Maybe.'

He faltered, shook his head, went quiet and his speculations fizzled out. They'd been clutching at straws all afternoon and, if the truth were told, since the very beginning of their investigation on that strange night he would never forget.

Carter felt the tension mounting and could hear his heartbeat. He and DC Jenkins had separated and then walked nonchalantly into the station concourse through different entrances. He was now placed at a table at another café opposite to where the target still sat. He pretended to read a newspaper, but kept his eye on the man and the bag, which was under the table. Not only had the suspect, and whoever else turned up, to be arrested, but the violin, if it was in that bag, had to be retrieved undamaged. This was no easy task given that two people had already been murdered and the instrument was relatively small and fragile. This could be a dangerous operation and he was more than ever glad that he hadn't said anything to Steph.

Carter raised his head to turn a page and took the opportunity to glance around. Two officers with special firearms training were in the café behind the suspect. They were the ones who would initially go in. A third man was observing the scene from the doorway of a clothes shop opposite. He seemed to be in conversation with someone on his phone, but was actually communicating with David Newton, who was directing the operation from a car beside the station. DC Jenkins was standing just inside a bookshop and newsagents next to the café and other police were hovering in the area. Carter noticed all the people milling around unaware of what was happening so close to them. It was like two parallel universes existing together. There were even people sitting at the café tables in innocent conversation near to the man being monitored – and that could cause a problem if things got nasty.

The suspect looked at his watch. He was a swarthy man with a beard, wearing jeans, trainers and a black jacket. He was drumming his fingers on the table where the empty cup of his long-finished coffee lay. He looked impatient; was there something wrong? Then he suddenly looked ahead beyond Carter and the drumming stopped. A figure wearing a heavy hooded coat and carrying a small case appeared and sat at the table opposite him. He placed the case on the floor near to the bearded man, who looked around. He seemed satisfied that they were not being observed and pushed the bag with his foot towards the hooded man, who took hold of the straps. The bearded man reached down and grasped the handle of the case.

David Newton heard the report of what was happening and gave the order to move in. Signals were passed between all the officers around the café. Carter could see the armed officers beginning to draw their weapons and then suddenly things burst into action but in an unexpected way.

Before the police could move in, a man who'd sat alone eating a sandwich near to the suspect – and being completely ignored by the police – stood up, produced a handgun and shot the bearded man twice in the chest. He slumped forward, dropped the case, and the killer grabbed at the bag under the table. By this time there were screams from witnesses and Carter stood up bewildered. The killer raised his gun again and seemed about to shoot the other man, who lifted his arms and cried.

'No! No!'

The armed officers pointed their weapons and shouted, 'Drop your weapon: we're armed police.'

The killer looked around and quickly turned his gun towards the police, who promptly fired, hitting him a number of times. He fell on to a chair, which crashed over. He bounced from the chair on to the floor and lay still. People were shouting and running away from the scene in all directions. In the café a woman was screaming hysterically while a man held her. The two men working in the café slowly reappeared in grotesquely comic fashion above the counter behind which they'd dropped to the floor when the shots were fired. The officers trained their guns on the man in the hooded coat, who was cowering in his chair and surrounded. Carter ran over to the café and pulled back the hood. A face was revealed – one that was normally the epitome of the cultured and urbane but was now terrified.

'Sir Patrick Jefferson,' said Carter. 'Well, well, I would ask you what you're doing here but I have a pretty good idea.' Jefferson clutched despairingly at the bag by his feet and darted glances around like a trapped animal. For a moment Carter thought he was going to try to run for it so he placed his arm firmly on the man's shoulder.

'Don't try anything silly, sir,' he said, reverting to formality. 'I think you need to hand that bag over to me.' Jefferson did not move and seemed incapable of speaking. Carter had to prise his grip off the straps of the bag, which he lifted on to the table. He unzipped it and lifted out a violin case. In turn he opened this case and removed the contents.

As soon as he saw the coat of arms on the back of the violin, he knew they'd at last found what they were looking for. He turned to Jefferson, who still said nothing; instead, at the sight of the Munsterhaven Strad, he burst into tears and cried like a baby. Another officer opened the case, which was stuffed with money.

'This one's still alive,' said one of the armed officers, referring to the one they'd shot.

'Good,' said Carter. 'Call an ambulance. We need him to lead us to the people behind this.'

In the interview room at the Met, a bedraggled, forlorn, but more composed Jefferson sat with his solicitor, faced by Carter and Newton. Newton was happy for Carter to lead the interrogation given the links with the Halifax case.

'What I can't understand,' began Carter, 'is why you got involved in this, seeing that you stood to inherit the violin anyway as soon as we found it. Or were you after it for yourself?'

It took a while for Jefferson to reply.

'No. I didn't want the Strad for myself; it was for the school. It was ours by right and . . .'

'That's what I mean,' interrupted Carter. 'Why didn't you just wait until we recovered it?'

Jefferson laughed cynically. 'You seem to have a lot of faith in your abilities. Look, the violin was stolen from Hamilton. The killers then have a problem, don't they?' He looked challengingly at the two detectives. 'How do they sell it? If it's put on the market, everyone knows it's stolen, so the only way is to secretly find some buyer who doesn't care about the criminal way it's been acquired and is prepared to keep it hidden for good. That's what we were afraid of: that it would disappear and we would never get it back.'

'Who's "we"?' asked Newton. 'You can't have organised this by yourself. Who was working with you?'

Jefferson appeared cowed by this and looked away.

'There's no point trying to protect anyone; you know we'll find out.'

'Lord Bromley, chair of governors at the school. He and I planned it, no one else. We were trying to help the school and now . . .' He looked down and despair returned to his face. 'We've disgraced it.'

'How did you contact this gang and what made you think they'd deal with you?'

'It was obvious after Martin had originally stolen the violin that he had contacts in that world. I didn't tell you, but he had a little office at the school and I went in and searched through his stuff. I found a list in a small notebook hidden behind a drawer. I went through, phoning the numbers, and eventually someone responded. They, of course, denied all knowledge of the violin, but said they could put me in touch with the people who had it. So it went on from there.'

Carter had an image of this posh principal of a music school negotiating with ruthless criminals. There was certainly a tougher, more worldly side to Jefferson than he'd imagined.

'But how could you afford to pay for it?'

'The problem they had is that because there would be so few buyers for an instrument like that, the price gets reduced. They couldn't hope to get what it would fetch in a legitimate sale. What we offered was a different kind of arrangement.'

'Which was?'

'We paid them a good price, but one we could afford, and then we would say that the violin had been mysteriously returned to us but we didn't know by whom. That way things could never be traced to them. If they sold it to anyone else, they ran the risk of the police hunting it down and eventually tracking it back to them. This way they were in the clear.'

'That's weak, though, isn't it? Very suspicious.'

'Maybe, but look at the history of these instruments: it's full of things disappearing and then being found again, sometimes without explanation. It's not at all impossible – and how would anyone prove otherwise? Lord Bromley's a banker; he arranged the financial side and there would be no trace of any transactions. We had a package prepared, which we were going to say had been left at the school. It doesn't matter how suspicious you were; you'd never have been able to prove anything.'

'So you had to pay one and a half million pounds for something that was your own anyway?'

'The alternative could have been losing it forever. Possessing a violin like that gives the school enormous prestige and if we ever fell on really hard times we could sell it for far more than we'd paid.'

'So what went wrong? What the hell happened at the railway station?'

Jefferson faced the detectives again.

'I don't know. I arrived as planned with the money. Their contact had the violin. It was all going according to the arrangements. I've no idea who that other person was. He was obviously from another gang.'

'You were lucky to escape alive,' said Carter.

'Yes I suppose so, but . . . at least the school will get the violin back and it won't have to pay anything, whatever happens to me.'

Carter found himself feeling a measure of respect for the misguided man whose career and life were now in ruins. At least his motives did not seem selfish; he'd done it all for the school. It was a touching, old-fashioned but ultimately reckless devotion, which had cost him dear.

Back in the office, Carter reported back on the events of the day.

'Bloody hell! Straight out of a TV cop show!' exclaimed Oldroyd.

'Yes, please don't say anything to Steph. It got pretty hairy at that station café.'

'OK, but what was going on? There must have been two gangs involved.'

'It looks that way. Newton's got his team working on it. Once they've identified the mystery gunman they should be able to link him with something.'

'So the Strad's safe?'

'Yes.'

'And Jefferson was trying to get it back for the Bloomsbury School?'

'That's his story. Don't think there's any reason to doubt it. We've pulled in this Lord Bromley character; what a toff he is, but not above some dodgy financial stuff to cover their tracks.'

'What a pair of fools! You can't believe it, can you? Men like that getting involved with underworld criminals. I suppose you could say at least they did it for something beyond their own personal gain.'

'That's what I thought. There's going to be an almighty scandal when all this becomes public, but it'll all blow over. They'll take the rap and at least the school has got its violin back. I had a look at it; can't believe a bit of polished wood and some strings are worth all that money.' He was learning how to tease his boss in return for the merciless way Oldroyd made fun of him.

'I see British philistinism is still very much alive. And you wouldn't say that if it was one of those guitars. What are they called? Stratospheres or something?' countered Oldroyd, deliberately playing ignorant.

'Stratocasters, sir!' laughed Carter.

'Yes. Anyway, look after it and get Newton's permission to bring it back up here for a while when you've finished down there.'

'Why's that then, sir?'

'I'm not sure. The problem is we're still stumped about the first murder and maybe it might give us a clue.'

Carter couldn't see how but never questioned his boss's intuition.

'OK. Hopefully we should get some information on that when we've tracked down all the members of these gangs.'

'I hope you're right, but I'm not sure. I assume Jefferson denies any involvement with Muller's murder.'

'Yes and with Hamilton's. By the way, it looks as if Elizabeth Knott was right about Hamilton: he had got out of his depth. He could've been playing one group off against another, trying to get the highest price, and someone got tired of it, or maybe the news got out that he had the Strad and then he was vulnerable to the attentions of some really dangerous people.'

'Something like that. It's sad – the greed seems to have got him too, doesn't it? He stole his own colleague's violin. But just a minute – you mentioned Elizabeth Knott. I wonder if she's behind this after all?'

'We've thought about that, sir. We're going back to question her again; she must know something about these gangs.'

'Good. And when you do, go with a search warrant and go through the place really thoroughly, including possible hiding places. I've an idea you might find something interesting.'

Oldroyd and Armitage gave up at five thirty and went to the nearest pub. They sat at the bar, Armitage with a pint of bitter and a packet of pork scratchings and Oldroyd with a tonic water as he had to drive back to Harrogate. They sat in silence for a while, Armitage munching on his ultra-fatty snack. There was an occasional crunch and snap as his teeth bit through the crozzled bits of pig's skin. The case was still so prominent in their minds that it was difficult to talk about anything else.

'The next problem,' said Armitage at last, 'is we're going to have the supers on our backs. Tomlinson's been very patient so far, for him, but now it looks as if all the business in London's just about cleared up, he'll be getting edgy, wondering why we still haven't solved the first murder.'

'I've not heard anything from Walker. Things must be quiet over there or he'd be wanting me back.'

'Lucky for you. I know what's going through Tomlinson's mind: he doesn't want to lose face. The Met solve their part of the crime, but we can't solve ours. West Riding police look stupid compared to the Londoners. And he has some justification for that; the press are bound to take against us at some point.'

'It's all very well, but down there it was all straightforward gangland stuff; they don't have this ridiculous mystery to solve, and it's just as bloody intransigent as ever.' Oldroyd took an angry swig of his tonic water and felt like slamming the glass on to the bar.

'Ah, Chief Inspectors!'

Armitage and Oldroyd turned round to see Frank Dancek, again dressed in his distinctive hat, coat and scarf. He was smiling amiably.

'I'm very glad to see you here. I was about to get in touch. Can I join you?'

He pulled up a bar stool and sat between them after ordering a whisky. 'I see you have your beer; the beer in Yorkshire is very good, but I prefer the whisky from Scotland. We drank spirits when I was young, you know, vodka, schnapps and things like that.'

'So what do you have to tell us?' asked Armitage.

The whisky arrived and Dancek took a sip. Oldroyd could hear carol singers outside in the cold street.

'Oh, it's not new information, I'm afraid. I wish I could help you more. I take it you have still not found who did that in the Chapel?'

'No.'

Dancek frowned and shook his head.

'I was going to ask if it is all right for me to leave Halifax for a while. I know you said that we should stay here while the investigation is going on but you see it is nearly Christmas and I am planning to see people I know in London. I was hoping to get the train soon, maybe tomorrow, and stay down there for Christmas.'

Armitage and Oldroyd exchanged glances.

'I assume you'll be back in the New Year?' asked Armitage.

'Oh indeed. Just a Christmas visit, you know.'

'That's fine, then.'

'Good.' Dancek held up his glass. 'Well, cheers and a Happy Christmas to you both.'

'Cheers.' The two detectives responded.

Outside the choir were singing 'Good King Wenceslas'. Oldroyd looked at Dancek.

'Good King Wenceslas. He was a Czech martyr, wasn't he? In the tenth century or something?'

Dancek looked bemused. 'Was he, Chief Inspector? I'm sure you're right. I've never been very good at history.'

Oldroyd didn't reply. The carol singing went on. Dancek finished his whisky. 'Well, I must be off. Again I wish you both a Happy Christmas.' He performed a formal little bow to each of the detectives and left the pub.

'Fancy a beer?' said Armitage. 'Oh, sorry, you're driving, aren't you.'

'Yes – and I'd better get off; there's snow forecast for later, the roads might get bad.'

He left Armitage at the bar and walked through the streets back towards the Red Chapel and the Piece Hall to where he'd parked his car. A band was playing carols in the Piece Hall and the Christmas market stalls were busy. The first flakes of snow were fluttering to the ground. He looked wistfully at the Red Chapel. The lights were on and it was functioning again. It looked exactly as it had when he'd rushed down the street to get to the concert. If only he could be transported back to that night and could see what had happened. As it was, vague notions hovered tantalisingly in his mind and sometimes he could almost sense an answer to the conundrum. But it remained elusively at the edge of his consciousness.

~

Elizabeth Knott sat stony-faced in her sitting room. Her plans were in ruins and she was now desperately considering how to save the situation. The tragic *Cavatina* from Beethoven's Op. 130 quartet was playing. She'd chosen it in an attempt to heroically, but rather theatrically, defy her sense of doom. She'd known what the risks were, so there was no point complaining. If she kept her nerve there was still a chance. Godetia, sensing a negative atmosphere, was curled up in one of her hiding places behind the large sofa.

The doorbell sounded and she knew who it would be. Sure enough, through the CCTV she could see a group of men and she knew they were police when she recognised Carter. She pressed the door release; the buzzer sounded and she got up slowly but resolutely to meet her fate.

Carter, standing outside with Newton and two detective constables, felt energetic and determined. It seemed at last that they were getting somewhere. Newton's team had done a brilliant job investigating the gangs involved. Nash, the man carrying the violin to Jefferson, was traced back to a group which was then busted by the Met in a dawn raid. These turned out to be the people who had murdered Hamilton. The gun that had been used to kill the cellist had been found. The real prize, though, was the trail left by the gunman who'd shot Nash and nearly killed Patrick Jefferson. A guard had been placed on the hospital ward to protect this man and his potentially crucial testimony.

Under questioning he'd agreed to inform in the hope of receiving a reduced sentence. Newton was delighted with the result: the ringleader turned out to be Novak Djaic. He'd long been pursued by the Met but, as with so many gang leaders throughout the world, the authorities had never been able to link him with any of the crimes for which they knew he was responsible. He was arrested and the trail from him led, as Oldroyd and Carter had suspected, to Elizabeth Knott. The jigsaw pieces had fitted together very satisfactorily and here they were to arrest the final piece. But although this piece was a small, relatively frail figure and not a gangland heavy, Carter believed that she was as tough as any of them and just as ruthless.

The door opened, and Elizabeth Knott greeted them with a smile. 'Well, gentlemen, it's my lucky day. Four good-looking, hunky men all visiting me at once. What have I done to deserve this?'

Newton was having none of this banter, and cut straight in without any niceties.

'Elizabeth Knott? We're here to question you about the murder of Terence Nash, the theft of a valuable violin and the murder of Martin Hamilton.'

'I knew Martin Hamilton and you've already questioned me about his murder. I had nothing to do with it. I've never heard of Terence Nash and I haven't got the stolen violin, as I told you before.'

'I think we need to sit down,' said Newton, and pushed ahead into the sitting room without being asked. Knott followed, looking tense but controlled. This time there was no offer of coffee. She sat in her chair and the detectives virtually surrounded her.

'You haven't got the violin because we've got it, but that doesn't mean that you didn't try to get it. Do you know a man named Novak Djaic?'

Carter observed her face. The expression was steely and determined. There was just a slight flickering of uncertainty in the eyes. He sensed the rapid calculations she was making about exactly what to say.

'Yes. He deals in artworks and instruments. I've invited him to social events.'

'Have you dealt with him in the past?'

'What do you mean?'

'Have you ever bought instruments from him?'

'Yes, occasionally.'

'And have you ever had reason to believe that those instruments were acquired illegally?'

'No, never. I told the police before: all my instruments have been purchased legitimately.'

'Yesterday we arrested Novak Djaic and we're charging him with the murder of Terence Nash. The murderer was acting on his authority. He's in hospital but we have his testimony.'

Knott said nothing.

'Djaic claims he was instructed by you to get this violin. We know the story of what happened. The gang that Nash was involved in were contacted by Martin Hamilton, who had stolen the violin in Halifax. He was trying to get a higher price for it than they were prepared to pay so they decided on a different approach. One of their hitmen shot Hamilton and took the instrument. This gang then arranged to sell it to Patrick Jefferson of the Bloomsbury School, but Djaic must have had informers in the Nash gang who told him about the deal. He positioned his gunman to kill Nash and Jefferson and take the violin – and it would have worked had we not also got a tip-off. The violin would then have come to you, I assume for a pretty large sum. So there we are. It's a nasty story of violence and greed, isn't it?'

Carter continued to observe Knott as she listened to Newton's narrative. Her face became tighter and grimmer as the net encircled her.

'I had no involvement in any kind of criminal activity.'

'Of course you didn't *directly*. People like you always have their dirty work done by other people. But I think in this case we'll be able to prove at the very least that you were prepared to receive goods that you knew were stolen.'

'Djaic is a criminal and a liar; why should anyone believe anything he says?'

'Is he? Just now you admitted he was someone you'd done business with; so did you know he was a criminal, then?'

'I have no more to say. Are you arresting me for something? If so I need to call my solicitor.'

'We'll come back to that later.' Newton produced a sheet of paper. 'I have a warrant to search these premises as we believe there may be stolen property here.'

Knott laughed derisively. 'That's ridiculous; you won't find anything. How many times do I have to tell you that every instrument is paid for; I have receipts for them.'

'Good, well, we'll need to see them, but I think we'll start with your collection. I understand you store it upstairs.'

'Yes, by all means.'

Knott got up, led them out of the room and up the stairs. Godetia appeared from behind the sofa and followed them silently. Knott opened up the collection room and the detectives went in, Carter again noticing the bars on the windows. Knott switched on the lights and the instruments were illuminated in all their stunning variety and beauty.

'Someone tried to rob you recently,' said Newton.

'Yes, but I managed to disarm him. He was a chancer acting alone, according to the police.'

'Yes, we couldn't link him to any of the gangs.' Newton was looking around. 'This is a pretty impressive set up in terms of security. Is everything stored here in this room?'

'Yes, all in here.'

Carter looked around. He felt that Oldroyd was right: there must be other things that she was concealing, things she had to hide, but where? He felt a furry body brush against his legs and there was a meowing sound. Knott turned quickly to look.

'Godetia! Goodness me, how did that cat get in here? Godetia, out!' She bent down to pick the animal up, but it escaped her clutches, ran across the room and jumped on to an antique wooden table. It then stretched up on to the wooden panelling and started to scratch with its paws. Knott flew across.

'Godetia! Stop it! Get down!'

The cat pulled its paws down, and bounced them on a corner of the panelling. Suddenly and almost silently, a panel slid across to reveal a hidden compartment. The cat jumped down; Knott screamed and collapsed on to a chair. For the first time, Carter saw defeat in her contorted face.

'Well, well,' said Newton. 'What have we here? I take it you weren't going to show us this part of your collection?'

Knott did not reply. Carter saw that she was weeping. Newton examined the concealed button in the corner of the panel, then he reached into the recess and pulled out a battered violin case. He opened it and took out the instrument it contained. Carter was astonished to see the Munsterhaven coat of arms.

'I presume this is worth a bit and I wonder why you've got it hidden away?'

'Sir, I think I know what it is. DCI Oldroyd told me what we might find.' He carefully took the violin from Newton and examined it. 'I think this is the missing Munsterhaven Strad. Apparently it was stolen a long time ago in Vienna from its owner and it's never been seen since.'

Newton went across to the distraught Elizabeth Knott. He saw that she was broken, and so he spoke to her quite gently. 'I think we'd better go back downstairs; you have some explaining to do.'

Carter had to help her back down the stairs and into her chair in the living room. The guilty Godetia was nowhere to be seen.

'So how did you acquire that violin?'

'I didn't; it was my father.' She spoke very quietly. All the fire had gone. 'I don't know where he got it, but of course he knew it had been stolen.'

'So that's why it had to be kept hidden?'

'Yes.'

'So you already had a Munsterhaven Strad. Why did you want another and risk all this for it?'

She looked up with a tear-stained face. She smiled grimly and shook her head.

'You'll never understand. Can't you see? I would have been the only person in the world to possess two Munsterhaven instruments; the first person since the count himself to own more than one.'

'But you could never have displayed them.'

'That doesn't matter. I would have known they were there, in that recess. I could've taken them out and looked at them whenever I wanted. And now . . .' Her face twisted in agony. 'I've lost them both. What would Daddy have said?'

'So she was trying to add another Munsterhaven to her collection?' asked Oldroyd as Carter reported back to him.

'Yes, sir, even though she'd have had to keep them permanently hidden.'

'Good God; she would have spent all that money on something stuck in a hole in the wall?'

'So it appears, sir. Weird, isn't it?'

'Yes, human nature never ceases to amaze me with its strangeness. So what will happen to her? Has Newton got evidence to link her to the murder?'

'I'm not sure about that, but she'll probably go down at least for receiving stolen goods. DCI Newton's got a lot of work on now. He's got to liaise with the Austrian police. They've presumably got an unsolved case from the 1960s and he's also got to get the violin properly authenticated, but that's just a formality. Even I can see it's one of those Munsterhaven things.'

'It's all blown up at the Bloomsbury School: all in the papers; principal and chair of governors both resigned. I suppose they'll go down too.'

'Yes.'

'It'll depend on how leniently the court looks upon them because of their motives and the fact that they didn't use any violence.'

'That's what I thought; I felt quite sorry for that Jefferson bloke – he nearly got himself killed messing about with those thugs.'

'Ah, nice to hear the lad's got a heart.'

'Yes, sir. I'm as soft as anything deep down, you know. Wouldn't hurt a fly.'

'Well, I'm glad to hear it. At least the school will get the Strad back and it'll be played by someone.'

'Unless that RNATN still kick up a fuss about it, though I have to hand it to them: their tip-off was sound. We couldn't have intercepted the operations of those gangs without them.'

'That Abel Ashkenazi must have been building up his intelligence for years. He must know more than anyone else alive about the people who deal illicitly in artworks and stuff. I don't think they'll take this one any further. It can't be returned to the family and they can't suggest it's not being used in a worthy manner if students can play it.' He stopped and thought for a moment. 'Actually, that's given me a bit of an idea: maybe Ashkenazi might know a bit more about Muller and his Strad than he's told his people in London.'

'Maybe, sir, but I don't know how that would help.'

'You never know. Sometimes when you're in the dark you have to try as many ways as you can to get some light, however unpromising they might seem. The fact is, after all that's happened we're still not much further on up here.'

'No, sir.'

'And everyone you've arrested down there has denied any involvement in Muller's murder?'

'Absolutely: Knott, Jefferson, Djaic and all the heavies in the gangs; they all swear they had nothing to do with it. They insist they didn't get involved until Hamilton arrived in London with that violin. Added to that, I think we've eliminated Christopher Downton, which – apart from the Halifax people, as it were – leaves Stringer and Robson, but then we're back to the old problem: they may have had a motive but they couldn't have fired the shot, so they hired someone – and that still doesn't seem likely does it?'

'No,' muttered Oldroyd, with the utter weariness of a man who has gone round in circles so many times and come to the same conclusions. 'Well, at least we've narrowed it down. And up here I'm pretty sure Shaw and Taylor are out of it.'

'They were drug running, weren't they, sir? And all that music stuff was a front? So I was right: I suggested that, remember?'

'Yes, Andy, I do, though I don't know how serious you were at the time.'

'Aw come on, sir, credit where it's due and all that.'

'All right. So we'll have you back up here now. Have you asked Newton about the violin?'

'Yes, sir. He was a bit surprised, but he said it was OK as long as it's returned soon. It's a piece of evidence for the trials, which are coming up.'

'That's ironic, isn't it?' mused Oldroyd. 'It was the cause of those crimes and now it's going to help to put all the guilty ones away. I wonder if there is anything in this curse business?'

Carter laughed. 'You don't really believe that, sir.'

'No, I suppose not. Anyway, get yourself back up here as soon as you can; we've still got a crime to solve.'

'OK, sir.'

The call ended and Oldroyd felt a deep tiredness. He had to tell Armitage to contact Abel Ashkenazi in New York and try to get some information. Then he needed to go back to Harrogate. He had to speak to his wife. Hopefully he could make her feel better and bring about some reconciliation between her and Louise. Maybe when he'd done that, and rested, he would be refreshed and finally able to see the solution. He didn't feel optimistic about any of it.

Eleven

The 'Lautenschlager' Stradivarius of 1719 was bequeathed by Dr Alois Maria Lautenschlager to the Universität der Künste Berlin in 1943. It was in the possession of violinist Gustav Havemann at the end of the war but he was living in the Russian zone and the violin was taken by two Russian officers. The Russian National Collection of Musical Instruments in Moscow has a 1719 Stradivarius violin acquired in 1946, which appears to match this missing violin. However, there is currently no suggestion that it should be returned to Berlin.

Armitage was already in a lugubrious mood before the phone rang in his office. It was DCS Tomlinson, and Armitage's heart sank. He'd been expecting this. He knew that his boss was not happy with the progress they were making in the case and he was probably about to get a blast from his superior. And, yes, he did want to know what was happening, so for the umpteenth time he went over the case with him.

'And you say all of those arrested in London deny any involvement in the murder up here?'

'According to the Met.'

'So what's bloody going on, then?' Tomlinson's barking voice was painful on Armitage's ears. 'I thought we were sure it was all connected? Don't we just need to put in the final piece of the jigsaw?'

'Well, that's easier said than done. There might be a motive, but there's no forensic evidence to link any of them to the murder scene.' He didn't want to remind Tomlinson that they still didn't even know how the murderer had escaped from the building, never mind who it was.

'Look, you need to pull your finger out on this. I've got DCS Walker on my back wanting to know how long I'm going to need their man Oldroyd, not to mention the press which is having a field day with "Mystery Murder Still Foxes Police" and all that rubbish. We're beginning to look stupid. I mean there're two of you on this case, both with years of experience, and you can't crack it.'

'Well, we're doing our best,' said Armitage weakly.

'OK, well, if you don't get results soon we'll have to have a review of things.'

Armitage knew that that meant the humiliation of being removed from the case and someone else being put in charge. Tomlinson rang off and Armitage wearily returned the phone to its base and put his head in his hands. He'd never been involved in anything as difficult as this. He was relying on his old friend to produce some of his famous magic to get them out of this hole. The phone went again. This time it was an outside call.

'Chief Inspector Armitage.'

'Oh, Chief Inspector, I'm glad I've got you.'

Armitage's heart sank again but for a different reason. It was Gertrude Dobson. She was the last thing he needed at this point.

'Yes, Miss Dobson,' he said, through gritted teeth, 'what can I do for you?'

'Well, you see, I've remembered something else from that night, you know the one when that poor man was murdered.'

Well, what other night would you be ringing me about? thought Armitage impatiently.

'Now, I don't want you to feel you have to come out here again to talk to me, though it would be very nice if you came and that other nice chief inspector and his young sergeant. I'm always pleased to see people because you see it can get a bit lonely here and . . .'

'Well, Miss Dobson,' said Armitage, cutting in rather abruptly. 'I'm very sorry to interrupt you, but I'm rather busy today so if you could just tell me what it is you rang me for.'

'Oh, yes, I'm terribly sorry; I do go on a bit I know. Well, you see, he didn't lead the quartet in, and he always does that.'

'Who didn't, and what do you mean, Miss Dobson?'

'Mr Dancek; he's on the committee and he always likes to lead the quartet from the stairs to where they play, but that night he didn't. I think it was Mr Howarth who led them on.'

Armitage tried to remain patient.

'I know it doesn't sound very important, but you said if we remembered anything that was unusual I was to let you know, so I thought I'd ring and, well, that's all really.'

'Thank you very much, Miss Dobson; I do appreciate your help. Now all the best and I'll say goodbye.' He put the phone down before she could get him involved in anything further.

As Armitage was besieged by the serious and trivial, Oldroyd was making the journey yet again from Harrogate to Halifax. He was giving Carter a lift. Today it again looked very different to the evening when he'd driven anxiously through the darkness and rain to get to the concert in time. Now it was sunny and clear with a covering of snow on the fields. The gritstone walls showed black against the white. Sheep were eating from yellowish clumps of hay put out by the farmers.

'It's a lovely day, sir,' said Carter, who actually felt glad to be back in Yorkshire and looking over the wide sweeping landscapes he'd learned to love.

'Yes.'

Oldroyd, of course, also enjoyed such scenes but he was distracted by memories of another telephone conversation he'd had with Julia the previous evening when he'd arrived home exhausted. He never found those conversations easy. Ever since they'd separated he'd been trying to find a way back into her affections, to somehow convince her that he was sorry and his feelings for her hadn't changed. So far he'd failed; he knew she didn't trust him. So many times before they broke up, they'd sat down and talked about their marriage and he'd promised not to spend virtually all his time working. But he'd broken his promise every time as soon as he was involved in some case that was particularly demanding. It was the old cliché: devoted to his job as well as to his wife and he wanted both, like having a wife and a mistress.

This time he'd called her. He never knew what response he'd get, so he felt it was much easier if there was a reason to ring. He could ask her how she was after she was upset the previous time and – this was the difficult bit – he had to discuss Louise again and where she was going to spend Christmas. He was nervous as the phone was ringing.

'Hi.' He tried to start off brightly when she answered.

'Oh, hi.' Her response was downbeat and his spirits sank. She never seemed pleased to hear his voice.

'How are you? I just thought I'd ring and, you know, see how you are.'

'Well, I'm not bad; it was a relief to get to the end of term. So what's she up to at the moment?'

'She's gone out to meet a friend at the Bell.'

'And what's she using for money? I suppose you've given her some.'

'Well, not much. She did try to get a job in a bar but no luck.'

'Huh, I've heard that one before. You're a soft touch, Jim. She'll never learn the value of money if you keep giving in to her.'

'Well, I don't know; this is the first time this term. Anyway, I was ringing to sort out Christmas. She says she wants to stay here and go with me to Alison's on Christmas Day – and before you say anything, I haven't said anything to her about it, or put any pressure on.'

There was a pause. Oldroyd knew this was a blow to her, although she quickly pretended it wasn't.

'OK, fine by me. I don't particularly want to spend Christmas arguing with her anyway. Robert and Andrea will be here.'

'Are you sure you're all right about it?'

'Yes.'

'Look, she'll come round, you know she will. We'll get it sorted before she goes back to Oxford.'

'Maybe. She'll have to come back here at some point; all her bags are here. Is she planning to do any work before she goes back?'

'I've no idea. Look, it's no good discussing all this on the phone, why don't we meet up? I'll come over to Chapel Allerton if you like.'

'I haven't got time before Christmas, Jim; I've too much shopping and stuff to do. Maybe afterwards, in the New Year.'

He was disappointed. 'OK, well, Merry Christmas, then, if I don't speak to you again.'

'And to you.'

'Bye.'

'Bye.'

Oldroyd frowned at the memory as they drove past Shibden and he tried to put it out of his mind and focus on work.

'Well done, by the way. You've done a great job down there; I'm sure Newton was very impressed. If you ever fancy going back to the Met I'm sure he'd welcome you.'

'Thanks, sir. Can't see that happening, though. I think we're settled up here, you know, me and Steph. She sends her regards, by the way.'

'That's nice.'

They arrived in Halifax and spent the morning with Armitage completing yet another trawl through the same evidence without success. They went for a long lunch with Armitage to a pub and ate pie and peas. On the way back to police HQ, Oldroyd noticed that Carter was carrying a bag.

'What's in there, Andy?'

'It's Muller's violin in its case, sir. You told me to bring it back from London. I daren't put it down and leave it anywhere.'

Oldroyd had forgotten about the Strad.

'We should put that in security when we get back,' said Armitage.

'Not just yet,' replied Oldroyd. 'You go back, Sam. Andy and I are going down to the Red Chapel to have another look.'

Armitage looked at Oldroyd as if he was sorry for him.

'OK, if you think it'll do any good. We've been through that place so many times.'

'I know. Anyway, we'll see you back there.'

Oldroyd and Carter walked on in silence until they got to the Red Chapel. The bar was closed but they sat at one of the tables. Oldroyd sat back in the chair, thinking. Suddenly he heard a wonderful sound in the distance. The last concert of the year was taking place that evening and the string quartet was practising upstairs. He would have probably gone to that concert if he wasn't so bound up in this wretched, ridiculous business.

'Andy, get the violin out. Let me have a look at it.'

Carter got the case out of his bag and carefully removed the instrument. Oldroyd held it again and examined it intently. Could this masterpiece somehow give him the answer? He stared at it but nothing came to him and after a while he handed it back to Carter, who looked at it himself with curiosity. Although he'd no interest in that kind of music, it was impossible not to admire the craftsmanship.

'You know, sir, it's amazing to think that there are other violins in the world that look exactly like this and you wouldn't be able to tell the difference between them.'

Oldroyd sat up in his chair.

'What did you say?' His manner had completely changed and Carter was a little startled even though he was used to Oldroyd's mercurial changes of mood.

'Well, that there'll be others like it, because Stradivari . . . didn't he make, you know, make a few all the same?'

Oldroyd slumped back into his chair and stared ahead as if in shock.

'What's wrong, sir?'

'My God, Andy, my God!' Oldroyd was almost whispering.

Here we go for a dose of the dramatics, thought Carter.

'What, sir?'

'It's one of the oldest tricks in the book, and I've missed it!'

'What is, sir?'

Oldroyd slapped himself on the forehead. 'I've been a complete idiot. Of course! There was only one way it could have been done and they did it under my nose. I was here! And Stuart Atkinson unwittingly gave me another clue that I completely failed to see. Remember what he said about the way Dancek spoke!'

He banged his fist on his knee and then sprang to his feet.

'Come on. If I'm right we've been looking in the wrong place all along, as I thought. Why didn't I trust my instincts? We've been searching in the world of big money and ruthless international criminals, but the answer's much closer to home and we've overlooked it. We'll have to be quick.'

To Carter's surprise Oldroyd ran out of the Chapel and through the streets back to West Yorkshire Police HQ. Carter followed him, finding it hard to keep up. They burst into Armitage's office and interrupted him eating a piece of his wife's chocolate cake brought from home. He looked up, startled.

'Sam, get Immigration on the phone, quick!'

Armitage spluttered cake out of his mouth.

'All right. What's this all about, then?'

'I'll tell you in a minute.'

Armitage looked up the number and dialled it. He handed the phone to Oldroyd.

'Hello, Chief Inspector Oldroyd, West Riding Police. A colleague of mine, Chief Inspector Armitage, made an enquiry recently about a Frank Dancek, came to Britain in the 1970s. You remember? Good! Now, this is very important. I want you to put that name, Dancek, through your system again and see if anything else comes up.'

There was a pause as Carter and Armitage looked on quizzically and Oldroyd tapped his foot impatiently on the floor.

'It has? Right, give me the details.' Oldroyd smiled as he scribbled something down. 'Thank you; that's been very helpful.' He put the phone down. 'Come on, let's go.'

'Where, Jim?' asked Armitage.

'Dancek's flat – quickly – they might still be there.'

'They? Who's they?'

'I'll explain later, come on.'

They drove at speed through the streets to King Cross. Oldroyd leaped out of the car leaving the door wide open and rapped at the door of Dancek's flat. There was no answer.

'We'll have to break in, Andy.'

Carter put his shoulder to the door and soon splintered the frame.

'Have a quick look round in here,' said Oldroyd, pointing to the kitchen and living room. 'But I don't think you'll find anything. I'm going into the bedroom.'

Armitage went into the kitchen and Carter followed his boss, who went straight to the bedroom wardrobe and started looking through the clothes.

'Yes!' he shouted triumphantly. 'Sam!'

Armitage hurried up, panting, and Oldroyd pulled some hangers out of the wardrobe. He stood holding up two identical jackets, shirts and trousers.

'This is how Dancek was dressed the night of the concert; and here's another set of clothes exactly the same.'

Carter was starting to see what Oldroyd was driving at, but it still didn't make sense to him.

'But, sir, we've been through this; didn't you say it was impossible for anyone to dress up like Dancek and impersonate him?'

Oldroyd laughed.

'Yes, and why did I say that?'

'Because even if someone was dressed in the same clothes, Atkinson and the others in the bar would have realised it wasn't Dancek because they had a close-up view of his face.'

'Right, but what I failed to see, dunderheaded fool that I am, is that it wasn't just anybody dressed as Dancek.'

'Who was it, then?' asked a still bemused Armitage.

'It was his twin brother: there are two of them and they must be identical.'

They looked at Oldroyd across the table with expressions of quiet admiration. There was no fear or anguish, only a calm acceptance. The officers who'd arrested them on the train to London had encountered no opposition. Armitage, Carter and two DCs were also in the interview room.

Oldroyd stared back. Even though they were in their sixties, it was impossible to tell the difference between them. But they didn't seem like ruthless criminals. He composed his face into a rueful smile; for some reason he found it impossible to be harsh with them.

'Well,' he began, 'I have an idea this is about something that happened a long time ago. Am I right?'

The twins exchanged glances, and then a few words in German.

Frank began to speak in English. 'Yes, Chief Inspector, you're right. We'll tell you everything. You deserve to know.' There were the first signs of emotion on his face. 'Her name was Helga, Helga Weber.' The Maiden! thought Oldroyd.

'She was our sister,' blurted the other twin in a more pronounced German accent and then suddenly burst into tears. Frank put his hand on his brother's arm and waited for him to calm down before continuing.

'We're not from the old Czechoslovakia, Chief Inspector, we're German.'

Oldroyd had suspected this since his meeting with Dancek in the pub. The spirits Dancek had said they'd drunk when he was young sounded more German than Czech and his knowledge of Czech history seemed poor.

'We were born in East Berlin just after the war. There were three of us: my real name is Franz Weber, my brother's name is Helmut and our younger sister was called Helga. We were born into a very musical family. My father conducted the Kreuzberg Symphony Orchestra and my mother was a talented pianist. All through our childhood we are listening to music and singing together. As you know, I learned to play the cello. My brother learned the viola and Helga the violin. Our father played the violin too. We used to play quartets together, just simple pieces, you know, but it was a wonderful thing to create that sound.'

He looked at Oldroyd.

'I know you appreciate how special is the string quartet, Inspector.'

'Indeed. Please continue.' Oldroyd shifted in his chair. He felt strangely moved and excited. It was obviously going to be a long and fascinating story.

'Helga was by far the most talented of us and when she was eighteen she won a place at the Hanns Eisler music school. This was 1968. She was two years younger than us, brilliant, beautiful and also dangerously political. It was the year of the Paris student uprising and the Prague Spring. A lot of young people in East Germany were restless. Helga started to attend meetings where speakers called for greater freedom. The Stasi started to watch her. When she applied for permission to travel and perform in the West, she was refused, unlike other musicians at the school who were orthodox, like Reinhard Meyer.'

Oldroyd noticed a spasm of hatred cross his face.

'Meyer was also a brilliant violinist and he fell in love with her. They saw each other for a while. He was handsome and very impressive, but she found him cold, arrogant and very defensive of the regime. I saw them having furious rows about politics. He always supported the government, said socialism had to be defended. As if what we had was socialism.' Dancek shook his head. 'It was more that his family benefited from the system. They were all high-ranking state officials with privileges the rest of us didn't have. Eventually Helga left him for Gerd. Gerhard Steinbach was a cellist and he shared Helga's radicalism.

'We didn't see much of Meyer after that. We used to joke that he was sulking and lovesick somewhere, but he must have been furious and dangerously jealous and stung by her rejection of him.

'Things went quiet for a while. They all got their diplomas and Meyer got straight into the first violins of the Berliner Sinfonie; that was family influence at work again. Helga was top student at the Hanns Eisler. She passed everything with distinction, but she wasn't given a job and neither was Gerd. I'm sure Meyer used his influence to make it harder for them. She languished at home, depressed and frustrated. The only work she had was giving a few lessons to children of families we knew. My father suffered, too. He lost his position with the orchestra. He knew why but he didn't hold it against his daughter; he thought she was brave. He wasn't worried about himself at his age, more about what the future held for us. I think it was a mercy he died before what happened.'

Dancek paused, sighed and put a hand to his forehead. He looked exhausted with the effort of reliving these painful events.

'Meyer hadn't given up the idea of getting Helga back. He turned up at our flat in Kreuzberg several times. I was still at home. I was studying engineering and I'd not been granted a flat of my own. He pleaded with her to speak with him. Once or twice she let him in but it always ended in a terrible row and she slammed the door after him. I think he must have been offering to smooth the way for her to get a position in the music world if she went back to him. But there was no chance of that. She hated him and what he stood for even more as time passed.

'Eventually, she and Gerd decided to try to escape to the West. They contacted a highly secret organisation that circulated details of people it could trust about methods of escape. Highly dangerous, every attempt was risking your life. They got them false papers. Helga was to be disguised as a young boy. They took me into their confidence; they needed help and support.'

Oldroyd looked at the brother.

'Why not Helmut too?'

Helmut looked down and his distress appeared to increase. With a great effort he spoke.

'Inspector, I am not as clever as my brother and sister. I am leaving school and going into the army.' His English was not as fluent as his brother's.

'The army?' said Oldroyd in some surprise. Frank spoke for his brother.

'I know that sounds strange, Inspector. We talked about it as a family. We thought if Helmut joined the army it might take the pressure off us all. The authorities would approve; we would be showing that we supported the regime, at least in public.' He laid a hand on his brother's arm again. 'It was Helmut's sacrifice.'

'So because he was in the army she felt she couldn't talk to Helmut?'

'It would have been too dangerous for him to know anything. He would never have willingly said anything but if his superiors got to know that he was keeping a secret like that, well, he would have been shot straight away.

'I helped them to perfect their disguises. They had to be superb to trick the officials at the Tränenpalast.'

'What's that?'

Dancek's face took on an expression of intense loathing. Oldroyd saw a deep and ancient pain in his eyes.

'The Palace of Tears, Chief Inspector. It's a horrible kind of annexe, I think you call it, built on to the Bahnhof Friedrichstrasse in the centre of Berlin. Everyone travelling back to the West had to gather there and have their details checked before going through to the station platform. It got its name from the grief of people saying goodbye to their relatives who lived in the East, wondering when they'd see each other again.' He shuddered. 'If anywhere is ever haunted it'll be that place.'

Oldroyd looked around the room. There was total silence; everyone was gripped by the story.

'The day came, Inspector. They'd made all the preparations and then had to say goodbye. It was a terrible moment; we knew we might never see them again. We'd told my mother what they were planning. I know she understood why Helga felt she had to go, but her anguish was . . .' He shook his head and for a moment couldn't continue.

'I walked part of the way with them. I'll never forget the feeling, as if everyone we passed knew what was going on and would run to tell the Stasi. I dropped back when we got near the station. My stomach was churning. I can't imagine what they were feeling. From across the street I saw them enter the Tränenpalast, and that was the . . . last time I . . .' He sobbed quietly to himself and a uniformed constable handed him a tissue. He wiped his eyes and continued.

'There were lots of people milling around, the sound of trains rumbling over the bridge across the Spree and into the station. I didn't know what to do with myself. I didn't know when their train would leave, even if they managed to get on it. I assumed it would be a long time before we found out what happened. But it turned out we had the most accursed luck.' Now he sounded angry.

'I walked back home feeling completely drained and when I arrived I found Mother very agitated. Meyer had been at the house, this day of all days, asking to see Helga, asking where she was. It sounded as if he already had suspicions. When he saw Mother so upset it must have confirmed them.

'We don't know all the details of what happened at the station, but it seems they got as far as the platform before someone raised the alarm. Guards came running. Helga and Gerd knew they'd been discovered but they weren't going to give up so easily. There was a train moving slowly out of the station. Gerd grabbed Helga's hand and they jumped on to the buffers at the back. It was desperate, but they clung on and the train gathered speed. Shots were fired at them but missed. They would now have to jump off the train when it got to the West and try to dodge any guards. They never got the chance. The guards at the Friedrichstrasse had radioed ahead, and when the train passed near to the Wall they were shot at from a guard tower. They were both hit and fell on to the line. They died from the wounds later that day.'

The PC gasped; a violent surge of anger went through Frank Dancek. 'Those bloody Stasi pigs just left them there to bleed to death,' he shouted and slammed his fist on the table. 'They crawled off the track, but couldn't get any further. When the Stasi came to remove them they were locked together in each other's arms, dead.' He paused again and gave a big sigh. He was shaking.

'Two armed Stasi officers came to our apartment next day and as soon as we saw them we knew it was over and Helga and Gerd were probably dead. One of them just announced their deaths in an arrogant, contemptuous manner, telling us our daughter and sister had died with her traitor lover trying to escape to the degenerate West; the same old miserable clichés. Then they came into the house and searched it for incriminating evidence, but they found nothing. We were too careful for that.

'It was horrible, almost unendurable; all our hopes dashed. But it didn't take me long to work out what had happened. I knew straight away it was Meyer. I think he must have spied on Helga, stalked her, as we say now, without her knowing. Maybe he was trying to find something to blackmail her with. He must have somehow seen enough to make him think that something was being planned. When she wasn't at home that day, he alerted his contacts in the Stasi. We found out later from other sources that it was definitely him who tipped them off.'

Oldroyd saw that Helmut, who'd been almost silent throughout the account, was getting more and more agitated.

'Were you in Berlin at this time?' Oldroyd asked him.

'Yes.' It was a struggle for him to speak.

'And did you know what had happened?'

'Yes.'

'How?'

Helmut gave his brother an agonised look.

'I shot them.'

There were gasps from the people in the room.

'What!?'

'I . . . I didn't know it was them until later. I am stationed in Berlin. I am on duty at the guard tower on the Wall. We all had to do it; it was terrible. If anyone is trying to escape we are told to shoot to kill. If they thought we tried to miss, we would be shot ourselves. The captain I am with, he is a fanatic. We got word that two people are trying to escape on the back of a train. The line is going past our tower and the captain orders me to shoot. I . . . I . . .' His voice was starting to break, but he stumbled on. 'I still try to shoot low, to hit but not kill, just to wound and I am doing this but they still . . .'

He collapsed in tears and could not say any more. The grief was as raw and intense as forty years before. Frank put his arm across Helmut's shoulders and continued.

'Imagine what it is like to kill your own sister, Chief Inspector, and in those circumstances.'

Oldroyd thought of his beloved sister Alison.

'What happened next?'

'We were utterly shattered of course. My mother never recovered. She died within a year; that bastard killed her too. We never told her that Helmut shot them; that would have been too much.

'Helmut was expected to carry on, but he got sick. In the end they let him out of the army. I think they knew it was too much to bear. He came home. Our grief was intense, but we were also angry. We wanted revenge. Our determination was terrible; we didn't care what happened to us.'

'What happened to Meyer?'

Frank smiled bitterly. 'He disappeared, the coward. He must have known we were after him. There was nothing for him in Berlin now that Helga was dead. He must have used his contacts to move away and start a new life, probably somewhere like Leipzig, and with a different name.'

'Hans Muller?'

'Exactly.'

'But you couldn't find him?'

'No, we didn't know his new name then. We were completely frustrated and despairing. When our mother died we decided to leave Berlin too and escape to the West. It was like a tribute to our sister: if she couldn't make it then maybe we could. We were young, reckless with grief and anger but resourceful. We managed to get into Czechoslovakia and then to England. It was a relief to get to the free world, Chief Inspector. Then we decided to split up; we were living under false names and we didn't want to draw attention to ourselves, being twins. Helmut stayed in London. There were plenty of jobs in the markets; he worked at Covent Garden. I came up to Yorkshire and worked for engineering firms. Everything went quiet for years and years.

'It's curious, neither of us married; we were scarred inside, I suppose, and we had too many secrets that we could never share. But life went on. It seemed as if we would carry it all to the grave. Then one day a few months ago I was with Mr Watson, the secretary of the Music Society. He showed me the programme for the new season. There was a picture of the Schubert Quartet. I couldn't believe it: I recognised him immediately, even though of course he was much older. I went on to their website, searched around and it all fitted together. It was him. He'd come to England after the Wall came down in 1989; lots of people started to come to the West then. It was much better money, more opportunities. He also had secrets to hide, which could have come out now he didn't have the Stasi to protect him. He'd formed a quartet. I knew the Schubert Quartet, of course, but I'd never heard them perform live or even seen a picture. It's ironic; I had lots of their recordings, but none of the sleeves and cases had a photograph of them. I'd been listening to him play for years without knowing it was him. And he had this wonderful, rare violin. I started to wonder: how did he get that? And I realised it was probably given to him as a reward for what he did, for his loyalty. I tried to find out more about it. I called an expert at the V&A, and he confirmed that there had been a violin belonging to a Jewish family in Berlin. I knew it was the same one and that made everything worse; he was playing on an instrument stolen from a family who were murdered.

'I spoke to Helmut; we planned what we were going to do. It was also ironic that they were playing *Death and the Maiden*. It seemed a good omen to us, you know; we were getting revenge for our dead maiden, our beautiful . . .' He had to pause again as his voice faltered. 'And also for the poor Jewish people who were sent to the death camp.'

'No one around here knew I had a twin brother. He got the gun in London. A Dragunov is not difficult to get; Europe's been flooded with them since the Eastern Bloc is breaking up. We dressed identically, and I smuggled him into the Red Chapel earlier in the day, when there was no one around. He was in position up in the gantry when you all took your seats in the hall. I didn't lead out the quartet as I usually do; didn't want to risk Meyer recognising me.'

Here, Armitage shook his head. Miss Dobson's information had not been so useless after all: it *had* been significant that the man they believed to be Dancek hadn't performed his usual function.

'I also kept out of the artists' room. Helmut waited until the end of the slow movement; that seemed the right time to take justice.'

His sister Alison was right as usual, thought Oldroyd; there had been a reason why he was shot at that moment.

'I made sure I was sitting by the stairs and, as you saw, Chief Inspector, I ran off before anyone else after the shot.'

'Then you swapped over and Helmut ran out of the building.'

'Yes: I followed close behind him on the stairs and kept out of sight up against the wall at the bottom. While Helmut was speaking to Stuart Atkinson, I slipped into the toilets and then when I heard you talking I came out and pretended to be out of breath. It was easy to say that I'd just come back into the building when the police arrived. Everyone is in shock and nobody remembers exactly who was where. Helmut stayed in hiding at my flat until we thought we could escape. We were going to London for Christmas where we wouldn't be noticed. Helmut would stay there, I would return and everything would be back to normal. We knew all the suspicion would fall on the Munsterhaven Strad. Helmut deliberately waited until Meyer had put the violin down before shooting so that it would look as if the instrument was being protected and the motive was something to do with that violin. We were helped a lot by Martin Hamilton stealing it. We couldn't believe our luck. It looked as if it was all part of the same plan and you were certain to think that robbery was the motive. I tried to push you in the same direction, confuse you, by saying I'd seen Hamilton coming out of that instrument shop in the Piece Hall, but I hadn't. It seemed to work until . . .'

He looked at Oldroyd and smiled.

'It would have worked, but for you, Chief Inspector. If you hadn't come that night things might have been different. But it was too much to expect that you would miss the Schubert Quartet. I'm sorry that you never heard the last two movements. Meyer was a great player. It is a great loss to music.' He frowned. 'But not to humanity.'

Frank stopped. Everything went quiet. Oldroyd took a deep breath, trying to take in all he'd been told.

'It was a risky plan, though, wasn't it? What if someone had seen you together on the stairs?'

'Unlikely, Chief Inspector; no one hangs around on those stairs while a concert is on. When we got to the bottom it was only a second for me to get into the toilets.'

'What if there'd been someone in there?'

Dancek glanced at his brother. 'We took our chance. There were several ways in which things could have gone wrong, but Helmut and I were clear about a number of things. We had to avenge our sister and Helmut had to be the one to do it after what had happened. We believed it was justice; we tried to avoid being caught, but in the end we were prepared to take the risk and accept the punishment. That's why I was so concerned when you seemed to be thinking that Ruth might be responsible. If you had continued with that we would have had to confess. We would never have allowed an innocent person like Ruth to take the blame. We will plead guilty and see what the court makes of our story. At least it will be a court in a free country and not like the ones in East Germany.'

He fell silent. His story was finished. Oldroyd looked at them both and shook his head slowly. Then he took a photograph out of his pocket and put it on to the table.

'Is this your sister?'

Frank picked it up, looked at the picture intently and then appeared to be fighting back the tears again.

'Yes, this was taken just after she graduated. Where did you get this?'

'It was in Meyer's apartment.'

'So he never forgot her, despite what he'd done.'

'It appears not.'

There was silence. Oldroyd stood up.

'You will have a fair trial, and I wish you luck.' It was an unusual thing to say, unprofessional, but no one in the room demurred. 'Take them away.' The brothers were led away in silence. A memory flashed into Oldroyd's mind: what had he seen inscribed on the wall when he and Armitage explored the gantry on the night of that fatal concert? 'Vengeance is mine sayeth the Lord.' If only he'd realised then that that was a clue as to what really lay behind the first murder.

Oldroyd, Carter and Armitage gathered in the latter's office for the last time in the case. They were breaking the rules by drinking a whisky each in celebration of finally solving the case. Armitage had produced the bottle from the bottom drawer of his desk.

'What put you on to them, then, sir?' asked Carter.

'When you referred to there being some other violins just the same as this and you wouldn't be able to tell the difference, I suddenly realised we were thinking about the night of the murder in the wrong way. We thought either the murderer had got out of the building or he must be somewhere still inside, hidden. Only Frank Dancek had left the building, and there was nobody found inside, so this sent us on a fruitless search for hiding places, trapdoors, secret passages, ways out and so on. But the truth was, in a curious way, the murderer both did leave the building and yet at the same time he didn't. There were two of them and they looked like one person so he both left and stayed. I had thought for some time that maybe the answer was something to do with Dancek. His behaviour was so different from everyone else that night that something was suspicious; but Atkinson on the door was so insistent that it was Dancek who went out, and everyone else down there agreed, so I couldn't pin anything on him. He couldn't have been the murderer because he was sitting in full view of everyone when the shot was fired. Then I thought that maybe the person who appeared running down the stairs was someone who looked and sounded so like Dancek that you couldn't tell the difference. The problem was that, although that might work at a distance, nobody acting or dressed up could talk close up to someone who knew Dancek well, like Atkinson, and get away with it. So I was stuck again. Now of course I can see there was something that Atkinson said, if you remember, that was a clue: that when Dancek ran down the stairs and spoke to them his accent was more pronounced than normal, but of course that was easily explained at the time by the stress of what was happening. Now we've seen that Helmut's accent is stronger than his brother's. The other thing that was suspicious was Dancek's past. Like Muller, we knew very little about him, where he came from, his family, and it finally clicked when the identical nature of the violins was mentioned. I began to see what was possible; in the end the only way it could have been done. He could have a twin brother that no one had ever met who had shot Muller, and was the one who left the building. It was a daring plan, and I had no idea about any motive, but when I checked with Immigration they told me that there was another Dancek, same age as the other, who came to England at the same time. And then I knew that had to be the answer.'

Armitage and Carter nodded. The relief and satisfaction they all felt was almost tangible.

'Fantastic work, Jim; I'd never have got there without you,' said Armitage.

'Well, it should get Tomlinson off your back,' replied Oldroyd.

'Yes. By the way, we've had information from Ashkenazi, remember? Well, he confirms what Dancek said about Muller: his real name was Reinhard Meyer and they're pretty sure that he was given that violin by the East German state.'

'Good,' remarked Oldroyd with satisfaction. He was luxuriating in the relief of having cracked the puzzle.

'And also forensics found gunshot residue on the jacket of one of those outfits.'

'You can be sure that was the one worn by Helmut that night.'

'Yep.'

'It's all fallen into place in the end, thank goodness. Well, thank you for your hospitality, Sam; I'm going to miss coming over here every day.' This was not quite true, as Armitage knew, but he understood.

'Well, I'll miss you too, Jim. Why don't you pop in next time you're over for one of your concerts? I take it this hasn't put you off?'

'No, no. I have to admit, it will be very strange to sit in that place again, but the music's worth it.'

'Won't it freak you out, though, sir? Won't you be expecting something to happen?'

'No, once I'm listening to that chamber music I'm uplifted to another level. Nothing could keep me from it.'

Although this was true, Oldroyd expected never to be able to listen to Schubert's masterpiece *Death and the Maiden* in quite the same way again.

'So, sir, the first murder turned out to be nothing to do with the old violin after all.'

Oldroyd and Carter had gone to have a last look at the famous instrument. It would be evidence at a number of trials before finally returning to its new home at the Bloomsbury School of Music. It was currently being stored in a high-security room at Halifax HQ. Another dramatic episode had been added to the extraordinary history of the instruments made so long ago by Stradivari. Oldroyd had invited Armitage, but he'd declined. He seemed content and relieved that the case was finally solved and confessed to a lack of interest in the Strad. To him 'one old fiddle was just like any other' – and anyway, he had other work to be getting on with.

A duty constable unlocked a steel cabinet and took the violin case out. Oldroyd opened it, carefully took out the violin and put it under his chin. He did a flourish with the bow and pretended to draw it across. That must be the ultimate musical experience, to play an instrument like that made by a genius 300 years before. Reinhard Meyer had had that privilege; strange that a man who'd done such evil things was also such a sensitive and talented musician. But hadn't that odd dislocation been a feature of history? Hadn't the Nazis loved their Wagner and Schubert? And the murdering Mafiosi their Italian opera?

'No,' replied Oldroyd, coming out of his reverie and putting the bow down. 'But for a long time we thought it had to be and in a curious, ironic way it did give us the answer.' He held the violin in both hands. 'We were mesmerised by it as so many people have been: a "wonder of the world". It had to somehow be the motive. It was so beautiful and so valuable that someone must have thought it was worth killing for. As Anna Robson said, maybe it has a kind of curse.' He shook his head. 'All false assumptions. I should have known better, but we were also expertly distracted by Dancek. He did the classic thing that magicians do: misdirection.'

'How do you mean, sir?'

'He got us to look at something that was very attention grabbing and away from what had really happened. Just as the illusionist performs his trick while you're looking elsewhere. He got us to focus on a near-priceless instrument, on money and greed and possession. But it was actually about something much more precious than any violin: the lives of a young girl and her partner, brutally murdered trying to get their freedom. How do you put a price on that?'

He looked again intently at the violin, turned it around and over. He traced the curves with his hand, marvelled at the mysterious craftsmanship and ran his fingers over the famous varnish. He stared for the last time at the coat of arms of the count.

Then he put the Munsterhaven Strad back into its case and closed it.

It was the early evening of Christmas Day at the vicarage in Kirkby Underside. It was dark outside after a crisp midwinter day. As expected, Oldroyd was spending Christmas with his sister and daughter, and what better place than in what he called the 'Jane Austen' vicarage. It was pleasant to be able to retreat from reality for a time into the fantasy world of an Edwardian rural Christmas. The weather had obliged by depositing snow on Christmas Eve, so that the chocolate-box village was enhanced even more in its winter beauty. It only needed horses and carriages to be straight out of a traditional Christmas card.

Louise was asleep on one of the big sofas; she'd had a late night on Christmas Eve in Leeds and the Christmas dinner had finished her off. Oldroyd didn't mind that nut roast had been served instead of turkey; he was just happy not to be alone in his flat. He snuggled deeper into his armchair and was yet again thankful that he'd been able to finish with the case before Christmas and could now properly wind down.

'I haven't seen you so relaxed for a long while, Jim,' observed his sister, who was ensconced in a similar armchair opposite. They were both holding glasses of port.

'Yes, I'm so relieved that that business over in Halifax is done.'

'I can imagine.'

'You know, it's strange how, whenever I get to the end of a case like that one, it makes me reflect on life.'

'Why that one?'

Oldroyd thought for a moment.

'I suppose because it was so full of human complexity: violence, greed, vengeance, but also love, courage and family loyalty. It was like a Shakespearean drama.'

'Which is what the whole of life is and no one depicted it better than him. And where do your reflections take you on this occasion?'

Oldroyd sipped his port. 'Oh, nothing very original. It struck me that people who are overly concerned with acquiring money and possessions end up in tragic states. Elizabeth Knott living alone with that amazing collection that was only there for her satisfaction in owning it: meaningless. The others, like Hamilton and Djaic, getting involved in violence; Shaw dealing in drugs to keep up the pretence that he could live like a squire in a manor house with all the trappings. It seems to me that they were all missing the point of life.'

'Which is?'

Oldroyd gestured to Alison and to Louise.

'This: family, people, love; even if relationships aren't always perfect,' he said, thinking about Julia, from whom he'd heard nothing.

'Well, bravo, that's not a bad mini-sermon for Christmas Day – so when are you going forward for ordination?'

Oldroyd laughed.

'Do you think the Church would have me?'

'I think they'd be scared off by your notoriety.' Alison smiled and then looked more serious. 'I agree with you, of course, but the most tragic character in the story for me was Meyer.'

'Why?'

'He loved Dancek's sister – what was her name again?'

'Helga.'

'Yes. But when the love wasn't returned, he first of all tried to force her to have him and when he couldn't possess her he finally destroyed the thing he loved. That's truly terrifying: love turned to hate; the ultimate blasphemy, if you like.'

There were a few moments of quiet.

'Anyway,' said Alison. 'Let's put some music on. What do you fancy?'

'Let's have some carols,' replied Oldroyd. 'King's College Choir. Anything except *Death and the Maiden* – I need a break from that.' He laughed, and raised his glass.

'Merry Christmas, Alison!'

'Merry Christmas, Jim!'

Acknowledgments

I would like to thank my family and friends for all their support and encouragement over the years, particularly those who read drafts and made comments.

The Otley Courthouse Writers' Group led by James Nash has helped me to develop as a writer and given me the extra impetus to get things completed!

Some readers will recognise the Square Chapel in Halifax as the model for the Red Chapel in the story. I have attended chamber concerts here, and in its predecessor Harrison House, for many years and I would like to thank the organisers: the Halifax Philharmonic Club.

The West Riding Police is a fictional force based on the old riding boundary. Harrogate was part of the old West Riding, although it is in today's North Yorkshire.

J. R. Ellis

About the Author

John R. Ellis has lived in Yorkshire for most of his life and has spent many years exploring Yorkshire's diverse landscapes, history, language and communities. He recently retired after a career in teaching, mostly in further education in the Leeds area. In addition to the Yorkshire Murder Mystery series he writes poetry, ghost stories and biography. He has completed a screenplay about the last years of the poet Edward Thomas and a work of faction about the extraordinary life of his Irish mother-in-law. He is currently working on his memoirs of growing up in a working-class area of Huddersfield in the 1950s and 1960s.